www.islington.gov.uk

❧ISLINGTON

T 020 7527 6900

Islington Libraries

4/17

'C
in
w
in

'T
th
Ar

'Se
Pre
the
Fid
firs

'Wh
seri
puts
for

'The
wife ... in a forest with her throat slashed. In the absence of a
police force, the local coroner, Titus Cragg, is required to investigate
the death; it is a time of scientific discovery and Cragg seeks advice from
a young doctor, Luke Fidelis, who agrees to perform a post-mortem. He
has barely ... when he makes a startling dis-
covery, transform ... case of wife-murder
into a potential

...nday Times

'In the age before proper policing and forensic science, it takes a super sleuth to solve the riddle of the woman's demise. Enter Titus Cragg – the star of a gripping new crime novel series set in historic Preston.'

Lancashire Evening Post

'Preston's Cheapside may never be mentioned in the same breath as 221b Baker Street, but it is destined to become a familiar location on the fictional crime map of Britain.'

Lancashire Life

Dark Waters

Dark Waters

ROBIN BLAKE

Constable • London

CONSTABLE

First published in Great Britain in 2012 by Macmillan

This edition published in 2015 by Constable

Copyright © Robin Blake, 2012

The moral right of the author has been asserted.

A CIP catalogue record for this book
is available from the British Library.

ISBN 978-1-47211-591-1 (hardback)
ISBN 978-1-47211-592-8 (ebook)

Typeset in Sabon by Initial Typesetting Services
Printed and bound by CPI Group (UK) Ltd, Croydon, CR0 4YY

Constable
is an imprint of
Constable & Robinson Ltd
100 Victoria Embankment
London EC4Y 0DY

An Hachette UK Company
www.hachette.co.uk

www.constablerobinson.com

For Fanny

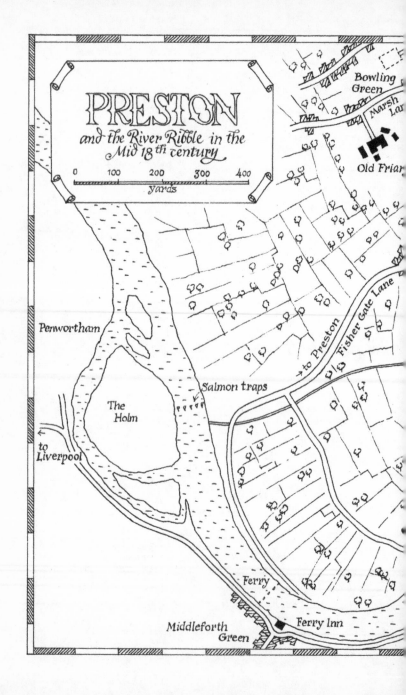

PRESTON

and the River Ribble in the Mid 18th century

0   100   200   300   400
yards

Bowling Green

Marsh Lane

Old Friar

Penwortham

Salmon traps

The Holm

to Preston

Fisher Gate Lane

to Liverpool

Ferry

Middleforth Green

Ferry Inn

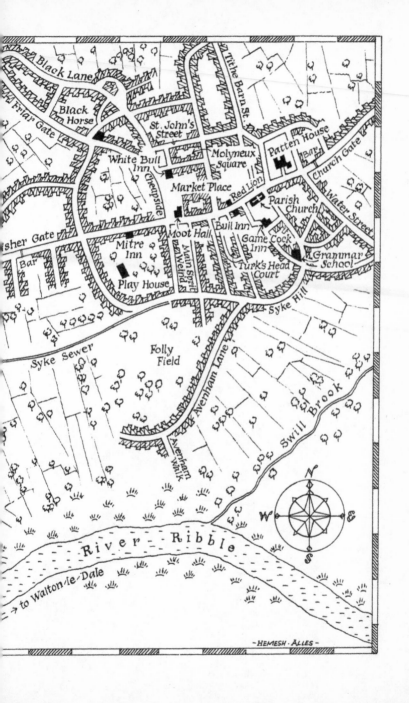

Chapter One

A HUMAN BODY IN the salmon traps was not such a rare event. The one they caught in the spring of 1741 was the fifth during my first eight years as coroner in the borough of Preston. On the other hand, from my point of view, there was something very particular and personal about the latest one. This corpse was my kith, if not quite my kin.

But I had no idea of that when the call to the riverbank came early on that Monday morning, exactly seven days before we were due to begin a week of voting in that year's general election. I immediately hurried out to perform the coroner's first duty – that of answering the summons to a questionable death, and judging the need for an inquest. On my way to the stretch of the river Ribble in which the traps were laid I naturally had to pass along Fisher Gate, where my friend Luke Fidelis lived on the upper floor of the premises of Adam Lorris the bookbinder. Reaching Lorris's door I mounted the steps and pealed the bell. If Fidelis was at home he could usefully come with me. When bodies floated in the river, the initial questions were always the same. How long had they been there? How far had they travelled? Dr Fidelis's knowledge of physiology, and such things as the progressive effects on a corpse of its total immersion in water, was far ahead of mine.

Mrs Lorris went up to tell Fidelis I had called and of course, as was his habit, my friend was lounging late in bed. I chatted for a few minutes at the foot of the stairs with Lorris and Mrs Lorris. He told me of his progress with my old childhood book of Aesop's *Fables* that I had brought to him for rebinding.

'I read the book through with Mrs Lorris before I started, and we were vastly entertained, were we not, my heart?'

'Oh yes, Mr Cragg!' Dot Lorris exclaimed, her face breaking into dimples of remembered enjoyment. 'Such tricks those animals got up to.'

'Yes, Mr Aesop was a clever fellow,' I agreed. 'He had a charming way of translating human nature into the behaviour of beasts.'

I glanced up the stairs for a sign that Fidelis might be stirring himself. There was none.

'There's some of the fables, mind, that a husband would do better not to put before his wife,' observed Lorris.

'Oh? And which are those, husband?' Dot challenged.

'*The Scarecrows and the Foxes*, for one. Remember it, Mr Cragg?'

I said I had a vague memory of it.

'That vixen,' said Lorris, shaking his head, 'she stayed under cover and let the fox run from the farmer by himself. There's little wifely love in that, or trust.'

'Trust!' laughed his wife. 'What was there to trust? He calculated that if both of them ran, his wife would be caught and he would get away. The farmer could only chase after one of them, and that would be the vixen, as she were the slower.'

'No, *she* calculated that if she stayed under cover, she'd save herself and damn the fox.'

'The fox damned himself when he lost his nerve,' was Dot Lorris's pitiless rejoinder.

Before the discussion grew too heated I turned it towards the election. Preston was excited at having a contested vote at last. In the previous parliament, and the two before that, our borough members had simply walked over, as no one could be found to stand against them. This time four men would be fighting over the two seats, making for a much livelier prospect.

After a couple of minutes of touching on the pros and cons of Whig and Tory we heard Fidelis's voice calling down.

'Cragg, I'm in my nightshirt, but come up if you like.'

Instead I called up to him.

'Get dressed, Luke. It's almost seven and I'm taking you for a walk by the river.'

'A walk? Before *seven*? Surely it can wait.'

'No. It is now or not at all.'

At length the tall, fair-haired figure of Preston's youngest and most adventurous doctor appeared on the stair. He was grumbling, as usual when asked to do a thing before eight in the morning.

'I only wanted half an hour more of sleep, Titus,' he growled. 'I was drinking until past midnight.'

In consideration of Luke's aching head I did not set too sharp a pace as we went along Fisher Gate and then, by a turning to the left, into the lane that passed the playhouse and headed down from the bluff along which the town is ranged towards the riverbank.

'Well, what is it?' Luke asked. 'I don't suppose this outing is for the improvement of my health.'

'No. It's for a body in the river.'

'Ah!'

We walked on in silence to the bottom of the steep path, before striking across the meadow beside the riverbank. But I sensed an increased spring in Luke's step. He was stimulated by the opportunity to assist me in my inquiries; more so, I think, than I was in leading them.

*

In many towns, the river is a high street. The buildings line up expectantly alongside it, waiting for trade to come across its wharves and quays, while locks upstream and down regulate the water for the traffic of lighters and barges. None of this is so at Preston, for the river is at a distance, and on a lower level. Abreast of the town to the south, it is at this point wide and, being close to the estuary, tidal. But it drains a great area of uplands to the east and, after heavy or prolonged rains combined with a tide, it can go so high that the water meadows flood up to 100 yards on either side. To keep its skirts dry, therefore, the town stays aloof on its ridge, a quarter-mile distant from the waterside, and it is possible to live one's life there without any particular consciousness of the river, except as a barrier to be crossed when travelling south, and the regular provider of fish suppers.

On this morning, breezy after yesterday's downpour, the current was big and tumbling, but it had stayed within the banks. A group of men wearing knee-length boots of greased leather were working the traps from boats that bobbed and pitched in the boiling stream. They were gaffing the last of the fish that had come into the traps during the night, and bringing them ashore to add to the neat row of those already landed. As we came near enough to see the display of salmon, like spears of bright polished pewter in the riverbank grass, we saw a gaggle of women in bonnets and full-length cloaks, advancing along the bank towards us, laughing and singing. It would be their job to pack the fish in rush parcels and carry them up to the market.

The women arrived at the same time as we did, and immediately their laughter died as they saw the thing lying stretched companionably alongside the row of fish, as if it were an enormous fish itself. It was wrapped in a net like a parcel but this did not fully hide the fearful truth: the head end was rounded, from which the shape swelled smoothly up to the belly in a small

4

mound before tapering away again. At the end where – had it really been a monster salmon – the tail should be, two splayed feet protruded. They wore the wooden-soled clogs of the countryman, strengthened like a horse's hoof with curves of steel nailed into them.

The sight provoked immediate cries of dismay from the women.

'Quiet yourselves,' shouted one of the men, as he carried the last of the fish up from his boat and slapped it down with the others. 'Coroner's here. You should be respectful.'

I asked who was in charge of the fishing party. It was the man who had just spoken, whose name was Peter Crane.

'Was it you that first saw it in the water?' I asked.

'It was. Me and the lad spotted it first.'

Crane nodded towards a youth who looked like a younger edition of himself.

'What time was that?'

'An hour ago, or a bit more.'

I took out my watch. It was half past seven.

'Before half past six, then.'

'If you say so.'

'And did you find him just like that?'

'How do you mean?'

'Wrapped in the net.'

'Oh, no. We wrapped him when we brought him ashore, like. Out of respect.'

Or, I thought, to stop him getting up and running away. It was a common thought: you can never be too sure of those that drown.

'Would you kindly uncover him for me now?'

It took three men to undo the parcel, so heavy was the body, and so well wrapped.

'Did you know him?' I asked as they struggled.

'Oh, aye, we knew him.'

'Who was he?'

'Don't think you won't know him yourself, Mr Cragg. Take a look.'

Finally, with two of them pulling his feet and a third at the other end hauling the net, they managed to disencumber the body. The dead man was wearing a coat, shirt, breeches and the aforementioned clogs. His grey hair was tied at the back. His eyes were closed.

'Good God!' said Fidelis. 'Look who it is.'

We all drew closer, and there was a murmur of recognition from the women. I knew the man better even than the others and, for a moment, was so disconcerted I could not speak. Not only did I well know his identity, I knew also that the contented impression conveyed by the corpse was false. For these were the mortal remains of poor Antony Egan, landlord of the Ferry Inn and the sadly troubled uncle of Elizabeth, my own sweet wife.

'Did you close the eyes, or were they like this when you found him?' Fidelis asked Crane.

'No, Doctor, staring open they were. I closed them.'

As a simulacrum of sleep it made the man look at peace, with the impression reinforced by the hands being arranged comfortably over the swollen stomach.

I knelt down on one knee beside him, opened his sodden coat and went through the pockets. They were empty except for a tobacco pouch, a few coppers and his watch, its chain securely attached to a waistcoat buttonhole. Then I stood again and looked at Fidelis who was on the other side of the corpse.

'He has his watch,' I said.

'He wasn't robbed, then.'

'When do you think he went into the water?'

'I doubt it was long he was in there.'

'Did he drown?'

'Let's see. Mr Crane, would you and your men kindly turn him over for me, and bring him round so his head's over the river.'

The dead man was placed, according to Luke's instructions, on his stomach with head and shoulders over the stream and arms trailing in it – the posture of one who throws himself down to drink, or a boy attempting to tickle a trout. Luke then crouched beside him and placed both hands palms down, with fingers spread out, flat on his back.

'Look at the mouth, Titus, while I palpate.'

I placed myself on the other side of the body and sank down on one knee, leaning a little over the water to see the profile of Antony's head. Luke sharply pressed his hands down three or four times in a kneading motion just below the ribcage and immediately water gushed up and out of the mouth, like water from a parish pump. Luke stood up.

'You saw it?' he asked. 'Lungs full of water. He sucked it in trying to breathe. It means he was alive when he went into the river. He died by drowning.'

I rose from my genuflection and considered for a moment. The cloud cover was disintegrating and patches of freshly minted blue sky had opened up over our heads. Then, in the east, the morning sun broke free and shafts of light set the swollen river surface glittering.

'Well, Luke, I have a ten-minute walk upstream ahead of me. It's a fine day. Will you come along, or have you other business?'

He said he had no patients to see immediately and would be glad to go with me. I asked Crane to get some sort of conveyance, and use it to transport Egan's body along the bankside path behind us.

'There will be an inquest but I see no reason why he can't lie at home, and be viewed there by the jury. There've been inquests at the Ferry Inn before. It's better that I go ahead, to break the news to his daughters. They will need time to prepare.'

Luke and I set off briskly to walk to the inn. It stood half a mile above the salmon traps, rather less than midway to the big stone bridge at Walton-le-Dale that bears the southern way for Wigan and Manchester. A road of sorts branched from that road to connect with the ferry stage, and for uncounted centuries traffic from the south had been transported across the stream in competition with the bridge. The Ferry Inn, lying on the southern bank, had served the needs of those waiting to cross, and a good business it had been, for the reason (which was really unreason) that, while a ferry crossing was cheaper than the bridge toll, many of those waiting to use it were happy to spend the saved money on drinking, eating, card playing and, sometimes, a bed for the night. So business had come to the inn as naturally as fish got into the salmon traps.

But under Egan its prosperity had progressively dwindled, to such an extent that for the past few years the inn had been hesitating on the edge of ruin. It seemed to keep going only by the tenacity and good sense of his twin daughters Grace and Mary-Ann.

'Poor Egan,' said Luke as we trudged along the bankside. 'I was drinking at the Ferry only last week, on my way back from a patient.'

'I hadn't seen him for a month or more,' I said. 'We see his daughters, of course, because they're Elizabeth's cousins. But we gave over inviting Antony two or three years ago. It had become impossible. What condition was he in – on the day you were there?'

'Same as always – no better, no worse.'

'I don't think he'd enjoyed a waking hour of sobriety for five years.'

'Is *enjoy* the right word, Titus? I enjoy a drink. But men like that can do nothing without a drink. Drunkenness is their sobriety. Their accustomed condition.'

'If so, what is their drunkenness?'

'Unconsciousness, I think. Oblivion.'

'Well, now poor Antony has found an eternity of that.'

'What made his life take the turn it did? Was he always a sot?'

'No. Once he was the model of moderation.'

'Then what happened?'

'The son that he cherished above all other creatures deserted him, and went south, without ever writing or sending word. And then, when word came at last, it was that the boy had died. His father took to drink because he could not bear to remember it.'

By now we had left the water meadows behind and reached the ferry's landing stage, on the northern side of the river. From here we had to cross to the inn on the far bank, which meant waiting for the ferry. We could see the flat, raft-like conveyance labouring towards us, fighting the flood as two men turned the great winching wheel that hauled the craft along the fixed rope stretched from bank to bank. A short distance upstream, smoke was rising from the chimneys of the inn, which stood among a small cluster of houses and trees known as Middleforth Green. The day had started at the inn as it did every day. There was no sign yet that this might not be one like any other.

The ferry made land with a crunch and lowered its ramp. Half a dozen passengers came off, and with them a cart laden with leeks, sparrowgrass, watercress and other market vegetables. The ferryman Robert Battersby, a fellow famous for his bad grace, tied off his ropes and came ashore with his son and crewman, Simeon, a muscular boy of seventeen. As they ambled towards the wooden hut in which they sheltered from rain and sold tickets between crossings, I stopped them and said we required immediate transport over to the Ferry Inn. He muttered something about his time-table but I cut him short, saying it was coroner's business and that as soon as he had transported me and Dr Fidelis, he was to return and await the arrival of a body from downriver, for bringing across after us.

When he heard this, a smile broke across young Simeon's face, and he began jiggling up and down.

'Another one gone in, is it?' he said, his voice lifting with sudden delight. 'Another sacrifice to the water? Oh, aye. She's a cruel one is the river goddess.'

'Shut it and don't be daft,' said the father savagely to the son, then turned back to me. 'Pay no mind, Mr Cragg. His head's full of nonsense. We'll take you now. It'll be tuppence.'

I gave him the money, and a warning.

'Let's have a little reverence when the body comes after, Mr Battersby, if you please.'

Chapter Two

THE FERRY INN presented a battered appearance, the thatch unkempt and the wooden frame seeming to sag from exhaustion. Inside, the stone flags undulated from wear, and the plaster of the unpanelled walls was cracked and darkened by decades of tobacco smoke. Going in, we found all the early-morning things that they do at inns being done now. The coppers were being scrubbed and the brass polished; barrels and milk churns rolled, pint pots clunked together in tubs of soapy water and birch besoms set about yesterday's floors, while sacks of new sawdust stood by, ready to give fresh covering. Windows were flung open and carpets were flogged. Backyard chickens squawked as they were pitched off the nest to give up their eggs.

In the hall we met a dull-witted boy, Toby, with disproportionately large feet. He was carrying a couple of long-handled warming pans, one tucked under each arm. I asked him if we could see either of his mistresses, but before he could spit out a reply one of them, Mary-Ann, came tripping down the stairs. She was a stringy, bony girl with the straightest hair you ever saw, and a markedly sharp nose. Yet she was as strong and capable a twenty-two-year-old as any in the world, and she had a musical voice, with the timbre of my favourite woodwind instrument, the oboe.

'Hello, Cousin Titus,' she cried when she saw us. 'And Dr

Fidelis. You'll take a glass of something. Have you had your breakfasts?'

'Your father—' I began.

'Never seen him yet this morning,' said Mary-Ann. 'Hogging his bed till late, as he does every morning. Business, is it? You and the doctor go into the parlour. It's empty but for the last of last night's guests having his breakfast, and his man has already carried down his luggage, so he'll be on his way. I'll send Toby up to root Father out – though whether you will get any sense out of him at this hour is doubtful.'

'It's not him but yourself and your sister I've come to see. Can she be found?'

'You want to see me and Grace together? But what for?'

By now we had walked ahead of her into the parlour, where the guest she'd mentioned was sitting alone with what remained of his meal, looking through some handwritten documents. A man of about thirty, with a mass of curly red hair, he nodded his head at us, but said nothing, while Mary-Ann turned back to tell Toby to fetch her sister. Then she came in, crossed to the guest's table and whipped the plate, knife and napkin away from under his nose, leaving him in little doubt that it was time to pay what was due, collect his traps and stretch his legs in the direction of the ferry stage. Abrupt was Mary-Ann, and always busy. It would be impossible to break my news until she became quiet and composed.

She paused a moment while the guest obediently drained his mug, gathered his papers and stood, then she bustled him out and across the hall to her business room. Overlaid by sounds from the kitchen, and the carpet beater's thuds, Fidelis and I could hear their conversation about the reckoning only as a mumble. We were standing together at the parlour window. The outlook was of the riverbank, with patches of scrub and a few willows, that sloped away from us down to the river itself, and of shallow tongues of shingle protruding out into the surging brown water. Beyond that we had a clear sight of the patchwork of gardens and orchards patterning the land on the other side as it rose to the line of roofs and smoking chimneys along the ridge – the houses of our town.

'How will they take this news?' murmured Luke as he scanned the view with only half of his attention. 'They think he is sleeping soundly in his room. This will hit them like a thunderbolt.'

'I don't know,' I whispered back, 'except that the man was already much despaired of by his family.'

I had heard Grace's voice, higher and lighter than her sister's, in the hall. A moment later we were turning to greet her.

How is it possible for sisters to be so alike, by which I mean such unmistakable sisters, and at the same time so different? Where Mary-Ann was angular, Grace was curved and charming; where the first was brown haired and had flawless skin, the latter was fair and carried a light but distinct strawberry mark across her lower face and neck. This is not to say either of them was more agreeable than the other; in character I liked them both equally, though in different ways. They were salt and sweet: Mary-Ann forthright and trustworthy, Grace shy and lovable. It was a twin-ship of complementary opposites, not of peas from the pod.

Grace greeted us happily, with a guileless smile for me, and (if I was not mistaken) the hint of a blush for my handsome friend.

'We are so glad to see you, Cousin, and Doctor. My sister says you have some affairs to discuss here. If so, you know you're better advised talking to Mary-Ann than to me. She has the brain for business. It's not much good saying anything to our poor father, either. He is very much reduced.'

I was able to let this remark go by without comment as Mary-Ann now came in, having taken her guest's money and seen him on his way.

'It's wonderful how some people will haggle over a penny while they shovel out their shillings,' she said. 'Last night that man paid a crown for a bottle of our best port wine. This morning he baulks at a penny farthing for the bootblack.'

She sat on one of the fireside settles and with a sideways movement of her head signalled her sister to sit beside her. Grace did so while Fidelis and I took our places on the settle opposite.

'Now,' Mary-Ann went on, 'my father is not in his room, Toby tells me. Happen he's gone out to the privy. So we can rely on being undisturbed for a few minutes.'

I cleared my throat in a lawyerly way.

'I am afraid your father hasn't gone to the privy.'

'Oh! How do you know that, Cousin?'

'Because we have just come from the townside riverbank, downstream by the salmon traps. He's been found there.'

'Eh?' broke in Grace. 'What is he doing there, at this hour?'

But Mary-Ann had more accurately picked up my tone of voice. She said, 'What do you mean, he was *found*?'

'They pulled him out of the river. I'm very sorry.'

At once the hands of both girls went to their mouths like sprung traps. After they had exchanged a look, Mary-Ann was the first to remove hers.

She whispered, 'So is he . . . ?'

'Yes, he's drowned, Mary-Ann. Dr Fidelis has confirmed it. I am truly unhappy to bring you this news.'

I studied their faces. Mary-Ann's eyes were wide, but her face was otherwise expressionless. Grace's was beginning to twist and crumple as the emotion took hold. The next moment she had pressed it into the palms of both hands and lowered both hands and head almost to her lap. She was whimpering.

'Oh, my poor father! Poor, poor Father!'

After a short interval, during which Grace cried and Mary-Ann sat immobile except for clasping and unclasping her fingers,

I gave them the facts as far as I knew them. Then Fidelis told them how we had laid the dead man on his front and the water had gushed from his mouth, showing he had tried to breathe while submersed in the river.

Finally I said, 'They're bringing him back here now, to lie at his family home. And I'll be calling an inquest to sit on the matter tomorrow. I'm sorry to trouble you with this at such a time, but this is the only usable place for the hearing. We'll need your largest room. The dining room?'

'Yes, of course,' said Mary-Ann. 'I'll see to it.'

A silence followed between us. Grace reached out and seized her sister's hand, gripping it tightly, as the two women cast down their eyes and thought about this change to their existence.

'You know,' said Mary-Ann at last, 'there's something fitting about it. He loved the river, my father. He adored it, I think, almost as much as he loved a drink.'

'He didn't, Mary-Ann!' Her sister was indignant, and suddenly shrill. 'I mean, he didn't *love* to drink at all. He hated it, because it had taken hold of him and wouldn't let go.'

She turned to Fidelis, her face pinched with distress.

'You understand that, don't you, Doctor?'

Fidelis nodded.

'Yes, I do, Grace. I've seen it very often.'

Grace gave an emphatic sniff.

'He couldn't stop, and it turned his brains to mush.'

'It did that!'

This was Mary-Ann again, taking her turn to break in. She'd allowed Grace's interruption without complaint, except to shake her head slowly, like a person walking into cobwebs. Now she threw off her dullness and was as animated as her sister.

'You know what he did every night of his life, Cousin Titus?' Her voice had tightened now into something like anger. 'He waited till the last customer'd been packed off, or gone up to bed, and we were well into clearing the tables. He'd watch us for a bit, then he'd put down his pint pot, he'd wipe his mouth with a napkin, and he'd drum the table for a bit with his fingers. Then his face'd light up as if he'd just had a new idea and he'd say, Oh! I think I'll take a turn outside.'

'Every night, you say?'

'Yes, and often as not, if you objected in some way, for instance that it was damp out, he'd say he wanted to see if the moon was shining in the water. Even with it cloudy, or on a new moon and not a sliver of it to be seen. He would find his way out – because *I* wasn't going to help him – holding the furniture as men do in a ship at sea. And he'd stay out till God knows when before finding his way back in. We'd often not see him till morning. That's how mushy his brains were.'

'Well,' I said, 'the moon in the water! It's an odd preoccupation, but harmless enough.'

Mary-Ann shook her head.

'But it wasn't harmless, was it? Just see what happened!'

Fidelis leaned forward, suddenly interested.

'So he was out looking for the moon in the water last night?'

'Course he was.'

Fidelis glanced in my direction. 'What time was that?'

'Quarter or a half after midnight,' said Mary-Ann. 'It always was. When you run an inn you have to keep regular hours. We serve no customers after twelve.'

'So he was out after midnight last night.'

'As I said, every night he was. Ask John.'

John was the ancient night porter at the inn.

'Of course, John. He would have seen your father last night, going out?'

'You must ask him.'

Mary-Ann's voice had tightened up, as if this conversation was becoming too much to bear. So I turned from her to her sister.

'And where exactly would your father go in his search for the moon in the water?'

'Down to the ferry stage, Cousin. He got a clear view of the water from there.'

'Did you not worry about him wandering out that way, inebriated?'

'He knew it as well as the way from his hand to his mouth. We thought—'

'We thought he could come to no harm,' butted in Mary-Ann, 'like you just said, Cousin Titus. We know better now, but too late.'

As they sometimes do, and in this case appropriately, the words 'too late' sounded like a funeral bell. We sat quietly for a while, feeling their resonance.

'He will miss the election, too,' said Grace, sighing deeply. 'He had plans. He spoke of going up in fellowship with a gang of folk from Middleforth Green and Walton, to do their voting. He would have so liked it. Oh, well.'

She sighed again. I got up softly and reached for my hat.

'We must go back to town ourselves now, Cousins, and be about our business. But I am sure Elizabeth will be down for a visit as soon as she hears the sorry news. I wish we had not been the bearers of it.'

In farewell, Luke kissed both the young ladies' hands. I am not sure if this was, in etiquette, the correct gesture, but it worked its magic. Mary-Ann smiled and Grace's cheeks again faintly reddened.

'About the inquest,' I said, 'we'll begin at noon, I think. And don't worry, I'll tell them not to expect too much in the way of victuals . . . the jury, I mean.'

But Mary-Ann stood and fixed me with an intense, beady look. She had recovered some of her fight.

'Cousin, we'll victual them royally, if that is what they require. We are glad of the business, aren't we, Sister?'

With a momentary smile and nod, Grace tearfully concurred.

'And I will come over a little before,' I went on, 'to speak with both of you and also any of your staff, especially John, who might have information about what happened last night. That way we can get the whole thing over and done. You will be able to bury him on Wednesday.'

The ferry stage was 70 yards downstream of the inn, along a continuation of the road from Walton. This road carried on westward along the riverbank to the riverside settlement of Penwortham and then, by a looping course, south towards Liverpool. It was a pitiful road, more like a lane, and the going was both rutted and potted.

'For a very drunk man in the dark this might be a challenging walk,' observed Fidelis.

'Antony must have been driven by a strong desire to come out here every night.'

'Is desire the right word, Titus?'

'I can't think of another.'

'I can. He was in an unhappy state at the end. "Mush" was his daughter's interesting word to describe his mind. But has "mush" desire, reasoning – will, even? No. Mush doesn't drive a man to do anything. It can't make plans, it can't look forward. But daily living requires these things. There must be some kind of structure in the mind, I think, or life collapses.'

Once Fidelis got hold of a theme, the jaws of his intellect bit so hard that they could not easily let go.

'Well,' I floundered, 'Antony got by because . . . I don't know . . . others – such as his daughters – made the frame of his life for him, maybe.'

'To an extent they did. But I am talking about something more fundamental than that. A person needs an inner skeleton to keep its shape, or it too becomes inchoate and falls apart. A suit of armour, say, worn on the outside won't stiffen it at all. We are not snails.'

'The brain is a bit like a snail, don't you think?'

Fidelis laughed.

'That's amusing, but inaccurate. I am not speaking of the brain, but the mind. That requires an intrinsic skeleton of ideas to keep its shape. For most of us this consists of hope, looking forward, schemes and projects and reasonable optimism. Without these, what remains?'

I had no idea what he was getting at.

'Mush?' I hazarded.

'Exactly. Mush.'

Still no wiser, I took him back to his original proposition.

'So what was it, in your opinion, that did cause Antony to come out here night after night to chase a delusion? I mean, if not that he just wanted to.'

'Habit, Titus. Habits were all he had left. He drank, he sat in the same chair, he said the same things, he went out to look at the reflection of the moon at the same hour. A hopeful, self-projecting man has no need of such repetitions, but the chronically unhappy can keep going only in that way.'

'He was certainly miserable, I can vouch for that. His son's death, then his wife's. But he had a few sparks of spirit left in him. You heard what they said – his plans for the election . . .'

'They'd have come to nothing, Titus, and you know it. His feeble thread of life was so reduced he had nothing but habits left to him, with not a sensible thought in between.'

'That is not a charitable estimate of my wife's kinsman, Luke. Though it may be true.'

'Of course it's true. The man was a helpless sot, was he not?'

With a sigh I let this go.

We came to a break in the left-hand hedge, on the opposite side of the track to that of the river, where there was a cottage standing a little back from the road. At the gate, leaning with a pipe in his mouth, was the cottager himself. His name was Isaac Satterthwaite and he was the local rat catcher. Isaac was sixty-five years old and fully bearded, but neither withered nor bent. Long ago he had been a soldier serving under the Duke of Marlborough himself, and even now his back was straight and military, his cheeks full, and his grey hair abundant enough to be drawn back and worn as a pigtail at the nape.

We stopped to talk to him.

'How do, Isaac,' I said. 'You've heard what's been found?'

'I have that,' he growled. 'Antony Egan's fell in the water and drowned himself. It's only a wonder it took him so long.'

'You didn't see him last night, by any chance? In the lane here, on his nightly walk?'

'No. Not last night I didn't.'

'Did you sometimes? He took the same walk every night, I'm told.'

'Aye, we've seen him out late before now, down by the landing, or in the lane. Always drunk.'

'Did you ever speak to him?'

He swivelled his head and spat.

'Before, I might have. Not now.'

'Before what?'

'A disagreement, a year or more since.'

'You fell out?'

He turned his head, this time the other way, and spat again.

'There was little to fall out of. We were neighbours, like, and sometimes I took a mug of beer at the inn. But he considered himself above a man in my line of trade, though he had not much cause to, when you looked at him. And then there was what they said about my granddaughter, who used to work for them. Well and good they could give her the sack, but to say . . . what they said.'

He straightened up and knocked out his pipe.

'Well, I must go in. Good day to you, gentlemen.'

Fidelis and I walked on.

'What was Maggie dismissed for?' Fidelis asked.

'I don't know. I heard nothing about it.'

'They must have given her a bad character. The old man took umbrage badly over it.'

I shook my head.

'I don't know. From what I've heard she's a winsome enough young girl.'

We arrived at the ferry stage, and found it deserted, the last of the market traffic having now gone across. I looked for the curly-haired guest who had earlier departed the inn, but Battersby had evidently transported him while we were in conference with the sisters. So Fidelis and I stood together alone on the slipway. It was here that the ferryman lowered his ramp to land carts, horses and livestock. Here too the southern end of the shore-to-shore rope, along which the ferry travelled, was attached to the top of a heavy post whose base was sunk deep into the riverbed. The wind was still gusting and the sunshine patchy. I looked across to the far side of the river, where one momentary patch illuminated the area near Battersby's hut. A knot of people had gathered there, watching four men who hurried towards them carrying a litter along the bankside.

The slipway was built of two parallel stone walls, 10 feet apart, which diminished in height as they sloped down to, and into, the river. The space between them was filled by earth and gravel to form a short but wide pathway into the water.

'I suppose he slipped off the side here,' I said. 'The water's deep. He got too near the edge and his feet went from under him, or he lost his balance.'

Fidelis crouched down, examining the edge of the walling.

'Could he swim?'

I almost laughed.

'Like a bag of nails. He wouldn't have lasted long.'

Fidelis moved to the other side of the slipway and inspected the retaining wall on that side. 'There are no traces to support your theory, Titus. He went into the water wearing iron-shod clogs, did he not? If it was from here he slipped, as likely as not we'd be seeing fresh scrapes somewhere on the parapet to show where his feet went out from under him. There are none.'

Having assured himself of this, Fidelis rose and joined me in watching the business on the other bank. The bearers had loaded the litter onto Robert Battersby's craft, then retired to the bank. But one of them immediately saw that they would still be needed on our side of the river, to carry the litter up to the inn. At this point they all re-embarked. Battersby wasn't happy. He argued with them, waving his arms and seemingly asking for their fares. None were paid and after a while Battersby realized he would be better off bringing the bearers across, but without tickets, than he would with no bearers and the need to make his own arrangements for the corpse when he got to this side. So at last, with bad grace, he cast off and he and his son began winding the travel rope. Antony Egan was coming home.

Chapter Three

∞

A s SOON AS he had made fast the ferry, and the litter was on its
way along the road to the inn, Battersby bore down on me
bristling with indignation.

'I shall bill you fivepence, Coroner, for these five crossings, and
another four for the men going back. I'm not doing good works
here. I've a living to make.'

'Five crossings?' I said. 'You'd charge a fare for a dead man,
Robert?'

Battersby pulled a printed card from his shirt pocket and thrust
it in front of my eyes.

'This here is my tariff sheet, see? It gives the crossing charge
for people, and stock, and carts, and horses, and donkeys, and
barrels, and bundles, but it says nowt about corpses. So I've to
decide. It's a penny per person, a farthing per large bundle. You're
a lawyer. What do *you* say it was that I just ferried over – a person
or a bundle?'

'Well, that's an interesting question. I am not sure the law has
a definitive answer.'

He shook his finger at me.

'And till it does, I'm billing you for a person.'

He returned to his boat and I looked around for Fidelis. He
was back on shore, surveying the riverbank on either side of the

slipway. Here, it was kept clear of reeds and thick vegetation and Fidelis was looking closely into the grass at a place on the bank downstream of the slipway.

'See this, Titus,' he called. 'I think I've found the place where he went in.'

He was inspecting two parallel muddy scrapes that went straight down the bank to the water, wide enough apart to have been made by a man's sliding feet. This was close to the end of the cleared section of bank, where it gave way to some denser vegetation of bushy blackthorn, gorse and bramble. The ground he was hovering over was patched with clumps of coarse grass, but otherwise the covering was weed, and it was this that had been disturbed by whatever had slid down.

'These are slide marks freshly made,' he observed. 'And there are additional indentations in the ground towards the bottom. And, look, a clump of grass has been half pulled up. He will have grabbed at it trying to save himself.'

'Where?' I said, hurrying towards him. 'Show me!'

Looking back on that moment, I see that I had forgotten all my feelings for Elizabeth's drowned uncle and his bereft daughters. I was immersed in the sudden feverish delight of wrestling with a puzzle. It was the lawyer in me coming out, the one who could trawl for hours through documents and witness statements in search of evidence to clinch a proof. Fidelis, as a physician, similarly absorbed himself in piecing together signs and symptoms to establish the truth of a disease. Though medicine and law have their differences in method and mentality, the doctor and the lawyer have this in common: the desire to connect disparate pieces of evidence and find the truth that links them.

I looked around the immediate area from which, conjecturally, Antony Egan slipped to his death. A small distance away, where the thick overgrowth began, I noticed something dark lodged in a blackthorn bush that hung above the bank, almost over the stream.

'What's that?'

I pointed.

From where he was Fidelis could see nothing. He climbed back up the bank to join me and squinted at the dark shape in the bush.

'I don't know.'

'It could be a bird's nest.'

'I doubt it. But let's see.'

A few inches taller than me, and with the help of a long stick that he found in the bushes, Fidelis was able to poke at the thing until it came loose, lodging fortuitously onto the end of the stick. He brought it down. It was not a bird's nest, but a very old black tricorn hat.

'Do you think this might be Antony's?' he said.

'By the look of it, yes.'

He handed the hat to me.

'Then it is evidence,' he said, 'to be kept safe.'

I turned the hat over and over in a melancholy and reflective way. It was not a pristine object: the nap was almost off it and the inside of the crown was shiny with grease.

'He did favour plain old hats like this. But there must be hundreds like it in Preston. Who's to say this one was Antony's?'

'His daughters. Ask them.'

'And even if it is his, how on earth did it get into the bush?'

By now Peter Crane and his men had come into sight, returning from the inn to re-embark on Battersby's ferry. As they stepped off the road and onto the slipway, I watched as each man in turn, almost in a ritual, met the brunt of the breeze by putting his hand to his hat. No sooner had I seen this than a solution to our puzzle presented itself to my mind.

'Suppose it was the wind,' I said. 'Suppose the hat was blown off his head.'

Fidelis considered.

'Yes, why not?' he said at last. 'Let's see. He came staggering drunkenly down here on his usual mission. A gust of wind whipped his hat off, and it went flying towards the river. He chased after it, slipped on the wet bank and caused these skid marks. He grabbed a tuft of grass but it came away and he could not save himself. He went splash into the water.'

'Yes, yes,' I said, feeling the excitement stirring in me again. 'And the hat flew up and ended in the thorn bush.'

'*Quod erat demonstrandum.*'

I thought for a moment.

'It is very persuasive, but we do have to be sure that this really is Antony's hat.'

'Let's go up and ask now, at the inn.'

The fire of curiosity was still burning and it tempted me. But then I pulled back, remembering the grief of the two sisters.

'No. They have enough to think about. I'll bring it with me tomorrow, and ask them then.'

There was a shout from Battersby that he was ready to leave. So we crossed back to Preston-side with Crane and his men, to whom I gave tuppence each for their trouble, and produced a shilling for the ferryman. He slipped it into his money pouch and turned to move away, but I took hold of his arm.

'What?'

'By my reckoning it's only elevenpence I owe you, Mr Battersby. Antony Egan made just the one crossing, as he'd swum the other way.'

With a rasping sigh Battersby returned me a penny.

'Robert Battersby is a proper Charon, Luke,' I murmured as we walked away. 'He charges a fare to dead men.'

'Charon? Who's that?'

Fidelis had a sharp mind, second to none when it came to

logical reasoning. He also had great knowledge of new discoveries in natural philosophy, whether published in the *Transactions of the Royal Society* or by any number of other corresponding clubs to which he subscribed. He also knew much about money and the banking system, about mathematics, music (he played the harpsichord with skill), chemistry and about fashion in dress, both male and (more surprisingly) female. Yet he had read hardly any classical authors, and his knowledge of poetry seemed to be confined to *Mother Goose*.

'Charon!' I exclaimed. 'You must know! The ferryman who took the dead across the river Styx to Hades, in the ancient myth.'

'Why should I bother myself with mythology? I am interested in what is verifiable: the truth of today, not the lies of our ancestors.'

'But literature is not lies!' I protested, though I was not sure I would be able to defend the proposition in a court of law.

Fidelis, having business elsewhere, left me on Fisher Gate and I made my way home to Cheapside. Reaching the Moot Hall, the seat of Preston's government which stood at the top of my street, I noticed a small crowd had gathered around a florid fellow, dressed in a gown-like greatcoat patched with different-coloured pieces of cloth, and embroidered with arcane symbols and zodiac signs. He was displaying an egg to his audience, which he then made a show of swallowing, before producing it from beneath the collar of the man who stood in front of him. This drew some applause so that, affecting to be encouraged, he now brought out a pack of cards and began to perform tricks of remarkable dexterity, repeatedly making fools of his audience's judgement – mine included. Even more remarkable, I thought as I walked up to my door, was how amused we all were to be made such fools of.

Going in, and remembering the nature of the news I was

bringing, I made an effort to quell my amusement. As it always was by this hour of the morning – just past ten – the house was aired, swept, refreshed and quiet. I found Elizabeth sitting in the kitchen with her handkerchief in her hand, and her eyes fixed on what lay in front of her on the table. As soon as I saw what it was, I knew that Elizabeth had already heard what I'd come in to tell her: a fresh salmon lay there gleaming in its dish.

'Oh, Titus!' she cried, rising and throwing her arms around me. 'I went to the fish stall for today's meal. They told me what happened. Poor Uncle Antony! How terrible to die alone. How more terrible to drown.'

I stroked her hair, kissed her ear and pressed her to me.

'There there.'

I don't know who first came out with the words of comfort that I had just uttered. What on earth do they mean? Yet for some reason they are the first that leap to the tongue when someone is crying in one's arms. Just the balm of a voice is all that's needed, maybe, the sound of another person paying attention.

'There there,' I said again.

'He was so unhappy, so . . .'

She could not finish the sentence, as a new wave of crying came over her.

'And now he has been released from his unhappiness,' I said.

She raised her head from my chest and looked at me.

'How did it happen?'

'I think, almost certainly, that he slipped on the riverbank, in the dark. He may have been chasing his hat.'

'His hat?'

'Yes. In the wind. And since he wasn't sober, well . . .'

'Didn't they miss him at the inn? Didn't they look for him?'

'They didn't know he was dead, or even missing, until I told them this morning. Your uncle had a habit of going out walking alone at night, and often didn't return until his daughters had gone to bed. Last night he didn't return at all. But when I called they thought he had come home safe, after they had all retired to bed, and was lying late.'

'I must go to them. And then I'll hurry to Broughton to tell Mother. I would like to get there before rumour does, though I expect I shan't be in time. Shall I stay the night and bring her back with me in the morning?'

Broughton was two or three miles out of town on the northerly road, so this was a good plan.

'Yes. I am sure your mother will want to attend her brother's inquest, and comfort her nieces.'

Calling our maid Matty, she left instructions for serving the midday meal, and asked the girl what she thought she might give me for my supper. Matty glanced at me, and then at the salmon.

'No. That had better wait until tomorrow, when I return,' Elizabeth said firmly. 'You are only fifteen and not yet ready to be cooking so beautiful a fish.'

The girl looked crestfallen.

'Don't worry about me at all, Matty,' I said firmly. 'You just feed yourself tonight. I'll take some supper at the White Bull.'

When Elizabeth had left, I crossed the hall and passed through the baize-covered door that separates our living quarters from my business rooms. In the outer room I found Furzey, my clerk, at his writing desk.

'Antony Egan of the Ferry Inn is dead,' I told him, as I passed him on my way through to the inner room, my own domain. 'They fished him out of the river – and I mean that exactly.'

Furzey did not look up from his writing.

'Then you'll need an inquest jury,' he said drily.

'Just so.'

I went through, leaving the door open, and sat behind my own desk. Three or four letters had come in and I began breaking their seals. All were on business arising from the legal practice I carried on alongside the coronership. When I had read them I looked up again and could see Furzey through the doorway, still bent over his writing.

'Will you bring in the summonses?' I called. 'I'll draft a list of names. I'll be looking for anyone from Middleforth Green and the south riverbank, as far as Penwortham I think. Antony was that well known, it shouldn't be difficult to get people to serve. And another thing, I want you to ferret out his will.'

I had, naturally, always acted for the Egan family and had drawn up Antony's will some ten years earlier.

'I'd better know what's in it before I see his daughters tomorrow.'

I waited patiently for Furzey to stop writing, but his head was still lowered and his pen still squeaked its way across the paper, line after line.

'Furzey!' I called. 'The summonses, please. We have only today to get them out.'

With some elaboration he finished the sentence he was on, wiped his pen and scattered sand across his page.

'I suppose the day will come,' he said, 'when you will finally employ two clerks. But not until you have worked me into an untimely grave.'

This was a common theme of Furzey's. He was a born agitator.

'I can't afford a second clerk, as you well know.'

'Can't, you say. Won't, I say.'

'Can we please get on with today's business?'

The jury summonses, in my father's day, were each of them laboriously handwritten. But when I took over the coronership I went to the printer and had him reproduce and print large numbers of these summonses, with blanks left for the names, dates and other details to be filled in, as occasion demanded. It was a bundle of these sheets that Furzey now brought in to me.

'See? Those are labour saving,' I pointed out. 'Without those, you'd be writing every summons out individually. So don't tell me your days are harder than they were.'

He merely dropped the sheets down in front of me.

'There is no such thing, in *my* opinion, as labour saving, Mr Cragg. When a man saves on one job, he finds another one waiting.'

With Furzey, one never enjoyed the last word. I sighed and asked again that he produce the Egan will.

The White Bull Inn stood at the heart of the town and I had only to turn left out of my front door, take the few steps to the end of Cheapside, and cross Market Place to get there. The inn stood on the north side, an old-fashioned wood-frame building, yet possessed of a sense of its own magnificence, and roundly contemptuous of puny rival establishments in and around town. From across Market Place the Moot Hall clock was striking six as I pushed hungrily through its swinging doors and smelled the roast meats turning on their spits, and the puddings steaming in the kitchen. The price would not be the cheapest but I would get a good supper.

From the middle of the big stone-flagged hall in front of me rose a wide oak staircase, to the left of which were the double swing doors that led to the grand dining hall, with its four tall windows ranged above Market Street. On the right, looking out on the market itself, lay two rooms, the taproom and coffee room.

The dining hall was reminiscent of our old hall at the Temple, during my student days. Diners sat at three rows of long tables running the length of the room, except for the High Table, which was arranged laterally across its end. Here the quality would be seated, not on forms as were the rest of us, but on high-backed chairs with stuffed seats. The wall behind the central chair displayed a great corporation coat of arms wreathed in lavish gilt foliage – the room was used for the largest of our civic banquets – and the rest of the available space on the walls was taken up with portraits of nobles and dignitaries connected with the town: the Earl of This, Lord That and His Worship the Other.

Even before going in I was aware of an unusual hubbub. Once inside I could see that the tables at the far end of the hall, including the High Table, were occupied by a rout of thirty or forty, gorging on a meal of roast beef, pickles and, to wash them down, superior ales from Burton-on-Trent. I recognized most of them as freemen of the town, with a sprinkling of out-of-towners unknown to me. Sitting at High Table in the president's chair was Sir Harry Hoghton, who had served as one of our Members of Parliament for longer than most people could remember. He lived at Hoghton Tower, 8 miles away. Beside him was a gentleman of about fifty who, compared with Sir Harry's florid bearing, was scrawny and a little lugubrious, and who looked nervously about him, picking at his food and saying little. This was Francis Reynolds, a Manchester man. For the last year he had lived largely in Preston, cultivating the electors – or trying to – in order to get himself in as Hoghton's fellow MP. Beside *him* to my surprise sat the curly-haired stranger who I had last seen being packed out of the Ferry Inn parlour by Mary-Ann Egan. He cut a confident, lively figure in this company, laughing and joking with those around him, proposing toasts and singing snatches of songs. I noticed him paying particular attention to Reynolds, hanging on any words the fellow spoke and drawing him into the general conversation whenever possible, while at the same time conferring closely with the man on his other side. This was Ralph Randall, Sir Harry's steward.

In addition to this party there were several other customers at the long tables, sitting in disparate groups of three or four. I was shown to a place at the other extreme of the hall from the election party, near the end of one of the long tables. I was opposite Nicholas Oldswick, a watchmaker and burgess, as well as a notorious litigant who in years past had been assisted by my father in various actions at the mayoral Court Leet, where local trading disputes and civil complaints were wrangled over. Oldswick had recently been made a widower and, being childless, took to supping at the White Bull, and other inns, for the company as much as the convenience. But tonight he didn't seem to be enjoying his meal very much, and was squinting with particular displeasure at the goings-on down the room.

'What's all this, Nick?' I asked as I slid into my place. 'Election treat?'

'Aye. Parliament is dissolved and the pig feeding has begun.'

'Well, we've known an election was coming, and we'll have a contest this time.'

'For all the good it'll do us. Pig feeding!'

I didn't entirely share his revulsion.

'Nick, it *may* do us good. We shall all enjoy it. How long since this town's had a contest in a general election – nineteen years, I think? This will stir the place up wonderfully.'

It had been evident for some time that Sir Robert Walpole, First Lord of the Treasury, would have to call a general election this year. Now for the first time since 1722 we were to have a fight in Preston, with Hoghton and Reynolds standing as Whig candidates against our other incumbent MP Mr Nicholas Fazackerley for the Tories, standing with a young newcomer, Mr James Shuttleworth. So there was a chance that, at the end of it all, the two members elected by Preston would for once be of the same party, and no longer cancel each other out as they had in the old parliament. I looked up the room at Reynolds, whom I had met only in passing.

'So Reynolds will get his chance at last,' I said. 'He's been assiduous enough in the last few months, working the town. What do you make of him?'

'Just another lackey of Sir Treasure Shovel. Speaks the King's German in his sleep, without doubt. He'll not get my vote.'

'I never thought he would, Nick. You've always been strong for the Tories.'

'I have, though there's some that call it the Country Party now. I won't be bought. There's plenty he might buy because that's all their politics is – people putting themselves up for sale.'

'Don't both sides do the same?'

Oldswick shrugged.

'A treat on one side's a bribe on the other, I grant you. But still, *I* know the difference, me.'

'Reynolds may be better than Hoghton, though.'

'He's forced to be. There's nobody *worse* than Hoghton. The man's hardly a Christian.'

Oldswick was getting heated now. He was beginning to enjoy himself.

'I once went over to divine service at his church in Hoghton Tower, you know – well, you'd hardly have called it *divine* at all. The barest church you ever saw. No candles on the altar, and you were not to call it an altar, but a table, always a table. And they speak of the Elect, you know, who will be saved at the Last Judgement while the rest of us troop off to hell. It's all been decided in advance, so they claim, before the world was made. Predestination.'

He took a sip from his wine glass and looked at me over its rim, his eyes sparkling as he became more voluble. He put down the glass with a little more force than was strictly necessary.

'And guess who they reckon are the Elect of this part of the world, Titus.'

'Sir Harry and his friends?'

'You have it. And not content with being elected to paradise, he sees himself as God's elected for this parliamentary seat. Of course, he forgets God's got no vote in the borough. So let them bid away for votes by giving feasts. I say they can be out-feasted.'

'Do you know the man on Reynolds's right? The red-headed stranger?'

'His name's Destercore, a political agent. They sent him from London to stick some backbone into Reynolds at the hustings.'

'Is there a Tory agent also?'

'Aye, we've got Thompson, that helped out with the Wakefield by-election in thirty-three.'

I had got a few mouthfuls of my steak pudding down when the speeches began. There was a string of fine phrases about the Spanish war, which had started a year or so earlier, after years of peace. Mention was also made of the plight of the new Queen of Hungary, who lived so far away that it mattered little what precisely was said, and there was much extolling of the yeomen of England, a class of person that has now entered the realm of the imaginary. No time was given I noticed to extolling the name of Walpole himself. Were Sir Treasure Shovel's fortunes on the wane?

After I had finished my dinner I went into the coffee room and wrote a note:

Mr Destercore:

As His Majesty's coroner for this borough I am inquiring into the sudden death last night of the proprietor of the Ferry Inn, where I believe you were staying at the time of the said death. If you have any information to provide to this inquiry please present yourself at the inquest to give testimony, which will be held tomorrow at noon at the aforementioned inn.

Titus Cragg

A few minutes later a reply came back scrawled on the back of the same piece of paper:

Sir,

I regret I cannot help you, knowing nothing of the event to which you refer.

Yr Srvt Denis Destercore

Chapter Four

I ARRIVED AT THE Ferry Inn at ten in the morning, with two hours to spare before the opening of the inquest. I intended to use the time to speak with the inn's nightman, and to form a clear idea of events on the evening Antony Egan had gone into the river.

John the nightman, who was great-uncle to the potboy Toby, was more than seventy years of age, a tall, skeletal figure with a pillow of white beard concealing most of his chest. His large, shuffling feet pointed outwards at the angle of a clock's hands upon a quarter past eight.

I apologized for getting him out of his daytime bed, then asked him where we could talk. He led the way to a small room off the passage back from the hall. It was not much bigger than a cupboard, contained a high stool and a workbench, and was lit by a small window that looked out onto the inn's backyard. Attached to the bench was a vice and cobbler's last, and on a shelf above, or hanging from it, were a collection of cloths, blacking, brushes, dubbins, waxes and shoe-mending tools. John settled himself on the stool while I leaned against the bench at his side.

First I placed in front of him the black hat that Fidelis and I had found in the riverside bush.

'Is this, or was it, your master's hat?'

The old man picked up the hat and peered inside. Then he held it at the extremity of his arm and cocked his head.

'Aye, I'd say it looks like.'

He spoke from his throat, in a voice that sounded like shifting wet gravel.

'You're sure it was his?'

'That's not what I said. I'm sure it looks like his.'

I took back the hat.

'So tell me what happened here on Sunday night.'

He looked at me as if he did not understand my drift.

'Same as always,' he said.

'Which means?'

'Which means what?'

I could not decide if he was being obstructive or obtuse. I said, 'John, why don't you simply tell me what you do here every night, before and after midnight?'

Looking up at the ceiling he took a deep, wheezy breath.

'All right,' he said, in a more conciliatory tone. 'Evenings I work on boots, if there is any. I polish them and mend them if mending's needed. Here in my boot room, I do that. If there's nothing of work for me I read my Bible. Then I come out for my duty at midnight.'

'Your duty?'

'I'm nightman. I sit by the counter in the hall till daybreak. Happen there'll be a late arrival to see to. Or an early.'

'And every night after the guests had gone up to bed, and the customers had cleared off, the master would go out for his walk, would he?'

'He would. Regular, he was.'

'And would this be before or after midnight?'

'Just a mite before, I reckon.'

'And he didn't do any different last Sunday night.'

'Likely he did not.'

'You're not sure?

He gave me another exasperated look.

'I told you. I come on duty at midnight. I was in this room until then, so how could I see him go out?'

'And you didn't see him come back in?'

He stroked his beard and gave me a long look, appraising or just thinking slowly – it was impossible to know with John.

At last he said, 'How could I have seen him come back in? He never did come back in.'

I tried hard to contain my impatience.

'All right. What happened during the night?'

He shook his head and sighed, looking at the floor.

'He drowned, so they tell me.'

'Yes, but I mean what happened here, at the inn? Did any guests arrive later? Were there any notable events?'

'Just the one man came after I started on watch, a servant following his master who'd arrived before him. On the journey up with his master their horses went lame so this man was left at Kirkham to sell the beasts while his master walked on. His name is Hamilton Peters. When he got here he asked for a bed but I turned him out of doors. Told him he was lucky I'd let him sleep on straw in an outhouse. But he was that tired he didn't argue with me.'

'Where did he sleep then?'

'On straw in the barn.'

'It's not very hospitable, is it? Why not let him in and give him a bed?'

John spoke guardedly.

'Maybe I didn't like him.'

He shrugged and opened his hands. I understood him to mean that he could tell me more, but it was not forthcoming.

'I was here next morning,' I said. 'I saw the gentleman his master having his breakfast but I never saw Peters.'

'He took first ferry. I saw him at dawn. He went up to his master for a few minutes, and then he cleared off. Said he was going ahead into town to find further accommodation.'

'Can you remember what time in the night he came in?'

'I don't need to.'

John eased off his stool and plodded out into the passage and back to the hall. I followed. The counter stood before the business room and beside it a comfortably upholstered hall porter's chair, from which one had a view of the front door on one side and the staircase on the other. I stood waiting at the counter as John went behind and inside, coming back with a ledger. He banged this down, opened it, licked his fingers and began leafing through the pages.

'It's all writ down,' he said.

'By you?'

I must have allowed the smallest hint of surprise into my voice because John stopped turning the pages and fixed me with a rheumy eye.

'I know my letters, Mr Cragg. But no, by them. That is our way at this inn.'

He found the place and turned the book so that I could read it. The page was divided into columns for the date of arrival and the time, a signature, the place where the guest had travelled from, and the date and time of departure. He pointed to the most recent entry.

27 April || *12.25 a.m.* || *H.P. servant of Mr Destercore (barn)*
|| *Liverpool* || *27 April* || *7.10 a.m.*

Immediately above I noted the entry for Peters's master in a different, more scrawled script.

26 April || 7.45 p.m. || Denis Destercore || Liverpool || 27 April || 8.10 a.m.

I took from my pocket the note I had received last night at the White Bull and compared the signatures. They were the same.

'What was his behaviour, this servant?'

'How d'you mean?'

'Was he polished, or rough mannered – how did he carry himself?'

'He was ill mannered and very ungrateful.'

'Really?' I tapped the entry in the register. 'Yet the hand of this servant is polite: an educated hand. Would you say he was educated?'

'No. To me he was foul spoken and rough.'

Before I swivelled the ledger back towards John, I looked over the rest of the page. Destercore and Peters had not been the only ones staying on the Sunday night: there were three other names – not an unusual number of guests. For most of the previous week there had been three or four putting up at the inn each night – late arrivals who slept there only because they could not cross to Preston by ferry until the next morning.

'There's just one more thing, John,' I said. 'You keep to your post here, in the hall, from midnight, is that right?'

'Aye.'

I pointed towards the inn's front door.

'And your master would come in by that door after his walk, plainly in your sight?'

'He would.'

'When would that be, normally?'

'Most nights he'd be out half an hour but, odd times, he did stay longer, I reckon.'

'Would he lock up after he came in?'

'Aye, unless he forgot.'

'In which case you locked up?'

'Aye.'

'So when he did not come back on the night we're talking about, you kept the door unlocked for him?'

'Aye.'

'Why did you not raise the alarm, or go out and look for him, when you knew he had been out such a long time?'

John appeared embarrassed. He leaned nearer to me across the counter.

'I didn't always mind him, see? Happen sometimes I had even nodded off when he came in, and never saw him at all.'

Then another idea struck him. He screwed up his face.

'But now I think on it, I did mind I hadn't seen Mr Egan come back yet. Then when I still didn't see him, I made up my mind he'd come in while I was seeing to that Peters, taking him to the barn, like. That is what I thought to myself at the time. But any road, I could not leave this post – not long enough for to go outdoors along the river path looking. I was on duty.'

I thanked John and asked him to stand by to give his evidence later. Then I went in search of Mary-Ann. She was sitting with her sister in their private parlour, which one reached through the kitchen.

'Where have you put your father to lie?' I asked.

'In his bedroom,' stated Mary-Ann.

'Dr Fidelis will be here soon and we will have a quick look at him together before the hearing. Now, do you know whose this is?'

I produced the black hat, which I had folded and tucked into my pocket. I straightened it and pushed the crown into shape.

'My daddy's hat!' cried Grace, seizing it from me. 'Where'd you find this?'

'Near the ferry stage. You're sure it's his?'

'Of course. Am I not right, Mary?'

She passed it to Mary-Ann who looked inside.

'Yes, it's his,' she confirmed.

'And you can testify that he would have been wearing this hat when he went out on Sunday night for his walk?'

'Oh yes, he always did,' said Grace. 'I'm right glad you found it.'

'May I have it back until after the hearing? I will need to show it to the jury.'

Mary-Ann handed it back.

'Will you tell us what will happen today?' she asked.

I explained the inquest's procedure. The jury would assemble at twelve and be sworn. They would then view the body, taking note of anything that could furnish clues as to how their father had died, before hearing the evidence of witnesses. Finally they would go into a huddle and come up with a verdict.

'What sort of verdict?'

'There are really only five possibilities.'

I counted them off on my fingers.

'Murder, manslaughter, self-murder, self-manslaughter and accidental death.'

Grace absorbed the information for a moment, and said, 'We had not thought it could be anything but an accident, had we, Mary-Ann?'

Mary-Ann shook her head.

'I cannot imagine what self-manslaughter is, Uncle.'

'I use it to mean when persons kill themselves but are not fully to blame. For instance, by reason of insanity.'

'Oh, I see.'

'I am sure, as you say, an accident is most likely in this case,' I said. 'But the inquest must be seen to consider every possibility.'

'Who will attend?' Mary-Ann asked.

'Inquests must be open to the general public but I don't expect many of them today, if any at all. Otherwise there will be just myself and Furzey my clerk, the jury members, the first finder – who was Peter Crane the salmon fisher, you know – and witnesses in this household. And other witnesses who may be called or come forward to assist. I shall certainly call Dr Fidelis.'

Mention the Devil, and see his horns. No sooner had I spoken than there came a knock on the door, and Toby entered to say that Dr Fidelis had arrived, and was waiting in the hall. I asked if we could be taken straight up to where the body lay and, two minutes later, Fidelis and I stood one on either side of Antony's bed.

He had been laid out in his nightgown, with a plain nightcap on his head, and his arms crossed piously across his chest. I put my hand under the body, lifting and manipulating it to enable Fidelis to pull the garment up to the neck. Then we looked down together on the naked remains.

'He has suffered many smaller accidents before this fatal one,' said Fidelis.

He was right. The body had an assortment of scars and bruises, scalds and burns.

'I have seen this at inquest on many a toper's corpse,' I said. 'They trip over, they set fire to their wigs, they bump into trees.'

'I see it on living persons, too,' added Fidelis.

He removed the nightcap and raised Antony's head to inspect it on all sides.

'There are a few insignificant contusions about the head, but they're old ones.'

'So you don't think he was clubbed over the head before he fell into the river?'

He laid the head back on the pillow and straightened his back.

'No. The only conclusion I draw from this examination is that it confirms what we already know. The man was a sot, who towards the end was near incapable.'

'Let us go down then.'

We found the jury assembling in the taproom, drinking beer and talking loudly about the inconvenience of inquest duty. I did not take them seriously because I knew they spoke like this only to cover up their happiness. Some of them must have known Antony Egan quite well and might have been sorry for his death. But that did not detract from the good feeling of having a holiday while, at the same time, virtuously performing a public duty.

I led the way into the dining room – good sized and well lit by two high windows – to find Furzey already established and writing busily at the end of a long table in the centre of the room, with an empty chair beside him. Here I sat, arranging the men on the forms six to each side, while another chair was left empty at the far end to seat witnesses as they gave their evidence. Mary-Ann and Grace Egan had their own chairs by the window, while another form ranged along the wall to my right was for witnesses after they'd spoken and others in attendance. Among those others were my wife with her mother, the sister of the dead man.

As if unwilling to let it interfere too far with drinking and eating, the jury was in a mood to get the inquest over quickly. Once they were sworn, I took them upstairs to view the body. There were some remarks made about its bumped and scarred state, some pious, others sarcastic; but they did not linger in the bedroom, and within a few minutes we were back in the inquest room ready to hear testimony from Peter Crane, followed by the two Egan daughters, the nightman and finally Dr Fidelis. None of this produced any unexpected information. Finally, with no further witnesses coming forward, I summed up, sketching Antony's sad condition, his habit of taking a late-night walk, the events of the fatal night, and of how the body was found next morning.

'I myself, in the company of Dr Fidelis, saw the body shortly after it was brought ashore, and the doctor has told us of the view he formed as a medical man, that the lungs were full of water. This meant Antony Egan was breathing when he entered the water, and his death was consequently by drowning. Dr Fidelis and I, as you have also heard, later inspected the riverbank beside the ferry stage, to which Antony invariably took his midnight walks. There we found signs that someone had recently slid down the steep, wet bank in the direction of the water. In a bush nearby we found Antony's hat and you have heard it discussed as a possibility that, nearing the ferry stage, the hat blew from his head and he chased it towards the river but, failing to catch it, slipped into the water and was carried helplessly downstream, drowning as he went. Your task is to decide whether a sequence of events such as this, or some other cause, brought about his death. Are there any questions?'

The foreman looked around the table but no hand was raised. When this happens I find that a jury is already of one mind, even before they have discussed the case among themselves. I therefore rang my handbell and rose, asking everybody who was not a jury member to leave the room so that the twelve could deliberate.

'Oh, Titus,' said Elizabeth, coming to me with her mother in tow as soon as she saw me entering the hall and shutting the door of the inquest room behind me. 'Tell us there was no foul play here. The business is horrible enough.'

'That is for the jury, my dear. But you heard my summing-up. I doubt they will contradict it.'

Five minutes later we received notice to return. The jury had reached a unanimous finding of accidental death. Furzey wrote the verdict on another of our printed forms and the paper was passed round for the signature of each juror. Finally I signed it myself and dissolved the inquest.

It was a satisfactory outcome. We had avoided the financially disastrous finding of self-murder, and the lurking uncertainty of murder. All that remained was for me to release the body for burial, and write my report. I signed the release (another printed sheet – there is no end to their usefulness) and gave it, with the battered old hat, to Mary-Ann.

'You may lay him to rest,' I said. 'This business is concluded.'

Of this I was utterly confident – and utterly wrong.

Chapter Five

M Y FIRST WARNING of just how wrong I was about the conclusion of the Egan case came within half an hour. Fidelis and I had just stepped off Battersby's ferry and begun the climb up the track to the top of the town, when the gate to one of the gardens lining the track swung open.

'Hissst!'

We looked. There was no one to be seen.

'Hissst!'

'Who's there?' I called.

Stepping into the aperture of the gate I saw, half hidden behind a flowering plum tree, a shape that I realized was Dick Middleton, cultivator of that particular plot.

'Well, Dick,' I said, 'come out and tell us what you want.'

The man who now edged into view was a slight figure in his fifties, who lived by selling produce from his garden, and by fishing for eels in the river, for which he had a permit from the corporation. He was also in his very nature nervous and retiring, a solitary fellow, for he had been born with a harelip that distorted his face and muffled his voice.

'How do, Coroner?' he said, with nods of his head. 'How do, Doctor?'

Fidelis and I gave him how-do in return and waited to hear what he had to say.

'I heard them talking,' he said at last, twisting his hands together as if this helped him squeeze out the words. His deformity meant that his mouth sounded blocked and his tongue impeded.

'Who did you hear, Dick?'

'Men after coming over from Ferry Inn. William Forrest and John Pitt, on their way up to town.'

'Yes. They were on the jury that sat over the body of Antony Egan this afternoon.'

'I know that. I heard, or rather I overheard, them talking to Poll Beattie, when they met her on the path.'

'Oh, yes? What were they saying?'

His gaze found everywhere to look but into our faces.

'They were saying that Antony were at ferry stage all alone, and his hat blew off his head, which he chased towards river, and missed it, and fell in.'

'Yes,' I said. 'That was the jury's conclusion.'

'And it's not right. It's not precise.'

'Oh? Why not?'

'I were there, see? I know it's not right.'

Fidelis and I exchanged surprised looks.

'You were *there*?'

'I was.'

'Where?' my friend asked. 'Be specific, Dick.'

'I was seated on riverbank. It were high tide, best tide for eels. I wasn't over there, mind. I was on this side of river. But I had the opposite ferry stage in the line of my eye. I could see all and I could hear a bit too.'

His tongue had loosened itself up, as if its very use made it freer.

'Hear what?' Fidelis persisted.

'Talking. Antony were talking. So that's why it's wrong, I'm saying. By the talking, I could tell there was someone with him.'

'Did you see this other person that he was talking to?'

Middleton widened his eyes and shook his head.

'Happen there was someone in the shadows, or in the trees. There must've been, if he were talking.'

'And what was he saying?'

'That I don't know, sir. I heard the voice coming and going, but missed the words in the water's noise and the wind. See, the wind were first class right there for finding eels on north bank. So I were just pulling in one of my traps when Antony came in my sight, and he were talking. I heard the sound of his voice.'

'What did his voice sound like?'

'It sounded vexed.'

'Like a lot of complaining . . . ?'

'Yes, that'll do. And here's another word: peevish.'

'And what time was this?'

'High tide, like I said.'

'But when by the clock?'

'Maybe midnight, or a little after.'

'And did you see Antony subsequently go into the water?'

'I did not. The eels were in the traps so I were busy for the next five minutes. When I looked again there were no sign of Antony. No sign of anybody.'

'You heard no cry or splash or other activity?'

'There are always splashes. Moorhens and such. And, as I said, the wind were blowing the sounds away.'

'Did you hear anything else?'

'I thought I did, Mr Cragg. Laughing, it might have been. Very faint it were, and happen I were wrong and it were a duck. I thought no more of it till now.'

'Why didn't you come forward and tell the inquest all this?' I demanded.

He touched his bifurcated mouth with his fingertips.

'With this, Mr Cragg, people don't believe what I say. It makes me, as they think, a double talker at the best, and a liar at the worst. So I can't ever be a witness, not in a court of law. I'll not be believed.'

'This changes things, Titus,' said Fidelis after we had left Dick Middleton and begun again to walk up the steep incline towards town. 'We must think again.'

But I had been less impressed than he by the fisherman's tale.

'Must we? I don't think what he said helps us towards the truth.'

'Surely you don't believe this nonsense about his harelip?'

'No, no. I don't think he's a liar, far from it. He is intelligent, though his tongue can't keep pace with his brain. But on this matter, I think, he must be mistaken. I don't think there *was* anyone else there. He said himself he saw no one.'

'I am not disputing that. Let's leave that to one side.'

'Then what is your point? I am not reopening the inquest just because a fisherman thirty yards away in the dark heard a few ducks and a drunken man doing what drunks do – talking to himself.'

'It isn't about whether or not he was talking to himself. It's about the wind.'

'The wind?'

'Yes. You heard Dick state that the conditions were best for finding eel on the north side of the river.'

'Yes, though I don't quite understand what he meant by that.'

'The ideal spot to set your traps is on the lee shore when the tide is high.'

'Is that the case? I didn't know that you were an eel fisher.'

'As a boy. But then there was something else, even more directly bearing on the matter. He said he could hear the voice coming across the water, but he missed the words because of the noise of the water, and the wind blowing them away from him. These reports taken together strongly support my idea that the wind was blowing from the north.'

'And what is the import of that?'

Luke clicked his tongue, exasperated at the snail pace of my thinking.

'It was blowing from Dick on one bank towards Antony on the other, Titus.'

I still did not grasp it. Now Luke, as he sometimes did when I could not absorb what was obvious to him, spoke slowly, as to a recalcitrant pupil.

'We have been blaming the wind, have we not? We have proceeded on the basis that Antony's hat was blown from his head and towards the river, precipitating a desperate attempt by him to catch it, followed by his fatal slip into the water. But if the wind was blowing from in front of him, if it was a northerly, as John Middleton's statement implies that it was, the sequence of events I have described could not have happened. If the wind blew his hat off his head at all, it must have done so away from the river, not towards it. The wind, I submit to you, is wholly innocent of this crime.'

I considered the argument.

'That is pretty, but I have an objection. If the hat wasn't wind blown, how did it get into the bush overhanging the water?'

Fidelis turned and punched me lightly on the shoulder.

'That's not an objection, Titus! That's the question we must ask. How do you think it did?'

'It would have to be some person that threw it there.'

'Yes, and perhaps that person was the one Dick Middleton heard Antony being angry with.'

I sighed.

'I suppose it may be so, Luke. But isn't it more likely that Antony threw it there himself? This doesn't change anything, in my judgement. No other person was seen. There is no proper evidence that such another person was there. And overtopping all that there is the problem of Dick Middleton as a witness. Even if you and I, and every other educated person in town, thinks that a man with a harelip can indeed be a credible witness, the people of Preston as a whole will still doubt him.'

'Damned superstitions.'

'That sounds rich in your mouth, Luke. Don't you yourself believe in angels, and Hail Marys, and Christ's body in a little piece of round bread?'

Fidelis perceptibly stiffened at my jibe.

'You are being unworthy there, Titus. Those are matters of religion; of faith, not reason. And, may I remind you that it's your wife's faith, as well as mine?'

In this he was perfectly right. Elizabeth, like my friend, was a papist. His reference to this made me regret my sally against the Church of Rome, though not the thinking behind it.

'Well, I am sorry, but I am not going to reopen the inquest. The only reason to do so is the testimony of Dick Middleton and he swears he won't testify. So we must let poor Antony rest there.'

Yet I found myself for the remainder of the day dwelling on what the eel fisherman had told us, and feeling annoyed that it might overthrow our convenient theory that the wind had blown Antony's hat towards the water, and caused its owner, in chasing it, to bank-slide into the river.

My mother-in-law would be having a bed in our house for a second night in succession, as her brother's funeral was the next day. Her being there meant I had no chance, all evening, to talk with Elizabeth about Dick Middleton's story. Instead I fretted about it in my own head until after supper (the salmon at last, roasted with herbs) when I dived into my library, and took down Izaak Walton's hymn and vade mecum to an activity that I am insufficiently contemplative to take up myself – *The Compleat Angler*.

Walton I found is an author riddled with contradiction. Angling is like poetry, he says in one place, and best practised by men '*born to the task*'. But I turned a few pages and found him arguing that '*as no man is born an artist, so no man is born an angler*'. Angling must then be learned, after all. Oh no, declared our riverside friend at yet another juncture. Angling is '*so like the mathematics that it can never be fully learned*'. I soon concluded that like every man ruled by one passion, Walton's confusion came from seeing his mania reflected in everything, and in everything's opposite, all at the same time.

But I had to allow he had authority on the practice of the sport and, turning the pages as far as chapter five, I read the following injunction:

'*Take this for a rule: that I would willingly fish standing on the lee shore.*'

I took 'lee shore' to mean the bank away from which the wind blows. Walton tells the reader that, since wind cools water, the fish prefer the warmest water they can find: that is, where it is sheltered from the wind by the riverbank – the lee shore. If Middleton was in agreement with Walton when he specified ideal conditions for eel fishing, he must have meant that the wind at the time he was fishing from the north bank had been at his back.

If that was the case, Fidelis's contention was confirmed. The wind on the night in question was from the north and, since Antony was walking on the south bank, it could hardly have blown his hat northwards into the bush where we found it hanging over the water.

With a sigh of perplexity I returned Walton to the shelf and myself to the parlour, where Elizabeth and her mother were companionably sewing. They were discussing Antony.

'He was always a crybaby,' my mother-in-law was saying. 'If something he wanted was denied him, or taken from him, he would sulk and sniffle for a week.'

She was a steely woman, with a sharp nose and a decided way of expressing herself.

'When my nephew took himself away, and then got himself killed, my brother could never leave off bemoaning his lot – a father deprived of his only son.'

'But that is a terrible loss for anyone, Mother,' Elizabeth objected. 'It is why Uncle drank – to forget it.'

'No, my dear. Antony drank so that others would be forced to remember, and so feel sorry for Antony for ever and ever.'

'Which his own death the other night put the seal on,' I suggested.

'Yes, it did. But it cannot have been deliberate, Titus,' the dead man's sister stated firmly. 'One may love a life of misery, you know, as much as a life of joy. And he did.'

'Then you think my jury was right to reject suicide today?'

'Oh, I am quite sure of that, dear Titus,' she said, bending over her stitching.

'Your mother is hard on the memory of her brother,' I said to Elizabeth as we lay in bed that night.

'She is of such a different temperament. And years ago he abandoned our religion because he hoped to be made a burgess, which she never really forgave him for.'

'Do you think she's right about his not having killed himself?'

'Didn't you know? My mother is always right.'

'So, like mother, like daughter,' I laughed.

I reached for her hand and described my meeting with Dick

Middleton, and the way it had destroyed my hypothesis of how her uncle's hat had found its way into the upper reaches of the waterside bush.

'Why does it matter, about the hat?' she asked.

'It is not just the hat, you see. The blowing away of the hat, and his chasing it, was a tidy explanation for why and how Antony slipped into the river. Now, if that doesn't hold any more, we don't know what happened. I hate to reach a verdict only to have doubts cast on it.'

'It was surely by some misadventure, at all events.'

'Could he have thrown the hat out over the river, I wonder, and in doing so lost his balance and slipped, while the hat blew back and lodged in the bush?'

Elizabeth took her hand from mine and, raising herself up until she was propped on one elbow, gave me a tap on the forehead with her finger.

'Now why ever would he do that? You will become brain feverish if you do not stop carrying on about this hat.'

'There's another thing,' I persisted. 'Dick Middleton heard Antony loudly talking. Who to?'

'Himself, Titus. Doubtless him*self*. Now here is a kiss. You have need for distraction, I think, or you will never sleep.'

Next morning I stepped out at nine to visit Miss Amelia Colley, a client of more than modest means who wanted to revise her will. The sky was grizzly, and there was a sharp, damp edge to the wind. Seeing a small crowd around the fountain at the centre of the Market Place, I strolled over to see what interested them. They were being addressed, from the steps of the fountain, by young Mr James Shuttleworth. This was one of the candidates in the election, standing in the Tory or, as some then called it, the Country Party interest.

Positioned just behind him, with four or five other supporting gentry and members of the council, was his father Richard, a dour, cunning old campaigner with a reputation for being a secret supporter of the Pretender's claim to the throne. This may not have been true, since politics have less to do with truth than with useful lies, and the elder Shuttleworth was a politician to the roots of his hair. He had represented the surrounding county of Lancashire uninterrupted as one of its two Members of Parliament for thirty-five years. He was going for the seat again this year, without opposition, alongside a new parliamentary prospect, Lord Derby's son James. In the previous election, seven years before, Richard had schemed to get his own son, his elder, to join him in Parliament as one of Preston's borough MPs, but the boy had inconveniently died of the smallpox a few weeks before the poll. Now the old crocodile's hopes were invested in his next boy, another James, who had come of age in the meantime.

James Shuttleworth was at a disadvantage, compared to his father, in that he had to fight to gain the seat, which brought his personal attributes into play. Though tall and with regular features, he possessed a reedy voice that struggled just now to make itself heard in the open air. He was talking about the Spanish war.

'England now fights,' I could just hear him say, 'merely in order to extort money from the Spaniard for his attacks on our shipping. Is this, I ask you, a just cause for war?'

He looked down at his notes, written on a piece of paper that trembled in his fingers. It was then that I noticed, at the edge of the crowd, the vivid red hair of Denis Destercore. The candidate looked up and began again.

'No, it isn't. Is this honourable behaviour? Is this how a gentleman conducts his business? I say it presents us to the world as little better than p-p-pirates.'

'Hoity-toity!' shouted someone from the crowd. 'Are you such a traitor?'

I looked and saw the interruptor was standing next to Destercore, a large man with a craggy, belligerent but handsome sort of face. It was my first view of the servant, Hamilton Peters.

'No indeed, sir, the opposite,' piped the youth, turning to address Peters directly. 'Do you not see? When we fight like that – for nothing but money – we do look just like pirates on the high seas.'

Despite the candidate's squeaking voice, his words sounded like good sense to me. But, emboldened by the intervention, bored by the speech and made rancorous by the cold, the majority of the crowd did not agree. One or two derisive hoots were raised, and shouts of 'Rubbish!' and 'Who cares?'

'But no, no, I assure you, we all must care,' squeaked the candidate, his face reddening. 'I-I-I mean as the great writer Lord St Albans once said—'

'Lord St Whose-arse?' came a reply, causing an outbreak of laughter. The voice was again that of Destercore's companion.

A cabbage stalk arced up into the air from the crowd and bounced off the fountain behind Richard Shuttleworth, striking his back. The old county MP then stepped forward and whispered urgently in his son's ear, before himself turning to the crowd and in stentorian tones bellowing for quiet.

'Pay heed to Mr James Shuttleworth,' he roared, hoisting his index finger high above his head. 'He is pointing out that not a penny of this Spanish lucre – supposing it is ever paid over – can possibly benefit you, the electors of this fine town. No indeed! Rather it will be poured straight into the already bulging pockets of the London shipowners and merchants. However, when you freemen of proud Preston do Mr James Shuttleworth the signal honour of electing him to represent this mighty borough in Parliament, let us assure you he will join with others to strain every muscle, every sinew, in opposing the government's connivance with these crooks, to stop this rotten war and, yes, yes, to reduce your taxes that are raised to pay for it! You cannot benefit from this war; only from ending it.'

This for the first time raised a cheer and a volley of clapping. The wily old roué had rescued the meeting for his virginal young son.

I walked on, reflecting on the excitement that this election promised, but also on the extraordinary disruption of town life it was going to bring. In the first few days the canvass would be frenetic. The list of freemen electors – about 700 of them – would be fought over and the credentials of each one scrutinized. One way or another votes would be acquired for this and that party. A market trader's debts would be paid off, and a dowry portion found for a shopkeeper's daughter. All the time the eating, drinking and jollity would be prodigious. And then as polling got started friendly persuasion would give way to bullying and broken heads, on the principle that if you can't laugh a man into voting for you, you must resort to hearing him squeal.

Chapter Six

'ARE YOU NOT EXCITED, dear Mr Cragg, that we are to have *Alfred* this coming Sunday?' cried Miss Amelia Colley, pouring me a glass of Madeira wine. 'Lord Strange is such a benefactor.'

Miss Colley was one of the numerous widows and maiden ladies who migrated to Preston in middle life, finding existence in a rented house (or, in less prosperous cases, a set of rooms) on Fisher or Friar Gate far preferable to a draughty dower house or ragged-roofed grace-and-favour cottage on some dull country estate. Sitting now in her downstairs parlour overlooking Fisher Gate, we were discussing an event that was exactly the sort of thing she had come to Preston to enjoy: a play that was to be staged entirely out of the pocket of young Lord Strange, Lord Derby's eldest son. It was in honour of his uncontested entry into Parliament as a county MP, as well as to mark the beginning of polling week in the town's contested election. While Elizabeth and I had invitations, I told Miss Colley we knew little of the work to be performed.

'Nor I, nor I,' said my client, with shining eyes. 'I expect it is one of Shakespeare's, and full of ghosts and women in male apparel, and there is sure to be a fool and at least one bloody sword fight.'

'No, I think it is a new work,' I told her, 'and with freshly composed music.'

'Oh, how delightful! It will be a fitting start to the poll, which is hardly less of an excitement. The first to be held since I came here. And not only that – we are to be the only town in all Lancashire that will actually vote. Oh, it is all so very gratifying, almost as good as a play, but with real actors and a wholly unknown outcome.'

I qualified my client's enthusiasm with a mild warning.

'It will be entertaining all right. But elections have their dangers, Miss Colley. I would counsel you not to go out into the street when the mob is abroad.'

She put her palm across her mouth.

'The mob!' she exclaimed. 'Abroad! Oh, how thrilling! And which side, if I may ask, will you be supporting in the vote?'

'I cannot decide. I find both parties rather disagreeable.'

She gave a tinkling laugh.

'You are playing me, Mr Cragg. I am sure you *have* decided. A man like yourself has a settled mind. Will you not take a piece of gingerbread?'

The gingerbread was cut into triangular mouthfuls. I selected one.

'Truly, I haven't,' I said, when I had chewed and swallowed. 'I wish we had something other than a choice between court-lackey Whigs and stick-in-the-mud Tories.'

'Well, that is certainly a novel idea. But are not the two parties the sides of a coin? What else can there be but heads and tails?'

'The law, Miss Colley. I am a man of the law. It seems to me the Whigs corrupt the law, and the Tories dream of no law at all.'

Suddenly Miss Colley patted herself above the heart and let out a slight coo.

'Forgive me, I am out of my depth, and must seem impertinent. But for a woman in my position, you know, impertinence is the seasoning of life.'

She took a delicate sip of wine.

'So, aside from your own preference, tell me, please, who is going to win the seats?'

'It may be close. We cannot yet tell which side has the larger treasure chest.'

'Treasure chest?'

'To buy the votes needed.'

'Really? And how much, may I ask, does it cost to buy a vote – yours, for instance, Mr Cragg, since you are still undecided?'

'My vote is not on the market, Miss Colley. Even to you.'

She laughed gaily once more.

'For shame, sir. As if I would ever want to buy it. And you a married man! But tell me what a reasonable person might sell his vote for, supposing one *did* want to buy it?'

'In money, three guineas will probably be more than enough. A shopkeeper in need of some capital might change his political coat for as much. But most are looking only for a feast, you know. They'll simply vote for the candidate who gives them the best roast meat. That is the deplorable system under which we choose our representatives, I fear.'

'Well, Mr Cragg, deplorable it may be, but it certainly simplifies politics, so that even a woman or child could understand it.'

Her eyes were sparkling and I saw that she had spoken archly. Women may stand in the shadows of the business but they are not blinded when they look into the light.

'Ah – politics,' I said. 'Yes, perhaps I am being too high minded. Politics is just an ordinary battle, isn't it? A battle of wills.'

'Oh, if I were not but an ignorant woman, I would so agree, Mr Cragg. And I might easily think it rather a low battle, nothing more than a fight to control the baser side of human nature.'

She put her Madeira glass to her mouth with a show of finality, drained it and discreetly smacked her lips.

'On which subject,' she added, leaning forward confidentially,

'I wonder if you know that Mr Francis Reynolds, I mean the candidate Reynolds, lodges at the address of Mrs Lavinia Bryce, my next-door neighbour. He has made the house his headquarters ever since he first came to Preston last year to establish his candidacy.'

'And how do you find Mr Reynolds, yourself?'

'I don't know the man, but I know Mrs Bryce. Very close, she is, about his comings and goings. But I think she's already sold him *her* vote, if you take my meaning.'

I was not surprised at the insinuation. Mrs Bryce was a widow of about forty, who had lived in town for three or four years. Even before Reynolds, she had been known for a certain freedom in bestowing her favours, and I guessed he would not be the first lodger to sport himself in her bed. I tipped the last of my own Madeira into my mouth, and judiciously cleared my throat.

'Perhaps we should move on to the business in hand, Miss Colley?' I said. 'Your will?'

Miss Colley's testatory second thoughts required little more than a substitution of names, since she only wanted to transfer her favour from one sycophantic (but in her eyes now disappointing) nephew to another, whom she considered (for the time being) more promising. The accompanying gingerbread had given me a thirst, which the Madeira had done little to slake, so, after leaving her house, I slipped into the Mitre Inn, which stood not far from her door on the opposite side of Fisher Gate.

Like people, inns and coffee houses each have their own character, which they acquire from their position and circumstances. In Preston, Antony Egan's Ferry had long been a skimble-skamble old place, living somnolently in the past; the White Bull was a fat, bustling establishment ready to rise to any challenge in the field of hospitality; and the Turk's Head Coffee House, a favourite of myself and Fidelis, was a centre of commercial and philosophical debate. The Mitre – universally known as Porter's to distinguish it from the Golden Mitre, another large inn on Market Place – had two faces. It possessed a rowdy labourers' taproom on the street and a larger and more comfortable parlour room. Although the latter could on occasion become equally rowdy, its prime quality was to act as a wellhead for London news and political argument among the better informed townspeople. It was first and foremost a Whig establishment, though the garrulous innkeeper Porter never himself expressed a party-political preference. Instead he acted as umpire in debates over the activities of Jacobites in the cause of the Pretender, the meaning of the Great Revolution, the Hanoverian succession and the policies of Sir Robert Walpole. This was where Sir Harry Hoghton would denounce the papistry of the Jacobites; Francis Reynolds would buy round after round of drinks; and outspoken Whigs like Isaac Satterthwaite, the scrivener Alphonsus Parr, the haberdasher Michael Drake and even my clerk Furzey, would gather to argue over the news. It was, in short, a forum for the pompous rodomontade of politics that Miss Colley had so archly mocked.

It was not yet midday and, though a scattering of the parlour tables were occupied by groups of men, their talk was low. I had just sat down with my pot of ale, when an inner door opened and Denis Destercore emerged, followed by the muscled Peters. Talking rapidly as they went, the two hurried diagonally across the room, past where I sat and towards the hall. Destercore was clutching an untidy armful of papers, one of which detached itself from the pile and floated down to my feet without him noticing. By the time I had retrieved it, and before I could attract its owner's attention, the hall door had slammed behind Destercore and his servant.

It was a sheet of foolscap, folded twice, and closely written over. I opened it up and saw that on one side the writing consisted of columns of names written in a careful, though informal, hand. I recognized all of them as men of Preston, and even saw after a moment that my own name was amongst them: *Titus Cragg (attny)*. I glanced again, up and down the names. Most had beside them only the man's occupation, but some were also attended by small queries, one of which was my own. A few names – but this time not my own – also had small points placed just before them, and among these I noticed that of *Nick Oldswick (wtchmkr)*.

I flipped the paper over and found further columns of hand-written names on the verso. Some but not all of these were known to me, and I realized these were not Preston residents but men living out of town, grouped under the place of their residence. They were treated similarly to the townsmen on the recto, some followed by queries, and others prefixed with a tiny dot. One name with neither addition was that of *Charles George (shmkr)* under the heading of *Broughton*. This was my father-in-law. I noticed that one name under the heading *Midd Green* had been scored out by a stroke of the pen. With an effort of scrutiny I saw it was that of *Antony Egan (innkpr)*. This was curious indeed.

I glanced around. No one had noticed me lift the paper from the floor. Quietly I refolded it, thrust it into my coat pocket and went back to innocently sipping my ale until it was time to leave for Antony's burial service.

Mr Brighouse, the vicar of Preston, read the prayers in his most aloof manner, somehow giving the impression that he had no knowledge whatever of the deceased, though in reality he knew Antony's circumstances well. There may have been more than 4,000 Prestonians in all, but most of us knew each other's business pretty thoroughly.

Innkeepers have a large acquaintance, even when they are abandoned to inebriation, so the church held a fair number of mourners.

After the book service, the box was carried out in procession to the churchyard for burial. As Elizabeth followed her cousins in throwing a trowel scoop of earth onto the lowered coffin, her eyes were damp with sympathy. Of the two daughters, however, only Grace actually wept, while Mary-Ann maintained a taut mouth and narrow eyes throughout. My mother-in-law, too, was dry eyed. Meanwhile my own thoughts kept returning to Destercore's list, and the black line that blotted out Antony's name.

We were providing tea at home for a select group of mourners. I shepherded Elizabeth and her mother, with the Egan girls and the vicar, across Church Gate and the short distance to Cheapside, and saw them through the door into the hall. Then I doubled back to the churchyard where many were lingering after the funeral to talk and exchange news. I collared Luke Fidelis and insisted he come back with me for the funeral tea, as I had something I wanted to discuss with him afterwards.

With his handsome appearance Luke was an asset at any social gathering, just as long as he did not get himself into an argument. His intolerance of stupidity had made enemies of many stupid men, and his religious beliefs put him to windward of many prejudices. On the other hand silliness in females he did not mind at all, and they most certainly did not mind him. Coming and going with cups of tea and almond cake for our guests I saw that he was entertaining three sisters who clustered around him with their fans whirring and their ringlets bouncing up and down and threatening to break loose from their ribbons. When this siege was lifted by their parents removing them home, my friend fell into conversation with Mr Brighouse. By now the company had thinned to half a dozen lingerers and I could hear enough to understand that they were discussing the election. As I joined them the vicar was commenting sourly on the banqueting involved.

'We cannot doubt that all this eating will lead to violence,

Doctor,' the vicar was saying. 'The blood of all the scourers and ruffians of the town will be excited by so much red meat. As an Hippocratic man, sir, you will understand the reasons for that, I suppose.'

'I don't think red meat charges their blood, Vicar. More to the point is the liquor.'

'No, Doctor, the main cause is the red meat, I am persuaded of it.'

'But it is not those who banquet that riot. Your scourers are the non-voters, whom it would be a rank waste of money to stuff with red meat. They are men whipped up by the words of their puppet masters, stung into action by their own impotence and enraged by too much strong beer.'

'Puppet masters? Impotence? I hardly think that smashing respectable law-abiding Christian windows can be classed as either puppetry or impotence.'

'Those who do it are without property, Vicar. They cannot vote, and this is their only way of taking part in public affairs. They are dancing to another's tune, to be sure, but it gives them the illusion that they're powerful in themselves.'

Brighouse pulled a severe face.

'I cannot agree. It sounds to me as if you approve of this criminal rampaging by the *mobile vulgus*.'

'Approval and disapproval are not matters for medicine. That is for you, the clergy. On this question I merely remark that it's natural conduct.'

'Yes, sir, it is indeed natural,' retorted Brighouse. 'And that is why it should be put a stop to!'

'A *Hippocratic* man, he called me!'

We had gone through into my office and Fidelis was laughing loudly about his exchange with the vicar. 'The fellow should be crowned with laurel, plastered with rosettes and fed with carrots. He is a prize ass.'

'You should hear him preach,' I said.

'I would rather not. What is it you want to talk about?'

I unlocked the desk drawer in which I had left Destercore's paper. As Fidelis looked it over, I explained how I had come by it.

'You remember the man, don't you?' I said. 'He was having his breakfast at the Ferry when we went there on Monday.'

'I do indeed. They're saying he's an agent from London charged with securing the election for Walpole's men.'

'That is exactly what he is, and these lists are very much to the purpose, though I can't see exactly how. What do they mean? My wife's uncle Egan is there, though his name has been crossed through – see? Our good Denis has been keeping his list up to date.'

Fidelis had put the paper down on my desk and was leaning over it, running his finger systematically down the names.

'You won't find yourself there,' I said.

He laughed.

'No, and I can see why.'

'Can you? The first names are all your co-religionists.'

'They are voters, or at least possible voters – possible freemen. I have no property and cannot be a freeman and so I do not vote. I would say this is part of an attempt to identify the voters of this town.'

'But the Catholics aren't voters at all,' I said, puzzled. 'You Romans don't vote because you cannot take the oath.'

'Yes, but some are freemen nevertheless. As the franchise here has always been that of the freemen, those must be included.'

There came a cough from the doorway to the outer office.

'That's not strictly true, sir, what you just said.'

It was Furzey, coming into the room to place a sheaf of newly copied documents on my desk. I was not surprised at his eaves-dropping for he had always operated on the plan that, in a good legal practice, the principal shares all intelligence with his clerk, willingly or not.

'Furzey, how is it not true?' I said. 'To my knowledge Dr Fidelis is right. Only freemen of Preston have ever voted.'

'Yes, but that is only to *your* knowledge,' he replied compla-cently. 'In this town, so some say, the right to vote was once possessed by all resident males with five, ten or twenty pounds of property – the amount having changed over the years. They say restricting the vote to freemen is quite a recent piece of cozenage, devised so that the corporation could ensure the outcome of an election – because, of course, the councilmen hand out the freedoms.'

'But I don't see the utility of this particular list of resident men. An electorate of freemen is, after all, what we have now.'

Furzey wagged his finger, as he must have seen me do many a time in court.

'But the old way has never been forgotten, sir, and may still be found to be the true legal way, if it is ever truly tested. The history of the Preston franchise was a great theme of my father's. He taught me to tell the difference between residents, householders and freemen. For fifty years and more, at the start of every contested election in Preston, one side or another has gone to Moot Hall and pored over the old charters to see where exactly the franchise lay. And I would not be surprised if Mr Denis Destercore is not readying himself to revive the argument again, for I think it may be his best chance of winning it for the Whigs. May I see the paper, sir?'

I handed it to him and he turned it once or twice in his hand, then passed it on to Fidelis.

'Dr Fidelis,' he said in the voice of a man conferring a bless-ing, 'you are quite right. It *is* a list of freeman voters – of the town on recto, and out of town on verso. I wonder if there is another list, on another piece of paper, for non-free residents such as yourself.'

'As a householder?'

'You are not one of those, sir. Does your wife cook your food exclusively on your own hearth, under your own chimney?'

'No, Furzey, regrettably I have neither wife nor chimney to call my own.'

'Then you are a resident but not a householder. Some have argued that the franchise belongs to householders, otherwise called potwallers, and some have claimed that it is conferred even more widely on six-month residents.'

He turned back to me.

'May I return to my writing desk, sir? I have much to do.'

I let him go and shut the door behind him.

'Your clerk really is a pearl of great price,' Fidelis laughed.

'Yes,' I said, 'and it's a price I pay daily. But let's go back to your point about what Destercore is up to.'

'Well, I think his idea is a sound one. Maybe Destercore has many lists of voters, of which this one comprises only freemen. It must have been drawn up with the help of Reynolds, who has been more or less resident in town over the last months. And they identify the voters under various circumstances – for instance, whether the poll remains only with the freemen or, as Furzey's been telling us, might be extended to these potwallers of his, or indeed to all residents.'

'But Roman Catholics can't vote anyway – they cannot take the oath. Why have a list of them at all?'

Fidelis reflected.

'Remind me how the election oath is used.'

'When a man comes before the returning officer to vote, he can be challenged to swear at length that King George is sovereign and the Pope is a rascal, or something like that. It is quite a convoluted form of words, I think.'

'Good! That's the point. "He *can* be challenged." It would take far too long for every voter to recite the oath. Only a selected few are challenged, and if you're a Whig you want to make sure that this few includes all Tory-voting Catholics. It is simply good election management to know who to challenge at the poll.'

'Why am I on his list, then?'

'Because of Elizabeth. They're playing safe in case you are one of us secretly.' He scanned the list of names. 'Note the query your name attracts. And you are not the only one here who doesn't himself worship with us, yet has a Catholic wife, or other connection. Destercore simply cannot afford to risk letting any Tory vote go through, if he can stop it.'

'Very well, though how Destercore knows I am voting Tory when I don't know myself is a mystery. But let's turn this over.'

I took the paper and laid it on the desk with the out-of-town names showing.

'These men are classified here by place of origin.'

'But what about these small dots placed against some of them? They must be significant, but I can't say how. Can you?'

I could not. Some secret form of classification, I suggested.

'I wonder if they refer to men with particularly vehement opinions,' suggested Fidelis. 'There's one against the name of Nick Oldswick – he'll never shift from his Toryism.'

'He won't. He told me so the other night.'

'And these others – where would you say they stood politically?'

'Many are solid for the Tories, as far as I can see. My wife's uncle had certainly always been an unshakeable Tory.'

'Right. So let's try the idea that they're men who can't be bought. Destercore'll have other lists of men who can easily be bought, and who might with difficulty be bought, and so on.'

'So this is all in the name of efficiency.'

Fidelis put his finger on the thick ink line under which lay the name of *Antony Egan (innkpr)*.

'And Egan's crossing-out tells us something more, does it not? The lists must have been compiled before Antony's death; that is, before Destercore arrived in town. Perhaps he brought them with him.'

'It makes another point too,' I added. 'The only thing that will reliably prevent these particular men's Tory votes is their sudden death.'

Chapter Seven

AN ELECTION IS a market in votes and, like any market, it brings visitors to town in hordes. Agents like Denis Destercore come from the distant south, with voters' lists and full purses, to invest their political masters' money, while freemen of Preston living in the countryside, or in the villages and towns round about, arrive eager to dispose their votes advantageously. This is the transaction at the heart of electoral business, but there is also a lot of activity in addition. Poor country people have the prospect of a few days of lucrative but honest employment as table servers, chambermaids, potboys, cooks and runners. And attracted too, like wasps to a jam pot, are bands of musicians and ballad sellers, hucksters, trinket peddlers and practitioners of legerdemain, like the one I had seen the previous day in front of the Moot Hall. Finally, but not least, are those who turn up just for the fun of it – for the opportunity to drink, sing, swagger, kiss girls, fist fight and in general throw off the traces, without having any notion of the Prime Minister, the Spanish war or the excise.

This is self-evidently not the time for a lone and very pretty young woman, such as Miss Lysistrata Plumb, to step down from the Wigan coach at the Red Lion Inn on Church Gate, and go looking for genteel accommodation for herself and the two boxes she brought with her. Yet this was exactly what had occurred at three o'clock that afternoon, shortly after which Miss Plumb was told by the innkeeper that his rooms were all occupied, most of them by three or more guests each, and that the same conditions would certainly obtain at the Bull, the White Bull, the Black Horse, the Golden Mitre, the Gamecock, and any of the other inns, unless a prior request for a bed had been received. Miss Plumb had made no such arrangements, but she refused to be deterred and set off to search for a room, leaving her boxes for later collection.

An hour and a half later she realized the innkeeper's pessimism had been justified. Miss Plumb had visited all the places he'd mentioned, and a few others, without success. Having been disappointed yet again at Porter's, she found herself standing on Fisher Gate, between Bryant's hosiery on one side of the street and Lorris the bookbinder's on the other, without a notion of where to go next. Her eyes were pricking with tears.

Just then she heard shouting from the direction of the Moot Hall. Turning to look up the slope of the street she saw a rout of young men, more than fifty of them, advancing down it, some carrying cudgels, others swinging lengths of chain. Hastily, every shopper and stroller in their way ducked into the nearest shop or tavern, where shutters and doors were quickly closed behind them – all, that is, except Lysistrata Plumb who, not knowing what to do, stayed rooted. Just a few seconds later, she was the only human being standing directly in the mob's path.

A tall man was leading this untidy phalanx, marching in front of them with his fist in the air and yelling slogans. It may seem strange, but the youths took hardly any notice of Lysistrata, despite her nicely formed figure and face, and her London clothes. They were like a river, flowing blind to any hindrance. Their intent was firmly fixed – to break up a meeting that somebody had heard was being held at Fisher Gate Bar – and, with their blood up to battle pitch, nothing they met was likely to interest them on the way.

Gesturing and roaring like brutes, they goaded each other as they marched onwards until the terrified woman was overwhelmed. Jostled and shoved and bumped by the rioters, down she went under their boots and clogs. No sooner had they rolled over this minor obstacle than they broke into a run and careered away cheering and yelling towards the bar, as if nothing at all had happened.

'Can you hear me? Are you in pain?'

A hand was supporting the back of Lysistrata's head, while another was at her wrist, feeling the pulse.

Her eyes came open and she became aware of the man's face, handsome and grave, floating just above hers.

'Good, you are conscious,' said Luke Fidelis. 'No, don't try to speak just yet. I am a doctor and I live in this house here. If you will permit me I shall have you carried inside where we may see if you are hurt.'

He beckoned to some men in the knot of people who had emerged from the nearby shops and were gawping at the fallen woman.

'Joseph Williamson, and you other men, come here and help me take her inside. She may be seriously injured so we must act with the utmost gentleness. That's it, you must support her with your hands, so don't be shy. Does anybody know who she is? No, thank you, Mr Bryant, we shall take her into Mr Lorris's premises, rather than yours, I think, since it is where I live and keep my medicines. And by the way, did I not see your apprentice Abraham in that mob? I was at the window and observed them pass, with the very serious consequences we now see. The boy should be ashamed of himself, Mr Bryant, and I hope you will deal with him severely.'

The scenes I have sketched were described to me by an excited Luke Fidelis in considerable detail. This was later that same evening, with a jug of punch on the table between us, at the Gamecock, the inn kept by Mrs Fitzpatrick on Stoney Gate. After our earlier discussion about Destercore's lists, Fidelis had left me at my office and gone home to his rooms at the top of Lorris's house and workshop. A few moments later he glimpsed Miss Plumb from his window, 'the most enchanting young woman you ever saw', standing alone in the street and giving all the indications of distress. His tenderness towards this sight gave way to alarm as the street emptied of shoppers and the mob bore down on her.

'I almost threw myself down the stairs, Titus, but was unable to reach her before they did. When we brought her inside I found bruises and shock, but nothing broken.'

'And who is she? What brings her here?'

'She says very little about herself. But she is not passing through merely in a day. Her intention was to look for a place in which to stay.'

'There's not much chance of that this week.'

'Not in the public inns. But she has had wonderful luck because the Lorrises have an empty room, and they have taken her in. The room is not normally let but they are charitable people and, after I'd explained Miss Plumb's predicament, they were very glad to allow her to have it.'

'So, you persuaded them.'

Luke gave me the laconic smile that I had noticed he some-times assumed when talking about attractive women.

'I did act as her advocate in the matter, yes.'

'You fancy her?'

Fidelis pursed his lips, to show he deprecated my turn of phrase, and shook his head.

'She is above fancy. She is a goddess of beauty, Titus, an angel to the angels. I think she may be my guiding star.'

I refilled our glasses from the jug of punch and raised mine.

'Let's drink to her, then. She has obviously made a mighty impression. To your guiding star.'

We drank and, at that moment, the ample figure of the landlady appeared beside our booth.

'Dr Fidelis, may I interrupt?' said Mrs Fitzpatrick. 'One of our guests who's in town on election business has been taken ill in his room. A bad way he's in, sir. Would you be kind enough to take a look?'

Fidelis again raised his glass to his lips, tipped back his head and swallowed the drink. Then without the slightest sign of objection he stood and picked up the leather bag containing his professional equipment.

'Please excuse me for a few minutes, Titus.'

The landlady took the doctor across the room to the door which led up to the ailing guest.

I looked around. The room was as busy and loud as I had ever seen it, with laughter, argument, anecdote and singing, with card players' calls and the clinking of money, glass and pewter. I noticed for the first time that my old nemesis Ephraim Grimshaw was sitting on the other side of the room. Dressed in a bulging red-and-silver-threaded waistcoat and a blue coat edged with golden piping, he was talking closely and earnestly with two men from outside the town, while referring to a document lying on the table between them. Grimshaw was one of the most powerful of Preston's twenty-four burgesses, our ruling council, by and from whom the mayor and two bailiffs are chosen each year. All of these men were strong for the Tories, and had contributed large funds to the coffers of Fazackerley and Shuttleworth in the fight against the Whigs, and London, and the schemes and machinations of Robin Walpole. Grimshaw had served more than one term as bailiff but he had relinquished that office last year, having fixed his eyes on a bid for the mayoralty that would next year preside over our most splendid civic occasion, the Preston Guild. To be guild mayor was the height of ambition for any politician in Preston, and for Grimshaw the coming election for a man to succeed the incumbent mayor, the corn merchant William Biggs, would be his one and only shot at the prize. Guilds are twenty years apart and even if he lived until 1762 he'd be far too old for the job by then.

You didn't have to be Nostradamus to guess what Grimshaw was doing tonight. In order to get his fellow Tory burgesses to hang the heavy gold chain around his neck at the next mayoral election he needed to anchor them securely in his debt. One way of doing this was by spending more freely than those on the Tory side in the election. The two out-of-towners he was drinking with tonight looked like brothers, and their document looked like a deed. Grimshaw was probably negotiating some land deal, no doubt highly advantageous to the brothers, in which the currency exchanged was not just money, but their votes.

There was a small commotion near the door and I saw that a group wearing Whig ribbons in their hats had burst in. They bullied their way into possession of the largest table in the room and began baiting Grimshaw and any other Tories in the room, singing anti-Jacobite songs and calling healths to King George, Lord Derby and Sir Harry Hoghton. After a while Grimshaw decided withdrawal was his best tactic. He rose, bowed to his co-conspirators and shuffled past the Whigs' table, to a barrage of whistles and insults. At the door he turned and shook his fist at the room in general.

'Ruffians!' he shouted before he left. 'Outrage and disgrace!'

A few minutes later Fidelis returned, interrupting my enjoyment of these activities.

'Titus, I think you should come and take a look, as coroner, at this man upstairs.'

'Why?' I said. 'Is the fellow dead?'

'He will be soon.'

As we entered the inner passageway, from which the stairs led upwards, a door swung open and a servant emerged carrying a tray laden with plates of roast meat. Fidelis caught the kitchen door before it closed behind the man and, without explanation, darted inside. He came out a few moments later carrying a small earthenware jar with a cork stopper.

'Come on,' he said, 'he's up here.'

The room was small, with space for a single pallet bed, a wooden chair and a narrow table on which a candle burned and smoked. Rhythmical groans mixed up with a rasping sound came from the bed, as the sick man struggled for his breath. The smell in the room was repellent, a rancid mix of sweat, faeces and vomit.

I could just make the sick man out in the gloom, a restless, recumbent form under the blankets. Fidelis returned to the door and called loudly for more light.

'Who is he?' I asked.

'Man named Allcroft, a farmer from Gregson. He's also got a good lot of land on the Fylde.'

The fertile, flat country known as the Fylde, which lay to our north-west, provided vast quantities of produce for Preston's market, meaning that Allcroft was likely a prosperous yeoman. At some point he must have acquired from the corporation the freedom of Preston, and a right to vote, which I presumed he had come to town to exercise in the election.

A serving girl came to the door with two oil lamps. Fidelis gestured her to bring them inside but she shook her head, and handed the lamps through the door to him. Once they were brought in, the detail of the room was revealed: the writing table with a jug on it and the remains of a meal, the tangled heaps of clothing and towels on the floor, the soiled bedclothes, the full chamber pot lying amid spillage and spattered vomit. Allcroft was lying on his back, wearing a linen nightcap saturated with sweat. His upturned face was fixed in an expression of horror, as if he could see a vision of hell burned into the ceiling. His throat pulsed and his mouth worked open and shut. It produced a single, hoarse request.

'Drink! Water! Anything!'

I reached for the jug, but Fidelis stopped me. He took the jug himself and sniffed it.

'That's beer. We'll leave it where it is.'

He called the servant back and asked her to bring up some cold milk with a raw egg beaten into it and a clean spoon. Then he pulled the chair to the bedside and sat down, taking his patient's wrist between finger and thumb.

The egg and milk arrived, though the girl would still not enter the sickroom. I took the jug and spoon and brought them to Fidelis.

'Did you recognize her?' I asked in a whisper.

'Who?'

'The girl. That was Maggie Satterthwaite, formerly of the Ferry Inn.'

He merely grunted, having more pressing matters to think about. Then he gripped the jug between his knees, lifted Allcroft's head, dipped the spoon into the mixture and put it between his patient's lips, carefully tipping the liquid onto the tongue.

'Mr Allcroft, I'm Dr Fidelis,' he said as he applied the spoon again. 'I'm here to help you. Can you speak?'

Allcroft's assent was little better than a croak.

'When did you first feel this coming over you?' went on Fidelis gently, now leaving the spoon in the milk and feeling Allcroft's pulse once more.

'Afternoon,' came the struggling reply. 'Ate my dinner. Went out. Felt queer, very. Vomited. Worse and worse. Came back.'

'How long after you'd eaten did you feel ill? Half an hour, an hour, two hours?'

'Don't know. Hour. Two. Three. Who cares? Give me a drink for pity's sake.'

'This is milk and beaten egg,' Fidelis told him, giving him more of it, then gesturing towards the table on which stood a soup plate with the congealed remains of some hotpot and potatoes.

'Is this all that you ate today?'

Allcroft seemed unable to answer in words, but he moved his head and momentarily closed his eyes in a way that indicated it was. Fidelis stood up and handed the milk jug to me.

'Would you nurse him for me, Titus?'

Gingerly I approached and sat down beside the bed.

'How dangerous is this, Luke?' I whispered. 'Surely there is contagion!'

My friend's reply was low and level.

'Possibly. But I don't think so. Just continue with the milk, a little at a time, on the tongue.'

Allcroft still lay with his mouth open, fetching his breath in rapid intervals. I copied my friend's earlier action, putting my hand under Allcroft's neck and raising his head to receive the drink. His flesh was clammy, as were his hair and cap, and I could smell the foulness of his breath.

As I got down to my task, Fidelis was busying himself behind me. Hearing the clink of metal on chinaware, I looked round and saw him bent over the table, scraping the leftover meal from the plate, and into the jar that he'd got from the kitchen. He closed the jar, then taking a small sampling bottle and a funnel from his medical bag, picked up the jug of beer and filled the bottle from it. Pressing home the stopper, he took writing materials from the table drawer and scrawled a few words and figures on a sheet of paper, which he then wafted in the air to dry the ink, before folding it.

'Titus,' he said, 'for a lawyer, you nurse the sick well enough, but now it's time for you to leave off.'

He handed me the paper.

'Will you go to the apothecary and ask him to make up this preparation and send it round here at once? Make clear that it is needed urgently.'

When I had tucked the paper into my pocket Fidelis handed me the bottle and jar.

'And will you take these to your house and keep them safe? I fancy it is the food that has poisoned this man, but it may have been the drink. Don't let anyone open them.'

'Of course. And you will stay here?'

Fidelis nodded towards the bed.

'I had better. No one else will come near.'

The street door of Thomas Wilson's apothecary shop was locked, but a faint light showed from a back room. I rapped at the window and Wilson himself came out to open to me, a man of about fifty wearing a cap and slippers, and holding a candlestick. When I handed over Fidelis's paper, and passed on his instructions, the apothecary accepted the commission without complaint. The hour was late, but no one successfully plies the druggist's trade unless he is willing to return to his mortar and his scales at the snap of a doctor's fingers, any time of the day or night. Wilson was regarded as one of our best apothecaries, if not always as the best of our men. He had spent years in London, where he learned his trade under the most capable masters, before returning to his home town with a wife and sufficient capital to open the shop on Church Gate.

He swung round and headed back to his inner sanctum with rapid, shuffling steps. I followed, shutting the door. As in all apothecaries', the air had a pungency like no other shop: a faint, dry, organic rankness mixed with something mineral, sharp though sweet. Wilson had slipped behind the counter and through the door on the other side, and there I joined him. The inner room contained a stool, a bench with pen and ink, and an open ledger in which Wilson had been writing. Above it hung a shelf holding his brass scales and other instruments for milling, measuring, heating and pouring, while the surrounding walls were lined with shelf upon shelf of labelled bottles and jars containing liquids, powders, crystals and roots – the raw materials of all medicine. Wilson had already placed his candle on the bench. Now he sat on the stool, pushed the ledger to one side and opened the paper, bending to examine it in the candlelight. His lips fluttered as he read the prescription.

'Ah, yes!' he said at last. 'I see the case very clear. The patient must be bad set.'

'He is,' I agreed. 'I've seen him. He's dying, I think.'

Wilson gave me a knowing look and indicated the paper.

'If he needs this, he must be.'

'What is the receipt for?'

But Wilson widened his eyes and shook his head, his loose jowls wobbling.

'My goodness, I cannot tell you that, Mr Cragg. That is a matter of confidence. My lips are professionally sealed. It is enough to say that the poor fellow must be very bad set, yes, very bad set indeed.'

He rose and scanned the shelves, finally reaching down a flask labelled *Spirits of Wine*, which he brought back to the workbench.

'You will send the preparation round to the Gamecock as soon as it is ready?' I said, watching as he took down a measuring vessel, inscribed down its side with a graduated scale. 'Dr Fidelis says the case is urgent.'

Wilson lifted the stopper from the jar and remounted his stool.

'Have I not indicated that I know the urgency, Mr Cragg? I will be ready to take the preparation there myself in fifteen minutes, if you will be kind enough to indulge me.'

I accepted the hint and left Wilson to his work, picking my way through the darkness with care for the bottle and jar that Fidelis had entrusted to me. A few minutes later I let myself into my office and locked Fidelis's samples inside a drawer in my desk, to await his collection in the morning. I felt considerably reassured now. I remembered Fidelis's words as he had handed them to me that, far from lying in the miasma of Allcroft's room, the sickness that had seized him was in his food and drink. I myself had breathed Allcroft's air for half an hour or more, but I had not eaten his food, or drunk his beer, and the thought made me feel lighter in my mind as I passed through the connecting door and into my house.

Chapter Eight

I WAS SITTING BEHIND my desk at the office, looking over some affidavits, when Luke Fidelis appeared shortly after ten the next morning. He was carrying a wicker basket, of the kind that might be used to transport small birds to market. This he deposited, without explanation, on the floor beside his medical bag and sat down with a heavy sigh in my client chair. His face was pale and drawn. I suppressed the desire to ask what was in the basket.

'How is the sick man?' I asked instead.

'No longer sick. May I have the samples you brought away with you?'

I unlocked the drawer containing the jar and bottle that Fidelis had entrusted to me, and handed them over.

'That is excellent news, Luke!' I exclaimed. 'So he's on the mend after all.'

'No, he's dead,' said Fidelis, finding room for the samples in his medical bag.

My elation subsided.

'So, it was just as you'd predicted.'

'Yes.'

'And in spite of your prescription from Wilson.'

His answer was a little brusque.

'That wasn't intended to cure the man, only to make him more comfortable until the end.'

'And the cause of death?'

He scrubbed his face with his hands.

'Look, Titus, it has been a long night. Might I trouble you for a plate of something and some small beer?'

I immediately hurried around the desk and raised him up by the arm.

'Of course, Luke. How thoughtless of me. Come into the house.'

Fidelis picked up his medical bag and followed me back through the outer office and into the house, where I sat him in the dining parlour and called for Matty to bring some breakfast. A moment later we were interrupted by a loud, importunate knock on the front door. Matty was piling food onto a tray for the doctor – food which, I am sure, she would willingly have spooned down his throat if he had asked her – and Elizabeth and her mother, who still stayed with us, had gone to market. So I was forced to appear at the door myself.

I opened to Denis Destercore, the red-headed political agent whom I had last seen sneering at the Shuttleworths' meeting in Market Place. His bearing was confident, straight backed, legs apart. His big-framed servant Peters stood behind him on the step below, holding a notebook, pen and inkhorn.

'Good morning, my friend,' Destercore began, smiling with an expression I had previously seen on the mouths of certain fish lying on the slab. 'We have not been introduced. I am Denis Destercore, friend to Mr Reynolds in the coming election. Today we are conducting the canvas, so I would be much obliged if you would tell me which of the candidates you propose to support.'

Destercore, with his lists and political intriguing, was interesting to me, in spite of his fish's smile and his presumption that I was his friend. So, instead of sending him away like the hawker that, in one sense, he actually was, I agreed to see him next door at my office.

'But it will have to be a little later in the morning. My clerk will make an appointment and, in the meantime, you may canvas him, as he too is an elector, and may even be one of your supporters. His name is Furzey.'

As my tone had been ostentatiously neutral, I was sure Destercore detected the ghost of mockery in it. He certainly did not like being put off, though there was not much he could do about it. So he produced a watch from his fob pocket and frowned at it.

'Very well,' he said, resuming his outward cheerfulness, 'we shall see you later.'

I went back in to find Fidelis eating slices of veal pie. He looked a good deal fresher and more alert.

'By the way, what's that basket you left in the office?' I asked.

'It is for you. I am hoping you might be visiting Middleforth Green again today, to see how your cousins are doing. If not, I shall have to go over myself, for I want to collect something from old Isaac Satterthwaite.'

'Well, you are in luck. I've been asked to call in on legal business. I can also call at Satterthwaite's on my way back, if you wish. But why will I need the basket?'

'To bring back the rat that I wish you to get from him.'

I was taken very much by surprise.

'A rat? What do you want a dead rat for?'

Fidelis shook his head.

'You don't follow me, Titus. I don't want a *dead* rat.'

'But surely any rat I get from Satterthwaite will be dead. He is a rat catcher.'

Fidelis laughed.

'He always has a few live ones that he's trapped. He uses them to train his terriers, and he also sells them. He is selling one to me. I have sent him a note with instructions to have it ready.'

'All right. If you really want a live rat, I shall bring one. Do you have any preference as to colour, age and gender?'

'Any, just so long as it is adult and healthy.'

'Will you tell me what it is for?'

But at this moment, between question and answer, I was thwarted. Elizabeth and her mother came in from market, and all discussion of rats was necessarily suspended. My wife took her produce straight through to the kitchen but Mrs George, upon hearing that Dr Fidelis was within, immediately rushed to the dining room to join us, without even taking off her bonnet.

'Now, Doctor,' she said, her eyes shining at the prospect of conversation with the handsome physician, 'tell me, is it true what I hear from my daughter – that you have been up all night at the Gamecock Inn bravely tending a dangerously sick man that's come to town to cast his vote?'

'I have, madam,' he replied, 'but the fact is my efforts have been useless.'

'Oh, dear! He has succumbed?'

'Yes, Mr John Allcroft died at eight this morning.'

At the mention of this name, she started.

'Mercy! Mr John Allcroft who farms at Barton and Gregson, was that him?'

'Did you know the man?'

'Certainly I did. Mr George has done business with him. I have visited Susan, his wife, and she me. We have all dined together. Oh, poor man, he's dead, is he? *Requiescat.*'

She crossed herself, and went on.

'We, that is, Mr George my husband and I, were hoping John would join us in religion, you know. The signs were there, increasingly.'

My friend had been calmly taking a sip of beer, but this startled him and he put down his tankard precipitately, slopping some of its contents onto the table.

'I wish I had known that,' he said, mopping up the spill with his napkin. 'I would have sent for Mr Egerton to give last rites.'

Mr Egerton was the Roman priest who lived, not so secretly, in Back Lane behind Friar Gate.

'Mother-in-law,' I said, 'what did you mean by the signs being there that he would change religion? Did he go to your Roman services?'

'No, he went to the English services, and he subscribed outwardly to the Protestant heresy, as it is in our view.'

She sniffed, and looked straight at me in a challenging way. I also subscribed to the Protestant heresy, and was proud of it, but I refused her bait.

'So what signs were in Mr Allcroft of incipient Catholicism?'

'Well, as I observed, he was very much like a Roman in his politics. He was really tenacious, he had a passion you could say, for our true king, our *Catholic* king. More than once have I heard him make the toast, you know . . .'

She looked from Dr Fidelis to me as she mouthed the words.

'*The king over the water.*'

Her reference to the Pretender did not anger me – I had heard such talk from Mrs George often enough before – but it did make me a little nervous. There were towns in other parts of the country where even to whisper such words might land a person in gaol. Northern parts such as Preston contained a larger proportion of Jacobites – there were even some in the corporation – and they were not averse on occasion to speaking their minds out loud. But that was in normal times. This was an election, when political sensitivity was much sharpened, and zealous Whigs like Sir Henry

Hoghton would cut savagely at anything that looked to them like sedition.

Fortunately we were able to venture no further down the Jacobite path, as at this point Matty came in with a note from Furzey. It read:

The politician is here waiting for you with his man. I have engaged you to see him at eleven o'clock, that is, in ten minutes.

At the same moment Fidelis jumped to his feet, his powers apparently restored by the beer and pie. He picked up his medical bag.

'I must be on my way, Titus. I am to be consulted at Mrs Parbold's in Water Street. Don't forget the rat!'

'But you haven't told me what it is for,' I protested. 'And what about Allcroft? If he has become coroner's business I need to know.'

'He hasn't – not yet, but we may settle the matter today. Come to my house this afternoon, and bring the rat in that basket I left in your office.'

Then he was gone.

The clock was pointing to a few minutes before eleven when I returned to the office. Destercore and his servant were waiting. I bowed to them and, asking their indulgence for a moment, told Furzey to follow me into my room. Picking some papers from his writing desk, he did so.

'What's in the basket?' he asked, nodding towards it.

'Nothing. It's for Dr Fidelis's rat.'

Furzey opened his mouth to speak, and then checked himself. I laughed.

'I know no more than you. Now, about this fellow out there.' I lowered my voice and cocked my head towards the door. 'I suspect he's come here from London to make trouble.'

'You would see trouble in a boiled egg,' whispered Furzey. 'He is an agent, that's all, a helper at election time. I see no harm in him. Now, I have done what you asked. Here.'

He handed me the papers he was carrying and I placed them in one of the desk drawers.

'While I am closeted with the master,' I said, 'you talk to the servant. Anything you can glean . . . you follow me?'

Furzey gave me a wink, called Destercore in, and left us. The agent sat opposite me at my desk, opened his notebook and helped himself to pen and ink. He moved in sudden jerks as if he were worked by a wound-up spring that released itself in short periods.

'You are Mr Titus Cragg, attorney. Is that right?'

I agreed that it was and he entered me in his book. It appeared, from the upside-down view that I had of it, that he was using a different page for each street, for I could make out *Cheapside* at the top of the page and the names of some of my neighbours in the list below.

'And for whom, may I ask, do you think your vote will be cast in the election?' he went on.

'You *may* ask, but I will reserve my answer.'

A subtle look came over his face.

'Does that mean you have a settled choice, but will not tell me? Or have you not made up your mind?'

'It means what I say – I reserve my answer.'

'Everyone will know your choice when you cast the vote, so why not declare it now?'

I shrugged.

'It is my preference not to do so.'

Destercore sighed in a cool display of irritation at my obstructing him. He dashed down a note against my name and abruptly sprang to his feet.

'Well, I must be on my way, Mr Cragg. I thank you for your time.'

'Before you go, Mr Destercore . . .'

I reached into my desk drawer and took out the list of voters that he had dropped at Porter's.

'I am glad to have the opportunity to return this to you. I happened to be sitting in the parlour room of Porter's Inn when you walked by. You dropped this paper as you passed, but left the inn before I could return it to you.'

For a moment Destercore's eyes narrowed and then bulged as he made to snatch the paper from my hand. But I jerked it fractionally up to evade his grasp. I wanted him to realize that I had studied the list.

'I see my own name is written here. I wonder what I may infer from that.'

Destercore's earlier cool had left him. He was definitely flustered now.

'It is merely a list, a projection of voting intentions. It is usual to prepare the canvas in this way.'

'I see. So now that I have reserved my own intentions, perhaps you will revise the list. And you might like to know that another alteration is due. I see you have already scratched out the late Mr Egan; now you can do the same office for a name lying a few places below his.'

I laid the list on the desk and put my finger on the name of *Mr John Allcroft (farmer)*. Destercore stooped to look at it, then straightened his back.

'I do not follow you, sir. What about Mr Allcroft?'

'I mean that he will not be voting in the election. He died less than three hours ago, at an inn on Stoney Gate.'

I picked up the paper and held it out, while looking steadily into Destercore's eyes. He whipped the paper from my fingers and stuffed it into his pocket, but he did not straightforwardly meet my gaze.

'I am obliged to you for that information, sir,' he said stiffly. 'Now, I must go. Good day.'

After he had left I again opened the same desk drawer. A second paper lay inside, written in Furzey's hand: the full copy that I had asked him to make of those lists. I took it out, dipped my pen and was just scoring a line lightly through the name of John Allcroft when Furzey came in.

'How did you do with Peters, the servant?' I asked.

'He was uncommunicative, on the whole. He is a Londoner, which I could already tell. He was engaged as Mr Destercore's servant only three days before making the journey here, so he professes to know little of his master. Of course I asked what he had been doing before his engagement.'

Furzey paused. I knew that he was deliberately baiting me.

'And what was that?' I asked, indulging him.

'Italy.'

'Italy? What do you mean?'

'I mean he was travelling in Italy, so he says, accompanying a young gentleman on the Grand Tour, but he would tell me no more about it, only that I would not be much interested.'

'Even though you were.'

'Yes. But when gathering intelligence it is vital to evince as little interest as possible, isn't that so? I had to let the matter drop or give the game away.'

'You did not even get the name of the young gentleman?'

'Of course I did. It was Lord Carburton.'

'Who is he?'

'Son and heir to the Earl of Powys. I would have thought you knew that.'

*

My wife's cousins had recovered sufficiently from the death of their father to become anxious about their own futures. Antony Egan had died with no property except his title to the inn. They wanted to know if the inn was now theirs. I was able to tell them that they were fortunate: their father had made an unsophisticated common-law will many years ago. As there was no son living, it allowed for his daughters jointly to inherit all their father's property.

'There is no entail or strict settlement, you see, so no need to search for a proximate male heir – by which I mean the nearest male relation of your father's blood. If your brother had been alive then, of course, the inn would have passed to him. Since unfortunately he is not, it is yours entire, my dears. You are your father's direct heirs and you may do as you wish with the inn.'

The sisters sat beside each other just as they had done when I had told them of Antony's drowning. On hearing what I had to say they grasped each other's hands in relief.

'Oh! That is a blessing,' Grace said.

Mary-Ann had another question.

'About the debts – we know we owe money to the brewers, and to a few suppliers else, but as long as we go on in business we can manage those creditors. We are only concerned in case our father owed other money, without telling us. Did he?'

I knew of none.

'The inn is not mortgaged, I can assure you of that,' I told them. 'It is possible some new creditor might still come forward but, as the matter stands, you are unencumbered. So, what *will* you do – sell or stay?'

Mary-Ann and Grace exchanged a glance and, as one, turned their eyes back to me.

'We stay,' said Grace firmly. 'This place is all we have, and all we know.'

*

Satterthwaite's cottage, from what I could see of it, was not opulent, but it was neat and orderly, with level flagged floors and a few solid bits and pieces of oak furniture. The tall, upright rat catcher led me through, from front door to back, and out into the yard. Going past the kennels, in which sharp-teethed terriers yapped and growled incessantly, he showed me an array of small wooden hutches behind whose wire I could see rodents of various sizes, as if they were exhibits in a menagerie. Some sat grooming, while others crept aimlessly back and forth, like debtors in gaol befuddled by gin.

'I have black rats, and brown rats, and white rats, Mr Cragg. The whites are not normal, they're freaks. But if you breed from them you get more white ones. I've been getting up a line of them – pretty, ain't they?'

I agreed, though only from politeness.

'I have followed the doctor's orders and picked one out for him – one of the whites. Here she is, a young female and ready for breeding if that's his fancy. I call her Athene.'

She was about 8 inches from nose to bottom, with a tapering, wormlike tail almost as long.

'Do you give names to them all?'

'Oh, aye. Helps me keep track. Heroes and gods, mostly.'

He rammed his hand into a thick leather gauntlet and opened a lid in the roof of the hutch, winking at me.

'Wouldn't do to get bit. Open your basket, if you please, sir.'

In a trice he had plunged his gloved hand into the hutch and brought out the rat, which flailed in his grasp and made frantic attempts to bite through the leather. Moments later she was lodged in my carrier, with the lid safely pegged. Through the basket weave I could see her cold rose-pink eyes glinting in the darkness.

He wanted sevenpence ha'penny for it. It seemed more than enough to pay for a common pest but I handed over the coins without comment and took my leave. Satterthwaite followed me as far as the garden gate, and watched me walk down the lane towards the ferry, gingerly holding the basket away from contact with my side.

The serving woman who opened the bookbinder's door took a look at the wicker basket I carried. I made no attempt to explain it, but merely asked for the doctor.

'Dr Fidelis says you are to go through to the back garden, sir, and to bring along –' she nodded at my burden – 'whatever you have with you.'

The creature was restless, scrabbling and giving out small squeaks from time to time. I smiled but gave no explanation, walking past the girl and into the hall, through the passage beside the stair and so by another passage to the back door, which gave access to the yard and washhouse. Beyond that stretched Lorris's burgage plot, a strip of land just as wide as his house, but stretching for thirty yards. The first part was laid out as a garden, with shrubs and beds and little bowers with seats on which members of the household could enjoy the air; the second consisted of kitchen garden and orchard and the third of a dovecot, chicken house, pigsty and rabbit run.

I found Fidelis at the far end, standing in the rabbit run. It was enclosed by tightly wattled hazel-twig hurdles and furnished with four rabbit houses or 'clappers', each similar to Satterthwaite's rat houses, but proportionately larger. These clappers had sliding doors to admit or exclude their inhabitants from the run, while the run itself had a wattle gate on twine hinges. With carrots and cabbage leaves Fidelis was patiently enticing the rabbits into their hutches before shutting them inside, then clearing the run of all food and emptying the drinking bowl.

'You have the rat?'

'Yes. She's called Athene. Satterthwaite says she's a fine specimen. I'll take his word for that. What do you want her for?'

'You'll see.' He rose from his crouching position and straightened his back. 'Give here the sample of beer from Allcroft's room.'

The sample bottle lay ready on the path, beside the jar from the inn's kitchen. I passed it over. Fidelis pulled the cork and crouched to pour the beer carefully into the drinking bowl. He stood again and now held his hands up to receive the carrying basket, which I also passed over the fence. Fidelis put it down and removed the pegs that secured the lid. Then, in almost a single movement, he flipped open the lid, skipped out of the rabbit run and clapped the wattle gate shut behind him. Together we leaned on the fence and awaited developments.

'What's this about?' I asked.

'You will see.'

Cautiously a whiskered nose poked above the rim of the basket, twitching busily. Then the sound of scrabbling was heard and the head of the rat appeared, followed by her body. In an instant she had clambered nimbly up the inside of the basket, slid down the outside and out into the open space of the run itself.

For a moment Athene sat up, like a lady in a theatre box, jerking her head around to take in the scene and holding her pink forefeet like two hands gripping a folded fan. And then she was off. She had picked up the direction of the rabbit smell.

She scuttled towards one of the hutches, stopping only to take a drink of beer from the bowl as she passed. Then she was running this way and that around the hutch in search of a way in. Finding none at the first hutch she quickly moved on to the second, and so on until she had unsuccessfully tested all four hutches.

'She hasn't had a drink or eaten today,' Fidelis whispered through the side of his mouth. 'I made sure of that when I wrote to

Satterthwaite. Now, she'd like a baby rabbit if she could get one, but she can't. Lorris would have my tripes else.'

The rat had now returned to the beer bowl and was taking a longer drink, while checking from time to time and looking round for danger. When she had had enough beer, she went back to her investigation of the hutches, running round them first clockwise, and then anticlockwise.

'Just look,' I said, marvelling. 'The beer is affecting her.'

'Yes, she is a little drunk. It's nothing serious.'

'What next?' I asked.

Fidelis took out his watch and opened it.

'We wait five minutes.'

During our wait nothing new happened. The rodent was as quick as ever, darting from hutch to hutch in sudden movements, interrupted by short periods of immobility, during which only her whiskers, nose and ears moved. Fidelis walked off, and came back with an old broom handle he had found. He propped it against the rabbit run's fence.

Dropping his watch back into his waistcoat pocket at last, he now took up the jar of old stew, and removed the lid. He opened the hurdle gate just wide enough and, placing the jar on the ground inside the run, used the broom handle to prod it towards the centre of the space. As soon as the stick was withdrawn the rat scurried across to investigate the jar.

Fidelis tied up the gate.

'Have I got this right?' I asked. 'You are giving poor Allcroft's leftover food to this pet rat of yours. You are testing it, I suppose. Do you know what for?'

Watching intently, Fidelis replied in a low voice.

'It may be I'll know in a few moments. And she's not my pet rat.'

'Yes, she is,' I protested. 'Only pets have names.'

'I didn't give her one. But with luck I shall soon give a name to how Allcroft died. Watch closely.'

The slate-grey clouds that had covered the sky since early morning now began to disperse and the sun came out just as the rat stuck her head inside the jar and began to gorge herself on the meat and other ingredients, all sodden or infused with the thick brown gravy. Fidelis took out his watch once more and flipped open the lid.

'Five minutes?' I asked.

He nodded solemnly.

It did not take as long as that. Less than a minute had elapsed before Athene, with the food by no means finished, made a few backward steps away from the meat to rest on her haunches, as if struck by a momentary unpleasant thought. She held the position for a few seconds, then abruptly fell down backwards, reeling or toppling in a spiralling motion away from the jar. Though she regained her footing, her body was convulsing now, and she was squealing urgently. She tried to run, but her buckling legs could no longer carry her, and she bumped to the ground on her stomach. Finally with one more shrill scream she rolled back onto her feet, leaped at least 2 inches into the air, twisted around and returned to earth belly upward. She did not move again.

Chapter Nine

F IDELIS WENT BACK inside the rabbit run and lifted the dead rodent by the tail. Surprised into silence by what we had seen, I watched as he collected the jar containing the remains of the food and closed it with the lid. Rat and jar were deposited in a sack he had brought with him.

'Come on,' he said. 'The performance is finished. Let us go to my room and talk this over.'

As we passed back through the flower garden, we came upon a young lady sitting in one of the bowers. This, I took it, was Miss Lysistrata Plumb. She was pale as paper but I had to agree with my friend that she was extraordinarily pretty.

'Good morning, Doctor,' she said in a voice that sounded husky and confiding. As Fidelis gave her a bow I noticed his face flushing to a rosy pink.

'Ah, Miss Plumb. Yes. I . . .'

For a moment he was at a loss for words – a rare event in itself.

'May I . . . may I introduce my colleague?' he said at last. 'That is, I should have said, my friend, er, may I introduce Mr Titus Cragg?'

She inclined her head graciously in my direction.

'How do you do, Mr Cragg?'

I also bowed, said I was well, and gave her the question back.

Instead of answering it she said, 'I heard your voices down at the end and wondered what you were doing.'

'An experiment,' said Fidelis, raising the sack in his hand.

'Oh? An experiment, how thrilling. What do you have in that sack?'

'Well, er, I don't know if I should say, it's . . .'

'It is material connected to the experiment,' I put in, to cover his embarrassment.

'Yes, in fact, a dead animal,' Fidelis blurted out, with immoderate suddenness as if he wasn't shaping his remarks very far in advance of opening his mouth. 'To be precise, I should say, to be precise, a dead rat, which I—'

He did not finish the sentence as now Miss Plumb stood up, her hand across her midriff.

'Oh! I do not feel well.'

Before either of us could react she had raised herself up, stumbled sideways and bent almost double, preventing herself from falling only because her hand had found the trunk of a shrub. Most unladylike sounds of retching and spewing followed, so that I hastened to avert my eyes from her. Fidelis, on the other hand, shed his nervousness in the instant and became the consummate professional. He handed me the canvas sack, and went to the lady's side. As the sickness abated he ushered her calmly back to the seat, whipped out the handkerchief that was tucked into her sleeve, wiped her mouth and chin and put the handkerchief into her hand. He then turned and looked carefully at the ground where the vomit lay. Finally he turned back to me.

'Titus, I must attend to Miss Plumb. Will you take that up to my rooms and wait? I will join you as soon as I can.'

Once again a conference between Fidelis and myself had been disturbed by a bout of violent sickness, I thought, as I mounted the stairs to his top-floor rooms. And though I carried the sack containing the corpse of Athene, and I had seen its connection, through the food, with the expiration of John Allcroft, the dread of contagion now returned to me. Perhaps Allcroft's death and Miss Plumb's sickness presaged an epidemic. Perhaps all Preston was now under threat.

To distract myself from these disagreeable thoughts I looked through the titles in Fidelis's library cabinet. It was a poor selection of not more than thirty volumes, almost all of them scientific and medical. I took out one by Dr John Arbuthnot – his *Essay on the Nature of Aliments* – because I remembered the author had been a great friend of two of my favourite authors, Addison and Pope, and had himself invented the satirical character of John Bull. I found little evidence of Arbuthnot's wit in this essay, which was disturbing rather than entertaining. His discourse on coffee has little to say of the delights of the drink but only stresses its 'acrimony' and has a list of its ill effects: 'palsies, leanness, watchfulness and destroying masculine vigour'. I thought of consulting Elizabeth as to whether I should moderate my coffee consumption.

Crossing to the window, with its southern view of the river and the country beyond, I picked out the roof of the Ferry Inn half buried in trees and with a thread of smoke rising from its chimneys. The sickness and death of John Allcroft, and the spectre of contagion that it raised, had put the Egan case out of my mind, but now I thought of it again, and with new complication. There was no chance of reopening the Egan inquest: the evidence on which I could act was too flimsy. But the fact that both men appeared on Destercore's list raised uncomfortable new possibilities, which I was pondering when Fidelis came in.

'Mrs Lorris and I have put her to bed and she is a little more comfortable,' he announced at the door, in the reverent tone of a courtier come from a royal sickbed. 'She is feeling ashamed now, as much as ill.'

'She must not have liked that we saw her vomit.'

Fidelis made for a chair and sat down. He leaned back and closed his eyes for a moment, as if infinitely weary.

'Vomit? It pains me to hear that word used about Miss Plumb. A *dog* vomits, Titus, not a lady.'

'Certainly, a dog vomits,' I agreed, 'and a man spews. What, then, can we say of a lady?'

Fidelis suddenly looked more animated.

'A good question, Titus. Most expressions that cover the matter are too colloquial. I would say she *disengorges*. Miss Plumb is unhappy that we witnessed her disengorging.'

I had to suppress my laughter. The word 'disengorge' was (to me) no less repulsive than 'vomit', but Fidelis had adopted it in all seriousness. He normally enjoyed satire, yet he never, I had noticed, made sport of pretty young ladies.

'I hope,' I said, to move the conversation on, 'that she is not sick in the way John Allcroft was. If there were contagion in this town—'

Fidelis cut me off. In spite of the success of the Athene experiment, he sounded out of temper.

'Allcroft did not die of contagion. He died of the food on his plate.'

'Which you know because of what happened to the rat?'

'Of course. When food kills a man or makes him ill it is either because it has gone bad of itself, or because something bad has been added to it. In Allcroft's case I am certain it was the latter. That is what our rat's death has told us.'

'I see. So in your opinion Allcroft did not die by accident.'

Fidelis shrugged.

'He might have done – for example, if something poisonous was tipped into his stew by mistake. But it is equally likely that he was murdered. I may learn more when I have made a minute examination of the remains of the meal.'

'But suppose the food itself was rotten, would not that kill the rat as well as a poison?'

Fidelis threw back his head in impatience.

'No, Titus. Rats eat rotten meat every day. They thrive naturally on what would sicken you or me, or even kill us. On the other hand, what we use *on purpose* to poison rats will certainly also poison us.'

I sank into the chair opposite Fidelis, a sense of dread slowly possessing me. I have always hated cases of poisoning, but this looked far more troubling than the usual family tragedy. Fidelis's logic was impeccable, but its implications were appalling. I could only hope he was wrong.

As soon as I had left the house I made my way straight back to the Gamecock Inn. Going directly up to Allcroft's room I found no trace of the dead man or his belongings. The odour of sickness still lingered, but the cause of it was gone. Allcroft's family must have come with speed, to remove his body and his traps back to his home.

I went down to the kitchen. The cook at the Gamecock had been in the job only a few months, since the death of Fitzpatrick. He was called Joe Primrose, a fellow with a bulbous nose who was always laughing. I found him at the great table, rolling out a quantity of pastry big enough, almost, to blanket a bed. I asked if we could talk where it was quiet and, with his usual geniality, he put down the yard-long rolling pin and led me past the range where soups and stews bubbled in copper pots, and meats sizzled in the broiling oven. We emerged into the enclosed yard, which was being crossed back and forth by men rolling barrels of wine off a dray. Stables and storerooms were ranged to right and left. Primrose crossed to the door of one of these and unlatched it.

'Hold onto your wig, Mr Cragg,' he sang out as he ducked inside.

The room was hung so thickly with hams, sides of bacon, pheasants and geese, muslin-wrapped cheeses, and sacks bulging with root vegetables, that we needed to stoop to avoid knocking against them.

'It's about last night's death,' I said, when we had disposed ourselves as best we could among the dangling stores. 'You know what happened?'

At the mention of death Primrose suppressed the cheerfulness that had been plastered across his face.

'Oh, yes. Guest fell sick and pegged out. But that's about all I know, Mr Cragg.'

'He'd been eating one of your hotpots.'

A passing frown troubled Primrose's brow for a moment, until his wide guileless smile returned.

'There's nowt wrong with that dish, you know, Mr Cragg. Very much called for, is that.'

'Did you make it the same way yesterday as you always do?'

'Yesterday? Yes, it were same as always, tasty and satisfying. There were a dozen or more that were served it. Tasty and satisfying, those are the two words we use for our hotpot.'

'I have reason to believe that last night there was a third apposite word. Tasty and satisfying, I do not doubt. But also *deadly*, Mr Primrose – that I think was the case when Mr Allcroft ate it.'

This time the concern darkened his face for a little longer. But it was not the black cloud of umbrage, such as most proud cooks would have taken at my imputation, only a flickering shadow of good-natured bewilderment.

'No, no, it can't have been the hotpot killed the poor gentleman. Like I said, a dozen or more had it.'

'And none of the others were poorly after?'

'Not that I've heard of.'

'Was there anything special about Mr Allcroft's portion?'

'No, it was straight out of the common pot.'

'Could anything have been accidentally spilled into it?'

'Get away! The serving girl brought a dish to me on a tray, I ladled out the stew, and she took it up to the room. Nothing could have happened to it without my knowledge.'

'Do you have anything about the place that would do a man harm if it *were* spilled into his stew?'

'But I just said, nothing was!'

'I know. But let's imagine the opposite case.'

Primrose chuckled like a man who enjoyed a bit of verbal stick fighting.

'I don't know what sort of thing you mean.'

'Any poisons, for instance?'

He cast his eyes down and to one side to give the matter thought.

'Not that I know of,' he said at last.

'What about powders or compounds you might use for killing pests? Rats, say?'

Primrose's expression brightened at the mention of rats.

'Oh, aye, rats,' he beamed. 'We don't like them here. They live under the brewery across the lane. We try to kill as many as we can.'

'Do you lay out poison?'

'I don't. We send for Isaac Satterthwaite. He knows what to do. If anything needs killing, whether it's a mad dog or a viper, he'll do it with pleasure, but especially rats. He does love murdering rats. But I doubt he's been murdering a man.'

'I'm not saying that. I was merely concerned in case there had been an unfortunate accident. How exactly does he lay the poison?'

'You can ask him in person. I gave him a slice of pie in the kitchen no more than a half-hour ago. He's been working at the brewery.'

I said I would do that and, as we dodged our way out of the storeroom, I asked, in as disinterested a way as I could, 'The serving girl you mentioned. Amelia – is that her name?'

'No. We've not got an Amelia here. It's Maggie. Maggie Satterthwaite. Matter of fact, she's granddaughter of old Isaac, you know.'

'Ah, yes! Of course. Maggie. And Isaac's granddaughter, you say? Well, well.'

I watched Primrose as he returned to his pastry rolling and then headed off to see if I could find the rat catcher himself.

The yard gates gave onto a little rutted lane that looped back to Stoney Gate. I went out of the gate and crossed the lane to Lacey's, one of Preston's four breweries, and here I found Isaac Satterthwaite, leaning in contemplative fashion over the mash tun with brew-master Ted Lacey himself. Also in the company was a skinny, desiccated fellow dressed in clothes that were not flamboyant but distinctly modish and elegant: the silver-buttoned waistcoat was of red damask, the shoes were expensive and the wig was a finely made 'natty scratch'. This was Michael Drake, the haberdasher, whose shop was next door, fronting Stoney Gate itself. The three of them were contentedly breathing the mash tun's fumes. Satterthwaite turned to me as I approached.

'How do, Mr Cragg? I did not think we would meet again so soon. Now have a sniff of this ale fermenting here. I was just saying to Mr Lacey and Mr Drake that it'll be a very manly one when finished.'

'It will an' all,' muttered Lacey, a man of few words.

'Aye, it will be a strong, fighting brew, will this, Mr Cragg,' confirmed Drake.

'And it's only to be had at the Gamecock,' continued Satterthwaite. 'What they call in London an *exclusive* ale.'

We discussed the various ales on offer in town for a few minutes before Drake left us, saying his dinner hour was done.

'I must attend to the shop. Shall we take our guns out on Moor Nook later, Ted? Does six o'clock suit you?'

The brewer's grunt implied that six o'clock was indeed a very suitable time for the slaughtering of rabbits. I took Satterthwaite's elbow and guided him into the yard.

'I should have mentioned it this morning, but we have a particularly bothersome family of rats under the house, so I've come over for advice about getting rid of them.'

'In such cases you call for *me*, sir. It's a dangerous business to dabble in, is rat catching.'

'What would you do?'

'The rat is my strongest and most wily enemy.' Satterthwaite spoke with steely severity. 'I have three lines of attack. My terriers, which you have seen, and very sporting they are to work with. Traps, which are chancy but they're the only way to take your rat alive. And laying poison, which for efficiently killing the animal can't be beaten. White arsenic. I get it from Wilson in Church Gate. It's a dangerous element, mind. You've got to keep it safe.'

'Have you used it about the place here?'

'I did on Tuesday night and I bagged a monstrous one, as big as a buck rabbit. I've just been putting some more down. Come and I'll show you.'

He took me round to the back of the building, where he slapped the wall.

'Other side of this is where the barley's kept. They can never get enough of it, rats. They get in through the drain here.'

He indicated an aperture low down in the wall.

'Why not simply block it up?'

'That's useless. They'd find another way. This is best because with this I know where to catch them. They will always run the easiest, quickest way. See this?'

He pointed to an earthenware pipe about 3 inches in diameter and 4 feet long lying on the ground beside the wall.

'I put the poison in that pipe mixed with some of Mr Lacey's best grain. I soften the grain first, of course.'

'You mean you cook it?'

'Aye. It makes it easier to mix, does that. And mark that pipe. It's got to be too narrow for a cat or a dog, and too long for a child to reach into, see? I'll never know how a rat as big as that got in, but it did, for it lay dead just over there by the water butt.'

I went down on one knee, planted a hand on the ground and lowered my head until my cheek almost touched the pipe's end. In this ungainly position I peered into the pipe. I could see light coming through from the other end but some substance partially blocked it about halfway along. I got up and dusted the dirt off my hand.

'I see just how you've planted the poison, Mr Satterthwaite. I will certainly call for you if our nuisance persists.'

I held out my hand and he shook it with military rigour but, as I was leaving, he called after me.

'I hope Dr Fidelis is enjoying his pet.'

I turned, momentarily at a loss to know what to reply.

'Has she settled with him?' Satterthwaite went on. 'Do you know?'

'Alas, she has not,' I replied. 'She has died.'

Satterthwaite looked concerned.

'Well, she were lish as a butcher's brat when I gave her over. What was up with her?'

'Nothing intrinsic,' I replied. 'Let's just say she gave her life in the cause of justice.'

I left him to scratch his head over this and walked back across the lane, and into the courtyard of the Gamecock. I had much to think about. Allcroft could certainly have been poisoned with the rat catcher's arsenic, but I had not proved the case. Even if I could do so, it would not mean of necessity that Satterthwaite was guilty. Anyone could have collected some of the poison, as long as they knew where and how he laid it – and it may have been no secret that he had done so most recently only last Tuesday night.

Of course, it had not escaped me that one of those perfectly placed to know such details was Maggie Satterthwaite – who was not only the rat catcher's granddaughter, but had served Allcroft with his meal.

I entered by the yard door, passed through the flagged passage and into the hall of the inn, where I was confronted by a tall figure coming in from Stoney Gate.

'Hello,' I said. 'You're Peters, Mr Destercore's man.'

He reacted with some suspicion though he clearly recognized me.

'That's right.'

'Well, your master will find this a friendly house. It's famous for its good ale.'

'I've tasted it,' said Peters. He had a genteel way of speaking, and his manner of dress, too, seemed a cut above that of a manservant. His buckles were of silver and his waistcoat's piping had woven into it gleaming strands of what looked like silver thread, not as thick or glittery as Ephraim Grimshaw's, but not the expected trim to the garment of a servant.

'You stop here?' I said. 'I thought you were at Porter's.'

'Mr Destercore's there, and I'm here. Now, if you would excuse me . . .'

So I let him pass. But our encounter had given me even more to think about.

When my conscience is taxed, or my understanding falls short, I talk the matter out with Elizabeth for, unless I do, I find it forms lumps in my mind that will not shift. That night, as we lay side by side with our heads resting on the bolster, and she having given me all the details of her mother's departure that day for Broughton, I told her the full story of my dealings with the Gamecock Inn and the death of Mr Allcroft.

'It was horrible. Blood, excrement, vomit, excruciating cramps – I am sorry, dear, but Allcroft died no ordinary death. It should have been subject to inquest, as I now know.'

'But it was a natural illness, wasn't it? There's been a fearful story going round that it was plague.'

'Utter nonsense. Allcroft was sick from what he ate. Death came to him in the form of a stew.'

'So why not put that to a jury?'

'I have a difficulty about that,' I said. 'The body has already gone from the town and out of my jurisdiction.'

'So what was wrong with the stew?'

'Luke has made a rather convincing case for its having been deliberately poisoned.'

'Poisoned! How?'

I told her about the experiment carried out that morning in Adam Lorris's garden. When she heard of the rat's demise she gave an involuntary laugh.

'Oh, dear! Poor innocent Athene. But how can Dr Fidelis be

so sure of his case? Some men are rats, as many women have found, but a rat is not the same as a man.'

'In much we are the same. If you hurt us we cry, if you cut us we bleed, if you hold us underwater we drown.'

'Yes, but a rat does not laugh, or write letters, or know God.'

'How can you be sure?'

'A rat writing letters, Titus?'

'All right, I concede there are no rat letters, strictly speaking. There might be a rat God.'

'That is irreligious, dearest.'

'Probably. I am not concerned with religion, but with facts, and they are these – Allcroft ate some food, the rat ate the same food, they both died. It is therefore my and Dr Fidelis's submission that a person, or persons, unknown laced that food with a poison, conceivably rat poison. I also adumbrate a possible connection of the culprit. Maggie Satterthwaite was the inn servant who brought the hotpot up to Allcroft's room, and who is also the granddaughter of Isaac Satterthwaite, our distinguished rat catcher and a man accustomed to the use of white arsenic in destroying rats.'

'Titus, will you please try not to address me as if I were the House of Lords? Just tell me in plain words why would Maggie, or anyone, kill Mr Allcroft? He was a most amiable gentleman, and my parents' friend.'

'I don't know, my love, but there is one dark possibility at the back of all this. Allcroft was on a list of voters kept by the Whig agent Mr Destercore, who has come here as Mr Reynolds's corner man in the election. I have seen this list. The names on it are those thought to be particularly likely to vote against Mr Reynolds. They are his political opponents.'

'You make this list sound so sinister. But isn't it normal for the parties to collect intelligence and tally the votes?'

'Of course. But it is definitely not normal for names on their lists to be murdered a week before the election. Elizabeth . . .' I took her hand and caressed it. 'You should know something else. Your uncle Egan's name was also on that list. I am wondering if he also was a victim.'

'But he died by misadventure. Your jury said so and you agreed.'

'But now I am not so sure. Especially when I recall that it happened the very night Destercore stopped at the Ferry Inn. And remember Dick Middleton's evidence.'

'You know what I think of that.'

'But if these were indeed murders – and if they were political – and that became even suspected here in town, there would be incalculable trouble. Mobs have sprung up and great houses been burned to the ground over lesser matters.'

Elizabeth had been resting on her side facing me. Now she rolled onto her back and lay for a few moments in silence. At last she went on.

'I'll grant you that Uncle Egan was a proud and deep-dyed Tory, when his head was clear enough to remember it. But the whole thing seems too fantastical. That Destercore has come here to murder Tories to alter the result! How could he? This is not a rotten borough with a mere six or seven votes. There are hundreds of voters here and to make a difference he would have to commit a mass murder, not just kill two or three.'

'Perhaps his tally tells him the voting will be that close.'

Elizabeth yawned and stretched like a cat.

'Well, I'll tell you something. Maggie Satterthwaite may be very pretty and perhaps not very wise. But she has always been a law-abiding girl.'

'She's not entirely good, though. She was dismissed from her place at the Ferry Inn – do you know why?'

'Ah! I wondered if that would be remembered.'

'Her grandfather remembers it. He is bitter.'

'Her dismissal was the decision of Mary-Ann and Grace. It was well founded enough but the cause was not her dishonesty.'

'What, then?'

Elizabeth hesitated.

'She fell in love, I think.'

'There's no disgrace in that.'

'She was found in bed with the man.'

'Ah!'

'Indeed.'

She yawned again.

'Now I must rest. Remember tomorrow is May Day.'

I leaned across and kissed her sleepy lips.

'Goodnight, then,' I said.

'Goodnight, sweet prince,' she murmured in reply.

Chapter Ten

O N MAY DAY the chill and rain that had gusted through the week gave way to warm air and sunshine. For most of Preston, this was to be a festive day without work. In place of the Friday market, a fair was to be held in Market Place, beginning at noon, with dancing, the crowning of the May Queen, amusement stalls, boxing booths, bearded ladies and much more in that vein. It was traditional for the girls to go out first thing, to scoop up morning dew with their hands and rub it into their faces, which they believed would give them soft skin. Then they gathered wild flowers for garlands to dress the town wells and the doorways of their houses. It was also customary to perform antics and play tricks, and shout, 'May gosling!' at those who were fooled.

It was not a workless day for me. My first act on entering the office in the morning was to write a note to Luke Fidelis. I had the idea of dining at the Gamecock, I wrote, and would he like to join me? This was sent by hand of a boy and, after I had been working for half an hour with Furzey on drawing up Miss Colley's new will, his reply came back that he would be seeing patients in the morning and at the same time developing an appetite for the meal he would be very glad to take with me at the inn. He suggested we meet at two o'clock.

By ten the will was drawn up and a fair copy in legal hand

had been made by Furzey. This I rolled up and then set off to Miss Colley's on Fisher Gate. My client greeted me effusively.

'Mr Cragg, have you brought my will for signing? How very genteel of you to come in person. You will take a glass of Madeira? I hope you like macaroons.'

While she saw to my refreshment I sat down at her dining table and unrolled the will.

'You must read it through before you sign,' I said.

'Oh, be a kind attorney, Mr Cragg,' she begged. 'Read it to me.'

'You really should peruse it personally before you sign, you know.'

'Of course I shall peruse it – after you have read it to me.'

'Very well.'

I began reading, taking a sip of wine and a nibble of macaroon between each clause. When I had finished I handed the document across.

'Please have a look over it and then we will need a witness to your signature.'

'I know the ideal person. I shall send word.'

She left me alone and went downstairs, returning after a few minutes.

'You must have another glass while we wait,' she announced.

'Only if you will engage in the meantime to look over the will,' I said.

It was agreed and at last she was sitting with the paper on her knee and spectacles on her nose.

'A beautiful hand your clerk has,' she remarked as she bent over it.

For the next few minutes she sat looking at the page. Though she exclaimed from time to time – at a name or an item bequested – she was not I think reading the document consecutively, but rather she was examining it, while remarking on one word or another as she randomly noticed them. I had seen this before in female clients of the gentry class. It was not that Miss Colley could not read; she believed reading in public to be somehow indelicate, undignified or unladylike. So she treated the document as if it were there to be appreciated just for its visual quality, like a fine engraving from Salvator Rosa.

Little more than five minutes had passed when there came a knock on the door and a lady swept in. She was voluminously dressed, and her face was heavily rouged and powdered. It was Miss Colley's neighbour, Mrs Lavinia Bryce.

'You require a witness to your signature, my dear Miss Colley? Allow me to be the one.'

She spoke heroically, as one volunteering for a gallant and perhaps suicidal military exploit. This tone amused Miss Colley, who tittered that she'd been in no doubt of Mrs Bryce stepping up to the line. However, certain social obligations had to be observed before the signing ceremony could take place. First the will was laid on the table, and Mrs Bryce was put at her ease in an uphol-stered chair. Then my name and person were presented to her and duly acknowledged, after which a glass of Madeira was placed in her hand and a macaroon offered – and declined on the grounds that Mrs Bryce found the biscuit excessively binding. Finally a certain quantity of conversation was to be made, and the topic that Mrs Bryce favoured was quickly apparent.

'We are all transfixed by the election, are we not? Poor Mr Reynolds, it is exhausting him extremely. I have to keep him constantly up to the mark, you know, telling him that the Great Prize is within his grasp and that he must not let his resolution waver. Without me I fancy he would have wilted by now. So many speeches to make, and bumpers of wine to drink, and banquets to attend.'

'Do the Whigs really think they can swing it?' asked Miss Colley. 'This town seems so very Tory to me.'

Mrs Bryce replied with a snort.

'The corporation is Tory. But Mr Reynolds says it's such a fretful long time since Preston voted, there's nobody really knows how it will go. In London they take it most seriously; they have set their eyes on us. Did you know, Mr Cragg, they have even sent an agent to oversee the vote on behalf of their party?'

'Yes, I did. I have met him. I—'

'A fretfully clever sort of fellow, I am told, and do you think they would bundle him up here if they thought the election was scuppered, and all Mr Reynolds's work here wasted and poor Sir Harry bound to be ousted from Parliament?' She inflated her cheeks and blew out a puff of air. 'Of course they would not!'

She swigged her wine.

'And Mr Reynolds is such a darling little man that I would be made quite ill if our efforts to keep him up to the mark were in vain. Now – what is it you would like me to sign?'

The May Day dancing was to begin at three and would be followed by the May Queen's coronation. The maypole already stood erected in the middle of Market Place, and carpenters were at work building a stage on the east side. A large oak branch, the leaves young and spring green, had been tied to the pole's tip, while coloured ribbons hung down from the top to the ground. A group of four young unmarried women of the town – the candidates for the crown of flowers the May Queen would wear for her procession through the town – had gathered around Barney Lostock, the fiddler and the master of the dance. He was giving out instructions for a rehearsal in the manner of a sergeant of dragoons preparing to attack. As his assault was about to begin, I strolled down to watch the dancers pick up the ends of the ribbons and take their positions around the pole. Barney counted to three and began to play a jaunty tune, upon which the girls began bobbing and skipping around the pole, two in one direction and two in the other. Gradually they wound their ribbons about its shaft until there was none left to wind, at which they made a smart about-turn on Barney's command and danced in the opposite direction, to unwind the ribbons again.

Standing next to me in the small group of passers-by attracted by the music and the pretty sight was Nick Oldswick, the watchmaker with whom I had supped four nights earlier at the White Bull.

'They're all supposed to be virgins – that's a joke,' he commented drily. 'But we must all agree to pretend, eh, Titus?'

I agreed that it was our civic duty.

'By the way,' he went on, 'I'm glad we met because I am thinking of consulting you.'

'Oh, yes? A legal matter?'

'I think so. A person tried to attack me last night, just after I'd locked up my shop.'

'What happened?'

'I had an urgent job in hand and had been working late by lamplight. It was eleven or so, very dark, with nobody about that I could see when I went out. After I'd locked up I dropped the key into my pocket and was setting off for home when this someone tried to brain me. He'd been lurking behind a cart that had a broken axle and so was parked for the night, pushed right close to the wall. This man, big he was, swung at me as I passed the cart with a heavy club, or whatever it was. By chance, at that very same moment, my foot tripped on a stone half sunk in the ground and I stumbled, with my head dropping forward, do you see? That stumble saved my life, Titus, and also no doubt my stock of gold in the shop, because the blow missed my head and hit the cart.

Then the man ran off. I don't know why. Happen he thought he heard someone else coming.'

'Who was he?'

'I don't know. I never saw him at all, except as a shape in the night. I was taken with such a shock that I did not think quickly enough. I did not call or run after him.'

'If you do not know his name you can hardly contemplate legal action.'

'It's not him I want to proceed against; it's the owner of the cart. Leaving it in that place was actionable. It greatly facilitated the attempted crime by offering concealment to the criminal.'

Did he have a case? The coming of the election had brought many strangers, some of them also malefactors, which made the present circumstances highly unusual for our town. Ordinarily the leaving of a broken-down cart in the street overnight would not be thought a mischief, and in my view the Court Leet would therefore be inclined to forgive the carter rather than condemn him. Furthermore, the attempted crime had not been seen by anyone else. Oldswick's hobby of going to law was so well known that, without witnesses to back up his story, he risked being derided, disbelieved and, in the end, out of pocket.

I told him as much, as delicately as I could. He huffed once or twice then made off, muttering about obtaining the services of a different lawyer. I turned back to the maypole and found that the ribbons were all but loosed from it, and Barney was terminating the dance with a decisive downward stroke of his bow. It was then that I noticed that one of the dancers was Maggie Satterthwaite. I went forward and drew her aside.

'Maggie, I hear you served poor Mr Allcroft with his dinner yesterday at the Gamecock.'

'That I did, sir, in his room.'

'Some say it might have been his food that made him ill. Would you know anything about that?'

'I just took plate up to him. I didn't cook it.'

She spoke sharply. I looked at her, but did not see evidence that she was hiding anything.

'Is there a way it might have had something noxious added to it, after it was put on the plate?'

'I don't know, sir. I just took it up straight from kitchen.'

'Was it served out of the common pot?'

'Yes, sir. I watched as Mr Primrose gave it onto the plate.'

'And how was Mr Allcroft when you delivered it up? Did he seem ill at all at that point?'

'I don't know, sir.'

'Didn't you see him?'

'No, sir, he was in coffee room. Half the people were there. They were discussing election lists, or the like, with that agent man.'

It took me a moment to realize whom she meant.

'You mean Mr Thompson, the Tories' agent, conducting his canvas?'

'Yes, sir.'

'How do you know Mr Allcroft was with him in the assembly room?'

'Because when I went back to kitchen I sent our boy Peterkin to look for him and tell him his food was waiting in his room, where he'd asked for it to be brought.'

'So the room had been empty when you left the food?'

'Unless there were someone hiding under the bed, sir.'

Our conversation went no further because now one of Maggie's fellow virgins ran across to claim her for a second trial of the maypole dance and I walked back to the office. I had heard enough to know that the theory of the deliberate poisoning of Allcroft had gained in credibility. But as to who was responsible, we were little further on. The food had been left alone in the room, if only for a few minutes: anyone might have gone in there and adulterated it.

I reached the Gamecock Inn ten minutes before two. It was almost deserted. News that a man had sickened on Wednesday after eating his dinner and died on Thursday, meant few would relish dining there on Friday. While every other alehouse and inn was at bursting point, the only customers in Mrs Fitzpatrick's dining room were a pair of newly arrived strangers and the stone-deaf tobacconist of Stoney Gate, Nat Parrott, eating with his neighbouring trader, Michael Drake, whom I had met at Lacey's the previous day.

I found the widow Fitzpatrick standing with Luke Fidelis, bemoaning her loss of trade. She greeted me volubly.

'Oh, Mr Cragg, how very good of you to patronize us once again! Is the Gamecock to be ruined by this staying away? All the prime meat I've bought in for the week will be ruined. We may salt some of it, but when, I should like to know, will I get my investment back? I've dug deep to pay for it all, extra beef, extra beer, preserved fruits and I don't know what.'

I told her I thought the customers would soon come back once they believed any danger had passed.

'But when will that be, Doctor?' she wailed, turning back to my friend. 'Another week and the election will be done and the people gone from town like the starlings in winter.'

'There is no knowing, Mrs Fitz,' he said, 'but I agree with Mr Cragg. I would be surprised if this sad death is not quickly superseded by other sensations.'

We took our seats at a private table and studied the bill of fare. Fidelis said he would have a cheese tart, cold roast teal and boiled salad.

'I shall order hotpot,' I said.

'Good God, man, that is a gamble,' he whispered. 'Isn't your name on Destercore's list? I could not promise to save you if you happen to ingest what Allcroft did.'

'Oh, I'm not ordering it to eat,' I said.

Mrs Fitzpatrick herself brought us wine and took our order for food. I asked for ham, cheese, pickled onions with mushroom ketchup, in addition to the bowl of hotpot which, I was reassured, was prepared exactly to the usual recipe. While we waited I enquired after the progress of Miss Plumb.

'She is completely better today.'

'And is she still angelic?'

Fidelis looked pained.

'Yes,' he said stiffly. 'That is the essential point about angels, Titus. They do not change.'

'One called Lucifer did, as I remember.'

To which he had no answer.

The food came and we set about our meat and cheese while the dish of hotpot cooled on the table between us.

'Have you had the opportunity to examine the remains of Allcroft's meal?' I asked.

He nodded.

'Yes – mutton, kidneys, peas, carrots, onion, cereals. I asked Mrs Lorris, who considered them the usual ingredients.'

'Cereals, you said? What kind?'

'Oatmeal and barley. Tell me where this is leading.'

'To our examination of this plate before us. I want to make a comparison, for I learned something suggestive yesterday.'

Fidelis leaned towards the plate, his face alert. I picked up a spoon and stirred it around in the hotpot, lifting out ingredients as the spoon encountered them. The presence of carrots was easily confirmed; then flesh, kidney, onions, peas each in turn revealed themselves.

'We have found the meat and vegetables,' I prompted. 'But what cereals do we have?'

'Oatmeal is all that I can see.'

'Good!' I cried, with (I admit) an unseemly show of triumph. 'This is coming out exactly as I hoped. The usual cereal used in hotpot is indeed oatmeal, as Elizabeth confirmed for me this morning. Barley is only sometimes used, for it is dearer. Here at the Gamecock, it seems, they content themselves with the conventional use of oatmeal only.'

Fidelis looked bewildered.

'But not in Allcroft's dinner, Titus. It contained barley, I swear it did.'

'Of course it did, Luke, and I think we shall find that is what killed him.'

Fidelis had been in the act of raising his glass to his lips. He put it down instead.

'How is that?'

I took him through my conversation on the previous day with Isaac Satterthwaite, stressing that, when working around the brewery, the rat catcher invariably mixed his arsenic with softened barley taken from the brewer's store. As Luke listened, a smile stole over his face.

'I understand you, Titus,' he said when I had finished, seizing the spoon from my hand and plunging it into the hotpot. He lifted it out heavily loaded with meat. 'And it's clever. It confirms my opinion that John Allcroft was murdered, even if we cannot yet say who did it.'

He shovelled the meat into his mouth.

'I have an idea on that score also,' I said, as I watched his jaws working.

Fidelis made a beckoning motion with his fingers.

'Tell,' he mumbled.

I described how I had seen the servant Peters in the hallway of the inn.

'He is staying on the spot, which means he might readily have been on the premises when Allcroft died.'

Fidelis, who had swallowed at last, was animated by this news of Peters.

'This is progress, Titus.' He tapped his chest at the place where the last of his mouthful was still descending his gullet. 'Excellent hotpot.'

'Well, suspicion must fall on Peters,' I went on. 'He could have seduced or corrupted Maggie and made her get the poisoned barley.'

'She may even have taken the plate of food to Peters's room, waited while he mixed in the poison, and afterwards taken it to poor Allcroft's as if nothing had happened. It could have been done in a minute.'

'And don't forget, Luke, this is the second death to have occurred near him. Peters was on his way to the Ferry Inn when Antony Egan went into the river. Both men were on his master's list of political enemies.'

'In other words this may all have been done by the manipulations of Destercore, in which case Peters is only the marionette.'

'But why? How could it help Destercore's party to kill one or two of the other side's voters?'

'Fear, Titus. Most of those coming into town will be Tories, won't they? Country people. If they fear for their lives they will not stay to vote, they'll hop straight back to their burrows like rabbits out of the rain. The Tory vote could be decimated.'

I considered.

'That's plausible. But we've had two deaths and there's been no flight to the countryside yet.'

'There is still time. Antony Egan's death may not have been part of the plot, but the poisoning of Allcroft was meant to look like a contagion, as you yourself thought it was when you first saw him. Another case or two like this and talk of plague will empty the town faster than a snake can spit.'

We drained our glasses and asked for the bill. When she'd brought it Mrs Fitzpatrick noticed the hardly eaten hotpot. She leaned across the table and sniffed it.

'There's nothing wrong with that!' she announced, straightening her back and challenging me with a proud look.

'Oh no, absolutely nothing, Mrs Fitzpatrick,' I agreed. 'It is perfectly delicious.'

'Then I wish you would tell folk, because this hotpot has got a bad reputation for itself, and all through no fault of its own. Clear its name for it – will you do that for me, Mr Cragg?'

I said I would do my best.

'Well, I have taken on many cases in my years as an attorney,' I told Fidelis, after she had bustled away, 'but this was the first time I've taken a brief from a dish of food.'

Fidelis laughed.

'And the first time you might boast that you've seen your client eaten, Titus.'

Chapter Eleven

T HE MAY DAY festivities were still under way as we walked out into the sunshine of Stoney Gate. With the swollen population of the town, most of them already intent on drinking and feasting, the holiday had quickly reached an intensity I had never seen before. From various points of the compass wild cheers and raucous singing reached us on the breeze from Market Place.

We parted at the top of Cheapside and, going home, I found Elizabeth waiting. She had seen the maypole dance and was now bonneted and ready to walk out with me to see the procession.

'Destercore is a villain, I am sure of it,' I told her, unable to rid my mind of dark suspicious thoughts. 'He has come here to murder voters with poison, and make it look like plague, and so frighten people out of town. I think I must take this to Mayor Biggs.'

'Can you prove it?'

'No.'

'Then do not speak to the mayor, Titus. Not yet. The man's fool enough as it is. There's no knowing what extremes he may go to if he thinks his party is under attack.'

As we came out of the house a group of men were hurrying towards Fisher Gate, calling to each other about some exciting event happening further down the street – an altercation between two gentlemen, which was evidently worth running to see. Curiosity quickened our own steps as we followed.

Outside Porter's there was a ruck of people. I noticed Luke Fidelis standing on the fringe of the crowd and we went over and stood beside him. Even by rising on my toes I could not see what was happening, but Fidelis is taller.

'Dr Fidelis,' said Elizabeth, pulling at his sleeve, 'can you see what the matter is?'

'It is Sir Harry Hoghton and Francis Reynolds, squaring up to each other.'

'What, the two candidates? Don't tell me they are fighting!'

'Any moment now.'

I pushed forward between two broad-backed spectators until I could get a view. The two Whigs confronted one another like a pair of fighting cocks. Sir Henry was even redder in the face than usual as he stood there, bullish and obstinate; Reynolds was screeching with rage.

I could not catch all the words being spoken, but the injured party appeared to be Reynolds. He was rocking back and forth as a string of reproaches poured from his mouth. These he punctuated at intervals by reaching out and sharply pushing Sir Henry on the breast. His voice rose to a height of indignation and I heard him clearly for the first time.

'You double-dealing swine! You rogue! You villain!'

Sir Henry was neither backing down, nor retreating, nor in any way showing weakness. He talked back with what might, from the grim smile on his face, have been some choice satirical remarks aimed at Reynolds's personal qualities. So he stood his ground, with his dander up and his fists clenched, happy to argue if Reynolds was arguing, and ready to box, if it came to boxing.

The crowd was murmuring in rapt anticipation of the fight, when Denis Destercore came bustling out of the Mitre, with the look of a farmer whose milk cows have escaped from their pasture. He was not a big man but he pushed through the crowd like a strong one, until he had placed himself between the two antagonists, parted them and spoken fast and earnestly. The import of what he was saying was clear, even if the words were not: the last thing that the Whig cause needed was a falling-out between the two candidates.

I tapped the shoulder of a big man in front of me, an out-of-towner whom I did not know.

'Have you seen this from the beginning? What has happened? How is Mr Reynolds injured?'

'Didn't you hear?' the man answered with a coarse laugh. 'He's caught the old one planting cabbage on his patch. But the old one thinks it was *his* patch in the first place.'

I slipped back to Elizabeth and Fidelis.

'That fellow says Hoghton's been planting cabbage on Reynolds's patch,' I reported.

Luke laughed in delight.

'What a kitchen garden is this life!"

Then, through the screen of bodies, we saw an arm swing, and heard a cry and a curse, and at once the spectators were parting, making a path for Reynolds. Hoghton, comforted by the agent's arm around his shoulder, was holding a handkerchief spotted with blood to his nose, while Reynolds continued to breast his way through the spectators, his face a rigid mask of anger. As soon as he was free of us, he crossed the street and let himself into a house on the other side, violently slamming the door behind him. Just before the crash of the door I looked upwards at the windows overlooking the scene. There, standing at a top floor, I saw the figure of Mrs Lavinia Bryce peeping out from behind a half-drawn curtain. As she heard the door hurled against its frame she abruptly turned away, letting the curtain fall.

Elizabeth had laughed so hard she needed to straighten her bonnet.

'Did you know about this?' I asked.

'Oh, no! Not until this minute. Everyone knew about Mr Reynolds, of course, and his – how shall I put it? – his *arrangement* with Mrs Bryce. But it appears that Sir Harry was there before him and last night tried to reassert himself. Oh, what cock-fighting! What sport!'

I laughed with her. The effect this might have on the election I could not say, but no one could deny that it was as good as a comedy.

We made our way back by a roundabout route to Market Place where we found benches and tables had been set out in front of the White Bull. They were crammed with customers spooning up glasses of custard and supping mugs of ale while a succession of itinerant personalities entertained them. The latest was the Irishman I had seen performing card tricks the previous Monday morning – the prestidigitator of eccentric appearance. He was standing on a wooden chest and giving out a stream of speech to the crowd; Elizabeth and I stopped to hear his patter.

'It was a grave thing, what happened,' he was saying, 'a very grave thing indeed. The poor man died, as I hear, from eating a hotpot. A very *gravy* thing, that was.'

The audience roared with laughter, leaning into each other and slapping their knees.

'You laugh, my masters,' said the man. His raised finger and darkened tone of voice quieted them instantly. 'You would not, if you happened to have eaten that hotpot yourself. For you would be in the grave also. To eat such a friendly thing as a Lancashire hotpot and to die from it! How horrible. But do not despair.'

His hand whisked in the air then dived into one of his waist-coat pockets, producing a small bottle.

'This is, my masters and mistresses, is my very own Patent Paracelsian Preservative. It is made from a unique secret formula divulged to me by a German gentleman in Württemberg who had it directly from the lips of a descendent of the great and potent wizard Paracelsus.'

The crowd gasped as he shook the bottle vigorously.

'Yes,' he continued, 'from Paracelsus himself, who could turn lead into gold and do diverse wondrous things, all of whose secrets were entombed with him. But not *quite* all. One particular secret was not entombed, because I have it here, yes, here, in this bottle, which I can sell to you, any of you, at the extreme modest price of sixpence, yes, sixpence, just sixpence, sirs and madams. This here is the Quintessence of Quintessence, as the good doctor himself called it – a universal specific, a guaranteed guard against contagion, poison, snakebite and the bloody flux.'

Swaying now, and bending at the waist in an inviting way, he turned until he was looking behind him.

'Dickon!' he called, snapping his fingers, 'come here to me.'

A forlorn-looking, cross-eyed man with thin, tangled hair and the appearance of having swallowed his own chin, shuffled out of the crowd that hedged them round. The mountebank stepped from his box, stood Dickon there in his place and produced a spoon from another of his waistcoat pockets. He pulled the cork from the bottle with his teeth and poured a dose of the preservative into the spoon. Still using his teeth he returned the cork to the bottle.

'This here is Dickon, my particular young pal,' he said. 'I have been worried about Dickon this last twenty-four hours, that is to say, it was his health worried me. Why? Because isn't he after partaking of that hotpot, that selfsame hotpot that did for the unfortunate deceased already mentioned? And did Dickon not guzzle the fatal stew at the very same time, and at the very same place, to whit the Gamecock Inn in this town, as the unfortunate deceased had done? He did, my ladies and gentlemen. Indeed he did.'

The crowd groaned. Every eye was fixed on the human exhibit standing before them. With his loose knees and drooping head, he looked as if he might fall dead on the spot at any moment.

'But fear not, my valiant, and be of cheer,' the speaker went on, now addressing Dickon directly. 'For with the irreplaceable assistance of my Patent Preservative you shall be reprieved from what will otherwise be a certain and agonizing death.'

He turned back to the crowd, leaning forward, swaying, and looking confidingly from eye to eye. 'I have been dosing him every hour, every hour most regularly, since he told me the unwise thing he had done. Now it is time for the next ministration.'

He returned the bottle to his pocket and, reaching up with his free hand, tweaked Dickon's nose, pulling it upwards so that his mouth fell open. Neatly, he popped the spoonful of medicine into the mouth, released the nose and waited while the patient swallowed.

It was as if a sunbeam had reflected off Dickon's face and body. He lifted his head, and straightened his legs and his sagging back. A spark lit his eye, and he smiled.

'There, do you see?' crowed the mountebank, standing back and spreading his arms to display his handiwork. 'What could be easier and better? If it works for poor Dickon it will work for you. Now, who will buy? Sixpence a bottle is all I ask. Sixpence, only sixpence. Who will buy?'

He helped Dickon down from the box and motioned him to open it up, revealing a supply of bottles identical to the one in his pocket. In no time people were standing in line and, over the next five minutes, the Irishman did a brisk trade. The fellow had an extraordinary gift for the opportune, but his histrionics also provoked in me a brief meditation on the power of rumour and anxiety. It was that very power that (by Fidelis's reckoning) some-one was trying to use to sway the country electors into fleeing the town for fear of a fictitious plague, a non-existent contagion.

A blast of wind music interrupted my thoughts. Every head turned to see the obese constable of the town, Oswald Mallender, as he strode bedizened into Market Place in his uniform (tricorn hat with silver-and-gold trim, brass chain of office) and swinging his mace, ahead of a six-strong pipe band. This in turn preceded a procession of mounted burgesses, led by Mayor Biggs looking oddly shrunken in his own regalia, heavy with silver, brass and braid. There followed the four flower-decked floats of the candi-dates for May Queen, each pulled along by a team of her followers, and attended by phalanxes of mostly drunk young men. They had grown hoarse from shouting political slogans over the last few days, but were now roaring louder than ever for the girl of their choice. In the general political argument few of them had a vote: in this election their voices counted for everything.

The floats trained into Market Place and drew up in a semi-circle around the rear of the stage that had been put up on the east side. With magisterial deliberateness Mallender supervised the descent of the young ladies from their floats and their ascent to the platform. As soon as they were installed in full view the struc-ture became an island surrounded by a boiling sea of men and women, waiting for Mallender to make a formal presentation of the candidates, and for the winner to be discovered by public accla-mation.

The first to come forward was so nervous that she could only blush furiously, her eyes fixed on the boards. The next forced herself into the attitude of a saucy actress, with hands on hips and pouting lips. The youths gave her a cheer, but it was at least partly in deri-sion, for she was Judith, the niece of Burgess Grimshaw. The third candidate was too young and excitable. She bounced up and down on the stage and laughed like a child rope jumping, which provoked some good-natured handclaps. But it was Maggie Satterthwaite, the fourth girl, who made the strongest impression on the public. Her wide smile, pretty face and graceful body, as she turned and waved this way and that, won by far the largest volley of cheers and whistles.

There was no doubt about the result. The shock expressed on Ephraim Grimshaw's face told the tale in full: it was the look of a man that had been overbid in a thoroughbred horse auction. His girl – what you might call the official candidate – had come a distant second. It was Maggie Satterthwaite who the people wanted as their Queen of the May, and all that remained was for her coronation by the previous Queen, a girl from Cadley called Eliza Tempest, who was standing by in readiness, wearing a crown thickly woven from spring flowers. A huddle of burgesses conferred at the back of the stage, with Ephraim Grimshaw talking urgently in the middle of them. While waiting for the announcement, the crowd sang and called out, 'Mah-gee! Mah-gee!', 'Send her to Parliament!' and other ribaldries. Then, in what looked like a prearranged signal, I saw Grimshaw nod at the constable, who waddled across to Maggie and spoke a few close words. Maggie clapped her hand to her mouth and took a frightened step backwards as Mallender reached out, gripped her by the wrist of her raised hand and began drawing her towards the platform steps. There were cries of protest and outstretched hands from all sides, which the constable batted away with his free hand. I looked again at Grimshaw. Having placed himself behind Mayor Biggs he was speaking rapidly into his ear while pushing him forward.

The noise diminished to a low grumble. Biggs cleared his throat, looked round at Grimshaw as if in search of courage, then fixed his eyes on Maggie, now halfway to the ground in Mallender's unyielding grip. She was sobbing in bewilderment. Biggs raised his eyes and surveyed the crowd. I had never estimated William Biggs highly. He had all the self-regard that drove his friend Grimshaw, but lacked the other's boldness, energy and enterprise. To compare the two men in their appearance confirmed that impression: Grimshaw's features were broad, with mobile, small and cunning eyes; while Biggs had a narrow, unconfident face, a beaky nose and the rolling, vacant eyes of a horse.

'Now, hear me, please – IF YOU PLEASE – hear me!' Biggs began, in a quavering voice. 'I am sorry to inform you that one of the candidates for May Queen – I mean Maggie Satterthwaite here – is, well, she is *disqualified*.'

The crowd roared back its disapproval.

'It can't be helped, it can't,' Biggs went on. 'Now listen to me! Here is the reason. Word has reached us – we have intelligence, you see – that she can no longer pretend to be a maid. So of course—'

His words were engulfed in a storm of hoots and popular denunciation.

'Not a maid?' they shouted. 'Get away! None of them's that! Had her yourself, have you?'

But Biggs persisted.

'No. By the most ancient tradition, I have to tell you, it is required that the May Queen must be a – a – well, a virgin pure.'

He spread his palms wide.

'So we have no choice. She must be excluded.'

He drew himself up and declaimed as if to the sky.

'So now, I go on to perform a very happy duty. It falls to me as mayor to give news that this coming year's May Queen is to be—'

But before he could pronounce the name that would ring with such satisfaction in Burgess Grimshaw's ear, the crowd's anger and frustration overflowed. The mayor looked down and saw that

Maggie had been wrenched from Oswald Mallender's grasp and hoisted onto the shoulders of two strong young men. The girl's slim figure wilted and swayed like a reed but gradually her tear-stained face began to smile and then to laugh. She was borne at a jog trot away into the square, three times around the well and the obelisk, and then back in triumph to the stage. To the mob's delight they found that the burgesses had begun fleeing the scene in alarm. The last to launch himself from the stage onto his horse's back was Grimshaw, his face set in a hard scowl as he beckoned his niece towards him and hauled her down bodily to sit behind him. Then he began forcing the animal through the melee with rough curses and shouts of 'Make way!'

No sooner had Grimshaw exited the stage than Maggie was deposited back on it. Her two remaining defeated rivals still stood at the back with Eliza Tempest, none of them knowing what to do. The young men who had chaired Maggie round the obelisk were in no doubt, however. One of them spoke to Eliza while another brought a stool and placed it at the centre of the stage. Maggie was seated on the stool, flanked by the other two girls as maidens of honour. Then Eliza stepped forward. In spite of the unusual circumstances, she was determined to make all she could of this, her last duty as May Queen. With a flourish she removed the chaplet of flowers from her head, raised it high to show the crowd, and spun like a dancer through 90 degrees to face Maggie. She held the crown for a suspenseful moment over her successor, then lowered it. As she removed her hands and stepped back, a jubilant cheer rose from the throats of the people. They had seen the crowning of the Queen of their choice and, no less happily, pricked the pomposity of the corporation.

I admit that it made me happy too. The look on Grimshaw's face as he rode through the rout of people had prompted a memory of what my father had once told me. Not so long ago bulls and bears had been baited in this very Market Place by mastiff dogs, for public entertainment. As a boy my father had been taken to see the last bear to have been baited there. It was kept in a cage with iron bars but, he said, it had not looked dangerous in the slightest, only rueful and chapfallen, like a gambler who had gone 'all in' at cards, and lost the hand. That is a fair description of the look on Grimshaw's face as he rode home, with his niece riding rump.

Half an hour later I stepped into the office, meaning to complete a little paperwork. I had pulled out my desk chair without looking down and, on sitting, was aware of something round, followed immediately by a sharp crack as my weight crushed it. Moments later a damp viscidity was soaking into my breeches. I stood up to investigate: I had sat on, and broken, a large raw egg, concealed under a cloth.

'Furzey, come in here!' I called. My clerk came in. I pointed to the crushed shell and mess of albumen on my chair.

'What in heaven's name is this – this – this mess?'

'You have sat on an egg, sir. A goose egg.'

'A goose egg? How did it get there?'

'I put it there.'

My voice rose almost to the pitch of a roar.

'You did *WHAT*?'

Furzey's face was without expression. He regarded me for a few moments, then turned and shuffled back towards his part of the office. At the door he turned once more, his face a mask of gravity.

'I beg to inform you, sir, that you are a May gosling,' he said.

Chapter Twelve

CONSIDERATIONS OF DIGNITY should not come between a man and his journal. So sitting late that evening to write up the events of the week by my library fire, I did not withold an account of Furzey's May Day goose egg. I even appended a gloss from Mr Spectator that '*a Jest is never uttered with a better Grace than when it is accompanied with a serious Countenance*'. That was the essence, in effect, of Furzey's character: frivolity disguised as black mourning.

As I wrote I reflected on the puzzling week that had passed. In the course of it I had dealt unevenly with two unexpected deaths, holding an inquest into one – with what I now thought doubtful results – and not acting in time to proceed to inquest on the other, when it appears that I should have. As long as the two cases were firmly separable from each other I could tell myself they were merely instances of unsatisfactory luck. Only if they came together might they become magnified into a concatenation of bad judgement.

I told Elizabeth as much later that night.

'To have two humps is not a burden to the camel,' I said. 'But now they are merging into one – a great towering single hump – and it weighs heavy on the spine.'

'My poor camel!' teased Elizabeth. 'Depressed by such heavy metaphors.'

I sighed.

'You joke, but my ill luck's beginning to look more like ill decision.'

She touched my hand more sympathetically.

'No, my dearest. How it looks to you is one thing. But no one else will see my uncle's drowning and Mr Allcroft's sudden illness as tied together.'

'Because they don't know the facts as I do. And as does Luke Fidelis.'

'What are these facts, then?'

'They are few, but of importance. They all lead back to the same family, you see. Maggie Satterthwaite resented being sacked from her job at the Ferry Inn. Isaac Satterthwaite lives on the road between the inn and the place where your uncle went into the water. It could have been Isaac that Dick Middleton heard him talking to that night. Isaac's method of poisoning rats looks the same as that possibly used to poison John Allcroft, at the very inn where Maggie now works.'

'That might all be nothing but circumstance. If Uncle simply fell into the water, and Allcroft also died by accident, or illness, your connection melts away into chance and change all round.'

This time I groaned.

'Yes, I know. Chance and change. But what keeps me awake is the chance that they both appear on the Whigs' list of Tory voters. So does Nick Oldswick, and he told me this morning that a man took a swing at him with a cudgel in the dark. And if these men died or were attacked because they were Tory voters, that would indeed change everything.'

'These may be unconnected events. Are there not scores of others on the list, Titus? And the election surely cannot swing on there being two or three fewer Tory votes.'

'I know, I do know. But knowing does not make me easy in my mind about this business.'

'Then you must settle your mind, Husband. You must go on inquiring until you get to the truth.'

It was later as I lay in bed, still turning these things over in my head, that I saw the need to know more about John Allcroft. If indeed he was murdered, it might still have nothing to do with the election, or with Antony Egan. It might be a private matter. Or even have to do with the passion for the Pretender that, as my mother-in-law put it, possessed Allcroft. I turned over to sleep, resolving to apportion Saturday morning between a visit to Allcroft's widow and a further conference with Fidelis.

John Allcroft had originally farmed at Barton to the north-west of Preston, near to Elizabeth's parents. But in about 1735 he had inherited a second parcel of land, which stood on the diagonally opposite side of town, at Gregson. The farm was substantial but had been neglected and was in need of close management, so he and his wife had gone to live there, putting an overseer into the Barton house to look after their Fylde interests.

Gregson lies out in the country towards Hoghton Tower, so it was in that direction that I was bound as I crossed Walton Bridge at half past eight next morning. I immediately put the chestnut mare into a smart trot along the Hoghton road. I aimed to interview the widow and be back in town by midday.

After making enquiries for her at Gregson, I was directed to the village of Hoghton a couple of miles further on, where my quarry had gone to shop and pay a visit to a cousin in that village. Arriving there and spotting her almost immediately, coming out of the grocer's with some small purchases, I dismounted and, tying my horse to a rail, approached her with a greeting from my mother-in-law as the easiest method of falling into conversation. She consented to my suggestion that I carry her packages as far as the cousin's cottage, which lay at the village end.

Mrs Allcroft was a haughty woman. She was just two days widowed and yet, when I asked her about her late husband, she seemed more anxious about his reputation than his passing.

'My husband was a leader of men, Mr Cragg. That was his character. When he spoke, men listened. When he took action, men took it with him. When he told of consequences, there were consequences indeed.'

'In what field would that be? In farming and husbandry, perhaps?'

'He had strong views in that direction, most certainly. But I refer to the world of affairs. Only last week he called a meeting here in Gregson and twenty-six attended. Think of that. Twenty-six, no less, coming at his bidding.'

We were at that moment walking past the Hoghton Arms. I indicated it with my thumb.

'At this inn, was it, the meeting?'

She almost spat at the suggestion.

'There? John would lose a thousand head of Cotswold sheep before he set foot inside there. On principle. No, the meeting was at the Royal Oak.' She gestured towards the rising ground beyond. 'Over the hill.'

'And what was the meeting about?'

'Why, to make a compact to go to Preston and all to vote against that heretic Hoghton in the election. To oust him from Parliament where he does nothing good, only play lackey to the criminal Walpole and the Germans.'

'The men attending must have been freemen of Preston, then, if they had the power to vote. I did not know there were so many of those hereabout.'

'As well as John, twelve of them are free in Preston. The rest came to listen to the argument, and by the end all of them were in agreement. He was that satisfied when he came home, was John. "That's a baker's dozen of votes secured against that Geneva-soaked so-and-so," as he told me. "Now we must do the same all round."'

'Geneva-soaked, did he call him? Surely Sir Henry does not drink gin, Mrs Allcroft.'

'It would not surprise me if he did. But it is the impiety of Genevan religion that he imbibes in greater quantities. And he expects all his tenants to imbibe it along of him.'

'Well, not being tenants, these twelve men were free to do and think as they liked.'

'Indeed. All freeholders, they were. They even outfaced Hoghton's steward, when he had the effrontery to burst into the room and rant like a madman that his master was God's candidate and any man who opposed him was damned to hell. My husband stood up and wilted the man's linen in a minute. Now I am obliged to you for carrying my things.'

By a change in demeanour, rather than by any word – in the manner of a duchess, perhaps, at the York Assembly Rooms – Mrs Allcroft let it be known that our conversation was at an end. I put in a last question as we reached her cousin's gate.

'Mrs Allcroft – one more thing. Why did you so quickly collect your husband's remains and take them home for burial?'

She turned on the path and pulled the gate shut between us.

'Because that's the proper thing, Mr Cragg.'

'Did you know that as coroner it is my business to inquire into any unexpected deaths?'

'I do that.'

'Do you not think your husband's was unexpected?'

She was suddenly overtaken by emotion.

'It was a blow,' she said with a catch in her voice. 'A mighty blow. But all death comes to shock us, which we are taught we must endure.'

I decided on a hard line: I was damned if this high-minded matron, widowed or not, was going to elude me.

'This was no ordinary death, madam. I must warn you that I am considering opening an inquest, and if I do I shall require your husband's body.'

She gasped.

'What can you mean?'

'I mean an exhumation. I will send you fair notice. And now I must go. Good day, and thank you.'

Leaving her standing and staring, with mouth open, at the gate, I doubled back up the street to my horse.

Riding home I listened to the sound of the hedgerows bustling with bird life. What the naturalist delightfully calls nidification was in progress everywhere: the bird couples were darting into the foliage with their beaks crammed with twigs, straw and moss, then flinging themselves out again a moment later to fetch more building materials. With the election uppermost in my mind I wondered if birds, like men, have their politics. They certainly seem to chatter together a great deal as they go about their business, and my father had told me as a child a story of a strange assembly called a Crow's Parliament, in which hundreds of crows would meet together, for what reason no one knew for sure, but on occasion, it seemed, to peck one of their number to death in a brutal attack. I was frightened by the story, but he assured me it was absolutely true. I had never had the opportunity to verify this, but now I got it into my head that I would do so, when the opportunity arose.

Coming into Cheapside I found the stallholders in the Saturday market already packing up, though it was not yet noon. There was a difference in the air, or in the general mood, but it was hard to define.

After dismounting I crooked my finger at a boy who was loitering nearby: this was Barty, a trustworthy urchin who made his way by doing errands for me and others in the neighbourhood. I handed him a halfpenny and the reins of the mare, telling him to walk her over to the livery stables that I used.

'Say they must give her a good rub. She's brought me home pretty smartly from Hoghton.'

'Right, Mr Cragg, sir.'

'Good lad. But what's happening here, Barty? The market's already packed up.'

'It's this sickness they're talking about, sir.'

'Sickness? What sickness?'

Barty shrugged.

'I just heard them talking about some sickness.'

'Here in town?'

'I reckon so.'

Barty was no fool, but you couldn't expect a boy of ten to interest himself in such matters, so I let him get off with the mare and walked directly to the lodgings of Luke Fidelis.

'Doctor's been summoned out, sir,' I was told at Lorris's door. 'So busy he is. It's been one call after another all morning.'

'Do you know where he has been called to this last time?'

'Yes, sir, it is Mr Oldswick the watchmaker. He's been taken bad, was the message.'

Taking the lane that connects Fisher Gate laterally with Friar Gate at a fast pace, I was at Oldswick's within five minutes. The window displayed a pasteboard sign saying 'Closed', and the door was locked. I rang and after a minute's delay Oldswick's ancient footman came crook-legged to the door, wiping his hands on his apron. I stepped inside.

'Hello, Parsonage. Is Dr Fidelis here?'

Parsonage screwed up his watery eyes, apparently to read my hidden intentions. I have found that all experienced servants do this, having the strongly developed sense, rightly or mistakenly, that their betters rarely if ever deal straight with them.

'He *was* here, Mr Cragg,' he stated.

'When did he leave?'

The bent old man half turned to glance at one of the several clocks in the shop.

'Eighteen or nineteen minutes since.'

'Do you know where?'

'Gone chasing another case of sickness, I think it was.'

'This is most strange, Parsonage. Are there many in town suddenly stricken today?'

'How would I know, sir? I have been entirely engaged in the care of Mr Oldswick.'

'When did he fall sick?'

'In the middle of the night.'

'And what is wrong with him?'

Parsonage replied only that his master was, in sequence, poorly, properly poorly and most vilely poorly. I pressed him and he gave a brief account of his master's staggers, and his aversion to having the lamplight near him. I suggested he return to his nursing duties and retreated to the pavement outside, looking up and down the street in case I saw Luke going about his business. Not finding him I decided to return to his lodging and wait.

I had barely turned once again into Fisher Gate than I was tapped on the shoulder. I turned to find Miss Colley, bonneted and booted, on her way back from market.

'Oh, Mr Cragg, there's hardly an egg, nor a piece of bacon, to be had.' Her voice was trembling, though whether from excitement or fear I could not tell. 'The market men have gone home.

Is it true we have the contagion in town? After what happened to that out-of-town man the other night, and now people going down with the sickness all over, everyone's affrighted.'

'Miss Colley, you must calm yourself. I cannot believe it has developed so vastly in a few hours. But I have been away on business this morning and I do not know anything. Perhaps you should go indoors and stay there until you can be sure it is safe to go abroad.'

'That is a good idea, Mr Cragg,' she trilled. 'You always give such sound advice.'

In answer to my knock, Lorris's servant opened the door with apron pressed to nose. She was plainly reluctant to let me in, but I insisted and she backed away from the door, then scurried away to her basement as I entered. I closed the door behind me and went up to Fidelis's rooms to await him.

The longer I waited the more perturbed I felt. I had smiled at Miss Colley, yet this was not something likely to amuse most Prestonians. Fixed in the memory of our town was the great sickness of 1631. Our oldest grandfathers would relate tales of how it had been, told to them by their own grandfathers. In the course of that fatal year all trade and marketing in Preston ceased; a pest house was established, in which more than 200 were incarcerated; and, in cases where whole families were visited by the contagion, they were boarded up sick in their own houses until they died. In the midst of all these cruel, futile measures 1,000 townspeople succumbed. There had never been such a disaster in the town, yet all were conscious that it might one day return in all its biblical fury. My father told me that, when the 1631 sickness was over, the survivors gathered in St John's church to give thanks and to hear the incumbent vicar preach a sermon on the text 'We had been as Sodom and been made like unto Gomorrah'.

By the time Fidelis at last arrived, I had imagined the worst without being able to control myself: the horror of my Elizabeth reduced to the degraded state I had seen in Allcroft – sick and imprisoned at home, or rather entombed there and left to die. There was a certain shame in this abject fear. Just a few rumours of contagion and I was sweating. I resolved to hurry home and tell them to stay in at all costs and see no one. But not until I had seen Fidelis. I had to know what he knew.

He came bustling in, throwing his wig down with the expression of a man preoccupied with many tasks.

'I can't stop. I have some drugs to collect and I must go out again.'

'What is happening? What is this epidemic?' I asked.

He went to the wall-mounted shelves and took down a jar containing a white powder. He moved to his scales and rapidly weighed out a measure.

'I've been to five bedsides already today. I believe my colleagues are equally busy. There are perhaps twenty victims of this to appear so far.'

He poured the powder into a paper, made a twist of it, and repeated the process from the contents of another jar.

'What do they complain of?'

'Violent vomiting, explosive incontinence, delirium, photophobia.'

'Like Allcroft! You realize what this looks like? That the town is victim to some epidemic pestilence.'

'Yes, I can see what it looks like. But I am not sure that the appearance coincides with the deeper reality. I still have in mind our other suspicion.'

'You mean, what we suspected about poor Allcroft? But it looks wrong now, doesn't it? Come now! How do you poison twenty or more people all at once? Surely this is some dreadful disease.'

By now Fidelis had placed the two papers in his bag, picked

up his wig and was preparing to go out again. On his way to the door he stopped before me and tapped me on the shoulder.

'So it looks, I know. But I have an idea that I need to prove, Titus. I will come to your house this evening with my results – will that satisfy you? Meanwhile, I must ask you to let yourself out.'

And he was gone.

Seized as everyone now was with the policy of avoidance, I was not surprised to find the common parts of the Lorris house hushed and deserted as I passed down the stair. For the same reason I was not expecting to be waylaid by any of its inhabitants, yet this is what happened, on the landing halfway down.

'Mr Cragg, sir!'

The voice came from behind a door that was a few inches ajar.

'Yes. Who is it?'

The door creaked a little further open and Miss Lysistrata Plumb showed herself.

'It's me,' she said.

I bowed and said, 'Of course it is!'

'May I speak to you, please?'

'I am at your service.'

She came out and closed the door behind her.

'We cannot talk here, but I am sure the sitting room will be available. Come.'

We found the room empty. Miss Plumb sat in an upholstered armchair beside the unlit fire with her hands crossed over her knees. I brought an upright chair from the wall and placed it before her.

'What would you like to talk to me about?' I asked.

I judged her to be about twenty-three years old, an age at which a woman's beauty – in my eyes, anyway – is set at its most heart melting. And she was indeed a beauty, with regular classical features in an oval face, though with lips perhaps fuller than the average marble from Greece and (unlike the statues again) with eyes alive and sparkling. At the same time she had an assurance about her that commanded respect.

I waited for her to speak.

'I have heard that you and Dr Fidelis are friendly.'

'Yes. I think of him as my closest male friend.'

'Then I wonder if he has spoken to you of anything . . . any matter in regard to myself?'

This was ticklish. Fidelis had not sworn me to secrecy but when a man unburdens himself of his feelings about a lady it is usually in the nature of a confidence. I took a cautious lawyerly line.

'He has indeed spoken of you. For example, after you had been taken ill the other day, he gave me the good news that you were feeling better. I hope that is still the case.'

In answer she only smiled and inclined her head.

'Well, I shall confide in you,' she went on, 'even if he hasn't. I believe that Dr Fidelis has fallen in love with me. There! I've said it.'

She gave a small laugh, of embarrassment I suppose.

'I see,' I said in a measured way. 'I wonder what reason you have for the supposition? Has he, in fact, declared himself?'

'No, that is the annoying thing about it. If he would only speak, I could respond in an appropriate way. Instead, I am left uncertain what to do.'

'Must you do anything – at this stage, I mean?'

'Why, yes, of course I must. Dr Fidelis is a kind man and a fine physician. I cannot leave him to wring his heart over me indefinitely, and to no purpose.'

'No, that would be a shame. Does he have no hope, then?'

I had not meant to ask this, because I was afraid it would leave me in possession of information I'd rather not have. But Miss

Plumb had virtually invited the question and I could see she was bent on answering it.

'Well, when you know about that, you will understand why I wanted to speak to you. I am hoping to employ you as a go-between.'

Employ me! I thought. This was a girl with spirit.

'As an intermediary?' I suggested.

'As a message bearer. And the message is the same as the answer to your question. Naturally, I cannot deliver it to him directly without Dr Fidelis raising the matter first.'

'Naturally. So what is the message?'

For the first time she showed a slight sign of discomfort, studying her hands rather than looking at me.

'The message is that . . . I have the highest regard for Dr Fidelis and find him a most agreeable gentleman in every way. But . . .'

Now she did turn her face to me and I saw in it a struggle between emotion and a kind of philosophical pessimism.

'But I am connected to another, you see. I am not free.'

'You are married? Should I call you Mrs Plumb?'

'No, not married. But in every other way . . .'

She left the sentence incomplete, and in doing so gave it a great deal more meaning than if she had finished it. She let her pause hang in the air and then went on.

'So you see, if he were the most eligible hero in the most charming storybook, he must still be barred from my affections, and I from his.'

'I think he will be distressed,' I said.

'And he will want to know the name of the gentleman, no doubt. But –' lifting her hand from her lap she waved her finger from side to side – 'I cannot tell him. That would be impossible as things are at present.'

'I will take your word for it,' I said. 'But may I ask about yourself? What is your reason for being in Preston? Is the man you refer to here? Is that why you have come?'

'Yes, but I shall say no more. I am bound to him, and doubly bound.'

Doubly bound? She was speaking in riddles. What did they mean?

'So,' she continued, more briskly now. 'May I take it you will let the doctor know of the position? And take the greatest pains, if you please, to spare his feelings.'

I nodded.

'I shall break it to him as delicately as I can, Miss Plumb. But I doubt I can spare him all pain. He is, I fear, very susceptible.'

'I am sure you will do your best. Now, I believe our business is over.'

We rose and she bobbed decorously. I gave her a bow and so departed, with the feeling that, though she had seemed to take me into her confidence, I had learned very little indeed about her.

Chapter Thirteen

STROLLING BACK TO the office I had a fancy to see how Nick Oldswick was faring, and again took the cut-through to Friar Gate. The streets were all but deserted and most of the shops were shuttered. People were sequestered, awaiting news of the epidemic.

This time Parsonage allowed me into the shop. He was breathing heavily through an open mouth and I waited while he caught his breath. I could tell he had something to impart.

'The bailiff's constable,' he gasped when he could close his lips at last. 'Constable Mallender called. Mr Oldswick's summoned. A council in Moot Hall. All burgesses are called in. But Mr Oldswick's in no condition to—'

'What – the corporation's meeting?' I broke in. 'On a Saturday? What's it for?'

The corporation burgesses including the mayor and two bailiffs govern every part of the townspeople's lives. They regulate our trade, instruct us in morality, decide our disputes, give us our holidays and keep order in the streets. Oldswick, as I think I have already mentioned, was one of them.

'All to do with this sickness, so the man Mallender said. But Mr Oldswick's—'

'Not well enough to attend, that is obvious,' I interrupted again, remembering why I was here. 'So how is he? Any sign of hope?'

'No, sir, I am afraid for his life. I'm in a right blether in this house. If he dies, what happens to me?'

'Let's think about Mr Oldswick first of all, shall we? Can he speak?'

'Oh, aye. He can speak. But he's raving, sir. Keeps asking me the time. And says someone's trying to kill him. And when I say there's no one here to kill him except for me, he begs me to tell him the time again. He's dead afraid of dying. And he won't eat but he wants to drink every five minutes. And he can't make water easy. So it makes him dead uncomfortable, but soon I'm feared he may just be dead.'

'Have you had the doctor back?'

'I have that. I *had* been giving Mr Oldswick the medicine, but—'

'What medicine?'

'That medicine Mr Oldswick himself brought home yesterday.'

'If he brought medicine home he must have been feeling sick already. You said he fell ill in the night.'

The servant's face went blank.

'He said nowt to me, sir, until night-time. Any road, Dr Fidelis said I've to stop the medicine, and it was better only to keep watering him and give him a beaten egg or warm milk. Which Mr Oldswick didn't mind as he said, when he could still talk, the medicine tasted sickly sweet, but with something bitter in it too. He didn't like it.'

'So Dr Fidelis has been back here, since I called earlier?'

'Not him,' said Parsonage. 'That's what he said for himself this morning. But Mr Oldswick got no better on that so I sent out for Dr Tewksbury. He came and said, what good is warm milk and egg and water? And he said this man's heart's racing and he must bleed him. So he did that, and then *he* left. But he did no good, neither. And I've not seen a shadow of a doctor since.'

153

'All the doctors are very busy. But if I see Dr Fidelis, or indeed Dr Tewksbury, I shall ask him to call back.'

I walked home through unnaturally quiet streets, amused in spite of everything at the thought of the prostrate watchmaker constantly asking for the time. As Shakespeare points out, we are all dyed through and through with the colours of our trade. On my own deathbed will I be babbling questions of the law?

I entered the office, where I meant to spend the afternoon absorbed in a dispute over title to a property off Friar Gate, whose origins were 500 years old, which meant back almost to the beginning of civilized life in the town. After more than an hour reading my client's papers, it was clear I would have to look at the Burgage Rolls, and to do that I would have to cross the road to the Moot Hall.

Attempts had been made over the years to clad this ancient building with a more youthful appearance, and even to endow it with the grandeur of modern improvement: an outer covering of brick over the primitive materials used in its first construction; a portico on Church Gate surmounted by a frieze of plaques carved with the heads of worthies. But nothing could prevent the place creaking inside like an old body. Here and there beams had sagged and stanchions begun to twist as the black oaken bones of the building dried out, and its lath-and-plaster flesh grew cracked and worn.

Passing in through the empty hall, from which rose a substantial oak staircase to the council chamber, I could hear from above the sound of the burgesses arguing, their voices heated and occasionally rising to squeaks of panic. I bypassed the stair, however, and entered a passage at the back of the hall that eventually led to the vaults where the records of the corporation were kept. This was a suite of rooms behind a thick nailed door, dusty but tolerably dry, whose gatekeeper was the Clerk of the Records, Atherton by name.

There was no sign of him at his writing desk in the anteroom, so I tried the archive door itself, which was unlocked. I heaved it open, and called out the clerk's name. My voice fell dully and without echo in the labyrinthine chamber, stuffed as it was with rolls of vellum and leather-bound ledgers heaped together in a maze of racks. Getting no answer, I ventured in but found no one there. Atherton, it seemed, had deserted his post, but it did not matter to me. His function was to locate requested documents and sign them out on removal, to prevent their loss. But I knew where to find the rolls I was looking for, and I could consult them on the spot.

The Burgage Rolls were preserved in a part of the cellar space that was far from the door and out of its sight, yet fortunately close to a light through which came some pale rays of afternoon sun. By this I inspected the rolls and wrote some notes. I had almost finished the work when I felt the faint breath of a cold draught on my neck and felt sure someone had opened the door.

'Atherton – is that you?'

There was no reply.

Five minutes later I had finished my note taking and replaced all the rolls. Returning to the antechamber I found a man sitting at Atherton's desk bent over a sheet of paper and writing, while consulting the open ledger in front of him. It was Denis Destercore.

'What are you doing in the Records Office?' I demanded. 'What are you copying, without the say-so of the clerk?'

'The clerk is not here.'

'I know he's not here, which is why I guess you are copying without his leave.'

'I might say the same of you.' He nodded to the papers in my hand. 'I see you have been copying from the rolls.'

'I am a lawyer in practice here in town, whereas you—'

'Have equally legitimate business. I may be a stranger but, as you know, I am acting as agent in the election.'

'What are you copying?'

Destercore sighed impatiently.

'Though it is not your affair, I am not. I am proving. And I have done it before, with Atherton's approval. Look if you like.'

He laid down his pen and lifted the book to show me the gold-leaf title printed on the spine: *Liber Liborum Prestoniensis*, the register of burgesses, or freemen.

'You are tallying the names of freemen against the voters on your lists – is that it? You are testing their rights to vote.'

Destercore only looked at me with a steady, challenging gaze, then picked up the pen once more.

'Now, if you will excuse me,' he said, laying the volume back on its stand, 'I need to get on.'

I left him to it, thinking that, for all I knew, he had the mayor's or a magistrate's authority to be where he was, and doing what he was doing. I gave some thought to his manner towards me. Destercore had not been impolite – the rudeness had more likely been on my part – but nor had he been imperturbable. There was a taut quality to the man suggesting that he felt threatened or was afraid that at any moment his performance would be found in some way wanting.

A little further along Church Gate, near the entrance to Water Street, were the premises of our bookseller Sebastian Sweeting. I could see even at this distance that his shop was lit, and found myself being drawn helplessly like a moth towards that welcoming illumination. I had not forgotten my musing earlier in the day about the politics of birds and, in particular, whether it was true what my father had told me of crows holding a solemn parliament or court. Still curious about the matter I entered, thinking I might find some book or information on the subject. The proprietor was seated, as usual, on a stool behind his counter with a large snuffbox before him, from which he took a pinch at intervals. He was alone. The remarkable fact about this bookseller was that one never saw him read so much as a single sentence from any book, yet he had in his head a complete inventory not just of all the volumes he held in his current stock but, it seemed, of all the books he had ever sold, with a thorough working knowledge of their matter and content. I was confident he would be able to tell me (and perhaps sell me) something on the subject of avian politics.

He greeted me with a laconic grunt, and swivelled the snuffbox in my direction. This was his invariable behaviour when a customer entered, for Sweeting projected a level appearance at all times, excited or surprised by nothing. I took a pinch, sneezed, and made my enquiry. For a moment he paused to think, then without a word wandered into the recesses of the shop, manhandled a ladder into place and ascended to a shelf almost at the ceiling, from where he plucked two fat folio volumes.

'This has something for you,' he said, lodging the books with difficulty under his arm. He began to descend the ladder, taking elaborate care. 'But if you want to buy it, it'll cost you.'

Arriving with his heavy freight he thumped the two books down on the counter, with a sound like distant cannon fire. The impact raised a cloud of dust and caused an atmospheric vibration that rattled the windows. On the edge of a narrow shelf above the other end of the counter a small bottle wobbled, then fell and shattered on the counter top. It had contained a syrup-like liquid, which was now oozing around the glass shards.

Sweeting quickly seized the two tomes and transferred them to a vacant chair, then went for a brush and mop-cloth. I carefully picked up the largest glass piece, which still had the bottle's handwritten label attached. '*Paracelsus, his Patent Preservative*,' I read, *'supplied exclusive by Thos. Shackleberry. Firmly eschew all imitations! 6d.'* Clearly Sebastian Sweeting had been in the Market Place yesterday, and had paid his sixpence to the mountebank. This suggested there was an unsuspected side to the urbane, unruffled Mr Sweeting. I dipped the end of a finger into the spill and dabbed it onto my tongue. I tasted sweetness, with herbal and other flavours that I could not identify.

'How is Mr Shackleberry's Patent Preservative?' I asked, dropping the glass onto Sweeting's pan as he swept the sticky glass fragments into it.

'Oh, I don't know,' he said, mopping with his cloth at the remaining stickiness. 'I gave some to Mrs Sweeting last night and she says it was very pleasant, and could she have some more? Well, I thought, that won't answer. There's cordials and tonics on the one hand, which is frivolous, and there's stinging galenicals and bitter pills and drenches on the other, which is serious physic. And I'm damned if I've paid sixpence for a mere bottle of sweet tonic. I took the bottle from her and told her she could have no more as I was going to return it to the fellow and demand my money back, which I have now saved myself the trouble of. Oh, well. Now, this book . . .'

He put on a pair of spectacles.

'Take a look, won't you?'

I opened the first of the volumes and found the title page.

THE
WORKS
OF
GEOFFREY CHAUCER

Compared with the Former Editions,
and many valuable MSS

Sweeting tapped the page.

'I swear you will find a treatise in verse here called *The Assembly of Fowls*, or maybe it's *The Parliament of Birds*. Very interested in birds was Chaucer.'

I turned the pages until I found the list of contents.

'It's a finely printed edition in two volumes, on good paper,' Sweeting went on. 'But there's something unlucky about it. It took years to bring it to press and killed two editors in the meantime. That was twenty year ago, of course.'

He paused, perhaps realizing that he would not sell the book too quickly with a patter like that. He began again, more persuasively.

'But there has been nothing like this before, you know. It's the first edition of Chaucer's writing that is printed in plain Roman type, not the Gothic. Very difficult to read, is the Gothic, specially on top of the poet's antique English. So to have it in the Roman type, well, it is a great benefit.'

My finger found the item he had referred to earlier: *The Assemblie of Bryddes*. Looking further down I traced the different episodes of the pilgrims' tales, told by each one to entertain the others on the road to Canterbury: *The Knight's Tale*, *The Squire's*, *The Prioress's*. It was when my finger reached *The Man of Law's Tale* that I decided to buy the book.

'It would be much better if that fool Tewksbury did not go about bleeding people,' said Luke Fidelis when I told him of my visit to the Oldswick house.

'You don't believe in its efficacy?'

'Our blood is in us for a reason. I cannot see any purpose in taking it out.'

'But letting blood is an old-established practice. Didn't Dr Galen recommend it?'

'That Roman windbag! For God's sake, Titus, he thought the heart was some kind of furnace! If he saw fever, he let blood because he thought it was overheating. If he found heartburn, he did the same. Now that we know the heart's a pump, the whole theory collapses.'

'Tewksbury must have some reason—'

'Reason doesn't come into it. It is the laziness of habit. Doctors like him are devoid of all reason, all ideas and all method.'

'Old Parsonage says you yourself are recommending water, raw egg and warm milk. How do you know they will work?'

'I don't. But I do know they will do no possible harm.'

I thought of poor Allcroft, and the milk I had spooned into his mouth.

'Luke, you said earlier that you were on the track of this new illness, and you had to verify it. Have you?'

'Yes, I am sure of it. It is something I discovered at the bedsides of the first patients I saw this morning.'

He drew from his pocket a medicine bottle, which he gave me to examine. I saw that the label was inked with exactly the words I had just read from the broken bottle in Sweeting's shop.

'One or two people told me that they had purchased this so-called "Preservative" and dosed themselves with it, but it had been singularly useless. At first my only thought was, how could it be otherwise? But suddenly I realized I might have stumbled on a common factor in this outbreak. I have spent the afternoon revisiting all the patients I saw earlier and what do you suppose?'

'Go on.'

'Every one of them that's ill has been dosing themselves with it.'

'You can see why, with this fear of contagion. They thought it would preserve them.'

'But what if it should really do the opposite? What if it should ruin them?'

'Ruin them? A quack medicine?'

'Yes, if it happened to be the primary cause of the illness. Do you see?'

Then I remembered my visit to Oldswick, when the disease was at its height with him.

'Old Parsonage did say something about dosing his master with some medicine he brought in on Friday. It must have been the same.'

'It was. I told him to leave off, as I have now told everyone.'

I examined Fidelis's idea from every angle.

'Well, it is certainly paradoxical. A salve to make you sick – a poisonous palliative.'

'Ha! Yes, though whether it poisons by accident or knowingly I cannot say. Our only way to settle it is by interviewing Mr Shackleberry himself, which we must do anyway if we are to put a stop to any further mischief. Will you help me find him? I know this is not strictly coroner's business, but—'

'It will be if anyone dies.'

'That's right. So where shall we find him?'

'We will start with Oswald Mallender. If anyone knows, it will be him.'

As town constable, Mallender was expected by his masters the burgesses to give regular reports on incomers, together with estimates of their wealth and the degree of nuisance they might present. His self-importance alone ensured that he enjoyed this task more than all his others, since it gave him the opportunity to lord it over people who did not yet know what a fool he was.

We found him at home, in his house in Tithe Barn Street, where he was being fussed about in front of his parlour fire by Mrs Mallender, a woman even fatter than himself. It was not an opulent dwelling: two rooms below and two above, with a cramped attic for the servant. Indeed, the whole house seemed cramped with these two filling every room they stood up in.

'How can I be of service, gentlemen?'

'Do you know the whereabouts of the mountebank Shackleberry that's been here in town doing card tricks and the like? He was selling a quack nostrum in Market Place yesterday before the May Queen's election.'

'The Irish fellow? Yes, I know him, of course.'

'He had an assistant with him, a feeble-minded fellow called Dickon. Can you take us or direct us to them?'

'Let's see . . . why do you want this man?'

'Because his so-called preservative is no such thing. It is noxious and suspected of being the cause of this outbreak of disease.'

Mallender looked from one of us to the other, smiling as in kindly tolerance towards the idiocy of others.

'Oh, no, sirs. No, no. The corporation has met on this point and all agree that the sickness is a dangerous contagion. Those who have tried to combat the outbreak with extraordinary measures, such as this good man Shackleberry, have even been commended by the Mayor, and are to be treated with the greatest indulgence—'

'Fiddlesticks,' broke in Fidelis, irritated beyond measure. 'The man should not be indulged. He should be put in irons.'

'Not in the eyes of the corporation, sirs, and it is with the corporation's eyes that I must look. Their worships have also issued a slate of measures against this contagion—'

'Say this poisoning! It is *not* a contagion.'

Mallender wagged one sausage-like finger.

'Hold up, sir! Will you contradict the corporation? They will not have it! Against this *contagion*, they say again, measures are planned and will be enacted with dispatch in this emergency. You may read them.'

He produced a paper and handed it across. It was headed *Contra Pestis* and contained a dozen numbered orders for such things as the establishment of a pest house, the control of laundry, the closing of the theatre and rounding-up of stray dogs. These methods had been used traditionally to combat the plague: the most extreme of them was the provision for people to be shut up forcibly in their homes.

'God forbid that it should come to any of this,' intoned Mallender with sanctimony. 'In the midst of all this election activity, and Lord Strange just arrived in town for his grand theatricals tomorrow. Yet we must be ready.'

'This is so much rank shit!' said Fidelis passionately, throwing the paper aside so that it floated down and landed close to the fireplace at the feet of the seated Mrs Mallender. Seeing her, as if for the first time, he bowed and apologized for the word he had used.

'Oh no, don't mind me, Doctor,' she tittered. 'I like to hear a professional man swear, I do.'

Meanwhile with laboured breath, Mallender had stooped to retrieve the note.

'You must have greater care, Doctor, with a fire in the room. This paper has corporational authority. If it had been burned that would have constituted a contempt. This paper is to go to the printer tomorrow, with a special dispensation to work the press on a Sunday. That is how serious the corporation takes this matter. And, *nota bene*, Dr Tewksbury attended them and was consulted.'

'Dr Tewksbury!' snorted Fidelis. 'They might as well consult a horse's arse.'

This conversation was leading nowhere, and I decided to put a stop to it.

'Well, if you are acting under the advice of another medical man,' I put in smoothly, 'there is nothing more to be done here. Mr and Mrs Mallender, we bid you a very good night.'

Out in the street Fidelis began to laugh.

'"Corporational authority"! The man thinks he *is* the corporation. So, what do we do now? We are checked.'

'Come back to my house and drink some wine. We will think of something.'

After Fidelis had greeted Elizabeth, I showed him into the library and slipped into the kitchen to fetch wine. I found Matty sitting at the table with a spoon in her hand and a small bottle in front of her, of a colour and shape that I knew well. She had already poured a dose into the spoon, and was now opening her mouth and holding her nose, ready to receive it.

Chapter Fourteen

I THINK THE MIND is a closely packed archive of impressions, memories and fears, tens of thousands of them, and every one tightly scrolled and tucked into its proper place ready to be consulted if necessary. But sometimes, for some reason, one of these bursts its ribbon and springs open quite spontaneously. Something like that happened to me then. Elizabeth and I had brought up this girl in our service, from a snotty child on a farm to the dignity of womanhood itself, and we had loved her and cared for her from the start. But now all at once I had a horrid vision of her death, lying in the same filth and degradation I had seen in that room in Stoney Gate.

With a cry I stepped forward and, in dramatic fashion, raised my hand and dashed the spoon from Matty's hand. It went flying across the room, rang like a bell as it struck one of our Delft jugs on the dresser, then came down on the floor. The spoon's contents spattered across the table. Matty screamed.

'Sir! What did you do that for?'

'That is a very dangerous preparation, Matty. Dr Fidelis believes it may be putrid.'

Matty blinked as her eyes filled with tears.

'But I thought there was no harm, because they've been taking it all over.'

'Precisely, Matty. And people have been falling ill all over – do you understand?'

I seized the bottle and went through to the stone sink outside the door, where I poured and flushed the contents away.

'How much of it have you had?' I asked, returning to her.

'None, not yet.'

'Thank God!'

'I only just got it, you see. But I'd been that worried about this sickness, so I sent Barty out to get me a bottle. He said he knew where to find it.'

'Did he? Well, that is very good news!'

Her tearful face turned into a puzzled one.

'But you have just told me—'

'Get Barty for me, please. I must see him immediately.'

I gave Fidelis the news as I poured out two glasses of port wine.

'I should have thought of it myself, Luke. Young Barty goes everywhere, and his eyes and ears are as keen as a cat's.'

We had had time for just two glasses when Barty appeared. I asked him if he had been tempted himself to sample Shackleberry's potion and he denied it.

'Let people spend their money how they like,' he said. 'But I think that's a naughty old man.'

'That does you credit, boy. What did I tell you, Luke? Now Barty, we need to see the fellow. Will you take us to him?'

Barty led us to a tumbledown house on Sprit Weind, occupied by Hugh Scratch, an old sailor so congested in the lungs that he could no longer go to sea, nor do any but the lightest work. I knew Scratch to be always desperate for money, and he would take the Devil himself as lodger so long as he was paid his due.

Mrs Scratch, who opened the front door, was a small woman with restless, birdy eyes. I asked after Shackleberry and she gave us a taut smile.

'He's here. But you'll not get a splinter of sense out of him.'

'Can we see him?'

'Of course you can *see* him. It's talking to him that you won't be able to do.'

'Why is that?'

She stood back from the door to make way.

'Come in. You'll hear for yourself.'

The kitchen fire had a single smouldering log, giving minimal cheer. Scratch sat beside it, leaning slightly forward, as if in the expectation of an imminent event. I said how-do, to which his only reply was to hunch his shoulders and surrender to a spasm of retching coughs. When this had passed his wife cocked her head and pointed upwards. A tearing sound was penetrating the ceiling from the room above. It sounded like a rusty bucket being dragged across a gravel beach.

'That's him,' said Mrs Scratch. 'Drunk every night, he is. When he's awake there's no shutting him up either, but that's his talking. Asleep he only snores, and Scratch and me, we're lucky to get a wink of sleep.'

'May Dr Fidelis and I go up to him? Perhaps we can bring him to his senses?'

'Good luck to you.'

The room in which we found the mountebank was sparsely furnished: two wooden beds covered in rough straw mattresses, a table and chair, a washstand, and a hat-and-coat stand were all the furniture. Shackleberry was sprawled across one of the beds, his chin bristled, his brow greased with sweat and his gap-toothed mouth as wide as an opera singer's in full spate. But Shackleberry was singing only one note, and less musically than a blacksmith's rasp.

I called his name and, when he didn't respond, went to the bedside and shook his shoulder.

'Wake up, man, wake up.'

But though I continued to shake him for half a minute, he could not be roused. I looked over the table, on which lay writing materials, some books and a sheaf of foolscap paper. I noted the titles of the books: *The Alchemist* by Ben Jonson, *Works* by Lord Rochester and *Penkethman's Jests: or, wit refin'd, containing witty sayings, smart repartees, apothegms, surprising puns, with other curious pieces on witty and diverting subjects* . . .

'Take a look here,' said Fidelis, just as I was turning Penkethman's pages to see for myself whether there was any real wit in them. My friend had gone down on his haunches to examine a collection of objects that lay together on the floor beneath the vacant bed. He began pulling them out: a brass-bound chest, a copper pan, some implements and various bowls, bottles, jars and packages.

'I recognize that box,' I said. 'That's what he stood on in Market Place to give his speech about Paracelsus and his universal cure. And he kept stocks of the preservative inside, to sell.'

'I reckon he made the mixture right here,' said Fidelis. 'This is the pan he mixed it in. And if I'm not mistaken these are the ingredients he used.'

He picked from the floor the shell of a hen's egg, and a bowl containing some brown granules. He licked his finger and dabbed for a sample, which he tasted.

'Sugar. Eggs. And here's the dried-out remains of some milk.'

'Were they making pancakes?'

He laughed just as he was putting his nose into one of the paper packets, with the result that a black dust puffed out.

'Not with this. It's tea. And these are nutmegs.'

'Tea, hen's egg, milk, sugar, odd spices. There's nothing unusual there.'

'But what about this? It has a particular smell.'

He showed me a small blue paper packet, which seemed empty. I sniffed it, finding a warm pungency coming from it.

'Is it horseradish? Or maybe ginger?'

'I rather fancy it is something a little more dangerous. I think it might be—'

'Stop! Stand up there!'

The voice came from behind us. It was not Shackleberry's, as his snores continued to rend the air. Fidelis and I turned, and saw standing in the door the man Dickon, Shackleberry's drooping foil, whom I had last seen with his disappearing chin and matted hair, meekly taking his medicine in the Market Place.

'What are you?' he challenged. 'Thieves? Trespassers? Shall I send for the constable?'

For an alleged idiot, he spoke as sharply as a thorn. I looked him up and down. His clothes were not luxurious, nor yet were they of the raggedness I had seen on his back on May Day. He wore a Quaker hat, a green coat over a yellow waistcoat, and a clean shirt and stock.

'Neither,' I assured him. 'We are visiting your master.'

A sneer rippled across his face and he jerked his thumb towards Shackleberry.

'My master? You mean this sot? The man's deluded about many things, but not so far gone as to think he rules me.'

He removed the hat and hung it on the hat stand. His hair was neatly brushed and his eyes seemed no longer to look across each other, as they had yesterday.

'But I saw you both yesterday, in Market Place,' I objected. 'He presented you as his . . . well, he gave the impression you were his employee. Mr Dickon, isn't it?'

'No, sir. Andrews, that is my name. Mr Richard Andrews, if you please. And do remember, it is not Shackleberry who directs Andrews, but the other way around. If not for my care and attention to his accounts he would have gone to gaol long ago. And if not for my care and attention to him, he would have died of drink before that. What you saw yesterday was only play-acting.'

'Play-acting?' objected Fidelis, 'But you sold this nostrum of yours on serious terms. You made claims for it – Paracelsus, and whatnot.'

Instead of making reply Andrews went to the bed and pinched the snorer's nose. Shackleberry spluttered explosively and rolled away from his associate to lie on his side, a position in which he breathed more quietly. On his return to us, Andrews's demeanour had changed. There was now a certain quickness in his step, a dancer's lightness, and he was smiling.

'It was a genial deception, good sirs. A May Day prank, that's all. It was not meant to be underhand. It was for the harmless comfort of the uneducated only, in this worrying time for the town. No one expected well-schooled people such as yourselves to imbibe it.'

By now I was allowing the man a slight admiration. He was handling us with some skill.

'I am a doctor,' said Fidelis. 'And I can tell you that—'

'Oh, really? A doctor of what?'

'Of medicine, sir, and I believe this stuff you're peddling is far from medicinal.'

'But it has nothing of harm in it!'

'What is in it, then?'

'Oh, this and that, you know? Common items, though not cheap. We invested quite a sum of money. It is based on black tea, and has milk, plenty of sugar and honey, a few herbs and spices.'

Fidelis held up the empty packet in which we had found the strong smell.

'What about this?' he said. 'This was not a spice.'

Andrews's face twisted uneasily for a moment.

'Oh, yes, that too. A small amount.'

'What was it?'

He shrugged.

'How would I know?'

'You used it without ascertaining what it was?'

'It came from an honest source.'

'You did not hear it called by the name belladonna?'

'Belladonna? No, it had some Latin name. I never learned Latin in my life.'

'*Atropinum?*'

'I don't know. We only put it in to give a proper kick. A good mixture has to have a kick, we find – it may quite properly consist largely either of foulness, or of sweetness, but it must give a kick, or it does not appeal.'

A degree of confidence had returned to his voice as he expounded this theory. Fidelis shook the packet relentlessly in front of his face.

'If this contained *atropinum*, its kick might kill – I'd rather be kicked by my horse.'

Andrews took half a step back, on the defensive again.

'That can't be true, sir. I know for a fact that it is given by physicians.'

'Yes, but advisedly, man! It is a powerful poison. Where did you get it? I do not think you dug it out of the ground. It has been dried and powdered before it was put into this packet, and probably mixed with something neutral. You bought it prepared and ready, didn't you? What was this "honest source"? Did you bring this with you, or obtain it here in town?'

Spreading his hands, Andrews patted the air, a gesture of conciliation.

'Look, let's not quarrel. I'll tell you. Shackleberry meets a fellow in a public house and he says some doctor's been giving out a medicine containing this powder of which, seeing as we're in the medicine line ourselves, he himself can procure some for us. So we think, yes, it's a good idea. Let's put in a real drug – something the doctors themselves is using. Perhaps you yourself use it, eh, doctor, for the good of sick folk. Can't do harm, then, can it? Or if it do, we're blaming you doctors that's recommending it, ain't we? So we got it off him. But I'm not saying what it is, because I don't rightly know.'

He indicated his associate.

'It was him that got it, not me.'

'Do you still have a stock of this medicine?'

'The last bottle went out earlier. A boy brought me sixpence and took it away.'

'Mr Andrews,' I said sternly, 'should it be found that you have, knowingly or unknowingly, been implicated in selling a noxious mixture you will be in serious trouble with the mayor. You must desist from this trade. I repeat, make no more bottles of this so-called nostrum. You understand?'

Andrews's spread-out hands, and his smile, were wide and conciliatory.

'We cannot make more, sir, even if we wanted. We never had too much of that ingredient the doctor last mentioned, and we now have none at all. So it would lack the kick, and without the kick—'

'By God!' spluttered Fidelis. 'You speak of a kick, and people are lying prostrate and may die. Have you no conscience?'

Andrews made his eyes wide.

'I swear it was all done in good faith, and to do good to the town.'

'How many bottles of it did you make?' I asked.

'Two dozen, at most. We sold most of 'em on May Day. Couldn't shift the goods fast enough. We soon wished we'd doubled the quantity, I can tell you.'

'You may thank God that you didn't,' said Fidelis. 'As you may that you did not drink the stuff yourself.'

'But he did!' I exclaimed. 'I saw it.'

Andrews gave us his foxy smile.

'Yes – and look at me, good sirs. I am none the worse. You could call me fit as a fisherman's cat.'

'That is as may be. But you will not feel so well when this is all over,' I warned. 'The mayor's court will not see your actions as being in good faith.'

'But they were.'

'No. You did this only to make money, and you disregarded all consequences. We will have to speak with Mr Shackleberry further when he is sober. In the meantime, goodnight.'

Before following me through the door Fidelis lingered for a last question.

'Oh! Just one thing, Andrews. Where and when was it that Mr Shackleberry met the unnamed person who promised to obtain *atropinum* for him?'

By this time I had started down the stairs and Andrews's reply was lost to me, as Shackleberry's thunderous snores resumed.

Barty was waiting for us outside. I gave him a penny.

'I want you to watch this house. Watch for the two strangers – I mean the ones you got the mixture from. I want to know immediately if they try to leave. There'll be two more of these for you if you last out until morning.'

Barty took the money and, reaching into his shirt, pulled out a leather pouch hanging from his neck. There was no great clink of metal as he dropped the coin in. This was a boy not used to being paid in anything but farthings.

'I'll do it, sir.'

Fidelis and I set off.

'I don't understand how Andrews did not make himself ill,' I said. 'I myself saw him swallowing this mixture in Market Place on Friday afternoon.'

'You thought you saw him swallowing it. It was probably cold tea. These men are sleight-of-hand artists – remember? And they wouldn't waste their valuable commodity in merely demonstrating it.'

'Andrews claims he doesn't know where Shackleberry got the special ingredient. I suppose he's lying about that too.'

'Perhaps he doesn't know, though I think I do.'

'Andrews also denied that it was called belladonna.'

'Poisons invariably have aliases. Belladonna. *Atropinum*. Deadly nightshade.'

'Deadly nightshade! Good God, is that what I saved Matty from?'

'What were the symptoms we found in the patients subject to this sickness?'

'I only know what old Parsonage told me about Nick Oldswick. He had fantasies. He didn't like being near the oil lamp. He couldn't stand up straight. Headache and fever and slurred speech.'

'That's not a bad summary of the effects of deadly nightshade. Now, Andrews said Shackleberry had been told, did he not, that this powder was recommended by a doctor? Assuming he meant a doctor from this town, I propose that Andrews was referring to myself, though he might not have known it.'

'Yourself?'

'Yes. A very small amount of *atropinum* was in the preparation I sent you to order for me from Wilson the other night. It has the ability to act counter to certain of Allcroft's symptoms. So think – this is what may have happened. There are rumours in the town of a new contagion after the death of John Allcroft. These two tricksters form the idea of using their play-acting skill to sell some cheapjack mixture. But first they have to concoct one. Then Shackleberry meets an informant at a public house who mentions that doctors are prescribing *atropinum*. Shackleberry asks who can supply this *atropinum* and his informant, in drink, says he can. Who could this informant be, Titus?'

'Well, it can only be Wilson!'

'Precisely.'

We had now come to the door of Fidelis's lodging, where I said goodnight. It had been an arduous day for both of us and, though he pressed me to come in and take a glass of wine, I could hear the weariness in his undertone.

'No, Luke, I am tired, and so are you. We must talk this over tomorrow. Will you have dinner with us at home? Good. Does half past twelve suit you?'

As soon as the door was shut behind him I began to walk home. Passing Porter's, I was struck by the riot of chatter, rowdy argument and hoarse singing that spilled out of the place. It seemed this scare had Prestonians either cowering indoors with their prayer books, or drinking themselves into a stupor at an inn or alehouse, for the drinking establishments were the only places lit up as the evening advanced. There will always be some people who defy fate. Or was it that people thought, if they had to die, it were better to do so drunk?

I was thinking about this when a customer came staggering out of the inn and we collided. He had rebounded off me with a look of astonishment on his face and started babbling about the election, and only then did I realize that this was Thomas Wilson, the apothecary himself. Seeing he was in no condition to manage it alone, I took his arm and engaged to bring him safely home.

As most people knew, in this town with few secrets, Wilson was a drinker very different from my wife's late uncle. Not for him the steady imbibing day by day that had slowly unglued Antony

Egan. Wilson was one of those men who are drawn in almost equal degree to drunkenness, and to sobriety, so that the two continually struggled for supremacy over his soul. Day by day he was the most principled of men, conscientious in his work, faithful to his wife, careful with money and respectful towards God. But once he began to imbibe he could not stop.

To find him at this moment, and in this state, was rather convenient. I wanted to know more about the intelligence Fidelis and I had just been gathering from Richard Andrews, and I was now presented with the chance to talk to Wilson on the same matter with his guard lowered. I seized on this chance, interrupting Wilson's incoherent rambling, and shooting a direct question at him.

'Thomas – I wonder if you have had any recent call to dispense a quantity of unmixed poison?'

His answer, if it was an answer, came obliquely, flying off his tongue like water shaken off a dog's back.

'Goat. Bloody champion cocksman. *He* thinks he is. Nay, but I know better. I. Do. Know better. See, the man's a eunuch. Practically speaking, a eunuch.'

He groped upwards with his free hand until he found the side of his nose. He tapped it.

'Because I know. Because his man came into the shop. His man. He bought something. I know what it is for. Pure poison but there's always those who think it answers all their deficiencies.'

He could hardly pronounce this last word, so thick was his tongue with drink. I stopped and turned him towards me, looking him directly in the face.

'Thomas, so you *did* give out some poison.'

'I did that. Only a little of it. But there's always those . . .'

'Did Shackleberry tell you why he wanted this poison?'

He looked puzzled at the question.

'Shackleberry? Who's that?'

'The Irishman that you met,' I told him patiently. 'Whom you talked poisons with, and agreed to supply. Remember?'

This was another chance shot on my part. While there was not much hope that a sober Wilson could admit to such a transaction, I wondered if a drunk one might.

The apothecary's face briefly flickered to life and then clouded again. He waved his arms.

'Oh, yes. No. Not talking about him. The other.'

'Oh? Who is that?'

He did not reply and I repeated the question as we stumbled on towards his shop. After a few paces he was talking again.

'Goat. Lewd, that's what. Sir. Cocky. Cocksman. If that's the man for the job, God help us all is what I say, Mr Cragg.'

'Who is this, Thomas?' I pressed. 'And what job?'

But the meandering flow of Wilson's thoughts was not to be diverted.

'Nay, they cannot choose him because before they start talking about me talking about poison let 'em talk about him wanting it. And I know for what, I do. Eunuch.'

When we arrived at his shop I was no wiser about who and what he was talking about. I steadied him in position with a hand on his shoulder while I patted his pockets with the other until I found his keys. Unlocking the door, I hauled him into the front of the shop and lowered him into the comfortably upholstered leather armchair, there for the use of customers waiting for their preparations to be made up. He sat gratefully slumped, still muttering but only half conscious, and hardly aware that I was still with him. I lit a candle and went into the back of the shop thinking to call Mrs Wilson down from the living quarters. On the apothecary's workbench lay an open register, to which I gave a glance as I looked round, and then quickly returned to when I realized its import: this was Wilson's drugs book. Not all those in his trade were as punctilious as he in recording what they sold, and to whom.

I felt excitement burn, as along a fuse, from my brain to my fingertip as I ran the latter down the list of the apothecary's transactions over the last few days. Here might lie the proof of what Andrews had been saying. Counting the columns from left to right Wilson's system was to list the date, the name of the customer, the item purchased, the quantity and the amount paid over. Taking a pen and a sheet from a pile of scrap paper I jotted down the items that had been sold on Thursday, two days earlier, leaving out only the cost, as being of comparatively little importance.

> Miss Bilsboro. Valrn 8 oz. Adder's tng oil. 10 drops.
> Lord Drb's man. Turps Clystr. 8 fl. oz.
> Mrs Coupe. Her peppmnt draught. 1 pt.
> Mr Priestley of Bamber Br. Lavdr in susp syrp. 1 bott.
> Dr Tewksby. Prescr rcpt no. 334. As per.
> Mrs Singleton. Ldnm. 6 fl oz.
> Boy pro H.H.? Cnthds pdr. 10 grn.
> Lady Pinklb. Oil of clv. 2 oz. Rose Wtr salve. 6 oz.
> Dr Dapperw's man. Tnct casc 2 drachm.
> Jos. Boothby Esq. Hngry wtr 8 oz.
> Strngr. Grnd Atrp 2 scrp agg. 100:1 ½ lb.
> Miss Wellson. Her own linctus. 1 bott.
> Mr Jon. Johnson. Sprt jnpr ½ pt. Florence oil 8 oz.

I had still not finished copying the full record of Thursday's business when I heard the voice of Mrs Wilson.

'Wilson? Is that you?'

She was calling from upstairs and in the same instant I heard her tread on the stair. Hastily sanding the paper and folding it into my pocket, I stepped away from the bench at the very moment that the apothecary's wife appeared at the door.

'Oh, Mr Cragg, is it?' she asked.

I felt like a boy caught with his hand in the raisin jar.

'I met Thomas outside the tavern,' I explained hastily. 'I have brought him home, as he is a little the worse, I'm afraid.'

Immediately she fluttered with concern.

'Where is he, where?'

I indicated the front of the shop and she hurried through to minister to her wine-stricken husband, scolding him and petting him by turns. I followed her and asked if I could be of any further service. I couldn't, so I made my excuses.

At home I found the household preparing to go to bed.

'Two volumes have arrived from Mr Sweeting,' Elizabeth told me. 'They're in the library.'

I went through with a lamp and unwrapped and opened a volume of my new Chaucer. Flicking through it at random, I found myself looking at the description of the Man of Law:

> *Nowher so besy a man as he ther nas*
> *And yit he semed besier than he was.*

I smiled. I knew lawyers like that, but it had certainly been a busy day for me. Yawning, I shut the book and carefully slid both volumes into a vacant space on the shelf.

Chapter Fifteen

First thing next day, which was Sunday, when Elizabeth was at her Mass, I walked down to Nick Oldswick's house to enquire after his health. Rain had returned during the night and many puddles slowed my progress. Parsonage opened the door of the watchmaker's shop, his face gurning at me in an approximation to joy.

'I suppose you want to know how he is, Mr Cragg.'

'Naturally I do, Parsonage. He is better?'

'Aye, better is one word. Asleep is another. And beneficial is a third.'

'Beneficial?'

'To myself, sir, to myself. He is so much better that I reckon I am not now imminently to be cast into the dark with nowt but the corns on my feet. Glory and praise, sir, I am saved!'

He neither raised his voice, nor spoke more quickly, as he said these triumphal words. Parsonage was too much the seasoned servant to crow or gabble, yet his lugubriousness was edged with undoubted relief.

'You should give praise that Mr Oldswick's saved, you know, not yourself.'

Parsonage rubbed his nose thoughtfully.

'It's the same thing, as I see it,' he said at last. 'If he gets sick, it hurts me and puts me in fear. If he gets better I am relieved.'

'Well, if he's sleeping now, I shan't disturb him. Will you tell him I too am relieved he is out of danger?'

As I was turning into Cheapside on my way home, Barty came running up to me, splashing through the wet.

'Mr Cragg, sir, those men, they've gone! I took shelter from the rain and they left the house before I came back, for I never saw them go. When I asked about them in the morning they weren't to be found.'

'Do you mean they've packed up and gone, or just gone out?'

'Packed up, sir. Disappeared you might say. I'm very sorry I missed 'em, sir.'

'What time did it rain?'

'Between three and five, sir, by the church.'

'I don't blame you for taking shelter, Barty. I would have done just the same. You have earned your money anyway, just by coming to tell me.'

I handed him his promised coins.

'Shall I find out where they're gone to?' he asked eagerly. 'I can, I think.'

I grasped him by one of his bony shoulders and steered him in the direction of my house.

'Come in with me for a wash and Matty will give you a bite of breakfast. After that, if you can run around and discover what road these two rogues are travelling, I will be in your debt again.'

At our own breakfast Elizabeth told me about a stranger, Mr Thomas Arne, who had appeared at the Roman chapel.

'He's a Londoner, and a musician. A finely dressed figure in a wig that was not cheap, and the finest velvet coat I have ever seen. He's here to give tonight's performance. Mr Egerton begged him to play something for us on our old spinet after Mass, and he did.

You should have heard it, Titus! His fingers raced up and down the keyboard. Our own Miss Gerard is a beginner by comparison, and I have always thought her playing rather good. She herself was a little put out by his performance, but he charmed her and all was well.'

'He sounds notable. We'll enjoy the music tonight, I think.'

'He was notable for something else, Titus.'

'Oh? What was that?'

'For his left eye. It was blacked – I believe he had been fighting. When I looked carefully at his hands as he played the spinet, they seemed grazed around the knuckles.'

'Fighting? Over what?'

'Titus, how could we ask, with any degree of propriety?'

At mid-morning Elizabeth accompanied me to divine service, as was her loyal habit, and, when it was over, I let her walk home ahead of me to see to dinner while I delayed. I wanted to intercept Mayor Biggs, who was for a long time locked in conversation with the vicar. It was fully five minutes before he broke free and I was able to secure an audience amongst the gravestones.

'I have heard that you intend to publish an advertisement today, giving instructions about this supposed contagion,' I said.

'True enough,' he acknowledged, 'though it is less about the contagion than against it. *Contra Pestis*, you know. Because of the danger it poses, we've allowed the exception of having our injunctions printed and posted on the Sabbath.'

During his not very distinguished mayoralty Biggs had cultivated the habit of using 'we' when speaking as mayor. I suppose he would defend this as an expression of the corporate will of the burgesses, but with it came the suspicion that he imagined himself royal. In Preston, as in many towns, there is the pretence of democracy but the continual reality is the pompous rule of a few small men tricked out like kings.

'I wonder if you should not hold the advertisement back,' I urged. 'At least for the moment. A new explanation for the sickness has just been discovered, and must be tested.'

'You say "tested". We cannot test every crackpot idea, Cragg. I suppose you are going to tell me we are catching this contagion from birds, or bats, or something equally ridiculous.'

'No. I am saying that it is no contagion at all, but only the effect of a quack medicine that was sold here on May Day, in Market Place.'

'A quack medicine? You cannot mean the preparation that the very skilled Mr Shackleberry brought here for our town's sole benefit.'

A man who rises to a position higher than the limits of his competence and courage must somehow cover himself. Biggs did so by pretending to a mysterious, lofty and unchallengeable cleverness: to knowing all answers while finding them not worth the effort of explanation. The unintended effect was to make him look very much like the fox in so many fables, whose cleverness is far less than he imagines. Biggs's smile at this moment was decidedly vulpine.

'I do,' I said firmly. 'Dr Luke Fidelis has been finding on his rounds that the sick were in fact those that drank Shackleberry's so-called preservative, rather than the other way, as should have been the case.'

Biggs, still wearing his foxy smile, winked and tut-tutted.

'Dr Fidelis, you say? Still a very young physician, I think, and green in judgement. We, on the other hand, have Dr Tewksbury, who has been in practice for thirty years or more. He assures us this is a dangerous contagion, and measures have to be taken to counteract it. So it would hardly be sage of us to ignore his advice. We would be blamed for the neglect of the town's health.'

'I'm not saying do nothing,' I insisted. 'But don't threaten to board people up in their homes, or lock them in a pest house. Tell them quite simply, if they do have a bottle of Shackleberry's medicine, to throw it away at once.'

Biggs tutted again and shook his head, causing the tails of his wig to flap.

'No, no, that's quite impossible, Cragg. People have spent sixpence a bottle on it. We cannot then tell them to dispose of it like some poison.'

'But it *is* poison.'

'So you say. We do not agree!'

At this moment Ephraim Grimshaw joined us, his Sunday finery even more splendidly gilded and silvered than his weekday suit.

'What do we not agree?' he boomed, clapping Biggs on the back and making the chain of office rattle. Grimshaw did not similarly greet me. He did not approve of me. He thought I was in some way subversive, because I stood outside the sway of the corporation.

'On the nature of the present wave of sickness,' I said.

'Mr Cragg has just seen fit to tell us,' said Biggs, 'that we should not publish our agreed points towards defeating the contagion.'

'Not publish the points?' protested Grimshaw. 'But you must.'

I repeated for Grimshaw's benefit what I had told Biggs.

'You blame Mr Shackleberry?' Grimshaw spluttered. 'You are wrong, sir. He is a benefactor of the town and in receipt of a ceremonial vote of thanks from the burgesses. He would no more poison us than throttle his own grandmother.'

'Have you met him?' I asked. 'His grandmother is in constant danger.'

Grimshaw's small eyes narrowed to slits.

'Look, Cragg, you are not in a position to joke about this

outbreak of sickness. I've heard that you allowed the only dead body to be produced by it to slip through your fingers.'

'And Shackleberry's slipped through yours. He's—'

But Grimshaw was not to be interrupted. He was jabbing his finger in the air in a rather menacing way.

'Bluntly, Cragg, you're not an elected officer. Stick to your rotten-ladder accidents and drunks in the river. These higher matters of public policy and common profit are not for the likes of the coroner.'

Before I could reply he had swung round to face Biggs once more.

'Now, Mr Mayor, if I may, a word about the arrangements for this evening's grand event. Would you leave us, Cragg? This is a matter of importance.'

The grand event was the musical entertainment *Alfred,* designed as the curtain-raiser to the week of voting, which would begin the next day. It was going to be performed in the town's theatre by a company of actors, and an orchestra of string and wind, all laid on by Lord Strange. It was this young nobleman that had secured the services of the fashionable Mr Thomas Arne to come from London to direct it. Biggs might be intending to close the theatre, but he didn't dare do so before his young lordship had had his evening of fun.

At home I found Fidelis awaiting me in his riding clothes. He looked pale and strained.

'I have come to make my excuses,' he said. 'I must miss dinner, as I have been called to Hoghton Tower. A member of the house-hold has fallen sick.'

'Can't you stay for your dinner first?'

'No, the matter is urgent. May I call in later, on my return?'

'Of course. The afternoon will be wet and we're not going out.'

His forehead was furrowed and, though professing to be in a hurry, he seemed reluctant to go immediately.

'You seem distracted,' I said. 'Is there something the matter?'

'Yes. I think there is.'

'And?'

'It is Miss Plumb, Titus.'

At that moment a shadow seemed to flick across his handsome face. He looked suddenly haunted.

'Has she become ill again?' I asked.

'I don't know. Possibly. I don't know where she is. She has gone.'

'Gone?'

'She was not in her room this morning. She did not sleep there at all last night. I was shown the bed by the Lorrises and that much is evident. But she said not a word, only wrote a note to say she did not want any supper in the evening, and was tired and not to be disturbed. That was during the afternoon. No one saw her go out of the house, and no one knows when she did go out.'

He picked up his hat and riding crop. This was the moment when I might have given him Miss Plumb's message. But he was in a hurry and I missed it.

'I am sure she will return,' I said.

This lame reassurance was spoken as I saw him out of the door, and onto his horse.

'I wish I did not have to go to Hoghton, Titus, else I could be looking for her.'

He mounted and rode off, with his medical bag bouncing on the horse's rump. Then, before I could shut the door, young Barty appeared.

'Mr Cragg, sir,' he said, 'the two men you asked about. They were seen at Bamber Bridge this morning at six, walking, with a donkey.'

'A donkey, is it? Well, they must be going south. Thank you, Barty. I think we can say good riddance.'

'Will you not give chase, sir?'

I shook my head.

'It's hardly worth it, Barty, and not a job for me at all events.'

I asked if he wanted to come inside for a bite, but he said no, he had to be somewhere else. He was a secretive boy. I did not know precisely where he slept.

I told Elizabeth about the unaccountable disappearance of Miss Plumb, but she implied she thought it some small impediment that kept the young woman away, of little moment. She was more interested in the absconded mountebanks, and wanted a close account of the previous evening.

'Do you mean to say that the underling Dickon is really the master?' she asked when I'd summarized the events of the evening. 'I cannot believe it – he looked the perfect idiot.'

'That was his intention.'

'Well, of course, I can see it now. A true idiot could never be as perfectly suited to that role as a false one.'

'Exactly. Andrews is the brain of the enterprise; Shackleberry is only the showman. His tongue may be golden, but his mind is tarnished by drink.'

'Should they not be pursued, though? They appear guilty of terrible poisoning.'

'Accidentally, I think. Or even unknowingly. It is the person who gave them the poison that we want to find. Though, as coroner, I need not make even that my concern unless and until someone dies. And the mayor won't take action. He thinks Andrews and Shackleberry are fine fellows.'

'But one person *has* died, Titus. John Allcroft.'

'That was before Paracelsus's Patent Preservative made its

appearance. If the mixture is the cause of the general sickness in town, Allcroft must be the victim of someone else. But who?'

'Could it be the same person as him that conveyed the famous kick to the preservative?'

'I don't know that. But I do think I know who it was that provided the ingredient you mention.'

'Oh, who?'

'I will tell you later. I want to make a few more inquiries first.'

In the afternoon, I brought my new Chaucer into the parlour so that my wife and I could read together the poem that had induced me to buy it – *The Parliament of Fowls*. Sometimes we stopped to puzzle over the strange vocabulary – 'make' instead of 'mate', 'slit' for 'slide' – but we got in the swing of it soon enough.

Expecting to be plunged straight into the world of birds and their politics, I was surprised to find that it began with lines about love.

> *The lyf so short, the craft so long to lerne,*
> *Th'assay so hard, so sharp the conquerynge,*
> *The dreadful joy alwey that sit so yerne:*
> *Al this mene I by love.*

It was Elizabeth who, with her eyes shining, opened mine to the genius of the poetry.

'I think those are very beautiful lines, Titus. It is true for many that love is a "dreadful joy" though it is a surprising phrase – a paradox, isn't it?'

'Yes, or it might be called an oxymoron.'

Without a word she rose, gently took the book from me and placed it on the floor.

'But our love is not an oxymoron,' she whispered. 'It is *only* a joy.'

Then she sank into my lap to kiss me, her fingers digging into the back of my neck as she pulled my mouth fiercely onto hers. It seemed a long time before she finished kissing me.

'Love does slide away, as Chaucer says, from many,' she said, drawing away at last and looking me hard in the face, 'but it shall not from us, unless we let it. But your poet is right to say that life is short: we must remember that too.'

'I do. How can I forget it, in my profession?'

'So, let's go on with the reading.'

It was apparent that Fidelis had regained some of his good humour, when he stood on our doorstep an hour and a half later. From the sparkle in his eye it even looked as if he might have been laughing.

'Have you found Miss Plumb?' I asked, thinking this must be the explanation.

His face clouded for a moment, and then lightened again.

'No, I have not, and shall not. I have told myself, if she can go away without a word, I must resign myself to being nothing to her.'

'I should tell you she—'

But once again my attempt to pass on Miss Plumb's confidence was stalled. Fidelis raised his hand.

'No, Titus, not another word about her. Tell me instead, is there any news of the mountebanks? Have you interviewed Shackleberry?'

'No. The pair gave Barty the slip. The last we heard, they were at Bamber, headed south. But come into the library. I have something to show you.'

We went inside and I related my adventures of the night before, once I'd left Fidelis on Fisher Gate – how Wilson had talked of dispensing poisons and how I had later copied certain details out of his dispensing ledger. I soon had Fidelis's complete attention.

'You have the paper that you copied onto?' he asked.

I opened the drawer of the escritoire and produced the paper. Fidelis took it and laid it on the desktop. He studied it.

'These are the sales he made on Thursday, is that right?'

'Not all of them. I was interrupted in my writing by his wife. There were at least as many that I didn't have time to write down.'

'Never mind. I think we have the salient ones.'

'They are all impenetrable to me. I hope not to you.'

'No, indeed.'

Fidelis was smiling and nodding to himself as he ran through Wilson's notations. It brought to mind a musician casting his eye over a stave of notes and hearing the tune in his head.

'See here?' he said at last, putting his finger on the paper. 'Between Mr Boothby's Hungary Water and Miss Wellson's linctus, what do we have?'

I looked. The item was, '*Strngr. Grnd Atrp 2 scrp agg. 100:1 ½ lb.*'

'What does it mean?'

'It means Wilson *was* dispensing poison. "*Atrp*" can only be *atropinum* – the root of the deadly nightshade.'

'And on such a scale – half a pound!'

'Yes, but only two scruples of the active ingredient – the *atropinum* grounds. It is normal when a dangerous poison is sold to the public to mingle it in a certain proportion with an inert substance such as acorn flour – here it is a hundred to one. When one is dealing with very tiny amounts of a noxious element it is very easy to use too much, and perhaps kill someone. By this method even a good pinch of the stuff will deliver only a minute dose of actual poison.'

'And I suppose he writes "*Stranger*" because he couldn't admit in his records that he knew Shackleberry.'

'Yes, he may have been covering his tracks. The effects of

atropinum closely mirror the symptoms we saw yesterday across the town — hallucinations, loss of balance, fear of bright light, constipation, retention of urine, extreme thirst and all the rest. If Wilson had written the name Shackleberry in the left-hand column he might be exposed as the source of poison. He may not have been sober when he wrote the record, but he was not completely careless.'

'We don't know he was drunk.'

'He met Shackleberry in an alehouse, and Shackleberry certainly drank.'

'Does the entry tell us anything else?'

Fidelis rubbed his hands together with undoubted relish.

'Yes, it does — but not about the Patent Preservative.'

'What, then?'

'It is a marvellous chance that you show me this, Titus. It tells us not only what Wilson might have meant last night in his drunken ramblings, but casts medical light on the bedside I was called to today. May I have a pipe and I will tell you?'

Chapter Sixteen

So we smoked, and Fidelis narrated. He had arrived at the outer gate of Hoghton Tower, still without knowing the name of the stricken person he was summoned to attend. Ralph Randall, when he came out to admit him, was silent on the subject. With the horse entrusted to a groom, the steward conducted Fidelis across the outer court, through the second gate and into the inner court, which they crossed to the door of the tower itself. He again asked Randall the name of his patient, but received no reply, except to be urged to quicken his step.

Passing through the hall, Randall led the way up the stair and along a corridor, well windowed with leaded panes on one side and panelled in oak on the other. He opened the door at the end, stood aside, and gestured Fidelis to pass through. He then shut the door, without following the doctor inside.

Sir Henry Hoghton was lying beneath the covers of the great canopied bed, wearing a nightcap and gown. But far from enjoying a peaceful rest, he was writhing in agony, groaning and continually licking his lips. At sixty years old, he had a face with a purple-tinged complexion, and a certain pop to the eyes that gave him an air of permanent grievance. On this occasion, at least, there was an easily seen reason for the grievance. His nose was swollen and his lower lip was split.

There was no one else in the room, so Fidelis presented himself at the bedside and asked Hoghton how he was.

Sir Henry muttered something inaudible and when Fidelis asked again, the stricken man impatiently roared, 'See for yourself, and damn your eyes!'

He threw back the sheet and blanket. Through the linen of his gown Fidelis could see the full extent of the problem: the parliamentary candidate's *membrum virilis* stood in a condition of gigantic and pulsating erection.

'The bugger won't go soft,' stuttered Hoghton. 'Been like that for twelve hours! It's got harder if anything. And it burns, man; it burns like some damnable fire's got into it. I can't piss. I can't do anything, not with my tool like that. It's intolerable. It's hell. It doesn't feel like mine any more. You must do something.'

Fidelis raised the nightgown to examine the engorged member. Gingerly poking it, he asked if this had ever happened before.

'Course it hasn't. Always been perfectly normal in every way. Never a cause for complaint.'

Fidelis observed that there must therefore have been something different, some new influence, in this instance. Had he been stung by an insect or plant, eaten or drunk anything unusual, or done some other activity immediately before it happened – dancing, riding, bathing – or boxing, perhaps?

'Boxing?' Hoghton roared. 'Don't be bloody absurd. And I wasn't playing ring-a-roses either. Use your wits, if you have any. What do you think I was doing?'

'You were . . . with a lady, then?'

At which Hoghton writhed around again and, without answering, demanded again that the doctor do something.

'So what did you do?' I asked my friend, between laughter and suspense.

'I relieved the bladder. I had been wondering if this stubborn erection was being maintained by pressure on either the prostate gland or the urethra. So I used a catheter, and presto! It worked. I drew off the urine and within a few minutes the member had noticeably deflated.'

'He was cured?'

'Not quite, but I thought matters would improve from there. I suggested that a cold compress, even a cold bath, might help soothe the burning, and that the discomfort would slowly dissipate. But there was not much more for me to do except tell him plainly that the influence which had caused this would be best avoided.'

'How did Sir Henry take your warning?'

'Growled and griped at me, but admitted nothing. So I left him, after I had treated the split lip and the nose, about which he was equally unforthcoming, by the way. I'd looked at his knuckles, and the joke of it is they were abraded. It seemed he really had been boxing.'

I remembered what Elizabeth had been telling me in the early morning.

'Another gentleman, I hear, has been seen this morning with signs of fist fighting on him.'

'Yes. As you know, I normally attend the chapel for Sunday Mass, and I saw him. Mr Arne, his name is, and he is half Sir Henry's age. Of course, there is disorder of all kinds at the moment, but I would say if the London musician and the parliamentary candidate had been fighting each other, there's not much doubt who would have come out on top.'

'But the blow of a fist could not have brought about Sir Harry's other embarrassment.'

'There have been stranger effects in physiology. But the truth, which I already suspected, is different. See this?'

He brandished the paper on which I had copied Wilson's transactions, then laid it on the desk again. He pointed to the line that read, '*Boy pro H.H.? Cnthds pdr. 10 grn.*'

'That means ten grains of *cantharides* – half a scruple – in powdered form, sold to a representative of a certain H.H. I think we now know who that is.'

'What's *cantharides*?'

'Spanish fly, to you, crushed and powdered. It is a powerful irritant to the sexual organs, which is why it is reputed to be aphrodisiacal. But its general effect is less pleasant – not as dangerous as *atropinum*, but if two or three scruples of this were imbibed at once I would expect it to be fatal. What Wilson gave out was less than a mortal dose, but enough to produce the symptoms that I saw in Sir Harry. Indeed, I suspected he had been taking *cantharides* as soon as I saw the urine.'

'Why?'

'Because it was streaked with blood.'

'Did he admit that he'd deliberately tried to stimulate his organ?'

'Of course not. Kept repeating that he couldn't account for his embarrassment. But this must be what Wilson was telling you in his drunkenness, when he talked about a eunuch, and all that. It was Hoghton.'

'And what else did he call him? Sir Cocky Cocksman. Was all this for the benefit of Lady Hoghton, do you suppose? It seems unlikely.'

It certainly did. Sir Henry's wife was an austere Presbyterian lady, older than himself. She was rarely seen in Preston.

'It does, rather,' agreed Fidelis. 'More likely he anticipated a joust with a younger woman who, he feared, might prove more passionate and demanding than he could manage. Wilson provided him with what he hoped would starch him up.'

'It did more than that.'

We laughed together, and Fidelis looked happy, and I let go

another opportunity to tell him what had passed between me and Miss Plumb. The woman had apparently gone, and I did not want to remind him of her.

Of course, I would later wish that I had.

When we approached the theatre that evening, the mood round about was rowdy. A group of Tories had gathered on one side of the entrance to taunt any Whig supporters as they arrived for the drama. An opposing group had similarly formed on the other side to bait the Tories. And in between were our deputy constables, the Parkin brothers, walking up and down and keeping the two groups apart, their poles of office held horizontally at waist level in the defensive position.

As in all theatres, the main interest for the audience before the play began was – the audience. We sat in our rows passing comments to each other about who was sitting with whom, what on earth young Mrs Skimble was wearing, and whether old Mr Skamble had accidentally dropped his wig in the jakes before coming out. Eventually the curtains across the stage parted for a moment and the slim, tall figure of a man slipped through to face us. The flickering footlights made him look at first sight like an actor, and it took us a moment to realize that this was Lord Strange himself. He waited for us to settle, then spoke out in a clear voice.

'We beg to present a play of noble sentiments, with uplifting music – written expressly by my very good friend, Mr Thomas Arne, who also undertakes to direct the orchestra. It is the Prince of Wales's best-loved play and it will surely inspire the people of Preston to cast true votes in the interests of our nation. I'll warrant it, or call me a turnip.'

The final touch of bathos raised a general laugh, and a cheer somewhere at the back. Then, to the astonishment of all, His Lordship performed an athletic leap across the orchestra pit, landing in the space in front of the first row of seats where – as our poor theatre does not run to boxes – Lord and Lady Derby, his parents, were sitting, and where a vacant seat was kept for him. The jump itself was graceful, but the landing was not. He came down in front of the plump and bejewelled Lady Pinkleby and pitched forward into her lap with such impetus that, if it had not been for the shield of her fan, her bosom would have received a smack from his face.

The young nobleman disentangled himself from the lady, receiving an even bigger cheer from the rowdy element. He seemed not a bit embarrassed but, smiling and bowing an apology to Lady Pinkleby, raised his arms in a wave to the audience at large, and sat down. He indicated with a hand signal that he was ready and the small orchestra produced the first chords of an overture, the time beaten for them by a smartly dressed man of about thirty – Mr Arne. Since his back was towards us, I could not see the bruised eye socket.

As soon as the overture had played itself out the curtain opened on the scene: a long-ago England, in the course of being conquered by a heathen army of Danes. At the centre of the stage stood an ancient oak tree beneath which, huddled under a blanket, lay the fugitive, ragged, all-but-defeated King Alfred, waking from an exhausted sleep. A chorus of spirits now appeared to the sound of solemn strains. '*What proves the hero truly great*,' they sang, '*is never, never to despair.*'

The words braced Alfred, even though the ill fortunes of war had cruelly separated him from his loving wife, Eltruda. He was further braced by the appearance of a sort of philosopher–hermit, perhaps domiciled in a neighbouring cave, who began to conjure visions of Alfred's great successors, although, paradoxically, they were figures out of history to the present audience: King Edward III, Queen Bess and King William of Orange.

Alfred was braced by these exemplars tighter than a lady's stays. He swore by God to cast out flatterers and be the common father of his people, a patriot king. Men naturally take from art what pleases them, so the jibe about flatterers sailed unrecognized past the government's supporters: they were busy gloating at the impossibility of patriotism in the skulking family of Stuarts. At the same time their opponents heard only the denunciation of flatterers, and thought how they hated 'Robbing' Walpole.

I feared that Miss Colley, full of hope for ghosts and violent sword fights, would be disappointed by the play. I looked around but could not see her, though I did catch the eye of Luke Fidelis in the row behind ours. He swivelled up his eyes and discreetly tapped his mouth with a flat hand.

Then something happened to shake him out of his boredom. Onstage, Alfred cupped his ear, saying, 'But hark! Methinks I hear a plaintive voice.'

The orchestra struck up once more, and we all heard it: a weird, wavering soprano drifting over us from somewhere off the stage:

> *Sweet valley say where, pensive lying,*
> *For me, our children, England sighing,*
> *The best of mortals leans his head!*

As his ear caught the sound, the best of mortals at once adopted an attitude of amazement, and no wonder for, trilling fervently, a young woman now edged onto the stage – a palpably lovely young woman, dressed in a gown of red silk, with her golden hair crowned by a chaplet of wild red roses.

I blinked. Probably my mouth fell open. This was undoubtedly Alfred's great love, the beautiful Queen Eltruda. But it was also, and even more incontrovertibly, my friend Fidelis's great love, Miss Lysistrata Plumb.

Whispers rustled through the stalls as the song unfolded, with the men in the audience marvelling sotto voce at the singer's charm. Her voice was highly distinctive – ethereal at the high end, breathy and corporeal in the lower notes. I could hardly imagine what Fidelis's thoughts must have been at the idea of Miss Plumb – Lysistrata – exposing herself onstage. It rather contradicted his image of her as an angel to the angels, for actors and actresses are certainly not angels. Their whole purpose is to deceive – not to be what they seem, or to seem what they are not – which is not too far from being a professional immoralist like Richard Andrews, though with the important difference that we disparage him and applaud them. I looked around to see my friend's reaction to the reappearance of his guiding star. He had turned as white as a goose feather.

Alfred was even further invigorated by his reunion with Eltruda. In life, people can reach this conjugation of the spiritual and the sensual only in fleeting moments of bliss; in the drama, on the other hand, they regularly achieve it, with the understanding that after fall of the curtain bliss will prolong into eternity. The play *Alfred* was now beginning to rise and sweep like an ocean wave towards just such a finale. As our protagonist's love for his wife is fulsomely reaffirmed, so his political rhetoric swells. Alfred's previously wan hopes of defeating the pagan Dane now wax and harden in a heroic final speech, passionately foretelling the triumph of liberty and safety across a land guarded by the deterrent power of Britannia's navies. He promises an end to lawless roads, and a new age of learning and the arts, '*whose humanizing Power / tames the wild Breast, the injurious Hand restrains / and gives vagrant Lust to taste the matchless Joys / of Kindred, Love and sweet domestic Bliss*'. The poetry was bad, but I admired the sentiments. They had nothing of the sordid lubricity of the Whig merchants' 'free' trade, or the brutishness of so many Tories; they painted instead a picture of laws passed with liberal consent, wise judgement by our peers, and an absence of dread throughout the land.

When the speech was finished, Mr Arne struck up his band once more, and Alfred launched into a closing song – and such a song! With its memorable tune and stirring words, I admit I had never heard the like before:

> *When Britain first at heaven's command*
> *Arose from out the azure main . . .*

I think I speak for most of the audience that heard it. As we listened we felt alternately the heat of emotion and the chill of the sublime and, upon each stirring repetition of the song's chorus of 'Rule Britannia!' – famous later but until that night unheard at Preston – the hairs on the back of my neck prickled. Mr Arne may have seemed like a dandy with a predilection for fisticuffs, but in reality he was a musician with a genius rare enough to rival Mr Handel's own. His glorious song had me believing, for a few minutes at least, that all the paradisial promises we had earlier heard Alfred make could be kept after all. The wild applause, whistles and calls for its repetition – it was heard three times and might have gone three more before we'd had enough – told me that most of the theatre felt much the same.

When the performance was done at last, several dozen select members of the audience crossed the road to the Lamb and Flag Inn and climbed to the long upstairs room for supper. This was by special invitation of Lord Strange – though, I would guess, at his father's expense. The seating was free-for-all and I found Elizabeth a place on one of the ladies' tables, before crossing the room to find a vacancy among the men for myself. At one of the men's tables I saw Fidelis sitting with a group that included Nick

Oldswick. But, there being no spare place, I looked around the other tables and saw one beside the hunched figure of Thomas Wilson. It seemed an opportunity too good to pass up, and I sat down there at once.

The apothecary did not look happy. He played moodily with his glass of wine more than he drank from it, and seemed to have scant appetite. He was one of the few to have taken a sour dislike to *Alfred*, with particular reference to its connection with Prince Frederick.

'Prince Fred's favourite play? No wonder it is. I bet he's rumpled every girl in the theatre company and especially the beauty in the red dress. Prince of Quails, I call him. They talk about him being spit-polished up to be the Great Patriot King when his turn comes. King Alfrederick? Yes, and my arse wears boots. He's a useful dupe, Cragg, and I mean that with the greatest respect for the House of Hanover. I receive papers from London from time to time and they tell me Fred has a toadying group of lords around him, who encourage him to hate his father the king, and egg him on to conspire at every turn against Sir Robert. Well, that's the last thing our country needs, with the French king building barges and kitting out men to invade us, and the Spanish king putting ever more guns on the water to blast our navy off it. Our only safety is in prudent finances, and a standing army, not bleating about law and citizen juries.'

'You express yourself strongly. You will be casting your vote for Hoghton and Reynolds, I take it.'

'I have always been against the Tories, me. A Whig to the core, like my old dad. That's why I don't like to hear this blatant politicking in plays. That speech at the end was not dramatic, it was a Tory electioneering rant.'

'But if it had been a rant in praise of Sir Robert . . . ?'

Wilson widened his eyes and thumped the table.

'No, no! That is my point, Cragg. The Whig party does not indulge in such canting tricks as to dress up a political meeting as a play. But the Tories, now! You would put nothing past them.'

'Do you not think politics are very like the drama, though? Roles are acted in much the same way.'

'Yes, by the Tories!'

'By both sides, I think. Besides, Lord Strange's family are hardly Tories. I would say the theme of the play we saw tonight should be acceptable to all. It spoke admiringly of things that any man of goodwill ought to admire.'

'I think not. It had nothing to say about business, nothing about finance, nothing about trade, nothing about fearing God. It speaks not of lowering the national debt or preserving the land tax. Instead it insults our lawful and good king by making him equal to Danes that worshipped the sun and wore horns in their helmets.'

I might have pointed out that the song 'Rule Britannia!' did speak of trade. 'Thy cities shall with commerce shine', I recalled, was one of its assurances. But I did not. Wilson would not be shaken off his platform by a line of verse.

I noticed a falling-off of conversation throughout the supper room, and grateful for a chance to leave the subject I turned to see the Derbys entering, followed half a minute later by their son, our young host. He made his way towards the high table, bowing to right and left with seigneurial assurance, as his guests called out their appreciation for the supper and the play. Wilson's lips curled in a sneer. Like *Alfred*'s original patron, young Strange expected one day to inherit great power and prestige; like Prince Frederick, he was at home with wits, musicians, artists and, especially, playwrights and actors. And this preference was most strongly underlined, tonight, by the companion on his arm. Still wearing the same red silken dress and tripping proudly by his side, her face a picture of pure serenity, was Lysistrata Plumb.

Wilson's single comment was uttered like a judgement.

'Libertine!'

Chapter Seventeen

B Y HALF PAST nine Lord and Lady Derby had left, allowing the older members of the party to drift away after them to their early beds. Space was cleared for the younger guests to dance, as Mr Arne's men assembled in a corner, with viols, clarinets, trumpet and sackbut at the ready. At his first sight of these preparations Wilson rose. I had been unable up to this point to turn our conversation in the direction I wanted – towards Shackleberry, and where he had obtained his belladonna. In hopes of still doing so I tried to detain him.

'No, Cragg,' he insisted, 'I must go. I cannot endure dancing.'

He stalked away and I rose too, looking around for Luke Fidelis. Sitting alone by the wall, he was holding out his glass for a serving man to refill. As I crossed the room to take the place beside him, the music struck up and we watched Lord Strange take the floor with his scarlet-gowned inamorata, both of them beckoning others to follow and form the dance. One of those who did was Mr Thomas Arne with, as his partner, the actress who had taken the role of the peasant wife.

We watched the dancers break into a vigorous gavotte, Luke viewing the proceedings moodily, even truculently. The musician and his actress made a striking couple: he a neat figure, dressed to a pitch of fashion that fell just short of extravagance; she red lipped, full bosomed and with a pert upturned nose. I judged her to be the older: over thirty-five to his (I guessed) about thirty years. Formally they were employer and employee, but their eyes and glances told a different tale.

At the other end of the set were Lord Strange and Miss Plumb. His face was a study of impassivity, almost complacency, while hers glowed with happiness. It was clear why she had travelled down to us on her own. She could not have come in her lover's carriage without provoking the kind of gossip that easily spills over into scandal, particularly at election time. And I guessed that she was not a regular member of the acting company. Lord Strange would have imposed his mistress on the manager who, however unwilling to accept her, would have had no choice but to bow to the wishes of the man paying the bills. Lysistrata's few days' lodging at the Lorrises' were an expedience. As soon as her lover arrived she had gone to him at Patten House, to the extreme detriment of Luke Fidelis's hopes. Seeing her again, seeing the truth of her situation, had shattered the mask of recovery he'd been wearing earlier in the day. Feeling for him, I gently nudged his arm.

'You must not take it badly, Luke.'

But he was taking everything badly, even my sympathy.

'What? That she is Strange's mistress? That she is carrying his child?'

I was astounded.

'His child? What on earth do you mean?'

'The signs were unmistakable but I was blind to them.'

For a moment I was dumbfounded. Then I remembered her words to me at Lorris's house. *I am bound to him, and doubly bound.* So that was the second bond: her unborn child.

'Can you not merely accept it?' I suggested. 'Plot a new path for yourself?'

He looked at me with incredulity.

'*Merely?*'

'I mean—'

But Fidelis was not in any mind to listen. He jumped to his feet with clenched fists and for a moment I thought he was going to wade into the middle of the dancers and carry out his threat against Strange and Miss Plumb.

Instead he bent stiffly and hissed close to my ear, 'I know what you mean. Not for the first time, Cragg, you show your powers of understanding to be limited. Goodnight!'

I watched him walk stiffly from the room. A few moments later my wife came over to claim me for a dance.

'I've been talking with two unhappy men tonight,' I said to Elizabeth. With the last dance done, the last cup of punch drained, we had walked home. Now we were preparing for bed. 'First Wilson, the apothecary, except that he did all the talking – I could hardly get a word in. He abhors all of that – song and dance, players, Lord Derby's son and heir. I wondered what made him come out tonight. Why was he there?'

'He is a divided man, Titus: a puritan when sober and a devil when drunk. I have never liked him. Was poor Fidelis your other misery? I saw him leave the room looking woeful.'

I told her that he thought Lysistrata was expecting a child. She took the news without a hint of surprise.

'That would explain much. No wonder he is despondent.'

'When I commiserated, he left me with an angry parting shot. He wanted to wound me.'

I told her what Fidelis had said, and at once Elizabeth reached up and pinched my cheek.

'Don't be sorry for yourself, Mr Cragg. Be sorry for poor Luke. I think he wounds himself more than he does you. But he will recover, as sure as green leaves, and in the meantime you must reflect that he is quite right – your understanding *is* limited. Will you help me with these ribbons?'

She turned her back to me, and I began to loosen the bands tying her hair.

'And what did you ladies talk about?' I asked. But as I released the hair I could not stop myself from kissing the slim neck beneath, and running my lips down the delightful bumps of her spine.

'May I tell you later?' she whispered, arching her back like a cat.

When at last we came to rest, Elizabeth lay contentedly in my arms.

'The ladies were all a-flutter about His young Lordship,' she murmured. 'They could not formally approve of course, but they were excited by the thought of him having a mistress. And of the two of them doing – what we have just done.'

'Prurience trumps prudery. What did they make of Mr Arne and his music?'

'They liked the music immoderately, and the same for his appearance. The black eye seemed to inflame them even more.'

'What is the report, then? Don't tell me you still haven't heard how he got it?'

'Oh, I have. The ladies knew. Miss Malcolmson heard it from Miss Langford, who got it from Miss Colley, who heard it from Mrs Bryce.'

'And?'

'Well, it was like this. With all the inns in town full, the theatre company stopped last night at Hoghton Tower. Sir Harry's disapproval of plays is only for public show, it seems. You noted the actress who played the peasant girl, and who danced this evening with Mr Arne? Her name is Belinda. During the evening she attracted her host's attentions, and during the night he got into her bedroom. He was trying to – you know.'

'We saw the same thing last week, with Mrs Bryce and Mr Reynolds. He is incorrigible.'

'Well, he had not got very far along when Mr Arne interrupted him. Coming suddenly into the room, he saw what was going on and violently dragged Sir Harry off the bed. Sir Harry took a swing at him and boxed his eye, but of course he came off the worst in the end.'

'And has not been seen out since. He is one of those men that tries his luck with any woman as a matter of course.'

'Yes, but possibly he didn't appreciate that Belinda is Mr Arne's girl. Or maybe he didn't care. I have heard it said that some libertines are inflamed by a woman just because she belongs to another man.'

I laughed.

'Sir Harry was inflamed all right. But not only by that.'

The next morning, the beginning of the polling week, men were at work early with saws, hammers and drills, getting the polling hall ready. The appointed room was inside the Moot Hall and, in normal times, it served as the courtroom, where the mayor conducted everything from civil suits and petty sessions to the grand ceremonials of the guild. This was an appropriate place because the election itself was, in part, a judicial hearing, with the mayor, in the guise of returning officer, sitting in judgement on the credentials of every voter who came before him. If there arose any doubt about his eligibility the mayor would question the man and either allow, or refuse, him. The recorder, his legal officer, was constantly at his elbow to give advice.

The scare over contagion had already blown away. When people first read the corporation's notices *Contra Pestis*, there was much understandable alarm. But this was soon balanced by the spreading gossip that the sickness had only visited those who drank Shackleberry's and Andrews's 'Preservative'. Within two hours there was hardly a Prestonian who believed any more in the second coming of the plague. As those who had been sick got up one by one from their beds – with none, mercifully, having died – the general mood changed from one of gestating panic to rising indignation, and a desire to see the mountebanks dragged back in chains from wherever they had got to and banged into the stocks.

Nick Oldswick must have recovered very well under Parsonage's care, since he had attended the play, and even Lord Strange's supper. I heard he had been conferring with the attorney Arsenius Tench about the prosecution of Shackleberry for attempted murder. Even Mayor Biggs had seen which way the tide was running. By morning he had give fresh orders to Mallender that he go through town, taking down the plague notices and spreading the word that if Shackleberry and Andrews should be seen, they were to be taken up and brought before him.

In the election the Whigs' hopes were beginning to shrivel. Neither candidate was seen on the hustings. The baronet skulked in his family castle and, at any mention of his name, men sniggered and ladies exchanged knowing smiles. Francis Reynolds had not been seen in public since the previous week, and there was speculation about what he thought of his election partner's fall into disgrace. Meanwhile, with no help from either of the Whig candidates, Denis Destercore was running around with increasing desperation trying to organize the party vote.

In the office, Furzey was crouched over his writing desk. I resisted the temptation to say anything about the declining fortunes of his party, and went straight to business.

'I've been thinking about John Allcroft's death, asking myself if we have been cowardly about it.'

He did not look up, but continued to scratch away with his pen.

'We are not cowards, sir.'

'Well, fearful, let's say. I simply cannot forget that he did not die naturally – and that I *knew* he did not within a few hours of the event. I wish I had held an inquest, and yet there are grounds to fear what such an inquest might uncover.'

'We should never be afeared of such matters. Our job is to uncover everything, whatever it might be.'

'No, it is not, Furzey. Sometimes, as you know, we must use discretion. Now, Allcroft was here for the election. In this election week, would inquesting him be against the interest of a fair contest?'

'What's your point, sir? The death had nothing to do with the election.'

'I disagree. I suspect murder, Furzey, which may have been done to affect the election result.'

The clerk raised his head from his copying for the first time since I had come in.

'The removal of one Tory from the vote cannot make much difference.'

'No. My wife has made the same remark. But this isn't just one voter. Mrs Allcroft told me that her husband had raised a group of out-of-town freemen, and that he would lead them to Preston as a single tally to vote against Sir Henry Hoghton: to help turn him out, is how they put it. So what about the other members of the tally, now without their tally captain? It is not too much to suppose that they might lose all heart, or run away out of fear for their own lives. And if that happened widely it *would* make a difference.'

Now Furzey laid down his pen and bit his lip, thinking.

'If there were people so devoted to Sir Harry's cause that they would kill for him, I think we must discriminate the cause from those people, and incriminate only the people. I speak up for the reputation of politics in general but also for the good of the Whig party which, as you know, I myself support.'

I sighed deeply.

'I am beginning to think you are right. It is a little late to open an inquest, but I can legitimately say that after Dr Fidelis's trick with the rat we have sufficient evidence in our hands. What we do not have is a body. And without that we can't proceed.'

Furzey shrugged.

'The body is there, sir. All we have to do is—'

'Yes, yes, I know.'

'Shall I draw up the order, then, sir?'

'Yes, Furzey. Reluctantly, but yes, I think you had better. And I shall go out to Gregson and inform Mrs Allcroft. But first, I really should pen a note to the mayor, to tell him again he's wasting his time looking for the two mountebanks in Preston.'

It turned out there was no need for me to send for my saddle horse. As I passed through the kitchen to get my riding boots from the boot room, Matty, who had been out early, told me she had seen Susan Allcroft in the town. So I dispatched Barty to run to her brother's shop on Fisher Gate asking for her. He was directed from there to Talboys the dressmaker's, where he found her, and she sent word – in a starchily worded note – that she would come in half an hour. Thirty minutes later, she was standing before me in the inner office, carrying a number of packages.

'Madam,' I began, 'I am afraid I have a duty to perform that is disagreeable to me, and must be repugnant to you. Won't you sit down?'

So she sat, distributing her purchases on either side of the chair.

'I have a deal of messages to run, sir, and would be obliged if you would come to the point.'

She had lost none of her sharpness.

'It concerns your husband's sad death. As you know I was with Dr Fidelis for a time while he tended Mr Allcroft's last hours.'

'Tended? Sat idly by, more like. Doctors!'

I let the jibe go by without comment. 'Have you reflected at all on the cause of his death?'

'Why should I? It was from falling poorly, a sudden violent sickness. Some people said he'd eaten putrid meat.'

'Would you not like to know for sure?'

'We are not always meant to know. So the Psalm says, "*Blessed is the man that maketh the Lord his trust*".'

'But it is important to know. If it was the case that he had a natural seizure, or the dropsy, or had eaten bad food, I would say, very well, read the prayers, ring the bell and bury him.'

'So we have done.'

'I know, but, as I warned you the other day, if there are any grounds to believe Mr Allcroft's death was not natural – any grounds at all – it is my duty to hold inquest over him. And I consider I now do have such grounds.'

'You may have grounds, Mr Cragg, but my husband's *in* the ground. He lies in the churchyard in our village. You're too late.'

'No, madam, as I also indicated to you, that is not quite the case.'

She flinched backward in revulsion.

'No – you're not going to—? You can't—?'

'Exhume him? Yes, I can, Mrs Allcroft, and I am going to.'

She started fanning herself furiously.

'Oh, heavens! Oh, dear! His funeral service has been read. His passing bell, his hymns at the graveside, his shroud and flowers, his deep grave filled in and headstone ordered. Oh, no! I cannot have it all again. I forbid his disturbance. I am his widow and I will not allow it.'

'I'm afraid it is not for you, even as his widow. The final authority on exhumation is with me alone. I do it very rarely and always reluctantly. But every now and then it is necessary.'

Now Mrs Allcroft was crying. This is not a very unusual event in a lawyer's office and so it was Furzey's idea to keep a stock of handkerchiefs laundered, folded and ready for such cases. He had even had his brother-in-law, a cabinetmaker, knock up a box of the right dimensions to hold them, with the words '*Daughters of Jerusalem*' inlaid in the lid. I now reached across my desk, lifted it and whisked out a handkerchief, which I offered.

'When will you do it?' she asked between snivels.

'Tomorrow, in the twilight. I will send a copy of the exhumation order to the parish sexton. He will do the digging and we will send a cart to collect the coffin. I assume he was buried in a coffin.'

'Of course! What do you take us for?'

The handkerchief was in strong use now, wrapped around Susan Allcroft's finger and dabbing at the flood from her eyes.

'What will you do with him?' she asked through thick snivels. 'Where will you take him?'

'Back here to town. He must be inquested where he died.'

This initiated another wave of weeping.

'All this way? Who is going to pay the cart, the sexton, and all?'

'Coroner's expenses, madam. I often find it difficult to extract them, but the corporation usually pays up in the end.'

I reached for one of the ready-printed sheets of paper and, dipping my pen, rapidly wrote out a witness attendance order in her name. When it was signed and sealed, I handed it to her and made sure she tucked it into her purse.

'The inquest will be on Wednesday morning, at ten o'clock, in the Gamecock Inn, Stoney Gate. We will need your evidence, Mrs Allcroft.'

I gathered up her purchases and steered her, still weeping, towards the door.

'Sometimes this process is of benefit, you know,' I said. 'As his widow you will feel that Mr Allcroft's death has been properly and respectfully examined, and not merely forgotten about.'

I had a feeling my words had not been heard, smothered as they were by another volley of sobs from beneath the handkerchief. But then came a change. In the outer office Susan Allcroft sniffed deeply one last time, straightened her back and handed me the wet ball of linen.

'You may try to steal my husband's body, sir,' she said in a voice that was now quite level. 'But I shall be ready for you. I'll not allow it, not for a moment.'

I tried to pitch my voice exactly halfway between gentleness and severity.

'I fear you cannot prevent me, madam. It is my clear duty, and that duty gives me authority. You must see reason.'

'Reason!' she fired back. 'How can I see reason where there is none?'

She stalked out. Furzey, who had given the appearance throughout this exchange of deaf application to his work, looked up.

'She means it,' he said.

'She is probably going to Rudgwick's to ask if she can stop me. They will tell her she cannot.'

'So we must hope,' said Furzey.

He was teasing. He knew the coronial law better than I did.

Chapter Eighteen

I HAD SETTLED DOWN to make my usual two pre-inquest lists, one being jurors and the other witnesses, when Furzey came in and dropped a printed bill on the desk under my nose. He withdrew without further comment.

I picked it up. It was headed, *CONTESTED PARLIAMENTARY ELECTION AT PRESTON. NOTICE OF RULES AND PROCEDURES*, and the authority at the bottom was that of Mayor Biggs. Below his name in small print it said that Oswald Mallender was charged with posting this bill on all public billboards, and in other prominent places such as large trees and wooden posts, and with handing copies in at the offices of attorneys and notaries.

I went back to the top and read the whole document. The electoral process was to start at midday when, by tradition, the mayor would cast the first votes, which he did before his deputy returning officer, one of the two bailiffs. Having revealed which two out of the four candidates he favoured (that they would be the Tories would be a surprise to no one) he would then take his place on the returning bench and begin to record the votes of the other twenty-three members of the corporation – a leisurely business as the self-importance of the burgesses meant that each of them swore the full oath – something that less exalted voters were required to do only if challenged.

This ceremonial would conclude the opening day of the election. The real business of recording the popular vote began on Tuesday. They would vote in tallies of twelve, raised by the parties themselves and based on the streets of the town. So for our own street, Cheapside, there would be Tory and Whig tallies, and one for those much fewer in number who chose, like me, not to declare their vote in advance. Organizing these tallies was a complicated business. Each had a tally captain – the role Allcroft had taken at the head of Gregson's tally of Tories – and his job was to marshal his men and ensure they marched to the polling hall in a single cohort at the assigned time. If any man did not do so, his right to vote could be taken from him. The bill in my hand gave the timetable for the voting of each tally, with Tories and Whigs taking turn and turn about. There were more than fifty tallies, which meant voting would not finish until the afternoon of Thursday.

During this time the disorder of the town could only be expected to increase. The march to the polling hall was a splendid event, a triumphal parade with flags, cockades, ribbons, and a trumpeter, if not a small band, to parade behind. This progress could be perilous. Opposing voters booed and threw missiles, while supporters cheered the voters on, and fights between the two groups were normal. It was the tally captain's most important job to prevent his own men from breaking ranks and joining in the fracas, in case they missed their appointment with the mayor and were not counted. But this, of course, was the sole aim of the opposing camp, using any means of provocation at their disposal.

I laid the paper down. Yes, it would be exciting. But many windows would be broken, and heads too, and for what? So that two men could go up to London and become the quintessence of pomposity.

*

At dinner my quandary over Luke Fidelis, and how to mend our quarrel, was at the front of my mind.

'What shall I do?' I asked Elizabeth. 'I must do something. Write to him? Present myself at his door? I feel I must pass on Miss Plumb's confidence, however belatedly, and despite his having now found it out for himself.'

'But he has quarrelled with you, Titus, and this will make it worse. He will be hurt that you kept the matter from him.'

'But I know he is distressed. Estrangement from his friends cannot but make this worse.'

'You must be careful. It can do no harm to write, but I don't think you should go to him in person. He is already angry with you. There's no knowing how much angrier he will be when he hears you did not divulge this message from Miss Plumb. Something irreparable might be said. So send him your white dove, and make your confession, but otherwise be patient and wait till he changes.'

I went to my office to compose the letter:

Dear Luke,

Elizabeth says that of course you are right, and my understanding is very faulty. However my conscience, vexingly, is in good order and it prompts me to confess that I have kept something from you that I should have told. It concerns Miss Plumb and though my silence about it until now may anger you yet more, I must tell you nevertheless, or it will always lie between us.

How should I put this? A narrative approach was the best, so I wrote down how Lysistrata had stopped me on the stair on Saturday and requested an interview; that she wanted me to pass on a message to Fidelis in confidence; that the message was that she knew he had grown fond of her; and finally that she could not be his because she was the mistress of another. I put a line through '*the mistress of*' and substituted '*pledged to*'. After further thought I crossed the substitution out and reinserted '*mistress*'. After all, I was writing man to man.

> *I did not keep all this from you maliciously, for I thought it would only cause you unnecessary pain, being already rather distressed about her. I see that I was wrong in this, as you are not a child. I wish I had told you what I knew, for in that case the lady's disappea ance on Saturday, and her evident connection with a certain Lord on Sunday, might have been a lesser shock to you. Please accept this as a heartfelt apology and a mea culpa. I trust our friendship is not damaged by it.*

Yours affctly, T.C.

I read it through and thought it would serve, so I made a fair copy. Then, just before I sealed the letter, I picked up my pen and added a postscript:

> *I am having Allcroft dug up. Come and see the corpse.*

I handed the letter to the Lorrises' servant girl on my way past the house, for I was now going back to Middleforth Green.

My thoughts were confused and I would have to straighten them out in time for the inquest. As Elizabeth had told me, my task was to uncover the truth about Allcroft's poisoning. But how could I do it without causing a riot?

The Ferry Inn was connected in my mind with the start of all this. When you have a tangled ball of string, it is good policy to get hold of the beginning of the string. In the present case, this was the death of Antony Egan – an event that at first seemed unconnected with anything else. By the time Allcroft died, something that tied the two men together had already fallen into my hand: both men were on Destercore's list of Tories.

After writing my note to Fidelis, I had been rifling my desk drawer for sealing wax when I noticed Furzey's copy of the list. I took it out. Thorough man that he was, Furzey had reproduced everything from the original paper – the queries, crossings-out and also the curious small dots that preceded some of the names. I looked at these dotted names again, trying to decipher the dots' meaning. Allcroft was dotted. So, I noticed, was Nick Oldswick, who himself had had a couple of narrow escapes in the past few days. The dots seemed to make these marked men. But what were they marked for?

I studied Uncle Egan's name. I could not see a dot. The other dots were placed a couple of eighths of an inch before the names they marked, and in Uncle Egan's case the cancelling line began at the same point. If there had been a dot, it would have been covered by the cancellation.

I picked up the paper and went through to Furzey. I put it down under his eye.

'When you copied this, did you copy also the dots in exactly the position where they occurred in the original?'

'Yes, of course. An exact copy, is what you said.'

'And Uncle Egan's cancellation line?'

'Yes, exact again.'

'Could there have been one of these dots against Uncle Egan's name, which the line of ink concealed?'

Furzey thought for several seconds, studying the place where Antony Egan's name was inked out.

'Of course there could. Anyone can see that by looking.'

'So in the original, was there such a dot?'

Furzey picked up the copy of the list and handed it back to me.

'How would I know?' he said. 'Ink blots out ink. It was a thick line. You could see the tops and the bottoms of the letters, so you could read the name that was cancelled. But these dots are smaller than the width of the cancelling line, you see? So, if it had been there, it would've been totally blotted out.'

As I now walked briskly down the track that led to the Middleforth ferry, I was thinking about marked men. If a man found a list of men, with some of them marked, and then two or more of the marked men died in suspicious ways, the inference would be obvious. But I only had one dead man who was definitely marked; I had a second who was dead and might have been marked; and I had a third, Nick Oldswick, who was marked and might – just might – have been threatened with murder, but was not dead. I knew that if Oldswick turned up dead, or if Egan turned out to have been marked on Destercore's list, then I would have good reason to treat the list as material evidence in an inquest. But evidence of what? Murder, certainly. And likely as not a conspiracy to murder. And suspicion of such a conspiracy would probably land Destercore in the dock at the next assizes in Lancaster Castle, on trial for his life.

But it was all too woolly, with too much unknown. There was no certain need to consider Oldswick as a possible victim. His assailant lurking behind the abandoned cart in Friar Gate might have been an unconnected threat, or an exaggerated one, for the clockmaker's own fancies had always been a greater danger to him than other men. And what was the meaning of the marked men on the list? Yes, it was a tangle. I wished that Luke Fidelis were with me to help straighten it out.

'My sister is up in town, Cousin,' Mary-Ann told me when I arrived at the Ferry Inn. 'But I am at your disposal.'

We were alone in the parlour, with teacups, pot and caddy at the ready between us.

'Thank you. I am about to inquest a gentleman who died on Thursday last at the Gamecock Inn. Mr John Allcroft of Gregson. Did you know him?'

'No, Cousin. I never met him.'

'You heard he had died?

'Yes.'

'And before that, had you heard of him?'

'Yes, I heard my father speak of him.'

'Your father knew him? That is what I have come here to ask you! You are quite sure?'

Mary-Ann's eyes stared at me without blinking.

'No, I don't know that he knew him. He may have. But I heard him speak of Mr Allcroft.'

'When was this?'

'Quite recently.'

'In what connection?'

'It was about the voting. I believe it was a few days after we heard that there would be a vote. Dad said something like, "I hear Mr Allcroft of Gregson is vigorous in his action against these Whigs." Whig Pigs is what he called them, if you will pardon the expression.'

I did so with a smile and asked, 'Did your father say anything more about Mr Allcroft?'

'Just that he was going to do as Mr Allcroft had done at Gregson and Hoghton, and get a gang together from here and Bamber Bridge. They were supposed to go across in a party and vote for the Tories, come election time. A full tally, he called it. I didn't take much notice at the time.'

'I remember your sister saying something about this when we

came here with your father's body. He used the precise word "tally", did he?'

'Yes.'

'That is very interesting, isn't it?'

'I don't know. Is it?'

'The tally is the collective name for a group of voters who march together to the polling hall under a so-called tally captain. Now your father was correctly informed about Allcroft. He *had* gathered a tally under himself at Gregson and Hoghton. What is interesting to me is that your father was intending to do the same here.'

'But he didn't.'

'No, he was not given the chance.'

'He would not have done it anyway.'

'He talked about it.'

'Talking isn't doing.'

'Had he ever acted as a tally captain before – in the last parliamentary vote, when he was younger?'

'I don't know. I was a small child.'

'Do you know if he made recent contact with any fellow Tory supporters who might have joined his tally in this election?'

'Cousin Titus, this tally of his was imaginary! I can't think why you are so interested in it. Are you trying to connect my father's accident in some way with what happened to Mr Allcroft?'

'Well . . . I beg you to keep this to yourself, Mary-Ann. Discuss it with Grace, if you like, but no one else, if you please.'

She nodded.

'Very well, I will tell you. There is a suspicion of poison in John Allcroft's death. And there is also a suspicion about your father's drowning. In spite of the jury verdict I now have reason to think there *may*, I say no more than that, have been someone else with him before he went into the river. And, if so, that same person *may* – with the same proviso – have meddled with Allcroft's plate of dinner.'

Mary-Ann stared, clapping her hands to her cheeks.

'You mean you think our dad was pushed in?'

'No, at this stage I don't. Only that eventually I may come round to thinking that, when I am further along this road.'

'But who? And why?'

Before I replied – not that I *could* reply – hot water was brought in, and Mary-Ann prepared our tea. I took the opportunity to broach the second reason for my visit.

'May I see your register of guests?'

She sent the serving girl out to get the book. I cleared the cups aside and opened it flat on the table. There was something here that I thought I remembered – or perhaps misremembered. I found the current page and then looked back to the guests of the previous week. I saw the most relevant two entries – about Destercore and his man. And then I looked above at the other names, and there they were, three, as I thought, that I had seen before: *Mr Chapman, T. Wilson, Richd. Gornall.* I put my finger on the middle name.

'Wilson,' I said. 'Tell me now. Is this by chance Thomas Wilson, apothecary, of Church Gate?'

'Yes, Cousin, it would be.'

'Now, that really is interesting.'

Mary-Ann shook her head.

'Is it? Mr Wilson often stops here on a Sunday night, after he has been at his card party.'

'His card party?'

'Yes, at old Satterthwaite's. Every so many Sundays they have a game at Satterthwaite's cottage. Other Sundays it is at Porter's in town, I believe.'

'When it is at Satterthwaite's does Wilson always stay here?'

'That's his custom, because he always misses the last ferry. He's the worse for drink, most times, so we have a bed ready for him to fall into.'

'What about these other two – Gornall and Chapman? Did they play cards also?'

'No. I don't know Gornall, except that he's a farmer in Ribbleton. Chapman's the chandler at Penwortham. He was riding to Kendal and took a room to get the earliest ferry across.'

She rang a handbell and the girl reappeared.

'Paula, will you send Toby in?'

She turned back to me.

'A little business I must deal with.'

She got up and slid open a drawer in a side table, bringing out a watch.

'My father's,' she said, showing it to me. 'It has not run since it went into the water with him. Grace was to take it this morning but forgot. I am sending it now with Toby to see if it can be mended.'

I took the watch from her – a good, solid fob of old-fashioned appearance. I squinted at the face to read the maker's name: *Wm. Oldswick, Preston* – our own Nicholas's father.

'He must have had this a few years.'

'He got it when he was twenty-one, so he used to say.'

'Here's an idea. Don't trouble Toby with this. Let me take it.'

So it was agreed but, as I left, another question occurred to me.

'Do you know who were the other regular card players?'

'No. But there must have been others, if they were playing four-handed cribbage. It wouldn't have made a game with just Satterthwaite, Wilson and Mr Destercore, would it?'

This brought me up short.

'Mary-Ann, are you saying Destercore was there, at Satterthwaite's that Sunday night?'

'Oh, yes, didn't I mention it? Wilson fell into conversation with Mr Destercore here at the inn, when he called earlier to secure his bed. He invited him down to Satterthwaite's but, being a stranger, Mr Destercore wasn't what you meant by a regular in the game.'

I trod a thoughtful lane back towards the ferry, with Uncle Egan's watch in my pocket and a bushel of new information in my head. I had drawn up a mental list of six witnesses whose evidence I thought the Allcroft inquest jury should hear: Mrs Fitzpatrick, her cook and kitchen boy, Luke Fidelis and the Satterthwaites, Isaac and Maggie. Now I considered adding a seventh – Thomas Wilson.

Having reached the Satterthwaite cottage, I let myself into the garden by the gate. Old Isaac was a considerable gardener. He had a mass of woodland bulbs growing beneath fruit trees that were themselves laden with blossom. It was a warm day and the air felt almost sticky – sweet with scent and the buzz of insects. I knocked on the cottage door, setting off one of the terriers inside, who scrabbled around behind the door, barking. But the old man did not appear. I peeped through the window, and could see the oak table at which the men had presumably played their cards, no doubt while jesting, smoking, drinking and talking politics. Isaac may have been a rat catcher, but he was well travelled and, in his way, a man of discrimination. I guessed it would have been port wine and not porter beer that they drank.

That Satterthwaite and Wilson were friendly was not a surprise. Both men had returned to Preston after spending long years away, and one was the other's customer in the supply of rat poison. They also happened to be opinionated supporters of the same political party, though I would have guessed that was not a question of two men thinking just alike, but of an alliance between different temperaments. Satterthwaite's Whiggism came out of his military past. He had seen more than enough slaughter, rape and mayhem to become chary of military adventuring, perhaps on grounds of pure humanity, or of not liking to see useful lives wasted. Wilson was first and always a businessman, who thought the accumulation of wealth was a man's main reason for being alive. As I had heard the night before, he supported Walpole's long peace because he saw the policy as good for trade and stability – and in the end for himself.

Destercore had sat at that table too, talking politics between hands, gathering news, compiling lists. Who were the other members of the card school? I was already prepared to wager they would not be Tories.

I made my way back to the ferry and during the crossing questioned Robert Battersby in case he knew anything about these card games, whose players he must have transported to Middleforth from time to time. He told me he couldn't tell me owt, but perhaps he simply wouldn't. I had offered him no money and there was a general assumption in town that Battersby's habitual surliness had a mercenary origin.

Oldswick put on a pair of spectacles and examined the timepiece.

'This is an old one.'

'It belonged to poor Antony Egan.'

'Did it indeed? Went in the river with him, did it?'

'Yes.'

He opened the back and looked closely around the works, with his eye no more than an inch away. He looked for as long as a minute without making any comment, then snapped the case shut and took off his spectacles.

'There'd not be much problem if it were just water, but it's not. The case has taken a few knocks and there's damage inside. I'm surprised the watch glass is intact.'

'Can you make it go again? His daughters are anxious to have it working.'

'Oh, aye, we can make it go. We built the bugger, didn't we? We'll rebuild it if we have to, only it won't be a quick job.'

'What shall I tell them you'll charge?'

'Let's say three shillings, maybe three and six. If it looks like being more I can tell 'em by letter.'

I watched as he wrote out the receipt, and, though I can't say what association it was that prompted me, I suddenly had the idea.

'You'll not have much time for the shop, with the election going on.'

'No, it's madness.'

It was a very bright idea, or so I thought, and it concerned Destercore's lists.

'When are you polling, yourself?'

'Eh, they don't get to Friar Gate till Wednesday afternoon. My tally's due there at three – not that they'll keep to the timetable. It could be anytime after that.'

He handed me the receipt for the watch, and I tucked it into my pocketbook.

'I heard you're acting as a tally captain.'

This was my bright idea: I had heard no such thing, but I had to test the theory. Oldswick sighed, as one burdened by responsibilities.

'Oh, aye,' he said. 'I've been waiting all my life to do it. In twenty-two it was my old father who acted for this end of Friar Gate, when I was still his apprentice. He died soon after. I never thought I'd have to wait nearly twenty year till my turn came around to captain the tally.'

A few minutes later I was on my way back to the office. I found my step quickening involuntarily with excitement about what Oldswick had just told me.

Chapter Nineteen

At the office I asked Furzey if there had been any word from Dr Fidelis. There had not.

'Do we have a working jury for Wednesday morning?'

We had.

'And an inquest room at the Gamecock?'

No, because Mrs Fitzpatrick was being obstructive. Said she was too busy and had no room to spare.

'I'll talk to her in the morning,' I said. 'I may as well give her the witness summons at the same time, and those for the other witnesses from there – Maggie Satterthwaite, the cook Primrose and I think the kitchen boy. His name's Peterkin. I'll also be seeking out Isaac Satterthwaite during the day, so will you prepare his summons too?'

Furzey reached for a printed form and dipped his pen.

'That would be Joseph Primrose?' he said, with affected weariness.

'Yes.'

When he had written this he reached for a second form.

'And Mrs *Kathleen* Fitzpatrick?'

'Yes. And don't let me hear that tone. You should be grateful that I'm serving these summonses myself, which saves you a lot of effort.'

'I like serving the summonses. They get me out of here.'

'Well, we also need one for Dr Fidelis, which you can take to his address on your way home tonight.'

Furzey frowned in surprise.

'Are you two not drinking together tonight? It is one of your regular nights.'

I did not reply, but went into my office and sat at the desk, wishing I *were* due to meet Fidelis. I wanted to share with him my bright idea. I took the copy of Destercore's lists from the drawer and opened it out. I went through the names for a few minutes, until Furzey brought in the completed witness summonses to be signed. Without a word he placed the pile of them on top of what I was studying.

Impatiently I pulled the foolscap sheet out from under the summonses. I couldn't keep this to myself any longer.

'Look, Furzey, I've had an idea about these marks against the names of individual men. The ones that we were talking about earlier on the list you copied. I think I know what they mean.'

'The Tory tally captains?' said Furzey.

I almost dropped the paper.

'Furzey! Don't tell me you already knew the dots were markers for tally captains! Why didn't you tell me?'

Furzey shrugged and said, 'Why didn't you ask?'

'How long have you known?'

'I knew that some of the names with dots next to them were tally captains, and all on the opposite side of the vote from my own convictions. It is reasonable to infer that they all are.'

'Which ones definitely are?'

He pointed to half a dozen names, but didn't want to linger to discuss them.

'I have to go out now,' he said, retreating towards the outer office. 'There's to be a speech by Mr Reynolds.'

'Is Reynolds back on the hustings? I suppose Sir Henry's absence is the reason.'

'I wouldn't know that.'

It was not until after I had heard the street door slam behind him that I noticed Furzey had forgotten to pick up Fidelis's witness summons. Separating it from the others, I wrote a second letter to Fidelis. Having heard nothing from him, I did not want a confrontation, yet he had to be served that summons and I decided to deliver a brief note at the same time:

> *Am enclosing with this your summons as witness to the*
> *inquest into John Allcroft. Particulars of the place are*
> *given. On a matter perhaps related, I believe I have got to*
> *the bottom of the 'marked' names on a certain Londoner's*
> *list of Preston voters. Would be glad of the opportunity*
> *to talk this over.*

Adam Lorris was at home when I called, but he told me Fidelis was not, which I was glad about. Before I saw him I needed some indication that he would be reconciled. So I handed the letter and summons to Lorris, and he assured me Fidelis would have it in his hand as soon as he came in.

'By the way, your book of fables is almost ready,' Lorris went on. 'I have found the most exquisite kidskin for it.'

But I did not want to stand around in the hall discussing Aesop so I said how much I was looking forward to seeing the book, then excused myself and left.

In our kitchen, I found Matty putting her feet up with her friend, a chatterbox called Dorcas, who was maid to our neighbour Burroughs, the cabinetmaker. Elizabeth had allowed the girls some tea. I had gone in to see if the shoes were ready that I had left for Matty to clean in the morning. While she went to fetch them I helped myself from the teapot and asked if Dorcas had enjoyed all the excitement in town.

'The real fun starts tonight, sir. This far, we've only seen the half of it, they do say. There's big feasts all over town.'

She was a rosy-cheeked girl with a mop of curly hair, and a pronounced gap between her two front teeth.

'My uncle Charley's come in from Lytham. He's not voting. He's got work for the week at Wilkinson's pie shop. They're selling three times the usual pies and he says they're supplying three feasts tonight. There's a lot of talk at them feasts, which Uncle Charley says I wouldn't understand – speeches about ships, and speeches about cider, and speeches about the King of France. Uncle Charley says best put the King of France in a ship with a thousand gallon of cider and let him sail away, so long as folk can still get good food and drink and singing and jokes – specially about Sir Henry Hoghton. You heard the jokes going round about him?'

'No. What jokes are those, Dorcas?'

She cast her eyes down in a show of modesty.

'I wouldn't like to say, sir. Not to you.'

In the evening I sat in my library reading the new Chaucer and hoping Fidelis would call. By eleven I knew he would not, so I closed *The Man of Law's Tale* and went to bed, anticipating a busy Tuesday with an early start. But sleep was almost impossible as Elizabeth and I lay listening to the sounds of election fever disturbing the peace. From time to time a band of revellers swung past below us, yelling their slogans, the light from their flaming torches flickering at the window and around the darkened room. Further away there was an almost continual hubbub. More than once I heard singers make a drunken attempt at Mr Arne's patriotic song, not very accurately, and not getting far with it.

I must have dozed because the next thing I knew was Elizabeth sitting upright and giving me a shake.

'Titus! Some fellow is making a speech – from our doorstep!'

I slipped out of bed and crept to the window, furtively getting between curtain and glass. I could see a rabble of about twenty young men in front of the house, swaying and leaning on each other, some of them holding big flaming brands. They were loosely paying attention to someone who I couldn't see but who was, evidently, addressing them with his back to our front door.

'I'll shout down,' I said. 'This is intolerable.'

'No, no, Titus, you will do no such thing,' said Elizabeth, who was now at the other window. 'They could have those torches through our windows and burn this house in a minute.'

Immediately she was back under the covers.

'Come into bed, my love,' she whispered. 'Don't even let them see you. Anything might provoke them.'

'It's all right. They haven't seen me.'

But I did as she asked. Back in bed I lay still, trying to make out what their spokesman was saying, and which party the ruffians were supposedly standing behind. For a time this was impossible, so thick was the orator's tongue with drink. Then a remark came through more clearly, and I caught the meaning: he was lampooning Sir Henry Hoghton.

'What's Sir Harry need a Walpole for, eh?' we heard him proclaim. 'He doesn't, does he? 'Cause now, we hear, *he's got a great pole of his own*!'

This was greeted by howls of mirth and audible thigh slapping. After a few moments I could feel Elizabeth, too, shaking with laughter beside me.

*

I knew that, once we heard Luke Fidelis's evidence of the rat, the Allcroft inquest would be all about a possible poisoning. So I reckoned the jury should hear something about poisons in general, and a little in addition about poisons in Preston. Since Wilson was the obvious man for this, I had decided during the night I would definitely call him to give evidence. It would be of added interest to me to have the apothecary answering questions. How would he answer my suggestion that he might be the source of the poison in Allcroft's case? What would he say to the suggestion that he had already been the supplier of *atropinum* to unscrupulous men? Would he sweat, develop a tic in the face, stammer his replies? Or try to swagger his way out of it? From such telltale minutiae momentous matters turn.

On my way to interview Mrs Fitzpatrick at the Gamecock Inn, I therefore called at Wilson's shop to give him his summons. As he looked at it his mouth dropped open in surprise.

'What's this, Mr Cragg? Legal summons?'

'Yes, to attend the inquest on Mr John Allcroft who lately died at the Gamecock Inn.'

'What do I know about that?'

'I think you may know something, even if you don't know that you know it.'

A ray of understanding lit his face.

'Ah ha! There was that preparation Dr Fidelis sent down to me for that night. It was you yourself that came with the receipt, wasn't it, Mr Cragg?'

'Yes, it was me.'

'So that is what you want me to speak to the inquest about, no doubt. There was nothing amiss with it, I hope?'

'Not as far as I know, Mr Wilson,' I said cheerfully, content to leave him thinking he would be giving evidence purely on his skills as a mixer of medicines, and not his wider business activities as a purveyor of rat poison and other materials. 'Be there at ten in the morning, if you please.'

And so I left him.

The Gamecock Inn was recovering from a disorderly night. In the dining room some men took breakfast; others sprawled asleep, or sat and stared through bleary eyes, with cold pipes dangling from their fingers. On the other side of the hall, in the coffee room, groups of voters were beginning to come together in their tallies, ready for their appointments at the polling hall later in the day. Between outbursts of laughter and partisan singing, rolls were being called, and missing men enquired after.

In the office the innkeeper told me she could not spare a room for my inquest.

'It is not for today,' I explained, placing my coroner's requisition order on the table in front of her. 'The hearing is tomorrow. You do realize, don't you, that I have the power to insist, Mrs Fitzpatrick? This paper means you have to make a room available. I don't mind if it is your dining room, coffee room or dancing room, but you must let me have one of them.'

'I'll apply to the mayor—'

'The mayor has no authority in this matter. The coroner is a representative of the Crown, you know. I am not accountable to the corporation.'

She read through my order, written out in Furzey's prime legal hand. Then she planted her elbows on top of it and clapped her hands to her face.

'All right,' she said, when she'd rubbed her eyes. 'The assembly room upstairs. People have been sleeping there: I'll have to move them out.'

'Thank you. And here is something else for you.'

I now put the witness summons down on top of the room order. She glanced at it, and looked up at me in sudden fright.

'You want me to give evidence?'

'Of course. Mr Allcroft died under your roof, after eating one of your meals.'

'What'll I say?'

'Anything you know about Mr Allcroft and his end.'

'That's very little. He came last week, Tuesday. He said he'd have a gang of fellows out of Gregson coming at the weekend, and they'd need accommodation. They were all going to vote together, then go home, so he said. You were here with the doctor when he was taken sick, so you know as much as I do about that. And the next day when he was dead the family came and took him away, which I was very relieved about.'

'What happened to the gang of people he said were coming to join him?'

'They never came at all. I don't know why. We had three rooms set aside for them – not that I've had trouble filling them.'

'There, you see? It won't be too hard, giving evidence.'

Kathleen Fitzpatrick still looked suspiciously at me. She was a substantial figure in two senses: she was amply proportioned, but she was also a woman of authority, who knew well how to run a large inn like this. At least ten people worked for her every day, and she dealt astutely with her many suppliers. But appearing at a coroner's court was a very different matter – it was outside her own experience and its findings might put the business in danger. I was not surprised to find her wary of the process.

I mentioned that I needed to see Maggie Satterthwaite, Joe Primrose, and the boy Peterkin. Did I also have her warrant to go about the inn, look at the inquest room, and refresh my memory about Allcroft's bedroom?

'You'll find Joe and probably the boy in the kitchen. Go and look in the bedroom and the assembly room if you want, but then you'll wish you hadn't. Don't worry, I'll have it empty and clean by tomorrow morning.'

'And Maggie?'

'She doesn't work here now.'

'Oh? What happened?'

'She upped and left. I don't know why.'

So I went upstairs, to the bedrooms. These were on two floors, and ranged along a passage with a stair at each end – one an open oak staircase descending to the hall, the other a narrow, boxed-in servants' stair that led down to the kitchen and the courtyard.

The room in which Allcroft had died was at the far end of the second-floor corridor, the last before the entrance to the back stair. I tried the handle and found the door unlocked. It had been cleaned and reoccupied since I'd seen it last, and the new tenant was apparently another politician. He was not there but an open book lay on the bed, which I picked up. It was entitled *The Idea of a Patriot King* and a passage on the page that lay open had been heavily underscored:

> *To espouse no party, but to govern like the common father*
> *of his people, is so essential to the character of the Patriot*
> *King that he who does otherwise forfeits the title.*

A comment had been scratched in the margin: '*The true Charter of the Land!*'

Young Lord Strange would be delighted at this evidence that the ideas from *Alfred* were infecting the town. They were spreading like a genuine contagion.

Leaving the room, I walked the length of the passage from the back to the front stair, which I descended to the first floor. A man was sweeping the bedroom passage. This had fewer bedrooms than the floor above since a proportion of the area was occupied by the assembly or dancing room, which stretched across the width of the inn on the side overlooking Stoney Gate. This was to be the inquest room: I had a quick look inside to make sure of its suitability, but could see little in the gloom, except huddled shapes across the floor. The curtains were drawn and snores filled the fetid air, but it looked spacious enough for my purpose.

I walked the length of the passage again and dropped down the back stair to the kitchen. Joe Primrose must in the meantime have been told of the inquest – Mrs Fitzpatrick, I supposed – and he greeted me without surprise, and with the sunny lack of guile that was his hallmark.

'Give evidence? It's a good job you're not having this anywhere far away, Mr Cragg, as I do have dinner to prepare. But seeing as it is all on the premises, I shall be happy to oblige you.'

The kitchen boy Peterkin had been sent out to buy a bag of suet, but Primrose took his summons and promised to bring him to the inquest, by the ear if necessary.

When I walked out into Stoney Gate I had already served six of the eight summonses on my list, Fidelis having had his the night before. There remained Maggie and Isaac Satterthwaite to find. On a chance I turned left, away from Church Gate and towards the Grammar School, where as a lad I had struggled to construe Horace and suffered the tortures of Euclid. The lane on the left was Brewery Lane and on the opposite corner stood Drake's haberdashery.

Michael Drake, dressed for riding, had just come out and was locking his door. I approached.

'Mr Drake!' I called. 'I wonder if you have seen Isaac Satterthwaite today. I have a communication for him and would save myself the trouble of a ferry ride.'

Drake's eyes narrowed for a moment, and he shook his head. 'No, not seen him this morning.'

'Do you know if he is still engaged in destroying rats at Lacey's?'

'He's always engaged there, I am glad to say. The animals are a curse. They nest in my cloth. If Isaac did not continually attack them I'd be overrun.'

He made a move towards Brewery Lane and I accompanied him.

'Was it Thursday you last saw him – when I found you both at the brewery talking to Mr Lacey?'

'Aye, that would be it,' he said. He pushed open a gate that led into the yard of his premises. I saw a horse inside, saddled and waiting.

'Do you know when he inspects or resets his traps next door?'

'You'll have to ask Lacey that.'

'And you haven't seen him at Porter's? I know he regularly plays cards there.'

'Cards? No, I never seen him play cards. Now, I'd best be on my way. Good morning to you.'

I walked on to Lacey's and found the brewer supervising two apprentices as they scoured out a brewing tun, a process in which the boys climbed down naked into the vessel with brushes and buckets, watched from above by their master. I enquired after the rat catcher but Lacey, his eyes never leaving the two scourers, told me he had not seen him. Before leaving I strolled around the building, to the place where Satterthwaite had shown me his trapping technique the previous week. I crouched to look at the pipe in which he had rammed his doctored grain. It was now empty.

It was only after I returned past the shuttered haberdasher's that I wondered why Michael Drake had not opened for business today.

*

Less than an hour later Battersby deposited me on the southern shore of the river and I walked with rapid steps along the track to Satterthwaite's cottage. It was Maggie who answered my knock, her pretty face showing alarm when I handed her the summons, and told her what it was. Yet she asked me, with some grace, to step inside and we stood in the parlour, into which I had peered through the window on the previous day.

'You have lost your job, I hear.'

'Yes.'

'What happened?'

'I just wanted a change.'

'You mean after what happened to Allcroft?'

She looked down at her hands, that were clasped at her waist. I took her silence to mean yes.

'Are you living here with your grandfather now?'

'Yes.'

'You haven't found other work?'

'No. Why do you want to know all this?'

'Forgive me. I should put a check on my curiosity. Now, do you understand what this summons means? You are required to be at the inquest tomorrow morning and to answer the questions I put to you.'

'What sort of questions?'

'About what happened to Mr Allcroft. About the hotpot dinner that he ate. It will be nothing very different from what we talked about the other day in Market Place. You must not be afraid.'

'I won't be.'

'Excellent. Now, I need to see your grandfather. Do you know where he's working today?'

'He's not. He's having one of his voters' meetings. It'll keep him busy till evening. They'll be voting tomorrow.'

'Oh, yes?'

I took the election timetable from my pocket and we both inspected it. The Middleforth Green tallies, we saw, were due in front of the mayor at half past eleven on Wednesday morning. Voting took precedence over everything, and I knew my court wouldn't be able to hear his evidence until after that.

'Where are they meeting?'

'At Porter's.'

I looked at my watch. It was a quarter to eleven.

'I'll be on my way, then. Happen I'll catch him.'

Maggie walked with me to the gate.

As I passed through, I asked as casually as I could, 'Did your granddad play cards this last Sunday evening?'

'He told me no cards this week because of the performance at the theatre.'

'I didn't see him at the theatre.'

'He didn't go. Said it would only be a puff for the Tories, which I heard it was.'

'Mr Wilson went.'

'Mr Wilson is one that likes to have his prejudice confirmed.'

She was no fool, was Maggie.

'Who else played in your grandfather's regular card games, apart from Thomas Wilson?'

'It was just four. They played four-handed crib. There was Mr Reynolds, you know, and—'

'Reynolds? You don't mean the candidate for Parliament?'

'Yes, him. And the other one was usually Mr Drake, that has the haberdasher's shop in Stoney Gate.'

Well, I thought, as I walked back towards the ferry, it's been a proper little nest of Whigs, this game of four-hand cribbage. And Michael Drake had denied all knowledge of it.

Battersby was loading up on the far bank and I had to wait

for him. So it took me twenty minutes to get back across the river and another ten to complete the uphill walk to Fisher Gate. All the time my head was buzzing with questions. Why had Drake lied to me about the card game? And what about Reynolds – had he also been present on the night Antony Egan died? Satterthwaite knew the answers, but they would have to wait. If I brought that up now I would confuse it with the matter of the Allcroft inquest, which had to remain uppermost and separate.

I pushed my way into the inn on Fisher Gate. Porter must never have known such business: a brim-full apple barrel would have had more space to spare. I forced my way through the press to the landlord, who directed me to the adjoining room, a smaller one sometimes used for private dining parties. Going through I found at the least three groups of men distributed the length of the refectory table, quaffing, arguing and laughing, some sitting, others standing around them. One end of the table was occupied by a distinctive group of carousers, one or two of whom I recognized as coming from south of the river. At their head sat Isaac Satterthwaite.

A heavily built member of the company had stood ponderously up to render 'Fill Every Glass' in a deep, almost a growling voice. Satterthwaite was listening intently, and tapping his hand on the table in time. I touched him on the shoulder.

'Hello, Isaac. May I have a quiet word?'

He twisted in his chair and shushed me with a finger to his lips. I waited out the song. Later, we retired through an inner door, which gave onto the foot of the stairs. I handed him the summons and the rat catcher looked it quickly over.

'What does this mean? Tomorrow – attend the inquest into John Allcroft? What has this matter got to do with me?'

'We want to tap your expert knowledge.'

'About what?'

'I can't say any more. This summons requires you to attend as a witness, but I know that your tally will be voting, which takes precedence. May I ask you, immediately after you have polled, to come to the Gamecock Inn, where the inquest will be in progress?'

Satterthwaite grunted what might have been his assent, folded the paper, slipped it into his coat pocket and brushed past me as he went back to the dining room to rejoin his colleagues. I did not take exception to his curtness. My chance to hear him speak would come tomorrow.

Rather than force my way through the crowded rooms towards the street door, I went out by the rear and found myself in the dark and crooked alley that joined Fisher Gate with Theatre Lane. I turned left and began to make my way towards the light but was soon impeded by a stationary cart left unattended. As I edged with difficulty past it a figure slipped out from the black shadow of a doorway up ahead and barred my path. He was holding something like a cudgel or bat. A hat pulled low over his face made him impossible to identify.

'What do you want, fellow?' I called out in as commanding a voice as I could muster. I was now standing at bay, between the shafts of the parked cart. This meant it was impossible for me to take to my heels, and bluff defiance seemed the only stratagem remaining to me.

'To crack your head, Mr Lawyer.'

The voice was extraordinarily gruff.

'Why would you want to do that?'

I was expecting this to be a simple robbery, the town being full of strangers and some of them undoubtedly desperate.

'That's not for you to know.'

'You could have my purse instead. What is the need for violence? I cannot recognize you, so you will be quite safe getting away.'

I reached into my pocket for the purse and showed it to him.

'Give it over,' the man snarled, raising his weapon high. 'Throw it down, and then take your payment from this stick.'

A tremor of fear like a sudden chill seized me. Whatever I did, it seemed I was not going to escape the promised beating. I took a step backwards until I was pressed against the cart. My assailant advanced by the same distance, still brandishing his club and breathing out a mixture of sour beer and tobacco smoke.

At that moment he emitted a sound – 'Oof!' – and shot forward, cannoning into me. His weapon missed my head and smacked down on the cart. He was so obviously surprised by whatever had impelled him from behind that I had more than enough time to drive my knee into his groin, causing him to emit an exquisite yelp. I grabbed his arm and brought it down two or three times on the cart's tailgate until he dropped the cudgel. The next moment a hand grasped his collar and jerked him away from me. There was a tussle, punches were thrown, and all of a sudden the attacker was staggering away, pushing past the cart and going down the alley at a run, his silhouette shrinking in perspective as the clatter of his footfall died away.

'Hello, Titus. Are you well?'

Luke Fidelis was peering at me in the gloom.

'Quite well, thank you, Luke,' I answered. 'But I am obliged to you. I would not be very well at all, had you not come along.'

'I was passing and happened to look down the alley, where I saw the raised club. So I investigated further. Of course, I did not know it was you under attack until I pushed him in the back and recognized your startled face as he crashed into you. Who was the man?'

'I have no idea, but I have the feeling that it was not a chance encounter. He was sent to do me harm. Are you free? I would like to buy you a drink.'

We entered the Grapes, an inn on Fisher Gate less rowdy than the one I had just left.

I picked up the jug of wine as soon as it was placed on the table between us and poured. Then I looked at my friend and opened my mouth to speak. Before I could do so he smartly raised his hand.

'If what you are about to say concerns a certain young lady's confidence to you, I do not want to hear it. I have had your letter and I accept what it says. Now I want to forget all about it. I do not want it to disturb our friendship any further.'

'As if nothing had happened, then?'

'Yes.'

I raised my glass in a toast.

'I will say amen to that.'

He raised his glass in answer.

'Amen, and there's an end.'

'So, you will come with me after dinner to collect the exhumed corpse of John Allcroft from Hoghton?'

Suddenly Fidelis's eyes were sparkling.

'A pleasant afternoon ride in the country – what could be better?'

Chapter Twenty

∞

I T WAS GETTING on for five o'clock when Fidelis and I rode through the Church Gate bar and up towards the division of the road between the way that ran directly east towards the small settlement at Longridge, and the bridge road that turned south, crossed the Ribble and divided again, one way continuing to Wigan and the south, the other sweeping away east towards Hoghton.

Peter Wintly's cart, not being an especially sporting vehicle, had trundled off for Hoghton a couple of hours in advance in order not to be late to the graveyard. Fidelis and I on our horses came up to it 3 miles beyond Bamber and rode on ahead. We could get the exhumation started while Wintly caught up.

As we rode on we played catch-up of another kind.

'You heard, did you, that Shackleberry and Andrews have run away?' I asked.

'Yes.'

'They will be put in the stocks if they come back.'

'And I shall be there with a sack of bad turnips. You said in your note that you had made progress with Destercore's mysterious list. The names picked out with a dot, wasn't it?'

'Yes. All were people the Whigs believed would be Tory tally captains – resident freemen, and out-freemen.'

I told him how Allcroft's wife had characterized her husband

– as a leader of men, a determined and vigorous opponent of the Whigs.

'The sort of man whom, if the Whigs wanted to damage the Tory cause and didn't mind how they did it, they might have thoughts of getting out of the way,' mused Fidelis.

'As they might Nick Oldswick, and he was threatened.'

'But your wife's uncle is dead too, and he doesn't fit the type. He was not very formidable', mused Fidelis.

We tossed ideas back and forth as to whether and how Antony Egan's doubtful death might be connected with the election. On Mary-Ann's evidence he had spoken loudly about following Allcroft's example and drumming up a tally of local freemen to vote against the Whigs, but he would hardly be a principal target for the machinations of Destercore and his faction, though he was, of course, an easy one.

We had now crossed the bridge, and reached the fork in the road. As we took the left-hand way we passed a windmill, standing alone by the side of the road. It had long since stopped turning; the canvas of the sails was rotted and hung down in rags, the skeleton round which they had been wrapped exposed like the bones of a half-picked trout. All at once the front door of the mill opened and the figure of a man stood there, looking out with a certain expectancy to left and right.

'Good God! What is he doing here?' exclaimed Fidelis.

The fellow had gone back inside and I had seen little more than a tall man: my vision at a distance was not as sharp as my friend's.

'You recognized him?' I asked.

'Wasn't it the man Peters, Destercore's servant?'

'Was it? I doubt it. You must be mistaken.'

We left it at that and, for the time being, I forgot all about Fidelis's doubtful sighting. It was seven by the church clock when we rode into the parish, and then the village, of Hoghton, where Allcroft was buried. After the outright defiance of his widow the previous day, I had expected to meet resistance against the exhumation of her husband, which is why I had written to the parish constable, William Blenkinsop, seeking his assistance. He met us at the lychgate.

He was a little over thirty, and had a serious, even ponderous manner. I was glad that he was not one of those constables too old to run after a thief and too poor-sighted to recognize him afterwards.

'Susan Allcroft is a very determined woman, Mr Cragg,' he told Fidelis and me. 'If she does not want this exhumation, she will do all in her power to stop it.'

'Which is why we are glad you are here, Mr Blenkinsop, to maintain order and allow us to do our duty.'

'I have my deputy with me. We'll do our best.'

'Is the sexton here also?'

Allcroft's grave lay on the far side of the graveyard from the gate. All there was to see was a bed of freshly turned earth, sodden from the earlier rain, with as yet no headstone. We found the sexton beside the grave, leaning on a long-handled spade. There was no sign of anybody else.

'We have an hour of light,' I said. 'Let us get the job done.'

The sexton began to dig, with such energy as would have exhausted me in five minutes. But he plied his spade continuously for twenty, and had got down to a depth of about 4 feet when we heard a cry from the direction of the lychgate.

'Stop! Desecration! Blasphemy! Stop *at once*.'

Mrs Allcroft was running towards us through the gathering gloom, with two young women barely out of childhood trailing behind and wearing canvas cloaks with hoods. A white spaniel ran in closer pursuit, yapping at her mistress's billowing clothing.

Arriving at the graveside, the widow looked down at the sexton, and then up at the constable and his deputy, while she caught her breath. She was barely able to contain her fury.

'William Blenkinsop, this is an outrage. I hope you will put a stop to the coroner's unwarranted intrusion into my late husband's resting place.'

The spaniel was still yapping as Blenkinsop produced a piece of paper bearing my signature, which he showed to her.

'Madam, it is not unwarranted. This is Mr Cragg's very warrant and it is legally binding. We must proceed.'

'You shan't. Daughters, into your father's grave!'

Giving each other an anxious look, but not daring to disobey their mother, the two girls sat on the side of the grave and let themselves down beside the sexton, their lightweight shoes half disappearing into the wet earth. They stood awkwardly, one on each side of him, unsure what to do next. Pointing with her finger, their mother told them what she expected.

'Down, girls! Lie down! The sexton shall not dig this sacred earth. Lie down and impede him!'

It sounded as though she was talking to the dog, and indeed the spaniel did make a move to jump down too, but the sexton aimed a swipe at her with his spade and she sprang out of the way.

Susan Allcroft shook both her fists and stamped her foot.

'You dig up my husband and now you try to kill my dog. Lie down, daughters. We shall prevent this iniquity. Your father's great soul shall not be disturbed.'

Then she was bending to pet the dog, giving her a sugar lump from her pocket.

'Poor little Polly-dog. Did the horrible man frighten you?'

Incredibly, to my eyes, the Allcroft girls did at this point lie down, forcing the sexton to come out of the grave, for lack of anywhere to stand without stepping on them.

'Mrs Allcroft,' I protested. 'This is very undignified. Surely it is abusing your young daughters to make them act like this.'

'I wish I had my son Jotham here, sir. He would break your nose for you. Since he is occupied with business in town, I must manage with the forces that I have.'

Polly-dog had lost interest in us and was running in a wide arc around the graves, her tongue lolling. At this moment, a mangy, half-starved village mongrel appeared, who began joyously loping after Polly-dog and sniffing her rear end.

Blenkinsop addressed himself to the daughters.

'Please, young ladies, come out of there. It is unseemly.'

'Unseemly!' spat back the widow. 'What you do is unseemly. Say that you will desist at once, and I will let them come out.'

But now Susan Allcroft's attention, previously so fixed, became fatally divided. She caught in the corner of her eye the where-abouts of her spaniel, and immediately swivelled in horror at what she saw. The mongrel and Polly-dog had stopped running and were circling each other with unmistakable intent.

Mrs Allcroft hesitated. She glanced at her recumbent daughters, then looked anxiously back at the canine pair, who were at least 35 yards away. In the same moment the black mongrel planted his front paws on Polly-dog's back and waddled on his hind legs up to her rear. With his tongue out and teeth showing in a devilish grin he started to couple with her.

'No, Polly-dog! No!'

Faced with the ravishment of her pet by the village cur Mrs Allcroft temporarily forgot the prime purpose of her visit to the graveyard and set off, running again, towards the dogs. She was waving her arms and screaming at the spaniel to stop, but Polly-dog took no notice. Indeed, she showed every sign of enjoying herself keenly.

Fidelis crouched down beside the grave.

'My dear young ladies, your mother's looking the other way,' he said. 'I am sure you would rather be anywhere but here. So which of you will be the first to take my hand and be pulled out of there?'

The three parish officers were watching Mrs Allcroft and laughing and nudging each other at the sight. She had taken off a glove and was thrashing at the mongrel with it as she uttered a rhythmical string of curses. The poor brute would no doubt have liked to disengage but now, it seemed, he was not able. Polly-dog had somehow locked him inside her and the two animals could do nothing but circle around, their passion spent, in an exhausted parody of a country dance.

Meanwhile the Allcroft girls had been pulled from the grave. I was surprised at how little fear, or horror, they showed. Each had some work brushing the worst of the mud off the other and then they hurried away, not yet wanting to face their mother.

'Sexton!' I called and the man, still chuckling, returned to his spadework, while Fidelis strode over towards Mrs Allcroft and the struggling dogs. He knelt and reached towards Polly-dog's back-side. He made some manipulation with his fingers, and at once the mongrel sprang free.

'Bad Polly-dog!' The dog squealed at the rap on the nose she got from her owner. 'Dr Fidelis! How clever you are. How can I thank you? Bad dog!'

Fidelis picked up Polly-dog and tucked her under his arm. He gave her owner a slight bow, crooked his other arm for her to take and the two of them strolled back to us by a roundabout route. Superficially they might have been enjoying a polite afternoon in Preston's place of genteel recreation, Avenham Walk, but I could see that Fidelis was speaking rapidly to the woman. By the time they arrived at the graveside, the sexton had almost dug down to the coffin. Susan Allcroft's eyes were damp as she took back the dog.

She looked down into the dark slot of the grave, shuddered, and produced a handkerchief.

'Dr Fidelis has convinced me, in the nicest way possible, that I have made myself ridiculous. So I shall follow my daughters home now. There is nothing more I can do to stop this infamy, except to ask you please not to treat my husband with barbarism.'

Before she left I reminded her of the inquest.

'It starts at ten o'clock. I would be most obliged if you would be punctual.'

She did not reply, but turned smartly and marched away, with a chastened Polly-dog trotting behind. Mrs Allcroft might have been charmed by Dr Fidelis, but she did not like me at all.

'How did you unplug the dog? Some trick?'

We were riding back towards Preston as escort to the cart on which John Allcroft's coffin was being transported.

'Something I learned many years ago.'

'Which was?'

'You stick your finger in the bitch's arse, and she just lets go.'

'Why would she?'

'Well, wouldn't you?'

In Preston's streets the fire of election excitement had not died with the fall of night. The darkness flared here and there in torch-light as groups of men rampaged from one rowdy alehouse to the next, and the air resounded near and far with the human voice in all of its more extreme registers.

I had made arrangements with the churchwarden to lodge our body in the vestry. Having done so, I locked all doors, and gave instructions to the nightwatchman standing guard. Then Luke and I strolled past the Moot Hall and down Fisher Gate towards his lodging. On our right we passed a bakery and pastry shop, whose sign creaked in the wind. It showed a crusty round pie, with the words *WILKINSON FINEST BREAD AND PIES*.

'Our victim's brother-in-law's shop.'

'Is that where the son Jotham works?'

'Yes. They do a roaring trade with the election, I have heard.'

A minute later we reached the Lorrises' door and said good-night.

It had not been easy to assemble a full jury with all the other distractions to contend with. Furzey had found just seven men prepared to serve and with that we had to make do. I swore them in, invited them to choose a foreman, and then opened the proceedings by making a brief summary of the known facts. After this I trooped them outside and we made the short walk to the vestry, where I uncovered Allcroft's body for the nine to see.

'It's an horrible sight, is that,' said Gerald Pikeroyd, who had been chosen foreman. He put his hand to his nose.

'I'm not touching him, Mr Cragg,' protested Jack Barlow, hanging back. 'I'm not catching the sickness off him.'

'You don't have to touch, Jack,' I reassured him. 'You do your duty just by looking.'

'Did anyone know the man?' Pikeroyd asked.

'I knew of him,' said John Mort.

'I know his lad,' said Charley Booth. 'Jotham, who helps at his uncle's pie shop – his mother's brother's.'

'Good pies they make.'

'Allcroft was a hog farmer, see?' said Booth. 'Meat comes direct from him to the shop.'

'Does Jotham not like farming, that he works in the pie shop?' Martin Ware asked.

'Or does he not like his father?' put in Julius Treadwell.

'Or the old man not like *him*?' This was Booth. 'He sent him in the army as a fusilier. Now the boy's come back, but he still denied to have him at home.'

'They say,' said Edward Lillycrap, darkly, 'it's because Jotham's not his son.'

'Who says that, Edward?' I asked.

Lillycrap shrugged and shook his head.

'It's just something I heard.'

'You shouldn't be passing on unsubstantiated gossip. You are a jury, trying to reach a true verdict. Please be good enough to act like one.'

Lillycrap was chastened.

'Sorry, Mr Cragg,' he said.

'So do we find anything about this body that we should take note of?'

By now the jurymen were slowly circling the table on which the body lay.

'It stinks,' said John Mort.

'Like a drain,' agreed Jack Barlow.

'It's an horrible colour.'

'It looks angry.'

This was Julius Treadwell.

'You'd be angry, Julius, if you died like that.'

'But what I mean is, if we knew what he was angry at, it might help us.'

'Well, we don't, so it can't.'

'I'll tell you what I've heard,' said Mort, 'which is that he was very quick to take against folk. What I mean is, he was a great hater, and I'll tell you summat else.'

Mort paused, to give his information more dramatic effect.

'Go on, John,' prompted Pikeroyd.

Mort jabbed his finger towards the body.

'They say he hated no one more than Sir Harry Hoghton.'

'What for?'

Mort shrugged.

'Don't know. Happen it'll come out, though, in time.'

I could see there was little to be gained by prolonging the viewing.

Back in the courtroom I launched the proceedings by calling the dead man's wife to give evidence. She sat in the witness chair in a posture of reluctance, even of resistance.

'Mrs Allcroft, thank you for attending,' I said. 'You live in Gregson, do you not?'

She nodded.

'Can you tell me when your husband came into Preston, and for what purpose?'

'It's no secret. He came Tuesday of last week. He had brought together a tally of freemen voters for the election and he was in town to make certain arrangements beforehand.'

'What arrangements?'

'I couldn't say. As you men know, we women have little appreciation of politics.'

'Well, do you have enough to know which interest your husband's tally was voting for?'

'That is no secret. It was in the Tory interest.'

'For Mr Fazackerley and Mr Shuttleworth?'

'Yes.'

'And now, I must ask you to think carefully, because my next is an important question. Was your husband in good health when he left home?'

'Yes, of course he was.'

'Are you quite sure of that?'

'He was laughing and singing and waving his hat as he rode away. Do you not think that is a sign of health?'

The audience tittered. It was made up of no more than thirty inquisitive townspeople, who included, as I noted, the ever-present Miss Colley.

'Thank you, Mrs Allcroft,' I said. 'You may get down.'

Next I called Mrs Fitzpatrick, and picked up the story where Mrs Allcroft had left off.

'Do you recall Mr Allcroft's arrival at the inn?' I asked.

'Yes, sir. We had the room ready that his son had been in the week before to secure.'

'We have heard Mrs Allcroft describe his state when leaving home. Would you say he was in as rude health when he arrived here?'

'He was a pleasant, courteous gentleman.'

'With respect, that does not answer my question.'

'Yes, it does. He was agreeable company, which a sick man never is. That's why I don't think Mr Allcroft was sick when he first came.'

I accepted this with a nod.

'So when *did* he fall sick?'

'Next day, the afternoon.'

'After his hotpot dinner, which he had taken in his room?'

'There was nothing wrong with his hotpot. I've told you that before, Mr Cragg.'

'So you have, Mrs Fitzpatrick. But is the chronology right?'

'The time, sir? Yes, afternoon was when he felt poorly. He had been out but he returned to the inn and took to his bed. He was vomiting and worse.'

'When did you become aware of this?'

'Our kitchen boy was passing his door. He heard him groaning and made report to me.'

'You mean Peterkin, who is here to give his evidence this morning?'

'Yes. It was early in the evening. I went up to investigate and opened the door.'

'It wasn't locked?'

'It wouldn't lock, sir. The key had been lost some weeks since. A guest rode away with it in his pocket.'

'So you went in, and . . . ?'

'Oh, it was a horrible sight. He was rolling around on his bed and clutching his stomach and making horrible complaining noises. And the air in the room was, well, it made my own stomach turn over, I can tell you.'

'What did you do?'

'Nothing except open the windows and go down to Dr Fidelis who I'd seen come in with yourself. As you know, I asked him to take a look at Mr Allcroft.'

'Do you have anything to add concerning your guest falling so suddenly sick?'

'No, sir, I can't account for it except I swear there was nothing wrong with the hotpot.'

I let her go, asked Joe Primrose to take the stand and, after he was sworn in, raised the question of the hotpot.

'This is a dish of high repute in town, is it not?'

Primrose's ever-cheerful face beamed.

'Yes, Mr Cragg, it is that.'

'How do you make it?'

'Good long stewing, sir, in the cool oven, that's my secret.'

'I mean, what do you put into it?'

Primrose counted the items off on his fingers – shin of mutton, kidney of same, carrots, potatoes, onion, sage and oatmeal.

I stopped him there.

'Is oatmeal the only cereal you use in your hotpot?'

'Yes, sir.'

'No other grain?'

'I've known other grains to be put in, sir, but oatmeal will thicken just as well as anything, and it's what I prefer.'

I asked him about how Allcroft's dinner had been served, and he described how he had plated and covered it and given it to Maggie on a tray with a jug of beer.

'Is that the last you saw of it, when Maggie Satterthwaite took it from the kitchen?'

'Yes, we were that busy, I thought no more about it after.'

'And you served other portions of the same stew on that day?'

'I did, many another.'

'Did you hear of any other diner becoming sick afterwards?'

'I did not. Not a single complaint.'

I let Primrose down, and called Maggie. She came to the stand looking pretty, in bright clothes, freshly laundered: every inch the May Queen. I asked her to describe what happened when she'd carried Allcroft's meal to his room.

'The room was empty, and very messy. I put down the tray on his table and did a little to put the room to rights. But it would've taken too long to do it proper, so I gave up and went down to look for him. But I was called to another customer so I asked Peterkin to go and find Mr Allcroft and tell him his dinner was ready for him.'

'Had you interfered with the dinner in any way, between taking it from Mr Primrose and leaving it behind in the room?'

'No, I never even looked at it.'

'So you didn't see anything go into it – some contamination, I mean?'

'Some what, sir?'

'Some impurity, that shouldn't be there.'

'No, there were nowt like that. The stew plate were topped with a cover, to keep the food warm and flies out. Like I said, I never even lifted it.'

Now Peterkin stepped up and like any good kitchen boy proved himself pert and wholly unafraid of adults. He gave his evidence in a clear piping voice: that on Maggie's bidding he had sought out Mr Allcroft in the coffee room; that he had been deep in discussion with a few other gentlemen; that he said he would go up shortly; and that he had then continued his discussion, waving Peterkin away.

'Did anyone else in the room hear what you and Mr Allcroft said to each other?'

'They might've sir, easy. I don't know they did, though.'

'And did you later see Mr Allcroft go upstairs?'

'No, sir. But I went in the coffee room twenty minutes later, and he was gone then.'

So far the room had listened closely enough to the succession of witnesses, but there had been little to excite their interest. That was about to change.

'I call Dr Luke Fidelis,' I said.

There was a rustle of clothing as the female members of the audience craned to catch a good sight of the handsome doctor. Fidelis took his place in the chair with composure, and once Furzey had administered the oath, adopted a slightly forward-leaning posture, as one completely attentive to his interlocutor.

I asked him to describe the squalid condition in which he had found Allcroft that night and, having heard him out, asked what he had thought the matter with the patient might be.

'I considered in the first place it was most likely some contagion, as there was fever present, with vomiting, loose bowels and intense thirst. But these were also consonant with poisoning, so that was the other possibility I considered.'

'Just so that we are all clear, what do you mean by contagion and by poisoning?'

'By contagion I mean a disease passed by touch from one person to another.'

'Only by touch?'

'That is the strict meaning of the word. It has been used by some learned doctors for diseases that are transmitted through the air by means of steams or effluvia arising from a person already sick.'

'Thank you, doctor. Will you tell us, then, what poisoning is?'

'Poisoning is the ingestion of something noxious, to the point of sickness and perhaps death.'

'Must it be given deliberately to harm?'

'No, not necessarily. There is a general misapprehension that poisoning is the same as murder, or attempted murder. It is not. It can be by accident, and may even occur without the agency of a deliberate human hand – as, for instance, when a bucket of white lime falls into a well.'

'I see. Now, in the case of Mr Allcroft, did you resolve the issue?'

'Eventually I did.'

'On what side: that of contagion, or poison?'

'Poison, either from the hotpot he had eaten for his dinner, or the beer he had drunk.'

On hearing this word pronounced the audience buzzed with comment. Suddenly what had seemed a rather humdrum inquiry was turning into a possibly sensational one.

'And how exactly did you resolve it?'

'With the help of a healthy rat called Athene.'

For a moment the audience and jury were struck silent, not knowing what to make of this. Then a sniggering and whispering was heard around the room. Was the doctor jesting?

'That sounds most unusual,' I said. 'Please tell us more.'

Fidelis recounted in detail how he had reserved samples of the food and beer Allcroft had taken for his dinner; how he had then conducted the experiment on Athene, first by giving her the beer and then the stew; and how the rat had expired on the spot after eating the stew.

'And what did you conclude from this trial?'

'That the beer was good, but the stew was poisoned.'

This bald statement brought a collective gasp from the public section of the audience. I raised my hand to subdue the murmuring that followed.

'Poisoned with what?'

'There's a number of vegetable and mineral poisons that it could be. What I can say is that anyone who ate it, even a few mouthfuls, would have fallen violently ill and, depending on the quantity swallowed, might have died.'

'Which you suggest was the case with Mr Allcroft?'

'Yes, if he ate his dinner.'

'You quite rule out contagion?'

'What happened to the rat does that for me.'

'And did you examine the stew itself?'

'Yes.'

'Did you find anything unusual?'

'I found it contained barleycorns.'

'Barleycorns?'

'Yes.'

For the benefit of the court, which was now hanging on Fidelis's every word, I pretended to be puzzled.

'Barleycorns are not poisonous. Did you not find any poison?'

'I did not. To separate the poisonous ingredient from the rest of the ingredients, not least the gravy with which it must have combined, is beyond my powers, or those of any man so far as I know. However I do recognize a barleycorn when I see one.'

'But why did you find these barleycorns a surprising ingredient?'

'At the time I did not. But now that I have heard Mr Primrose's testimony, denying that his hotpot stew contained any grains other than oatmeal, I am surprised that I found some.'

No one, except myself and Fidelis, understood where this was leading, though by this stage everyone in the room wanted to know.

I released Fidelis and immediately recalled Primrose.

'Mr Primrose, consider yourself still under oath. Can you account for the presence of this barley that Dr Fidelis found in your hotpot?'

Primrose was looking confused. His usual laughing demeanour was replaced by a guarded expression, a suspicion that he was about to be accused of some dark misdeed, though he couldn't be sure what it might be.

'No, Mr Cragg, I can't. As I said before, I don't use it in stew. But there wouldn't be any harm, would there? I mean, if there *was* barley in it? It's a healthy food, is barley.'

'Yes, Mr Primrose, as far as I know it is. But do you use it for anything else in your kitchen? I mean, do you keep a stock of it?'

'I do from time to time, yes, but it is a dear enough grain and we would never use it much.'

'So might some barleycorns, let's say from your excellent storeroom – which as you know I have seen – have got into the stewpot accidentally?'

'I don't see how. And I would have noticed. I was serving it out all dinner time. I would have noticed.'

'Very well. Let us merely note at this stage how we have heard that the stew eaten by Mr Allcroft contained barleycorns, and that this was unusual. Now, I wish to call Mr Isaac Satterthwaite. Is he present?'

I looked around the room for the witness. There was no Isaac Satterthwaite. Looking at my watch I saw that it was twenty-five past eleven and realized that, if the vote was going according to timetable, he would be on his way to the polling hall with his tally. I whispered to Furzey.

'How long does it take a tally to go through polling?'

Furzey shrugged.

'An hour maybe. It depends if there are challenges from the recording officer. The Tory voters get through quicker, because the mayor gives them the nod. The Whigs, of course, are questioned like gypsies.'

I turned back to the court and rapped the table with my gavel.

'Mr Satterthwaite is, I believe, attending to his duties as a voter in the present election. I understand he will be available later. I shall therefore reconvene this hearing at two o'clock, when I hope we can hear him. Jurors, in the meantime keep your wits about you. Have your dinners, but no strong drink, and no idle gossip please. Adjourned.'

I gavelled the table again and Furzey intoned the order to rise. The court stood and, as I made my way out of the room, I could hear some of the remarks being made in the audience, as they strained to understand why I was calling the rat catcher to give evidence. There were murmurs suggesting I must be up to something.

But as I passed I heard Miss Colley confidently assert, 'Mr Cragg knows what he is doing, you may depend upon it.'

That was heartening. Unfortunately, I did not yet know what others were doing, and in that lay the downfall of my plans.

Chapter Twenty-one

As I left the inn, I found the air had thickened and, just then, a growl of thunder rolled around the sky like a loose cannon-ball on a moving deck. I was on my way to see how things stood in the voting, and to make sure that Satterthwaite would be able to give his evidence in the afternoon. At the Moot Hall I found that his tally had not yet appeared before the mayor, so I went on towards Porter's. I had made only a few yards along Fisher Gate when I was stopped by Nick Oldswick. He had heard report of the testimony given during the morning, and was agitated about it.

'Cragg, is it true John Allcroft was poisoned? The word is flying round town that the Whigs had Allcroft killed to stop his votes from registering – that would have made a dozen votes lost for Fazackerley and Shuttleworth. I call it an outrage.'

I did my best to damp this speculation down, saying the jury had yet to decide if there was anything deliberate about Allcroft's death and even if there was, the motive would still need settling.

'Fiddlesticks,' he cried. 'Everybody knows why Allcroft came here. He thought Sir Henry Hoghton a scoundrel, which is an opinion I see no reason to disagree with. And I never thought I'd see the day that a man should die because of his vote. These Whigs are blackguards.'

I walked on through a light drizzle of rain to Porter's, where I found the place still boiling with people, and plenty of beer being swilled in both the larger and smaller rooms. But on inspection I saw there was more coherence in the room than chaos. The large smoking room was subdivided much like a sheep market into little folds, in each of which was a group of men. They wore the usual party favours, rosettes and the like, and were being served drink from a tray carried by a serving girl. Each little flock had its sheep-dog, the tally captain, who worried around them, keeping them in a group, lecturing them when they looked as if they would get out of hand, leading them in songs and rousing toasts: 'Pretender to Perdition!' 'Up With the Land Tax!' A trumpet band was playing to the room on a raised platform. They had by now learned the music of 'Rule Britannia!', for it was being performed as I walked in. Someone had enterprisingly had the words printed on a broadsheet, copies of which were distributed around the room. With these to hand, the sing-along was deafening and joyous.

I stepped onto a bench to get a better view. Almost at once I saw the tall, white-haired figure of Isaac Satterthwaite. The rat catcher was being a very active collie to his flock. He patrolled the perimeter of their fold continually, having words in their ears as he passed, and occasionally stopping to address them as a group. I could see his determination that every man should go through the polling bar as efficiently as sheep through the tick bath. He was determined, that is, that every vote he had would be cast, at the very least; whether or not all would be allowed by the mayor was another matter.

I was considering how best to approach him when a loud call for attention cut through the general noise. It came from Denis Destercore, who had mounted the orchestra dais, shushed the musicians and now faced the room with his watch in one hand and a sheaf of papers in the other.

'Mr Satterthwaite! Bring forward your men, if you please.'

The rat catcher's voting detail pushed through the throng and out into the street. I followed them.

The rain was falling a shade more steadily as they formed up in the street. The change of weather had not yet chased people indoors and excited groups of onlookers still swarmed all over Fisher Gate. But the tally would be making plenty of noise to clear their path, being led all the way up the slope to Moot Hall by a bugler and a drummer. On the other hand any such martial music would likely attract the enemy, so a posse of young men was to march alongside the group with cudgels, to repel any attack. This protection was certainly desirable. Several of Satterthwaite's men were either old or sickly, one had a wooden leg and one was being carried by four of the able-bodied ones in a chair.

The drummer began to beat a marching time, the bugler joined in, and they were off. Keeping pace, I saw a few obstructors being pushed intemperately out of the way. Walking immediately behind the drummer, Satterthwaite was visibly the leader; his head constantly moved this way and that, alive to any threat. As we passed Lorris's house, I glanced up. Fidelis had returned home and I saw him leaning on the sill of his open window to watch. I was about to give him a wave when my attention was drawn back to the street. For now an animal roar was heard from a side alley and a band of five or six men broke cover to rush at the voters, waving heavy sticks.

As battle was joined, a bolt of lightning streaked across the sky, and a crash of thunder followed. Now the men were cudgel to cudgel: heads and bodies were clubbed, ribs were cracked, noses and scalps bled. With his protective screen engaged in this way, Satterthwaite ran past the faltering bugler and drummer, and turned to face his voters, hammering one fist again and again into its opposite palm, yelling at them purple faced to keep going. They responded with a defiant cheer and were on the move again. It was obvious as he bustled them along that their captain's only thought was for the objective, which was now less than 50 yards away. As an old soldier, perhaps he ought to have known better than to press on without protection; perhaps he ought to have sensed that the first attack was only a diversion, designed to crack off the flanking defenders like a shell and expose the soft inner body to the tip of someone's sword.

The second group of attackers gave even less warning than the first. They burst silently from an alley on the opposite side of the street, just as the rain began perceptibly to increase. As soon as he saw them bearing down on him, the bugler panicked and ran for his life, but the drummer, encumbered with his instrument, was caught. His drum was quickly punctured and sent rolling away, while its owner was forced to the ground where he received a summary kicking.

Meanwhile the ten members of the tally itself were having mixed fortunes. The able-bodied, including the four chair carriers, had taken to their heels, while the sick and doddery were taking whatever came to them. The one-legged fellow had his peg snapped like a twig, and the chair-bound one was pitched out of it onto the cobbles while work was begun on reducing his chair to matchwood.

A few of the public, including myself, started forward to intervene but were repulsed, as much by threats as fists. Satterthwaite, still in the midst of the melee, was now the focus of the assault. He had picked up a bit of the splintered chair and was beating one of his attackers frenziedly around the shoulders. When another of them leapt on his back, he roared like a sightless Samson and spun around and around, hacking blindly back over his shoulders with the chair spar to dislodge the man. At last he did so and flung him off, then looked around in despair for any remnant of his tally. There was none and seconds later his attackers had melted away even more suddenly than they'd appeared, their work complete. Another crack of lightning ripped the sky with a sound that might have been a second peg leg splintering, but much magnified.

Suddenly I saw Satterthwaite stagger and fall. I ran forward and knelt at his side, trying to see what the matter was. It seemed he had struck his head on the cobbles, for he was unconscious. I patted his rain-spattered cheeks and called his name for a moment, but found no response. Then I was aware of another figure kneeling on his other side, taking Satterthwaite's wrist between his fingers.

'It's no use, Titus,' said Fidelis in a low voice. 'I think you'll find he is dead.'

I stared at him.

'Don't be daft,' I said. 'He's just knocked out by the fall.'

Fidelis shook his head firmly.

'There's no pulse. He probably died on his feet.'

'I still say he might be only—'

'No, Titus, that's why you should always have a doctor by your side. You don't know a sleeping man from a dead one.'

As I surveyed the stretched-out form of Isaac Satterthwaite I was conscious that the fighting had now stopped as suddenly as it had started, and that the attackers' object had been achieved. Satterthwaite's tally of voters, even as their leader was falling, had been routed and dispersed.

'I didn't see what happened. He must have been taken with a sudden apoplexy . . . all that excitement. Or – wait a minute – wasn't there a flash of lightning? Perhaps he was struck. An act of God.'

Although it was raining quite heavily now, a curious crowd several people deep had made a tight hedge around us.

'Make way there,' called out Fidelis. 'And lend a hand. This man is mortally hurt. We must get him out of the wet.'

We took him to lie in the vestry at St John's, alongside John Allcroft, and I sent for his granddaughter to come urgently. While we waited for Maggie the rain drummed on the roof and Fidelis and I had the corpse to ourselves.

We both looked down at Isaac Satterthwaite, lying on the vestry table and looking peaceful.

I let a few moments pass, then said, 'What killed him, Luke? A stroke of lightning, or a stroke of apoplexy?'

'It wasn't either.'

'But there was no attacker anywhere near him. And there's no injury. Not a mark.'

'Isn't there?'

Carefully Fidelis took the bushy beard by its end, and lifted it so that it hung like a little white cloud above the dead man's breast and abdomen. He peered underneath. I also looked from my side of the table.

'See that?' Fidelis pointed with his finger. 'That is no act of God, but an act of man.'

At the end of his finger, immediately over the breastbone, was a neat, blood-rimmed hole. I had seen such a hole once or twice before in the course of my work. It was a bullethole.

'Good God! He was shot!'

'Yes. And the sound was masked by the storm.'

'Why did he not bleed more copiously? There was no blood spilt at all.'

'The ball stopped his heart instantly, before he even hit the ground. So – no heartbeat, no bleeding. It is not like a knife wound.'

I considered the matter. Luke was right in more than one way.

A shooting is wholly different from a knifing. Almost any of us could lay our hands on a knife, should we need one. It can be used without a thought: it is all too handy, easy to conceal, easy to wield. Not so a gun. Few people have one. It is unwieldy, and cannot simply be snatched up and used. First you have to load, charge, ram and prime. There's no killing so premeditated as a gunshot – unless it be a poisoning.

In time a distraught Maggie arrived. I waited until the storm of her crying had abated, then asked for a private conversation. It took place in the church porch.

'At first,' I told her, 'it appeared that your grandfather had been struck down by illness, or even by the lightning. But now we know someone killed him.'

Maggie's eyes filled again with tears.

'Who?'

'Can you think of anyone?'

'I don't know what to think.'

'We shall have to inquire into it, and I will in time hold a formal inquest. Unfortunately, as of course you know, I have another inquest in hand into John Allcroft. It will be hard and I am sorry, my dear, but you will have to give evidence once again. Will you be able to?'

She sniffed and nodded her head.

'Good. Have you anyone to look after you? Who is your closest relative?'

'I have an aunt married in Longridge.'

'If I send for her, do you think she'd be willing to come and take you home with her?'

'I think she would, sir.'

'Then I'll do it. In the meantime come into my house. You are welcome to sit with my wife and she will comfort you.'

*

Arriving back at the inquest a little late, I found that word of the latest death had already spread like a bad smell around town. People were treating my temporary court as a news exchange, for the numbers had swollen and the place was in an uproar of speculation and debate. The most popular opinion was that Satterthwaite had been struck by either a seizure or a bolt of lightning; only a minority promoted the idea that he had been murdered.

As I reached my place, Furzey pushed a piece of paper, folded and sealed, towards me. It bore the mayoral seal, which I broke. I read:

> Mr Cragg,
>
> *I should be obliged if you would wait on me at the Moot Hall this afternoon at four, after we have finished polling for the day. Urgent matters to discuss.*
>
> Wm. Biggs, Mayor

'When did this come?' I asked my clerk.

'Fifteen minutes since. What's happened? They're saying Satterthwaite's in no condition to appear.'

'That is one way of describing it,' I said. 'He's lying in the vestry alongside our Mr Allcroft, covered by a sheet. We'll have to manage without him.'

With a few raps on the table I brought the room to order, asked the jury foreman if all his men were present, and rose to speak.

'As the court knows, my first witness this afternoon was to be Mr Isaac Satterthwaite. But, as many of you evidently also know, Mr Satterthwaite has suddenly and unfortunately died. So I have no choice now but to call the next and final witness on my list, who is Mr Thomas Wilson.'

'Mr Thomas Wilson!' echoed Furzey, setting his tone at halfway between that of a drill sergeant and a light basso in the opera, and looking imperiously up and down the room.

At first in silence, and then amidst an outbreak of whispering, we waited for Wilson to stand and walk up to the chair. He never did and, when a full minute had passed, I asked Furzey to find young Barty, who I knew would not be far away.

'Tell him to run up to the apothecary's shop and enquire after Wilson. If the man's there, he is to remind him that this inquest requires him as a witness, and that he should come here without delay – that is, now.'

We had only ten minutes to wait before Barty returned, panting for breath and on his own. He came to the back of my chair and spoke in my ear.

'Mrs Wilson is by herself in the shop, Mr Cragg. She's not seen her man since last night when he went out to tavern. She's saying likely he's got himself drunk and he's laying up somewhere. She's in a right scrow about it, though, shouting and that. It's not my fault, I told her.'

'Well, thank you, Barty. I regret that you were shouted at.'

I handed him his tip and rose to address the court once more.

'It seems we must forfeit another witness,' I told them. 'I have just heard that Mr Wilson cannot be found, for reasons I do not yet know. So, I shall proceed to sum up what we have heard, so that you, members of the jury, can retire to decide the issue as best you can. So, let me begin with what Mrs Allcroft told us. Her husband came to Preston in good health on the twenty-eighth of last month . . .'

I took my listeners back over how John Allcroft had put up at the Gamecock Inn. Then, recalling the words of Mrs Fitzpatrick and the others working at the inn on the twenty-ninth of April, I detailed what had happened to John Allcroft before he died. After mentioning his hotpot dinner I brought in Joe Primrose's testimony.

'The stew has taken on some importance in this inquiry, as it was the last thing the dead man ate. Mr Primrose told us that he did not use barley but only oats to thicken the dish. Yet Dr Fidelis testified to the presence of cooked or otherwise softened barleycorns in the sample of the dinner that he collected from Mr Allcroft's room. We tried to establish how this unexpected ingredient could have got there, and it emerged that there had been a clear opportunity for some mischief to be done to it, since the food was left alone in the bedroom for a period of up to twenty minutes, awaiting Mr Allcroft's attentions. That mischief *was* done to it, somehow or another, was later demonstrated by Dr Fidelis. He told us how he fed a portion of the leftover hotpot to a rat, who died within a few minutes. I should add that the doctor invited me to observe this trial, and I can confirm that this is precisely what happened. I should also advise you that some vermin catchers have been known to mix poison with softened grains such as barley before laying it.

'You have the following options. You may decide that some poison was introduced into the food accidentally, or that you do not know how it was put there. On the evidence we have heard there is no suggestion that Mr Allcroft took his own life, but the possibility of murder remains. Weigh that possibility carefully.'

'We are very disturbed by the unfortunate killing this afternoon of Isaac Satterthwaite, Cragg. What do you have to say about it?'

Although it was still not four, I had taken the opportunity during the jury's deliberations to go up to the Moot Hall. The death of Satterthwaite had caused polling to be suspended for the day, and we now sat in the mayoral parlour.

'What can I say, Mayor? It has only just happened.'

'Well, I'll tell you what, we want answers to certain questions.

For instance, was he killed or did he die naturally? Was it an act of man, or of God? We cannot have this uncertainty. He was on his way to vote. If he was murdered it would look like an attempt to subvert the election, as a mine dug under the very foundation of our constitution and government.'

He raised a finger, liking the phrase enough to repeat it.

'A very mine, Cragg! And meanwhile we have another charge waiting to explode beneath us – this matter of Mr John Allcroft's inquest. It is being said everywhere that you have proved he was poisoned. There is the likelihood of public disorder. Accusations will fly around. More blood will be spilt.'

I could see Biggs's point, and I could see, too, what he wanted: early notice of the likely inquest verdict. He wanted, if possible, someone he could quickly have arrested, to show that he was in command of the situation. Not that I was going to help him out.

'I do not quite follow you, Mayor,' I lied.

'Well, I would have thought it was as plain as pudding, Cragg. Can you not see? Satterthwaite may not have been to our liking politically, but if he really was killed for political reasons it reflects badly on our conduct of the election. In the case of Allcroft, he was of our party. We must know if either man was murdered and, if that is the case, there will have to be measures to prevent any further deaths.'

At the root of the Mayor's nervousness was the fear of Parliament. Adverse reports might persuade honourable members in London to enquire into the result of Preston's vote, and perhaps to overturn it. Not only would a second ballot be an embarrassment, the expense would be crippling.

I said, 'I regret, it is not yet possible for me to tell you. The jury will inform me when they have made up their minds. On Allcroft they are meeting now. Only when a verdict is reached can I inform you.'

'And Satterthwaite?'

I admit that I was enjoying Biggs's discomfort. In place of its customary arrogance, his voice had taken on a supplicatory tone.

'I shall hold that inquest as soon as I can,' I told him. 'But of course I cannot know in advance what conclusion it may reach.'

Biggs spluttered but there was not much more he could say. I rose, telling him, if our business was finished, I must return to the court and await the jury.

Chapter Twenty-two

THEY CAME BACK having deliberated for a little over an hour. I did not think there was much doubt they would see the death as a poisoning. What I did not know was whether they would choose 'by means unknown' or the more dramatic 'murder by a person or persons unknown'. The former was the more rational choice, and it seemed to me that Gerald Pikeroyd was a rational enough fellow, who would not allow the fancies of Charley Booth or the tittle-tattle of Edward Lillycrap and John Mort to dominate proceedings. On the other hand, juries in my experience will always find murder if they possibly can.

'Mr Foreman,' I asked when they had settled themselves, 'have you agreed on a verdict?'

Pikeroyd cleared his throat.

'Aye, Mr Cragg, we have.'

'Will you tell the court what it is, please?'

'It's murder. Murder by poisoning.'

I glanced at Furzey, who was writing the verdict on yet another of his printed forms.

'Thank you. But I need a little more information. You must tell me if you believe you know who carried out the murder. I should add that you do not have to name anyone, and you really should not do so unless you are certain you are naming the guilty party, and not just someone who might have done it.'

'Well, we are very sorry, but we have no name for you. We don't know who was the killer.'

'Very well. So the verdict you are entering is "murder by person or persons unknown". Are you all agreed on it?'

'Aye, we are all agreed.'

'Thank you, Mr Pikeroyd, and thanks to you all. The jury is dismissed and may go. But first—'

Though the public were now beginning to stand up, talk, gather together their hats and umbrellas, I had not finished. I raised my voice to be heard.

'But first it is my duty to add one or two remarks, ladies and gentlemen. I congratulate Mr Pikeroyd and his colleagues on the verdict, and on the way they have acted in this matter. We do not know what this poison was that killed Mr Allcroft. Nor do we know who administered it, or why. I therefore have no arrests to recommend to the mayor and magistrates, and I will confine myself to saying that deliberate poisoning is a shocking crime. It is of necessity a case of malice aforethought, it is very devious and it is very difficult to detect. Human nature being what it is, a successful murder by poisoning can attract the attention of would-be imitators. In my return to the mayor I shall therefore suggest that the corporation investigate the supply of poisons in this town, and find ways of making it more difficult to get hold of. That is all. The court is dismissed.'

I struck the table with my gavel. As the audience began to bustle about – leaving, getting ready to leave, crossing the room to exchange views with others, or simply milling about in the way a herd does, hoping for something more to happen – I noticed Ephraim Grimshaw in conversation with Susan Allcroft and a podgy young man, dressed in black, who stood by her side. Grimshaw was holding the widow's hand and patting it consolingly. He was, of course, of her party, but Grimshaw was speaking as if he were also her friend – persuasively, emphatically, with wide eyes and head jabbing forward.

I moved towards them. As soon as he saw me coming, Grimshaw let go of the lady's hand and turned his crafty eyes in my direction.

'I call that a severe waste of time and money, Cragg,' he said. 'You have a murder, yes, but no murderer. What is the point of an inquest, if no finger is pointed? Mrs Allcroft and young Jotham here are sadly disappointed.'

Ignoring this I turned to Mrs Allcroft, and presented her with a paper.

'Madam, I have the honour of giving you your paper of release. If you would present this at the vestry, the body of your husband will be given to you. I have asked Peter Wintly to stand by with his cart.'

She took the release warrant with a sniff and handed it to her son, who unfolded it and scrutinized the wording as if it were a cryptogram. I bowed and, before leaving, took Grimshaw aside by the arm.

'I cannot pluck a murderer from the air,' I murmured in his ear. 'If you wanted conjuring you should have had your friend Shackleberry as coroner.'

At home I found Elizabeth in the parlour, sitting with a long-faced, wet-eyed Maggie Satterthwaite, still wearing her now incongruous brightly coloured dress. My wife, at her needlework, was chatting away on a cheerful note, while the girl sat silently, her posture rigid and her eyes fixed on the flames of the fire. I asked if word had come yet from her aunt, Mrs Sowerby, in Longridge.

'Not yet,' said Elizabeth. 'We expect the messenger to return by the moment.'

She stood and took my arm and steered me out of the room.

'Is it over, the inquest?' she whispered after she had closed the door.

'Yes.'

'Thank the Lord. When you were attacked yesterday I felt sure some people wanted the proceedings stopped. Now they are too late, and you, I hope, are safe. What was the verdict?'

I told her and she groaned.

'I wish it had been declared an accident. Maggie has been fretting about it being murder. She has been talking more about that than the killing of her grandfather.'

'She doesn't need to fear,' I said. 'There was no mention of her name in connection with the death. She is not accused.'

'Will you go in and reassure her? She has not said it in plain words, but I think she is genuinely afraid of arrest.'

She went off to bring tea, while I re-entered the parlour. Maggie had not stirred. I drew up a chair beside her and informed her in as gentle a tone as I could that the jury had decided Allcroft was murdered.

A tremor ran through Maggie's slim frame.

'Murder!' she said. 'But I didn't, Mr Cragg. I didn't!'

'No one is saying you did, Maggie.'

'Then who? Who *are* they saying?'

'They don't know. Nobody knows.'

She sighed, and the edge of her panic seemed less sharp.

'That's not true. The one that did it knows.'

'Yes, of course. But the official verdict is "by person or persons unknown". In most cases of such findings, there is never any more action. The person or persons are never found.'

'You mean there'll be no one arrested? No one tried and hung?'

'Probably not, I am sorry to say.'

'Oh!'

That last exclamation was hard to judge. I could not tell if it conveyed her interest, or its lack.

Elizabeth came in with tea, while I offered to explain to Maggie what I planned to do about her grandfather's death – when and where I would hold the inquest, and so on. But she shook her head slowly.

'Do what you like, Mr Cragg. You cannot bring him back and any road, he was old and his time had come.'

'But it hadn't, Maggie. You know, he did not die naturally. He too was killed by an unknown person or persons. I hope that we shall be able to identify that person but, like in the case of Mr John Allcroft, there is always the possibility that we shall not.'

Maggie did not reply, but returned her gaze to the fire.

At that moment we heard the door knocker pounding and Matty scurrying out of the kitchen and across the hall to answer it.

'That'll be the messenger with word from Mrs Sowerby,' said Elizabeth, who turned towards the parlour door expectantly. She hid it well, but I could see she would be glad to hand to another the responsibility for Maggie Satterthwaite.

There were voices in the hall, and the footsteps of several people. Then the latch sounded, the door swung open and Matty stood there, white of face. Immediately a bloated figure in a scarlet coat loomed up behind her, put his hand on her arm and eased her out of the way. Then the doorway was filled by the town constable, Oswald Mallender, holding his mace, a long silver-tipped bog-oak stick with a silver bulb at the top.

'Mr Cragg,' he boomed, looking around and taking in the whole scene. 'I see you are sheltering the girl Maggie Satterthwaite. I must inform you that I hold in my hand the mayor's warrant for her arrest. She must come with me.'

Maggie gave a short scream and bit her knuckles.

'Arrest?' I said. 'On what possible charge?'

'It is the regrettable one of murder, Mr Cragg. Deliberate murder.'

There was then a very strange moment. We all stood or sat motionless and silent as a sculpture gallery, with only the sound of Mallender's breathing breaking through.

'And who is this girl supposed to have killed?' asked Elizabeth at last, softly breaking the silence.

Mallender held up a rolled paper that was clenched in his fist.

'According to this document, ma'am, it is Mr John Allcroft that she is accused for the murdering of. And so, if you please, she must come with me.'

Mallender's relish was patent as he stepped into the room. For the first time we saw that he was accompanied by the Parkin brothers, his henchmen. I tried to bar their path to the girl.

'Who has accused her? This cannot have come from the inquest. There was no imputation made against her.'

'It is not for me to say, is it? But accusation has been levelled and it must be answered. Now, if you would make way, sir, I shall do my duty.'

Maggie's face was like a mask, as white as limewash. She stood and turned towards the corporation officer, and I had the unaccountable sense of someone offering herself.

'Then I must go, mustn't I?' she said.

'No! Stay, Maggie,' I cried. 'Mallender, give me the warrant.'

I unrolled the paper and quickly read through it. Maggie Satterthwaite's name was there; the words 'accused', 'murder', 'warrant', 'require' and 'take into custody' were all there too; and finally the signature and seal of Preston's leading magistrate, Mayor Biggs, was at the foot. With a sigh I handed it back. There was nothing legally wrong with the warrant.

'Maggie, I am sorry. I cannot prevent this. I am afraid you must go after all.'

And so the arresting party trooped from the room and through the front door, with Esau Parkin guarding one flank of Maggie, Jacob the other, and Oswald Mallender leading the way with his mace held in front of him.

'I'll come to you with food and drink, Maggie,' called Elizabeth as we watched them go from our front door. 'Don't despair.'

Maggie did not look back as Elizabeth held my arm.

'She is not much more than a child,' she said. 'Who could have laid such an accusation against her?'

'I have to meet Fidelis at the vestry. But first I will try to find out.'

I went back inside, seized my hat and went straight out again.

The mayor's clerk was determined to obstruct me.

'His Worship is engaged. He cannot see you.'

'Three hours ago he could think of nothing else but seeing me. Now he cannot see me. Let me write him a note.'

I leaned forward, plucked the pen out of the surprised clerk's hand and took a piece of paper from the pile by his elbow.

'You can't do that!' he screeched. 'That paper's property of the corporation.'

But I had done it, and was already writing. I didn't need to finish my note, however, because at that moment Biggs himself appeared at the door.

'Mr Biggs,' I cried, 'I am here in the interest of Maggie Satterthwaite. Who is responsible for this charge against her?'

'There is nothing untoward about it, Cragg. Mrs Allcroft will prosecute her. I told you of the importance we place on finding John Allcroft's killer. The peace must be preserved.'

'Is this the way to do it – with a sacrifice?'

'I cannot imagine what you mean, Cragg.'

*

I felt tired, overwhelmed, as I walked across to the vestry. I was in time to see Peter Wintly cracking a whip over his horse's bony rump, as he rattled away down Church Gate with the body of John Allcroft loaded behind. I let myself inside, and found the church-warden shaking his head as he circled the table on which Isaac Satterthwaite lay.

'I was hoping that we had done with corpses in here, Cragg. Is this a proper use of the vestry?'

'I fear it is not, Mr Fleetwood. But there is nowhere else. One day, perhaps, the town will give us an ice house dedicated to the purpose.'

Fleetwood scratched his head.

'A nice house, you say?'

Before I could put him right we heard a door slam and Fidelis came in, carrying his medical bag. I guided Fleetwood in the opposite direction, towards the door.

'The doctor must now examine the body,' I explained. 'He will have to perform various medical procedures so you may prefer to . . .'

Fleetwood was not inclined to argue, and left us.

Fidelis took from his bag a bolt of felt and unrolled it to reveal a set of steel implements, among which I saw tongs, knives and scissors, a saw and a heavy pair of shears.

'We shall see what damage the bullet did,' he said as he set to work. 'And we must have the bullet itself. Will you help strip off the upper clothing?'

Ten minutes later I was flinching as I watched Fidelis's actions: to see the human body butchered in this way, with saw, shears and knife, its organs exposed and some of them removed, its dignity and integrity destroyed, was awful. After a while he brought out Satterthwaite's heart and dropped it into a pewter dish that he'd taken from his bag.

'You see?' he asked, picking up the dish to show me the slippery organ. 'My supposition, just after the shooting, was right. This was a direct hit on the heart and it has been torn right through by the shot. It stopped beating instantly.'

He put the dish down and returned to the cavity he had opened in Satterthwaite's torso. For a while he seemed to be feeling around, and then brought his hand out, the fingers pincered onto a ball of lead dripping with blood and slime.

'Here it is.'

He held it up and turned it to catch the light. It was no longer perfectly round, but flattened, or rather dented on one side.

'It was embedded in the sixteenth vertebrum of the spine. That is interesting.'

'How?'

'It tells us something useful, if we are to identify the shooter.'

'What?'

'Not now. I must finish this and tidy the body up while the light lasts.'

It was almost dark, and I had had to go for candles by the time Fidelis finally returned Satterthwaite's heart to his chest, then closed and roughly sewed up the cavity. He had also completed a survey of the rest of the body, washed his instruments under the tap in the vestry, and rolled them up in their felt wrappings.

'Let us walk out to Fisher Gate,' he said. 'I will show you what I think happened.'

The street was largely deserted as we ventured out on cobbles that gleamed wetly underfoot. We reached the place where Satterthwaite had fallen, but images of that heated, chaotic scene were a little difficult to summon up now, in the cool of night. Fidelis paused for a moment and revolved slowly through a full circle, his eyes darting about.

'Good,' he said, 'this is the spot. Now, Satterthwaite was exceptionally tall and well built. We need someone similar.'

He looked up and down the street. Two men were unsteadily approaching, leaning against each other and singing a melancholy air. One was small and slight, but the other was a big bull of a man. In a few moments, Fidelis had befriended them. He learned their names – Bob and Bill – and persuaded them to join us in the centre of the street. The pair stood there side by side in drunken docility, until Fidelis detached the smaller one, Bill, from the side of his large friend, upon which the latter, deprived of his prop, fell to the ground.

We picked him up and returned his associate to his side, lifting Bob's meaty arm behind Bill's head and draping it across his far shoulder so that now his near shoulder nestled supportively in Bob's immense armpit.

'You saw Satterthwaite just before he went down?' Fidelis asked.

I nodded.

'What was his posture?'

'He stood upright. He had turned to look back down Fisher Gate to see where his followers had gone. But then just before he fell he turned again to look up the street.'

'We must get Bob in the same position. Stand on his other side.'

I stationed myself there and lifted Bob's free arm across my shoulders. So we shuffled the two men around until, swaying, they faced up the street, and towards the Moot Hall.

'A little more to the left,' I said. 'No, too much . . . that's about right. Rest there.'

Going behind us Fidelis touched the centre of Bob's lower back and told me to put my finger on the place. Then he returned to face Bob, this time indicating with his own finger a place above the drunkard's heart.

'This is where the bullet entered Satterthwaite. But it lodged lower in his body, where your finger is. So that is the line it took. Agreed? What does this tell us?'

'I don't know. What?'

'If we extend the line upwards from your finger through mine, we will see that he was shot from above, and probably from the north side of the street.'

'From an upper window?'

'Yes, but to come down at such a steep angle the bullet cannot have been fired from very far in front of him. It must have been from a house nearby. That one, I would say.'

But Bob's hand was draped across my head, tipping my wig and blocking my view. I lifted the hand and let it drop while ducking out from under Bob's armpit. As I straightened the wig I saw the house Fidelis was indicating, on Fisher Gate's northern side. It was Wilkinson's bread and pie shop.

'By God!' I exclaimed.

'Exactly.'

Behind us we heard a grunt and turned to see that, unable to sustain his companion's weight, Bill had collapsed to a kneeling position. Left without support, Bob was trying to keep his balance, his eyes bulging with effort. But the pull of gravity supervened and he too went down, tipping sideways like a foundering ship and sprawling on the cobblestones.

Fidelis and I got both men up and manoeuvred them to the side of the street where they could lean against a wall. I gave each man sixpence.

As we left the pair to make their own befuddled way to wherever they were going, Fidelis's face wore an almost imperceptible smile. This was an expression that I had last seen after the death of Athene the rat. It might have been read now as amusement at the expense of the two drunks but, in fact, it had a quite different quality: the satisfaction the mind feels after reaching a clever interpretation of obdurate facts.

'It is looking as if you may be able to build a case against Jotham Allcroft,' he said.

'We are a long way from that, surely. We only know he worked there.'

'He lived there, too, and most important of all he had the skill for the job. Have you forgotten that he was in the fusiliers?'

Chapter Twenty-three

I N THE MORNING voting resumed, its intensity only a little diminished by the fatal events of the day before. Meanwhile I held conference with Furzey at the office. We had two awkward questions to resolve: the timing of the Satterthwaite inquest and what to do about Wilson's failure to appear at the inquest on Allcroft. Wilfully not to answer a coroner's summons was an offence, which ought to attract a considerable fine. This money was due to the Crown, and I could have Lord Derby after me, in his role as Lord Lieutenant and Chancellor of the Duchy of Lancaster, if it came out that I had failed to pursue the miscreant and exact the fine from him. On the other hand, no purpose would be served by starting proceedings in the Duchy court if Wilson had a defence.

'We'd best go and see him, then,' said Furzey. 'He'll likely be nursing his sore head at home. We'll take his statement, and we'll see what it says. If it's pure drunkenness that kept him away, we can fine him.'

'Yes, we'll go this morning. But first, I want to think about this new inquest into Isaac Satterthwaite, and when we should have it. I have my strong suspicions about it and in the ordinary way, the sooner I test those suspicions at inquest the better. But the circumstances surrounding this case are not ordinary.'

'How's that? As I see it a man's dead, the doctor says he

was shot, so let's get it inquested and put our finger on the killer.'

'But the town is on a very short fuse, Furzey. It is full of factions, and this could set them at each other's throats. The killing of Allcroft is already causing more stir than is healthy, with talk of it being a political affair. The Tories are seething. I am not at all sure how the arrest of the unfortunate Maggie Satterthwaite is going to play with the people, either.'

'She's granddaughter of a self-proclaimed Whig. That's bad for her. He was an exterminator of vermin and handled poisons. That's doubly bad. And she put the poisoned dish in Allcroft's room. That's—'

'I know, trebly bad. Yet with the chamber door unlocked, anyone could have gone in there after her and mixed the poison into the stew. There's no proof it was Maggie, though in certain people's eyes you don't need proof, you just have to hate the girl enough and she becomes guilty. It would have been much better had she never bested Grimshaw's own niece in the May Queen contest, but she did. So there's more than enough of circumstance and prejudice to convict her, I fear.'

'The election will be well over by the time of the assize.'

'Yes, but in the meantime she'll be the focus for all sorts of discontent. Some will be for her and some against. The killing of her grandfather, on his way to vote, cannot fail to be seen by your Whigs as the same. Once the facts are out they will say it is some kind of retaliation for Allcroft.'

'So what do you propose to do?'

'Delay the inquest until after polling has finished. Biggs and Grimshaw will be delighted. They're afraid the election will be overturned and they'll have the trouble and expense of another contest. It's a pity to please them but it can't be helped.'

*

We found the apothecary shop closed, with the door locked and the window shuttered on the inside. I hammered at the door while Furzey peered in, trying to see through a gap in the shutters. At length Mrs Wilson came to the door.

'I must see your husband,' I told her. 'He failed to answer my summons to give evidence yesterday. It is a serious matter, I'm afraid.'

Even before I had got through half of this short speech Mrs Wilson was shaking her head.

'Wilson has never come home, Mr Cragg. I've not seen him, from when he walked out of that door on the night before last to go to the tavern, to this minute now. I begged him not to go out. I said there'd been more than enough drinking, but he wouldn't listen.'

'Have you enquired after him?'

'I went myself to the White Hart, sir. They said yes, he'd been in but he left at ten on Tuesday or soon after. Nobody's seen a whisker of him since and I don't know where to put myself for worrying.'

I exchanged glances with Furzey who gave an almost imperceptible shrug. He was right. There was nothing much we could do until the apothecary turned up. I told his wife I would let her know if there was any news, and we left.

There was news soon enough. We had been back at the office no more than five minutes when Dick Middleton the eel fisher walked in.

'I've got Wilson the apothecary for you, coroner, at my place.'

'You have? That's very good news. I need to speak to him. But how did you hear about that?'

'I didn't, and it isn't good news.'

'Well, it should be, Dick. Mr Wilson was lost, and now he is found, like the prodigal son, you know.'

'He's found all right. I pulled him from river this morning.'

This brought me up short.

'He was in the *river*?'

'Aye. I was early bringing in my traps, see, because tide had yet to turn and rightly I should do it at top of tide.'

'Come to the point, Dick. You pulled Thomas Wilson from the river, you say. You mean he's dead?'

'Oh, aye, dead as can be.'

'Ye gods, not another drowning!'

I collected my thoughts. I had just felt a kind of landslip around me, a sense that events might pass out of my control. It was necessary to act with decision.

'All right, let's go directly to your place. Furzey! Will you please get a message to Dr Fidelis and ask him to meet me at Dick's garden as soon as he can get there?'

On the way, Dick told me his story. He'd gone down to the riverbank and started to bring in his traps, when what he thought was a sack became snagged on his lines. He pulled until it came within reach and he groped underwater for it. Presently he found he had hold of a man's hand.

'I can tell you, I were properly frighted, Mr Cragg. I'm used to pulling in live eels, not dead people.'

When we came to his garden there was a small knot of curious people standing by the gate, standing on tiptoe to look into the garden and exchanging whispered remarks. For some reason people do speak in whispers in the presence of death, though I don't know why. Do they imagine they might wake the corpse with too much noise?

I told them to disperse, unless they could tell me anything about the death, which none of them could, and they shuffled off. Middleton crossed to one of his sheds, whose door was fastened with a padlock. He unlocked and opened up, to reveal Wilson's body sprawling in the wheelbarrow that he had used to transport it from the riverbank. The legs and arms dangled over the edges, and the head was canted at an unnatural angle. If I had not known he was dead, he might have just seemed dead drunk, and ready to be barrowed home.

'Let's get him into the light and out of that.'

I seized the barrow handles and wheeled him outside. Then, together, we lifted up the corpse, still sodden with Ribble water, and humped it onto a rough table just outside the shed, which Middleton used to gut his eels. Wilson was still fully clothed, except for his shoes. His mouth was open and his eyes stared, as if shocked at the sudden death that had come upon them. I tried closing the eyelids, but they kept springing open again until Dick offered me two flat stones the size of crown pieces, and I used these to weigh them down. Then we stood, one on each side of him, while I thought about death, its suddenness and its finality.

I knew Dick was following the same line of thought when he said, 'It's the same with eels when they're dead, Mr Cragg. Eyes stare at you, mouth gapes open. Makes you think.'

Luke Fidelis arrived ten minutes later, carrying, as ever, his medical bag. First he examined Wilson's head, peering close.

'He's taken a blow to the head. It would have knocked him out for certain, if it didn't kill him.'

He bent again to inspect the open mouth.

'What's this?'

He rifled in his bag until he came out with a case of small instruments, which he opened. He selected a pair of tweezers and applied them to Wilson's teeth. Wilson had had good teeth, browned but holding together. Fidelis's tweezers seized something from between the two front ones, and plucked it out. He held it up to the light.

'What would you say this was?'

'It looks like a piece of silver thread.'

'I think that is exactly what it is. But I wonder how it got between his two front teeth. Who do we know who wears silver-threaded clothing?'

'Burgess Grimshaw, on most days,' I suggested.

Fidelis laughed.

'Beware of prejudice, Titus. Who else?'

Suddenly I saw again the unexpected opulence of Hamilton Peters's waistcoat, when we met in the hall of the Gamecock Inn.

'Peters!' I said.

'Quite so,' confirmed Fidelis.

Carefully he preserved the piece of thread in his pocketbook and went back to work, extending his examination of the corpse from the head to the trunk, arms and legs. Stripping off the man's coat and shirt he turned the body onto its front and produced his listening trumpet, which he pressed to various parts of the back, applying his ear to it while thumping the flesh with his fist. Finally he stepped away from the table.

'Of one thing I am certain, Titus: that Wilson was murdered. Quite probably with a bludgeon. His body was then thrown into the river. The killer may have had in mind what happened to Antony Egan, and the outcome of your inquest at the Ferry Inn. He wanted people to assume the same of Wilson – that his death was a drunken mischance.'

'Perhaps it was, Luke. He might have struck his head on something while being swept along by the current.'

'He might well have – but if he did, it wasn't what killed him. There's no water in his lungs. Unlike the last corpse we recovered from the river, this one was dead when he went into it.'

'I am beginning to be alarmed,' said Fidelis, 'about the safety of the other two.'

We had left Middleton reluctantly in charge of the late Wilson, and were climbing up the lane in the direction of town.

'Which other two?'

'Reynolds and Drake. The only two left from the Sunday night cribbage game which, it seems to me, someone wants to exterminate.'

'I don't think we have enough facts to warrant the conclusion. You are suggesting a conspiracy.'

'Of course I am, Titus. Why not? Looked at in a certain way, all life is a conspiracy. One group against another. Politics. Religion.'

'Good Lord, could it be someone objecting to their playing a godless game on the Sabbath?'

'It's a possibility, I suppose. But the fact that all were of the same party, and one of them a candidate in the election, is more suggestive of politics.'

Fidelis had a point.

'Very well. First I must go to Mrs Wilson and tell her of her sadly changed station in life. But let's meet at your lodging in thirty minutes and we'll pay a visit to Mr Reynolds. He may still by then not have heard of this latest death, and it will be interesting to see if it frightens him at all.'

So I left him and hurried away to the apothecary's shop.

It has often been my task to bring news of death, and I have observed certain patterns in the behaviour of the suddenly bereaved. Some collapse like a tent whose ropes are cut. Others jut out their chins and put a brave face on it. And there is a third group that finds release in histrionic mourning, as seen in old Greek tragedies. Mrs Wilson had never heard of Sophocles, I am sure. But she played the news of her widowhood with extraordinary vigour and passion. She threw her apron over her head. She wailed in long, swooping vowels. She went around the room thumping and kicking the furniture, cursing fate and cursing too her husband Wilson for his inability to stay alive.

I made sure that a neighbour woman was at hand to provide her with a suitably condoling audience and, as soon as I decently could, slipped away.

Fidelis and I had to push through a small knot of troublemakers that had gathered in the street outside Mrs Bryce's house. Wearing oak leaves pinned to their lapels they jibed about murderous Whigs and Walpoleans, and called John Allcroft a sainted martyr, to which neither Fidelis nor myself made reply. Mrs Bryce made a face at them as she came to the door, at which they jeered.

'Those ruffians have been at my door all morning,' she said as she ushered us inside. 'They seem to think dear Mr Reynolds is in some way responsible for this poisoning at the Gamecock. Such nonsense.'

I asked after Mr Reynolds.

'He is in the music room, drinking coffee with Mr Destercore. So you and the doctor must come up and take a cup with us.'

Mrs Bryce's house was of four storeys, with two parlours. The one on the ground floor was for everyday callers, while the first-floor front room, equipped with a harpsichord, was reserved, in normal times, for evening entertainments.

At the door Mrs Bryce whispered, 'Poor Mr Reynolds is feeling fretfully hard pressed, you know, very hard pressed indeed. But he finds coffee steadies his nerves.'

Music had been temporarily abandoned and the room had become a staff headquarters for the election battle, with its harpsichord, side table and more than one of its chairs covered with papers containing lists of names, with incoming letters, memoranda and drafts of speeches. I recognized several notebooks like the one Destercore had been copying into at the Moot Hall on the previous Saturday morning.

Fidelis and I had agreed in advance to behave, at first, as if this were a polite call. Two or three chairs were cleared of paper and we sat in a semicircle at the fireplace while Mrs Bryce brought fresh coffee and buttered teacakes. Reynolds looked as his land-lady described – fatigued and rather bewildered – though he seemed amenable to a little distraction. Destercore, on the other hand, was hardly able to conceal his impatience at our interruption; he sat studying papers while swiping up his coffee cup at intervals to take hurried sips. I asked how Mr Reynolds and his party were faring in the vote.

'We struggle against heavy odds,' he said. 'The death of Isaac Satterthwaite is a blow and it cost me a dozen votes. Even worse, Hoghton will not campaign. He skulks at Hoghton Tower afraid of the jokes they will shout at him. Imagine that, will you? The sitting MP and afraid of jokes! He ought to think about policy not scurrility.'

'The view does you credit,' I said. 'But I wonder if, in politics, jokes are not a mightier force than arguments.'

'Oh, no! We cannot have that,' broke in Mrs Bryce. 'For then Mr Reynolds will never succeed, having not a – what shall I say? – not a *funny* bone in his body. Have another teacake, dear Mr Reynolds, it will build you up.'

Reynolds fetched a deep and gloomy sigh as he helped himself.

'My late mother used to say,' he declared, taking a half-moon out of the slice, 'that I never laughed after I was five years old.'

A moment of silence followed this curious statement, during which I wondered if it was time to broach the real reason for our visit. Then Reynolds himself, swallowing his mouthful, leaned forward and opened the way to me.

'Cragg, have you come nearer to establishing what happened

to Satterthwaite? There are shocking rumours that he was shot. Can these be true?'

I thought it best to evade the question.

'That will come out at the inquest. But I'm afraid we now have equally sad news about another of your friends in town.'

Reynolds was nodding lugubriously as he listened. I went on.

'I am sorry to tell you that Mr Thomas Wilson the apothecary has been pulled out of the river this morning. He, too, is dead. Dr Fidelis and I have just returned from examining the body.'

Reynolds froze, his mouth gaping.

'Tom Wilson? Drowned?'

'It looks like it.'

This was not a lie: it *did* look like it. I glanced at Fidelis, who gave me a judicious half-smile. I went on.

'I think you regularly played at cribbage with both Mr Satterthwaite and Mr Wilson. Do you have any reason to think anyone wished them harm? Or would do this to cause your party harm, for both men were actively of your party, I believe?'

The news of Wilson had turned Reynolds's face a greyish white. His lips trembled. He glanced at Destercore who, equally thunderstruck, had let the document he'd been studying fall from his fingers. Reynolds turned to him and spoke in a hoarse whisper.

'Peters? Is it possible?'

'The scoundrel!' growled Destercore, bending to retrieve his paper. 'By God in heaven, I shall see him hanged.'

I looked from one to the other.

'You know something to implicate Peters in this?'

Without reply, Destercore stood, went to the harpsichord, and took up a letter that lay there.

'Mr Cragg, I received this yesterday. Perhaps it is right that I acquaint you of its contents. It is from Lord Carburton.'

He cleared his throat and read:

'Dear Mr Destercore,

'*I have been ill the past few weeks and am only now able
to deal with correspondence. You ask about Hamilton
Peters, that was lately my factotum. I regret to say that I
cannot give him a good character. He was engaged to
accompany me to Italy and, although he carried out his
duties tolerably well, I discovered when we were back in
England that he had been deceiving me. My journey's
object was to see the sights of Rome; his, by attaching
himself to my household, to make contact with the
Pretender, which I believe he did on at least three
occasions. I learned this, only on our return, from
one whose business it is to collect intelligence about
Jacobite sedition. I accordingly dismissed Peters
from my service. I regret this unavoidably
tardy reply.*

'*I am, Sir, yours, etc., Carburton.*'

Destercore lowered the letter and stared unblinkingly at me.

'So you will understand, Cragg, when I tell you I have dismissed
the man, but too late, it seems. I had no idea that he was such a
villain, or I would have had him arrested and delivered to prison.'

'Do you know where he is now?'

'No. I gave him his marching orders in this very room. He gave
me in return a thin smile, with a certain derision about it, then
turned about and left the house.'

'It's true, sir,' said Mrs Bryce with emphasis, as if Destercore's
word were not to be relied on. 'It was the last we saw of the fellow.
He banged the door behind him and, you know, we lent him a
key because he was in and out of this house writing for Mr
Destercore, and he never left that key behind him, the thoughtless

so-and-so. So we can say it, can't we, Mr Reynolds? We never liked him.'

In reply Reynolds only grunted, uncomfortable at being publicly joined with Mrs Bryce in an opinion.

'Well,' said Destercore, 'it is no use taking this to the corporation to have Peters pursued. There is no direct evidence and the burgesses are Tories to a man. They will not act.'

There was no dissent from this and another silence followed, until Fidelis stood and made as if to stretch his frame. He strolled across to the window with its view over Fisher Gate and looked out for a moment, then spun around and produced his watch.

'I should be on my way, Mrs Bryce. Thank you for the excellent coffee.'

I too rose and made my farewells, but not before advising Reynolds and Destercore that I might need them as witnesses.

'The inquest may find Peters responsible, and then the burgesses will have to act,' I said.

'Huh!' grumbled Reynolds. 'The fellow will be miles away by then.'

Chapter Twenty-four

OUTSIDE THE HOUSE, on Fisher Gate, we lingered for a moment. Next door to Mrs Bryce stood Miss Colley's lodging and, next to that, Wilkinson's pie shop.

'I saw you observing from the window,' I said. 'Could Satterthwaite have been shot from Mrs Bryce's house?'

'No doubt of it.'

'Last night you were sure it was from Wilkinson's.'

'I'm sorry if I gave that impression. I could not have been sure. The mathematics of the bullet's trajectory are impossible to work out with precision, because we cannot know for certain the exact postural direction of Satterthwaite's body when it was hit. I considered the pie shop most likely for non-mathematical reasons – Jotham Allcroft works there, and we both know he has reason to blame Satterthwaite for his father's death. But, in truth, the bullet could have been fired from any nearby house on the north side.'

We began walking slowly towards my office.

'I hope you're not suggesting that Miss Colley could have taken the shot.'

He laughed.

'No – let's rule her out. But we now have two serious suspicions: one against Jotham, and the other, a new one, against Hamilton Peters. He had a key to the house, and could have entered privately, because neither Reynolds nor Destercore was in the room, since both were at Porter's organizing the tallies. The only question is – and it is a hard one – why would Peters shoot Satterthwaite?'

'Well, to swing the vote to the Tories, obviously. To frighten off Reynolds's and Hoghton's supporters.'

Fidelis shook his head.

'Don't be hasty, Titus. We are already suspecting Peters of poisoning Allcroft. Why? To swing the vote to the Whigs. So we must make up our minds. Did he kill Satterthwaite and Wilson for the Tories, or Allcroft for the Whigs? Or did he do none of the murders?'

I sighed. The new information about Peters was forcing us to adjust our view of all these deaths. Knowing Fidelis would pounce like a cat on an ill-considered reply, I spoke carefully.

'After hearing what Lord Carburton said about him, it does not look likely that he killed Allcroft. You heard my mother-in-law – who is not to be contradicted on the near side of never – maintain that John Allcroft was a staunch Jacobite: king-over-the-water, commemorative medals, Oak Leaf Day, all that. Peters had been in Preston before and if it was on Jacobite business, he would have known Allcroft's affiliations, and might have met him. And, if he did, he cannot have poisoned him, surely.'

'There's an "if" there, which would have to be resolved.'

'Why else would Peters come here?'

Fidelis did not reply, or open his mouth again for the rest of our walk.

At the office I instructed Furzey to collect Wilson's body and bring it to the vestry, then went through to my sanctum where Fidelis was waiting. He was humming to himself a tune which, after a moment, I recognized as 'Rule Britannia!'.

'Well, we know where we can begin to look for Peters, at any rate,' I said. 'And the windmill is not miles away.'

'We saw him there the day before yesterday, before he was dismissed. By now who knows where he may be? But anyway, I think his whereabouts are irrelevant.'

'You don't think Lord Carburton's letter means he should be pursued?'

'I see a paradox in the letter. It purports to damn Peters as a scoundrel, but I have come around to your view – that it tends to clear him, in these matters at least. I think we must look elsewhere for our murderer.'

'But he may still have murdered Satterthwaite and Wilson, surely.'

Fidelis wagged his finger at me.

'When I hear the word "surely", Titus, I at once look for the flaw in the assertion.'

Resolving never to use the word again in his presence, I persisted.

'The relevant point is, we now know that Peters is a Jacobite, a High Tory, who comes in disguise to the Preston election, having been here before a year earlier. Furthermore, shortly afterwards, we have a spate of suspicious deaths, including those of two prominent Whigs, one of whom was shot, possibly from a room to which Peters had access. How can he not come under suspicion?'

'Because the murders of Allcroft, Satterthwaite and Wilson are linked. I am convinced of it. Not to mention the death of your relative. However, I am curious to know what Peters was doing at the windmill on Tuesday.'

'At the moment we saw him he looked as if he was waiting for someone – on the lookout, in fact.'

'Who owns that old windmill?'

'I don't know, but Furzey will. Let's ask him.'

I called for my clerk but, unfortunately, he had already left on his mission to Middleton's garden. I say unfortunately because, had he been there to answer my question, I would have been spared a good deal of trouble later.

Fidelis had patients to see and I had a few matters of business to put in hand, which kept me occupied for another half-hour. Then I went through to the house for dinner.

No sooner had I sat down – to a good plate of mutton chops in caper sauce – than Elizabeth mentioned a subject I had quite forgotten in the flurry of recent events: Maggie Satterthwaite. The news was startling.

'I have been to visit her.'

'Oh? How does she?'

'I have not seen her. She is gone, Titus.'

'How can she have gone? Gone where?'

'Nobody knows. She has absconded.'

'From the town cells? That's impossible without bribing the warder.'

'She wasn't put in the town cells. They are so filthy that, when the aunt from Longridge arrived at last, she persuaded Mayor Biggs to consign her niece to house custody. Biggs lodged her with Oswald Mallender, who undertook to lock her safe in a room he has at home just for these occasions. Seemingly he didn't lock her safe enough because this morning, when his wife went in with Maggie's breakfast, the window was wide open and she had gone.'

'How?'

'Mallender is a fool, of course. The windows had barred gates across them. He swears the bars were secured by bolts on the outside, but he probably forgot to fasten them.'

'I doubt that. He is a fool, but a conscientious one. She must have had help from outside. You were with her yesterday. Did she talk much?'

'In fits. She is a contradiction, I think. She is very proud of being known as the prettiest unmarried girl in town, but burdened by it too. She is angry that the loss of her virginity has been made so very public. But she is not sad that it *is* lost.'

'What would be the point? Split milk . . .'

'What I mean is, she is not ashamed, Husband. She only complains about how the men of the town treat her, knowing as they do that she has already been with a man.'

'Which was one of them, presumably.'

'No, no. She swears it was a stranger passing through, a traveller at the Ferry Inn when she worked there – you remember?'

'Ah, yes – the reason for her dismissal by your uncle and nieces.'

'When he dismissed her, my uncle called her a common whore, or something like that, but the stranger who seduced her – I am sure she did love him, and still does.'

'A love wholly undeserved on his part, the rat. Did she name him?'

'No. She does not speak of him. She regrets only that now any man considers he can have her. Young and not so young, married and single, her grandfather's friends even – they all try their luck, it seems. She told me that now, without her grandfather's protection, she will be fair game for all, and eventually . . .'

She let that eventuality trail away into silence as we finished our meal. Then, as she loaded our empty plates on a tray, she added one further thought.

'I know I said Maggie was little more than a child. But now thinking about it, I feel something else about her – something reserved, or even hidden. But I cannot see it yet.'

'We all have something to hide, Wife,' I said.

I was holding the door for her to pass through with the tray. She paused and, turning her head, planted a kiss on my mouth.

'I sincerely hope you hide nothing from me, Titus.'

'Not from you, my love. From the world, perhaps, but not from you.'

After dinner I took a pipe and a few minutes in which to forget all this confusion of feeling, and dramatic incident, by reading my Chaucer. But the fabulous incidents from *The Man of Law's Tale* began to become entangled in my mind with the real things that Elizabeth had been relating to me.

Chaucer's lawyer tells of the bewitchingly beautiful Constance, daughter of the Emperor of Rome, who is sent across the Mediterranean to make a diplomatic marriage to a Mahometan sultan. Her charm, and her Christianity, antagonize the mother-in-law who has Constance cast off alone in an open boat. She drifts until she beaches in Northumbria, of all places, where the king, naturally, marries her.

I was already thinking of Constance as one of those girls who are too beautiful to be allowed to control their own fate. And sure enough, new mishaps come her way. A would-be seducer whom she has scorned takes revenge by murdering the king's mother and leaving the bloody knife in Constance's hand while she sleeps in the same room. The king returns and finds his wife arrested and awaiting execution. Despite his grief for his mother, he makes a thorough investigation, and '*by wit and sotil enquerynge*' uncovers the real evildoer.

At this point I was imagining myself as the King of Northumbria, subtly inquiring into a wrongful accusation – or, to put it the other way, I was thinking of the king as the town coroner. And then I came to Chaucer's words about what he had uncovered: '*al the venym of this accursed dede*'. '*Al the venym,*' I repeated, and suddenly asked myself, was Maggie's case the same – a pretty girl adrift in a sea of circumstance? A fury of false accusation? It was then that I made a resolution: I would do all I could for her.

Furzey was still not returned from his errand. I looked out of the window and my eye fell upon young Barty, just a few yards away. To earn a farthing he was shifting crates of chickens in the market. I went out to him in the hope he might have heard something about Maggie Satterthwaite's whereabouts. To my surprise, at the very mention of her, he took fright and tried to run away, but immediately stumbled over a chicken coop, and I was able to reach him and grab him by the ear. Enduring his squeals and curses as inflexibly as a press-gang sergeant, I led him back to the office.

Inside, I let go of his ear and told him to sit down on Furzey's writing stool. He did so, rubbing his ear, squirming in his seat, and avoiding my eyes.

'Barty!' I said sharply. 'Why did you run away from me? Have I ever harmed you? You know something about this matter – what is it? You must tell me or it will go hard with you.'

Barty looked at me at last, but defiantly.

'I don't care about me, so long as she's safe away and not hung.'

'I understand you want to protect her. Then tell me what you know.'

But he kept his mouth obstinately clamped shut.

'Listen, my lad,' I said, 'if it helps you to speak out, I am not sure in my own mind that Maggie is a murderess. It is Burgess Grimshaw who wants her prosecuted, and we all know he hates her for besting his niece in the May Queen election. I will make it my business to help her in the best way I can, by finding the real killer. Meantime, the very worst thing is for her to run, to be a fugitive, with a price on her. She will be caught and, because she ran, she will be found guilty. Do you understand?'

Tears welled up in Barty's eyes.

'I did it so she wouldn't be hung.'

'Did what?'

'I went to constable's house, sir, and found where she lay and climbed up and opened her window. She climbed out.'

'When?'

'Darkest time of night, sir.'

'Where did she go?'

Two glittery runnels were crawling, like snail trails, down his grimy cheeks.

'To her man. She's got a man, but she told me not to follow.'

'But you did follow, didn't you?'

'Yes.'

'And found out who this man is?'

'Yes.'

'What is his name?'

Barty looked down at the ground and said something in so low a voice that I did not catch it.

'Barty!' I said. 'Speak up. Who is Maggie's young man?'

The moment's silence that followed was broken by a peal on the brass bell that hung outside the street door. It was immediately followed by the opening of the door itself, and the entry of a young man of somewhere between twenty and twenty-five years.

'Mr Cragg?' he said, in a peculiarly shrill voice. 'We have met only briefly but, in case you forget, I am Jotham Allcroft. I would like a word, if you please.'

I looked at Barty, hesitating. The boy was in turn staring at young Allcroft as at someone who had saved him.

To erase this impression I reached for his arm and propelled him towards the door into the house, saying over my shoulder, 'Will you excuse us for half a minute? Come on, my lad. I haven't finished with you.'

Marching Barty into the kitchen I asked Matty to give him milk and some food and keep an eye on him, then doubled back to the office. Jotham Allcroft was standing where I had left him, with his hat in his hand.

'Mr Allcroft. Come through to my private office and take a seat. This has been a sad business about your father.'

We took our seats on either side of my desk, and I asked him what I could do for him.

'Well, here it is,' he piped. He kept his round, popping eyes fixed on me with unsettling intensity. 'There are stories going around which stem from the poisoning verdict by your inquest. I am concerned about these stories and I wish you to put a stop to them.'

'In what way?'

'They are slander, against me and my family.'

'In what way?'

'In the way of saying that Isaac Satterthwaite the rat catcher murdered my father for his politics and that he must therefore have been killed in revenge. Folk are saying I shot him. Me.'

He jabbed his thumb emphatically into his chest.

'You are consulting me professionally, Mr Allcroft? Is it that you wish to bring an action for slander?'

'No, sir. You mistake me. I know better than to go to law in this land.'

I looked him up and down. He had a fleshy, globular head, a face smooth as an infant and a bodily frame that was narrow about the shoulders and big arsed, giving him a pear-shaped appearance. His clothing was sobriety itself – a black coat and breeches, plain linen collar and a round-crowned, wide-brimmed black hat.

'Well, such talk is very regrettable,' I said. 'But there are no secrets in this town, I am afraid. Speculative talk cannot be curbed.'

'But the Psalm says it must. *Let not an evil speaker be established on earth!*'

'But it is mere tittle-tattle. No sensible person will listen to it.'

'Slander is slander, Mr Cragg.'

'Well, such talk does not come from me, or my family. It may – and I say only may – emanate from a member of the inquest jury, or the public attending the hearing into your father's death.'

In fact, it almost certainly was from the jury. Juries are impossible to silence. They may have returned an uncertain verdict but they will have debated the possibilities of guilt and blame, and will no doubt have talked about them in the tavern afterwards. Allcroft was not a fool: he knew this. He took one hand off his hat and pointed at me while thrusting his chin upwards.

'I tell you, put a stop to the slander yourself for I hold you and your godless jurors responsible.'

'Mr Allcroft, this talk is easily refuted. Even if the rat catcher did kill your father, which I doubt, it does not follow that you must have killed the rat catcher.'

'And indeed I did not kill him. But people keep saying I did. They have sharpened their tongues like a serpent – adders' tongues are under their lips, Mr Cragg. You must contradict them.'

I took a deep breath. The man's clothing was highly suggestive but the words he was using were definitive.

'I wonder if you would have had any reason or desire to revenge your father. You and he had seriously quarrelled, had you not?'

'Yes, we had.'

'And it was about religion.'

He grimaced.

'About that, and about everything. His politics were detestable. His religion was that of the Whore of Babylon.'

'And what is your religion, may I ask?'

'I make no secret of it. I am a member of the Society of Friends. We believe in peace. That is why I could never have used a gun, even if I had wanted revenge.'

'Yet you were a soldier, you knew how to.'

He sighed, closed his eyes as if to summon patience in the face of stupidity.

'This is the mistake everybody makes. I was a clerk in the pay division, Mr Cragg. I can, if I must, distinguish one end of a musket from the other, but it is all I know about that vile engine.'

'I believe you.'

This came out spontaneously and it was true. I had difficulty imagining a figure less like a fusilier than the one sitting before me.

'Is this why you left the army? You became a Quaker?'

'I received the Inward Light, yes, and of course then I could no longer stay.'

I rose from my chair and with a gesture of the arm invited him to do the same which, automatically, he did.

'Well, I can do this for you,' I said. 'I'll write to the jurors and warn them not to speak publicly of any of the jury's discussions and suspicions, beyond those expressed in their collective verdict. That, as you know, was murder but with no name whatsoever mentioned. Will that satisfy you?'

By now I had manoeuvred him into the outer office, and towards the door, using a method I had mastered with clients over the years: half leading and half ushering.

Young Allcroft hesitated. He was not calculating whether I was trustworthy in general – I doubted he would ever think that – but only whether I would keep my word in this instance. All at once he decided I had nothing to lose by doing so. He proffered a cautious hand.

'That will be acceptable. Would you be kind enough to send me a copy of the letter?'

We shook hands and I opened the door for Friend Allcroft to leave.

Chapter Twenty-five

L UKE FIDELIS WAS coming in just as young Allcroft was going out, and they almost bumped.

'Who was that little puritan duck waddling out?' Luke asked moments later as he crossed into the inner office and threw himself into my desk chair. 'I've seen him about town but never heard his name.'

'That was Jotham Allcroft. You are sitting in my chair, Luke.'

'Oh, very sorry.'

We exchanged places.

'Well, I'm surprised,' Luke said. 'Was that really the fearless fusilier, our possible sharpshooter? You wouldn't have thought it possible.'

'It wasn't possible. He was a pay clerk, Luke. He soldiered with the pen, not the sword.'

Luke gave a shout of laughter.

'The abacus, not the arquebus. Wonderful!'

'What's more he's a devout Quaker. And he and his father had quarrelled irreparably, so he says. I don't think, despite what his mother foolishly thinks, that he regrets his father's death at all.'

'Which, if we put all those beads in a row, makes it far from likely that he shot Satterthwaite, or that he even wanted to. And we're forced back yet again to consider the case of the mysterious Hamilton Peters.'

'Whom we must find. Are you free to ride out to the old windmill? I think that is the only ploy left to us.'

Luke leapt to his feet and said he'd fetch his horse. I thought of sending for Barty to get mine, when I remembered that he was already under my roof, waiting to tell me the name of Maggie Satterthwaite's swain. I went through to the kitchen to complete my interrogation and found only Matty there.

'He's gone, sir! He gave me the slip. I'm stronger than him but he's quicker. He had a glass of milk quietly enough at the table there and I had just turned my back to cut him some cheese when he was into the backyard and over the fence before I could blink.'

I immediately went through to Elizabeth in the parlour. When I gave her the news about Maggie she grasped the seriousness of the situation at once.

'If she runs, it will condemn her, Titus, whether she is innocent or not. We must find her, and that means first finding Barty and wringing out of him the name of the wretched man she has gone to. Leave that part to me. You must set about discovering the truth about John Allcroft's death, and don't you dare to come home until you have done so!'

She pushed me in the chest and I shook my head in bewilderment at her impetuosity. As if producing this villain was a simple trick I could perform, like Mr Thomas Shackleberry palming his cards.

While Matty went to the livery stable for my cob, I returned to the office and jotted a note for Furzey, to read whenever he chose to return, about the letters I had promised Jotham Allcroft I would write.

I instructed Furzey to write the letters and send them out, one to each of the jurymen in the Allcroft inquest. All must use the same wording, I emphasized. They must warn the men not to speak openly about the jury's private deliberations. I added something by way of explanation:

There has been slander against Jotham Allcroft in the inns and coffee houses, falsely saying he has taken revenge against Mr Satterthwaite. To stop this there must be no mention made of the Whigs' having plotted Allcroft's murder.

I wrote the note hurriedly, not as a lawyer would, but carelessly like an ordinary letter writer. I quickly placed it on Furzey's writing table and returned to the matter immediately at hand. I took another sheet of paper and quickly wrote out a summons for Hamilton Peters to appear as a witness at the inquest – further particulars to be notified later – into the death of Isaac Satterthwaite. Just as I was dripping the sealing wax, Matty put her head in at the door to say the horse was ready, and Dr Fidelis was waiting. I pressed the seal down, and slid the paper into my pocket. Then I locked up the office and mounted my horse.

Passing the Moot Hall we saw a knot of men gathered at the foot of the steps, being addressed by Oswald Mallender. He had a paper in his hand, from which he was reading in a loud and officious manner. Judging by the staffs in their hands I guessed they were deputies recruited by Mallender to form a hue and cry after Maggie Satterthwaite.

Riding at a trot it would take us about twenty-five minutes to reach the windmill. On the way I told Fidelis how and why the corporation had arrested Maggie, and about my surprising discovery of Barty's role in her escape. Fidelis was not interested in Barty, but he was in Maggie.

'Grimshaw has got it woefully, and hopelessly, wrong. She is not the killer of Allcroft. If she did anything at all to contribute to his death, it was unwittingly. There was simply no reason for her to kill him.'

But was there? I thought to myself. I remembered her words to Elizabeth, that all the men try their luck with her. She was Allcroft's chambermaid. Had he tried his luck? Had he even gone further than try, in the secrecy of that room? And in spite of all the assurance with which I had pronounced her innocent, I thought, yes, a woman might kill after being insulted like that. And, as coroners find again and again, a woman's weapon of choice is often poison. I said all this to Fidelis.

'Yes, of course, women do resort to poison,' he agreed. 'But I would guess only for certain crimes. What do you think? Poison is useful to a woman in any slow killing that she wants to look natural – infanticide for the burial insurance, the slow death of an oppressive parent or of a husband to get his money, that sort of thing. But here we're imagining – if I am not mistaken – a young girl who has suffered an insult. Her idea of vengeance will not be a quiet, stealthy death, but a public slaying. Of course she may cover her deed up, and deny her guilt. But in her heart she wants the world to know her victim has been killed deliberately for his sins. In such a case she stabs him or knocks him on the head, wouldn't you say?'

'Yes, but someone did poison Allcroft. We cannot get away from that.'

'Not with the motive of punishing him, merely of removing him. Did Maggie have any reason to wish for Allcroft's silent removal? I doubt it. We have not uncovered any connection between them, except that she brought him his meals.'

As ever, Fidelis's reasoning looked strong.

'In my heart, I agree with you. Talking to her I have felt her innocence, Luke. My Elizabeth is less sure. Her instinct finds something secretive about Maggie.'

Fidelis was smiling. We rode side by side and he punched me lightly on the upper arm.

'You know what I think of instinct, Titus. We should be suspicious of it. Animals have it so that they will perform the tasks of life without hesitation or question. People are well advised to steer clear of instinct, I think. If that rat had had the power of reason she would have looked into the question of why I was giving her this strange-tasting food, and left it alone. Instead she ate it by instinct and died.'

I refrained from asking what impulsion it was, if not instinct, that had made Fidelis fall for the charms of Lysistrata Plumb.

Instead I warned, 'Don't dare put in question my wife's instincts, Luke.'

Ten minutes later we crossed the stone bridge at Bamber and, taking the left fork, followed the course of the river towards Hoghton. Shortly afterwards the windmill appeared, still distant enough to look like the silhouette of a stout man with arms outstretched, standing proudly alone between road and river. By the time we had turned down a track of about 100 yards to reach him, this quixotic giant had dissolved. Now we saw only a soaring brick tower, tapering upwards towards a dome-like roof of heavily tousled thatch. Indeed, the mill's entire fabric was badly neglected. Grass, nettle and willowherb sprouted from places up and down its wall where the mortar had fallen out, while its sail frames displayed only a few tatters of remnant sailcloth. Birds flitted in and out of the thatched eaves at the very top, above the axle shaft, but of other life there was no sign.

We dismounted beside a stout arched door that was firmly shut and locked. Leading our horses around, Fidelis going one way and I the other, we met on the other side having found no sign of humanity. Equally spaced on the circumference of the wall there were three windows about 5 feet up and, much higher, four more lights. They were all blinded by shutters. Turning our backs to the windmill on that far side we saw that the river flowed past less than 30 yards away.

Fidelis's hand came down on my shoulder.

'Wait here, Titus. I see the way in.'

Handing me his hat he remounted his horse and placed it under the bottom edge of the downward-pointing mill sail. I would like to say he hauled himself effortlessly onto the frame, but in fact it was only with extreme effort and at the third attempt that, having stood up on his saddle, he heaved high enough to hook a leg around the lowest bar. After that it was easier. He was quickly on the wooden frame itself, on its inside, and going step by step upwards until he reached the central boss and the axle. This he stepped onto and across, and succeeded in squeezing though a ragged aperture next to the axle hole, where some bricks had fallen away. He was dangerously high on the wall but now, at least, inside the mill.

I waited. After a minute I tethered the horses to a bush and called out to him. There was no reply. Then I heard his voice and walked around the mill until I saw him leaning out from an aperture larger than the windows, which was positioned under a hoisting beam.

'Hello, Titus,' he called, with a wave and a grin.

Then he disappeared again.

Another minute passed, and then another. I could hear thumps and other sounds inside, but could not imagine what they meant. Had Luke crashed through a rotten ladder, or demolished a tottering gallery? I was just wondering what I should do if he broke his leg when the shutters over the ground-floor window nearest me, at the height of my head, creaked and opened. Luke Fidelis's face looked cheerfully out.

'Jump onto the sill and come in. It's rather dark in here but, with this open, we shall see well enough.'

I hesitated. Strictly, to avoid trespassing, I should have a warrant. But armed with my summons, I thought, and if we were careful and took nothing away, I would be able to justify this as coronor's business. So, from the back of my horse, I got myself onto the sill and was soon over the window ledge and inside.

The circular interior was filled with blocks of shadow, pierced here and there with shafts of light from above. Looking up I saw that Fidelis had descended via a succession of narrow galleries, attached to the walls and connected by ladders. As my eyes adjusted to the gloom I saw that, once, a wooden floor had stretched across the space at 20 feet above our heads, but woodworm or rot had brought most of it down, and we could see right up past the axle and gearing as far as the roof. Light rayed in from wide air holes placed between the top parapet and the roof itself. Pigeons burbled melodiously. A rodent was scuttling around somewhere.

'It's been a few years, I'd say, since they reduced corn to dust in this place,' said Luke.

At ground level, the original pulverizing gear had been cleared. The grinding stones were disconnected and put aside, two gigantic wheels of granite leaning aslant against the mill wall. The rest of the machinery had been taken entirely away and the central area was now occupied by three large heaps of crates, packages and bulging sacks, each covered like hayricks by sheets of protective sailcloth.

'It looks as if it's being used for a warehouse,' I said.

'Of what, I wonder. Let's take a look.'

Fidelis untied the ropes tethering one of the canvases and pulled it off. Then he seized a box from somewhere in the middle of the pile, pulling it out. The extracted box had been a load-bearing element of the structure, for there now followed a sound midway been a creak and a wheeze, and the whole pile tottered and collapsed in a choking plume of dust. Fidelis and I barely had time to jump out of the way.

'No matter,' I said, fired now with eagerness to know what was in these bags and boxes. 'Such a thing could have happened naturally. What's in there?'

Fidelis prised open the lid of the box he held.

'Combs,' he said. 'Three score of them, at least.'

I was loosening the string around the necks of two linen sacks.

'I have ribbons in this one and . . . lace in this,' I said. 'What's in that other?'

'Buttons. And these long rolls must be bolts of cloth.'

Searching through the fallen merchandise we found containers, some intact, other spilled open, containing fans, buckles, reels of cotton, needles, and balls of knitting wool.

'Well, it's obvious what kind of warehouse it is. This is an Aladdin's cave of haberdashery. It's—'

I interrupted myself and looked at him, and he at me, in a simultaneous moment of understanding.

'Michael Drake!' he said in a low voice. 'This is the haberdasher's warehouse.'

'By God,' I said. 'So what was Hamilton Peters doing here when we saw him?'

We surveyed the avalanche of female accoutrements that lay before us.

'I think we had better go back to town, and ask Mr Drake.'

I crouched and conscientiously began restoring some of the spilled goods to their boxes while Fidelis walked around the back of one of the two intact piles. I heard him moving about, the sound of a pair of shutters opening, and then his voice, again rather low.

'Titus. Come over here.'

He was standing before the window on the south side, whose shutters he had opened. Under it was a wide table covered in dark green baize – a cloth-cutting table, apparently, for there was a steel rule on it and a pair of shears, as well as an oil lamp. Fidelis had opened his pocketbook upon the table, and was picking something up from beside it between his finger and thumb.

'I think we have stumbled on the place where poor Wilson died,' he said solemnly.

He showed me what he had picked up. It was a silver thread which he had placed in his pocketbook beside the thread we had recovered from Wilson's mouth earlier that morning. They were exactly alike. Then his fingers pointed to the baize. It displayed a pattern of dark stains, dried and encrusted.

'That will be his blood. It scattered like this when his head hit the tabletop.'

'How do you know his head hit the tabletop?'

'Because I know what happened,' said Fidelis. 'Wilson was standing facing this table, perhaps looking out of the window. His murderer came up behind and struck him right handed with the bludgeon, or whatever it was, and he pitched forward, face down on the table. He then probably slid back towards the floor arse first as his legs gave way. His face was still squarely down against the cloth and, as he slid, his mouth was pulled open and the bit of thread probably snagged between his teeth.'

I looked again at the surface of the cutting table. There were several curly fragments of the same thread on it, glittering like stars as the light fell on them.

I said, 'It seems we have suspected Peters's waistcoat in vain.'

'Yes, though it was a damn good idea, while it endured.'

'The murderer may yet have been Peters,' I pointed out. 'We saw him here, after all.'

Fidelis went down on one knee to inspect the floor beneath the table.

'There must have been much more blood down here but, as far as I can tell, it has been cleaned away. It would be good to light that lamp and see better.'

I crouched down and could see no trace of any stain on the floor.

'The murderer, whoever he was, probably waited until dark,' Fidelis went on, who had now crawled right under the table, 'then he carried Wilson down to the river and pitched him in. What's this?'

I caught the whites of his hands reaching into the shadow and drawing something out. It was a long roll of blanket. We both stood up and he laid the roll on the table.

'It was tucked in by the wall. Difficult to see.'

'It's only a roll of blanket. Shouldn't we be on our way?'

'No, wait, there's a sausage in this roll.'

Carefully he unrolled the bundle. It was not a sausage. It was a full-length flintlock hunting gun.

Chapter Twenty-six

T HE SKY WAS still pale, though the earth was shadowed, as we rode back into town. The last of the votes had now been cast and the results of the election were to be announced on the steps of the Moot Hall the next day at noon. But the election-time mob was still out on the street, unruly and drunken, roaming around singing and squaring up here and there for sudden bouts of fist fighting. As the evening fell they began to light torches and braziers, and to establish fixed camps, four or five in Market Place, and others at the town bars, at the top of Stoney Gate, on the patch of common that surrounded the theatre and at other strategic places. The more prudent townspeople stayed within doors.

Riding in through the Church Gate bar past one such camp, I remembered that I myself had been due to appear at the Moot Hall at four that afternoon to cast my votes. With so much to think about, I had utterly forgotten to do it, but I didn't mind very much. As a fellow lawyer, whose legal knowledge I respected, Nicholas Fazackerly would have had my vote, but the other three men in the ballot weighed no heavier than feathers in my scale of things, and would have been difficult to choose between.

Eager to learn if Elizabeth had been successful in finding Barty, I brought Fidelis first to my house. My wife was sitting by the fire calmly stitching, while on a stool in the corner sat the chastened child.

'As you see,' she said, 'I have brought the boy back.'

'Where did you find him?'

'I asked around the market until I had an idea of the various places he sleeps at night, his refuges if you like. He has a big brother, a labourer when he can get work, that lives off Back Weind, but he only lets the boy stay odd nights. I went directly there but drew no luck, though his brother did tell me the secret of Barty's most favourite place to sleep – the hayloft at Old Shambles.'

She meant the loft above the livery stables, the same where my own saddle horses were cared for.

'So there I went next,' she continued, 'and there I happened to find him amongst the straw, didn't I, Barty?'

Barty shifted nervously on his stool, but said nothing.

'Well, young Barty,' I said, approaching the boy, and going down on my haunches to be at the same level. 'Do you know where Maggie is now?'

He shook his head, full of woe. I went on.

'You were just going to tell me something about her when we were interrupted. The name of the man she went to, after you got her out of the constable's house. But instead you ran off. Why didn't you wait to tell me?'

'To give them time to get away, see?' Barty's voice was hoarse and low, in the way of all children's who are close to crying. 'They're looking all over for her now, Mr Cragg. Constable's right angry and he's got deputies out.'

'I know. I've seen them.'

'He's sworn he'll break her head for her when he brings her in.'

'Has he? That's the sort of fat talk you get from Constable

Mallender. He'd be advised not to do any such thing. But, in case he does, would it not be better if we found Maggie first, and brought her safely back?'

Barty's head was sunk down, his chin on his chest. His hands clasped and unclasped as he mumbled something inaudible.

'What was that, Barty? Speak up.'

Barty lifted his head.

'Aye, if you could, if she's not got away clean.'

'Well then, let's do it. Who is this man of hers? What's his name?'

Barty sniffed, and the action seemed to help him make up his mind, for he straightened his back and spoke in a clear voice for the first time.

'It's Hamilton, sir, that's his name. That's who she says.'

'Hamilton?'

I shot a glance at Elizabeth, then at Fidelis, and finally brought my attention back to Barty.

'Hamilton Peters? The servant of Mr Destercore who you have seen around town on the business of this election? Is that the Hamilton she meant?'

'Yes, sir. That's him.'

'Good God!'

'There's something else, sir.'

'Yes, Barty.'

'I didn't do it on my own like I told you.'

'Do what?'

'I didn't get her out on my own. I was helping Hamilton – Mr Peters. Her room was on first floor, sir, and he put me up on his shoulders to climb in.'

'So she left with Peters, did she, when you got her down?'

'Yes, sir. But first he kissed her, sir.'

'Oh? In what way? Do you mean on the lips – a lover's kiss?'

Barty would not look at me. His lowered eyes were fixed on the floor.

'It were not like ordinary kissing but . . . like they were biting each other.'

'Indeed? And did they say where they would go?'

'I heard Maggie say, is it safe to go to Drake's. He said yes. Then they went off, after they told me to say nowt about it.'

'Shall we engage linkmen?' asked Fidelis.

We were preparing to go to Michael Drake's. It was now fully dark and, with so much disorder on the street, a couple of torches to light our way, and men carrying them to protect us, might have been useful. On the other hand it would take time to arrange and I was in a hurry.

I went into my library and from a high shelf took down the cherrywood box in which nestled a pair of duelling pistols. These had been presented to me by a lady, a year ago, as a keepsake for a service I had done her, and though I had in the meantime taken the trouble to learn how to load them, I had not as yet had any reason or any wish to fire them. Now I handed one gun to Fidelis, took the other myself, and together we loaded them.

'Just for safety,' I said.

At the last minute I decided to bring Barty with us, in case we needed an extra pair of eyes, or a runner. We walked out into Cheapside. To our left Market Place was thronged with election revellers, who were now predominantly Tories and crowing their anticipated victory. They were readying themselves to gambol through the streets behind the mayor, who would shortly be parading around town ceremoniously by torchlight, from bar to bar. He would be carrying the books containing the election results from the polling hall to be locked securely in the Moot Hall, before counting in the morning and the announcement of the result at noon. The fact that the polling hall and Moot Hall were one and the same place was no deterrent to the plan: what they wanted was a rousing procession, and the chance to wear their chains and finery. That they went round in a circle was of no consequence.

We turned our steps, however, not left towards Market Place, but right, completing the short distance up Cheapside and crossing the road slant-wise in front of the Moot Hall, where Fisher Gate became Church Gate. From there we passed into the narrower and gloomier Stoney Gate. The Gamecock as we passed it was lively enough with noise and bright lights while Drake's shop, just beyond it, showed only the dimmest of lights, probably just a candle, behind the drapes on the first floor. I pointed to a shadowed archway on the opposite side of the street and Fidelis and the boy stationed themselves there; then I rapped hard on the door, which was the entrance to the shop but also the front door of the living quarters. The door was glassed but a heavy drape was drawn across it.

Nothing happened. Then Fidelis slipped from his concealment and joined me.

'Someone raised the curtains a fraction, and then immediately dropped them again.'

'Anyone you knew?'

'I didn't see enough. But it was a woman.'

'A woman? Drake is unmarried and lives alone, except for his apprentice.'

At length I heard footsteps approach the door on the inside and a faint flicker of light shone through a chink in the curtain. I put my ear to the glass and heard a woman's voice speaking in an urgent whisper.

'Is that you?'

'Who else?' I hissed.

'What've you come back for?'

A bolt scraped above, and then another below, and the door opened. I pushed it wider and stepped in, followed immediately by Fidelis. As soon as she saw me the young woman gave a startled squeak and took a frightened step back into the room, her eyes wide and her knuckles in her teeth. We had found Maggie Satterthwaite.

'I used to be at my grandfather's to do the kitchen when he had his guests in for cards,' said Maggie. 'He wanted a fuss made of Mr Reynolds, him being a gentleman and candidate for Parliament. Everything would be proper on those evenings – best service, best crocks, a roast bird, Cheshire cheese, port wine.'

We were sitting in the shop, with Maggie's single candle on the counter. Fidelis and I had decided as soon as we had calmed the girl that we would wait with her.

'Who is it you were expecting?' I had asked. 'Are you waiting for Hamilton Peters?'

She had looked more than surprised at the mention of this name.

'How did you know about him?' she asked.

'There's a story to that, but it's your story we want to hear, Maggie. We have sympathetic ears. Go back to the beginning.'

She told us it had all started with her grandfather's Sunday-night card game. Originally four Whig friends used to gather but, when one of them died the previous year, they invited Mr Reynolds to make up the party as he had come to live in the town and was to be their candidate at the next election.

'When you served at table, was there much talk of politics?'

'Oh, yes, while they were eating and in between hands of cards, it was how to beat the Tories, how to get certain pamphlets on sale, all that. Not that I paid a lot of attention.'

'You mean you were not a part of these discussions?'

'No, I am very dull about politics. And they were only interested in me in a very different way – or rather one of them was.'

'Who do you mean?'

'I mean Michael Drake, who owns this shop.'

I exchanged a glance with Fidelis. We were perhaps coming to the heart of all this, and especially of why we had found her waiting alone in this house.

'He used to come and stand in the kitchen door to watch me work. He'd say he'd quit his hand and would rather look at me than sit and count the cards falling. And that's what he did, watch me, like a cat. I hated it. It made me feel prickly all over myself. He had that look in his eye. Then once he came right into the kitchen when I was at the sink and got hold of me and when I twisted around he kissed me. It was horrible. I told him, never do that again, and he said, yes, he would, first chance he got. So I slapped him hard as I could and said he was an old man and he disgusted me. I'm sure the sound of the slap carried to the room where the others were playing, but no one said owt, then or later. Michael Drake's eyes changed, though. Before, they were always mocking, like, but after that they were looking at me with hate.'

'Was it Michael Drake who was responsible for your . . . well, your disgrace at the Ferry Inn? The reason for your dismissal?'

She lowered her head.

'In a way, yes, sir.'

'How?'

'By putting Mr Wilson onto me. Mr Drake told him, after they'd finished cards one night, that he could have me, if he liked. I was easy, so he told him. Liar. That's how much he hated me. Well, I was sleeping at the Ferry Inn at the time and I had to help Mr Wilson back with me after the cards, and when we got there Mr Wilson didn't go to his room, but followed me to mine and . . . Well, they found him asleep on my bed in the morning.'

'Was Michael Drake also at the inn?'

'No. His old mother lives nearby. He would always sleep at her cottage.'

'And did Thomas Wilson force you on that night, Maggie?'

Maggie laughed.

'Oh, no! He were too drunk to do owt. But that's not what it looked like to them at the inn. Mr Wilson, he were a customer, he could do no wrong. So it must all be on me. I was a slut and a whore and all the rest. They give me the sack.'

'Can you remember the night Antony Egan fell into the river? There had been a card game that night, too, hadn't there?'

'Yes, course I do. But he never fell in.'

Fidelis leaned forward in his chair. The deeply shadowed room felt ghostly, hollow.

'How do you mean?'

'They did it. Drake, Wilson, Reynolds – or maybe not Reynolds for he had left on the last ferry, I think. My grandfather had gone to bed. The other two went out as I was clearing table. When they came back in for more to drink they were well satisfied with themselves. They had done something, but they would not say what.'

'But what about Mr Destercore and his man Peters? Didn't you see them that night?'

'We'd seen Mr Destercore earlier. He had come by to greet Mr Reynolds, and he stayed for a bit of supper but he was tired from journeying and went back early to the Ferry Inn.'

'And Peters?'

Maggie shook her head slowly.

'I never saw him, sir, not that night. But later I saw him at the Gamecock, and he'd be coming in and out of this shop. I think it were then that Mr Destercore had started to talk about John Allcroft, and how they could save more votes for the party by getting rid of him. Drake was all for the idea, but Wilson and my granddad didn't like it. I think that's why they were killed, see? They didn't like it and they would have told, that's what I think. Braver than me, they would've been, if they had told.'

She sniffed, and now I saw tears glistening in her eyes in the candlelight.

'So are you saying you had nothing to do with Allcroft's poisoning?'

'I did, but only without knowing it, sir, I swear! Drake pestered me for word on Allcroft, like where he ate his dinner, which I told him was in his room, and he asked me if the room was locked and I said no, because the key was lost.'

Luke Fidelis, who had been listening intently, cleared his throat.

'Maggie, tell me what you are doing here, now. Who are you waiting for?'

'Oh sir, I am afraid to tell.'

'Is it Hamilton Peters?'

'I can't, I mustn't—'

'Come now, Maggie. Is it Peters?'

'I have sworn.'

'That doesn't matter. An oath to murderers is no oath. Mr Cragg here is coroner. You must tell him. You must.'

'Very well, sir. Yes, it is. He is my friend, sir, my . . .'

'Your lover?'

'He does say he loves me, sir. And wants to take me away and protect me.'

'Was he to take you away tonight?'

'After the business—. After something that was to happen tonight.'

'After what?' said Fidelis, urgently. 'What business tonight?'

But Maggie was weeping now, with her head sunk down to her knees. Her words when they came out were broken, and difficult to make out.

'A terrible thing, sir, a wicked thing, though no worse than what they've done before. He said we would be miles and miles away by the time it came out that Mr Drake and him had done it. He said Mr Destercore and Mr Reynolds would never be prosecuted for it.'

'Done what, Maggie? What terrible thing were they going to do?'

Emotion was making her sob now, choking her words and making them very hard to pick out. Her speech, as I give it here, must be understood as being fragmentary and spoken with the utmost effort.

'It must be around about this time that they will do it, sir, this time of night. You can still maybe stop it, if it isn't too late. I cannot keep it to myself any more. It's the mayor, sir. They plan to shoot him, see, as he parades down Fisher Gate. Just like they shot my grandfather. I heard them talking, and they went out with guns, sir. They are that angry, they say the election's lost and the mayor's arranged it all by corrupting the vote and deserves to die. But you can stop them, you can, if you go quick. Mr Drake, he threatened me with death if I spoke out. Without Hamilton he'd have killed me anyway, I think, and blamed me for the poisoning. That's how much he hates me. But I'll not keep quiet now, not when it can still be stopped. If you go quick.'

By now, Luke had leapt to his feet, only a fraction of time before me.

'My God, Titus, it will be from the room at Mrs Bryce's, as Biggs passes below. We must get up there. The parade has probably started already. God knows where it is now!'

'Maggie!' I warned. 'You must stay here. If you go out you are in danger from Mallender's hue and cry. Stay exactly where you are, keep the door locked and admit no one until I come again for you. I shall say nothing of where you are.'

She nodded her head mutely, humbly. I felt she had returned to sanity. The villains had turned Maggie's head towards them by persuading her that, without their help, her case was hopeless. Now this influence was counterbalanced. We went out and I heard the rasp of the bolts behind us.

We left Barty to watch the house, with particular attention to the back entrance, and strode up Stoney Gate at the double, full of purpose. Well, I thought, perhaps Elizabeth's fears would be ground-less: Maggie had not run; she had not condemned herself. Instead she had forestalled a crime – perhaps – if we could get there in time.

My fingers touched the pistol in my pocket. I felt excitement, elation. It is this, I imagine, that charges soldiers up to go into action. There is a coil inside you hard wound, or if you prefer, a balloon tightly inflated, pent up, waiting for release.

We turned left into Church Gate and continued urgently along Fisher Gate, where we were increasingly impeded by knots of by-standers and routs of political enthusiasts. The sides of the street were lined with folk, some waving small Union flags, rather more with oak-leaf flags and other tokens of their opposition to our German monarchy. Evidently the mayoral progress had not yet reached this spot.

I looked down the length of the street, sloping away from us towards the town bar and then on to our small tidal port beyond. I could hear a band playing, and whoops and shouts. Great flaming torches, flaring in the darkness, were visible at the far end of Fisher Gate. I saw one particular torch go high into the air, and then come spiralling down into the hands of its bearer, to the hoots and applause of the crowd. This was the head of the procession.

'Come on,' shouted Fidelis, 'we are not too late. We must get to the Bryce house before they do.'

But our progress was being impeded by the people milling

around in the street and a moment later I had bumped and rebounded off one of them. I realized it was Adam Lorris.

'Eh, Mr Cragg,' he said, failing to read the signs of my haste. 'It's ready! Your Aesop. It's done. Shall I—?'

'Not now, Adam,' I said. 'I am in something of a hurry.'

I pushed on but then, quite involuntarily and without a spark of warning, the words of Elizabeth about Maggie – 'If she runs, it will condemn her' – and the fable Lorris and I had discussed on the morning they found Antony Egan in the river – the one called *The Scarecrows and the Foxes* – fused together in my head and exploded. By virtue of the association of ideas, or the concatenation of memory and experience, I suddenly saw their true significance for the present moment. Is *that* it? I thought. Is *that* what she's doing?

Immediately the tension began to leave me, the coil to unwind, the balloon to go flat. I stopped pushing forward and stood still in the midst of the turmoil, lucidly calm. *The Scarecrows and the Foxes*. Of course: how obvious.

I no longer faced down the street towards the procession but revolved on my heel to survey the view back the way we had come. Fidelis, who had gone ahead of me, now returned and grabbed my arm, tugging it.

'Titus! What are you doing? We have no time to lose. Come along!'

I put a restraining hand on his arm. All the urgency and hurry had left me.

'No, Luke,' I said. 'If we go anywhere, we should go back – but I doubt that is necessary either.'

'What, Titus? I don't understand.'

I looked at him, rather enjoying the moment.

'The game is played,' I said. 'The cards are back in the pack. The players have gone their ways.'

'Have you taken leave of your senses?'

'No, I have come to them. Light has suddenly dawned. There is no attack on the mayor. There is no murderous Whig plot, and in fact there never was. It is a pack of lies, Luke. We have been spun a yarn, and it is all a cock and a bull – or should I say a couple of scarecrows and a female fox.'

Chapter Twenty-seven

I T WOULD BE no great exaggeration to say that Luke Fidelis took this rather like a man interrupted in coitus. He was flushed in the face, blowing hard: I had never seen him so fired up and passionate of purpose at one moment, and so frustrated at the next.

He shook loose from my hand and made a step away from me.

'You *have* taken leave of your senses. I'm going on. The risk is too great.'

I found myself smiling.

'Give it up. There is no risk at all. It is all quite clear to me. None whatsoever.'

The fight went out of Fidelis at last. To go bursting alone into a house such as Mrs Bryce's – if, indeed, he got in at all – and to try to apprehend desperate men would be a very different matter from going in with one to back him up.

'Very well, Titus,' he said, brandishing his index finger in my face. 'But you had better have very good reasons for this.'

We moved down the street, more slowly now, until we stood with crowds of other spectators on the opposite side of the street from Mrs Bryce's house. This address was still subject to the attentions of a group of Tory zealots, shouting slogans against Hoghton, Reynolds and Walpole, and constantly raising three cheers for the 'martyr' John Allcroft.

'They are sadly deluded,' I said with seraphic confidence. 'He was no martyr at all.'

The torch throwers and the band approached with the coach immediately behind. Some in the crowd threw streamers of paper, which occasionally caught fire from a torch and caused screams of delight as they flared and died, like parodic streaks of lightning. As the mayoral coach came up, the band launched into the tune of the moment, 'Rule Britannia!'. I looked up at the two windows of Mrs Bryce's music room. On the right I saw a downcast-looking Reynolds with Mrs Bryce herself. She was at one moment laughing and cheering, because she could not help it, and at the next patting Reynolds on the shoulder, and running the backs of her fingers fondly across his cheek. On the left stood Denis Destercore, scowling down at the revellers. Though the results had not yet been announced, few held out any hope for the Whigs.

The mayor's coach drew level with the house. I was aware of Fidelis craning his neck by my side, but I felt quite complacent as the mayor rumbled safely on, past Miss Colley's and past Wilkinson's pie shop, and up the gently sloping street without harm or incident.

Fidelis turned to me and gripped my upper arm a fraction tightly. 'How could you be so sure?' he demanded.

'I had sensed something at Drake's shop, something not right. It was dark and impossible to be certain, and it wasn't until after we'd left that I knew what it was.'

'And?'

'That shop was a shell. There was no stock. A haberdasher's should be full of cloth, bolts of it, and boxes of ribbons and trinkets and suchlike lining the walls. That room where we sat had nothing in it that absorbed sound. It was hollow, empty. The stock was gone and it resounded.'

Fidelis thought for a moment. He was recalling the interior scene, when we were listening to Maggie's sad tale.

'Yes, you are perfectly right. I did not notice but, now you mention it, the place felt as if it had been hollowed out.'

'And I think we know where the goods that used to fill it are to be found now.'

'Yes. Those boxes and packages heaped up without any system.'

'I would say they were the whole contents of the shop brought higgledy-piggledy in three cartloads and dumped in a hurry.'

'But why? That's the question we must address now. Drake could tell us, but where is he?'

'He's running,' I said simply. 'Running, while Maggie lurks in the covert.'

'In the *covert*? What in heaven's name are you babbling about?'

I had not seen my friend at such a loss for a long time. For once he had been distracted from dispassionate observation – something with which the heart-melting prettiness of Maggie Satterthwaite had much to do – and now he was groping for a logical solution to a problem created by forces that were not logical.

'I read it in a story when I was a child. A fable. Come along. I know where we can get more information.'

'What about Maggie?'

'I think she will stop where she is but if not, there is no great danger in it.'

I led the way back to the Old Shambles, which we cut down before crossing to the north side of Market Place.

'So, where *are* we going?'

Fidelis was growing a little tetchy, his brain still unable to establish the connections that would explain my actions, or rather my failure to act. I admit I was rather enjoying his bemusement.

'Molyneux Square. I intend to look into Mr Drake's finances. And to do that we must find his man of business.'

Preston's three money-lenders – or money-scriveners as we called them – all lived on the substantial square built during the last century for the dwellings of Preston's richer merchants and professional men. The first address we tried was Frederick Taylor's, but he was not at home. The second was that of John Furbelow, where the door was opened by the old father, Ezekial, in his nightshirt and cap and with candle in hand.

Ezekial had himself been a scrivener in his day but, he told us curtly, 'I have never to my knowledge had any dealings with a haberdasher, sir. Goodnight to you.'

Finally we came to the house of Alphonsus Parr, a fellow bibliophile and genial friend of mine.

'Yes, Titus,' he said in reply to my enquiry, 'Mr Drake does indeed do business with us – or rather he did. Come into the library, both of you, and take some wine and a pipe.'

Parr's collection of books was twice the size of mine, and included many volumes that I would not have refused the gift of. But he collected more for show than I did and, settling into one of his comfortable chairs and looking around at the long, expensive sets of Milton, Shakespeare and Bishop Atterbury in folio, with their tooled bindings, I wondered how much he read them.

'What is it about Mr Drake that you would like to know?' Parr asked me.

'About his accounts, his financial affairs – anything you can tell us.'

Parr cleared his throat.

'Well, normally, that would be bound under the seal of discretion, as you ought to be glad to hear, Cragg. We professional men are nothing if not discreet.'

There was caution in Parr's voice. The scrivener's reticence is always a little different, I find, from that of the attorney or, for that matter, the doctor. When called upon to be discreet Fidelis and I can hide behind professional mysteries. But, since everybody believes they know money, the scrivener finds it harder to erect barriers of mystique between himself and the enquirer. He is forced back on the weaker notions of confidence and trust.

'However,' he went on, 'I believe I no longer owe a duty of discretion to Mr Drake comparable to what I would extend to you.'

He drew on his pipe thoughtfully.

'The fact is that Drake has been a persistent defaulter for years. He owes money everywhere. He raises mortgages and then does not honour the repayments; he borrows privately and does not pay back; he orders stock that he does not pay for.'

'Is he insolvent?'

Parr held up his hand, with finger and thumb a quarter of an inch apart.

'If you ask me, he is that close to imprisonment, Cragg.'

We returned once again to the town's centre where, under the portico of the Moot Hall, its main door now locked, Oswald Mallender had set out a table and an oil lamp, and was sitting with pen in hand puzzling over a large sheet of paper. I went to speak to him.

'Mr Mallender,' I said. 'Are you still commander-in-chief of the search for the absconded prisoner?'

He fixed me with his small eyes, upholstered with fat.

'Yes, I am still engaged in that business. We have looked all over, sir, and found not a hair of her head.'

He tapped the paper.

'I have listed here all the places my men have searched. I have now sent them out again and await their return. But it is my belief she quit the town as soon as she left my custody.'

'Really? Then she must have returned very promptly, for I have seen her in the past hour. I had thought you must have discovered her by now.'

Mallender looked up at me with increased suspicion.

'You saw her and did not report the matter?'

'I am reporting it now. I strongly recommend you try Mr Drake's shop in Stoney Gate. If you go there straight, I believe you'll find she is waiting there, ready for you to take her.'

We walked on, leaving the constable open mouthed.

'Is it not a bit hard, Titus, turning the poor girl in like that? You were previously convinced of her innocence.'

'If that is hard, she's harder, Luke. Parr's information has capped it for me. She's not a poor girl, she's a killer, I'm sure of it now. I also hope that having her publicly arrested once more will flush out her accomplice.'

'I would not think Drake – a debtor, dodging prison – will show himself.'

'Maybe not. But there is also her admitted lover, Hamilton Peters. That kiss Barty saw was not a trivial thing. What did he say? "Like biting each other." That's passion, is that.'

'Come into the Turk's Head and we'll have a bottle,' urged Fidelis. 'I want to talk this out.'

But I was too tired. It had been an extraordinary day, and a long one.

'No, Luke, go to bed. That's what I'm doing. We shall meet in the morning and when you have slept on it, you'll have the answer for yourself.'

'That is my worry, Titus – that I won't sleep on it. That you are condemning me to a sleepless night while I hunt for the truth.'

'Your brain's too quick for that, Luke. Just loose it and it will run down the hare.'

*

I woke at the late hour of eight o'clock. As soon as I'd returned the night before Elizabeth had given me soup and a few cuts of ham, and warmed a cup of punch for me, before sending me straight to bed to cure my yawns. It had been a deep and dreamless sleep and I rose feeling as sharp and shiny as a needle. The day, bright and clear, matched my mood.

Straight after breakfast I was in the office, talking to Furzey. He told me how he had lodged Wilson's body in the vestry, and how Churchwarden Fleetwood had wailed despairingly at the prospect of the parish giving hospitality to yet another dead guest. We discussed inquest arrangements, and I told him we could safely have the hearings on Monday, using the same panel of townsmen for both. I told him I would have to think about whom we should call: with criminal charges impending, these inquests might by Monday be reduced to formalities.

'Did you find the note I left about the letter to the jurors who sat on Allcroft?' I asked.

'Aye, the letters went out by six.'

'Good. I ask only because you were late back, or so I thought.'

'Not late. Voting. Not that it did any good. It seems we took a beating.'

'Yes, that is what everybody is saying.'

The letter to the jurors had been meant to placate young Allcroft, but it had another, unfortunate and unintended effect, which would have been avoided had I taken greater trouble in the drafting. The problem was in the words I had written in my note to Furzey: '*there must be no mention made of the Whigs' having plotted Allcroft's murder*'. I had meant these for a drafting instruction to Furzey, not as words to include in the letter. But Furzey had simply transcribed the phrase and, as I now saw, it was open to a grave misinterpretation: to the interpretation, in fact, that the Whigs *had* plotted against the Tories, and that I wished to suppress this.

Now, going out, I found talk of this all over town. Jurors had shown the letter to family and friends, and these had passed its contents on to others, with embellishments, until everyone was debating it, in a process that tended rather to defeat than to fulfil Jotham Allcroft's intentions. I was to meet Fidelis at the coffee house at ten, but first I called in at Wilkinson's bread and pie shop to see Allcroft and, if possible, explain that this new outbreak of gossip was more or less an accident of misunderstanding, inflamed by people's gross appetite for sensation.

When I asked for him, a little girl was told to take me through the shop and down the yard to the 'meat house'. At the yard's end, a gate gave onto a track, leading after a few paces to a group of workshops or sheds and three adjoining animal pens, in which porkers lay contentedly, half immersed in mud. The girl pointed to the nearest shed, and then skipped back the way we had come. As I approached the door, the sound of a human voice cursing inarticulately, and punctuated by violent thuds, could be heard. Upon entering I could not prevent my mouth from dropping open.

At a heavy rough-hewn table, a man with his back to me was savagely hacking a freshly killed carcase into joints, swearing furiously with, and between, each blow. He wore a long leather apron over a rough buffin shirt with sleeves rolled high and arms slathered with gore to above the elbow. Nearby, a second carcase was hanging by its hind legs from a beam above a bucket, into which dripped the blood from its recently cut throat. Two wooden tubs stood near at hand: one contained the red, blue, pink and grey coils of a pig's entrails; the other held the pig's head reposing in a mess of its own lights. The smell was a powerful compound of blood, sweat and manure.

'Mr Allcroft?' I called, stepping hesitantly through the doorway, for I was not yet sure it was he. The butcher jumped in his skin at the sound of my voice, then sprang around, revealing himself to be without question Jotham Allcroft, sober Quaker and former clerk of the fusiliers' pay division.

'You!' he said in his unmistakable fluting voice. 'You!'

He stood as if at bay, spattered with gouts of fresh blood, his baby face set in something between a snarl and a pout.

I opened my hands.

'Yes, but good heavens, I did not think to find you doing such work as this!'

He raised the meat cleaver in his hand and I took a flinching step back.

'What do you want, lawyer? What MORE do you want from me?'

'Well, I think I owe you an explan—'

I did not finish the sentence for without further warning Jotham ran at me brandishing the bloody cleaver above his head, and giving a squealing cry of pig-like fury. I somehow slipped to one side and his scything blow missed me, the cleaver burying itself in the door post with a splintering crash. At this point I would have taken to my heels but now, though struggling to pull the thick blade from the post, he stood square in the doorway between me and escape. I edged instead into the interior of the shed, taking shelter behind the butcher block. Having extracted his weapon at last, he pursued me there, aiming huge chops at the intervening air with the cleaver. I continued round the table until I bumped into the hanging carcase, which I crept behind. For a few moments I danced this way and that as he aimed blow after blow at me but struck only the hanging pig, which began gradually to be reduced to shreds.

Panting heavily now, he was forced to pause and draw breath, whereupon I saw my chance and made a run for the door. Unfortunately the tub of guts stood in my way. I saw it too late, tried to vault over it and instead caught my foot on the rim and went down, sprawling on the ground. I rolled over to see Jotham looming over me, the gory meat cleaver ready to strike down and, no doubt, part my head from my body.

At that moment, a shadow was cast into the room from the door, and a deep voice shouted, 'Hey!' Then some sort of heavy staff flashed horizontally through the air, striking Allcroft a heavy jab on the chest. I saw my attacker's face change from rage to surprise. So concentrated had he been upon butchering me that he seemed not to have noticed the shadow, or heard the voice, and the blow, catching him all unawares, sent him staggering backwards two or three paces until his progress was checked by contact with the guts tub. He wobbled there for an instant or two, but momentum had the last say and down he sat, his big arse plopping into the tub. The cleaver fell from his fingers.

Still on the ground I rolled over to acknowledge my saviour and saw a dirty scarlet coat, tricorn hat and a brass-knobbed mace of office: Oswald Mallender. For the first time in my life I was heartily glad to see him.

After helping me up, Mallender produced a piece of paper, which turned out to be a warrant. Holding this up as he might a lot at auction he solemnly intoned, in words that must have been of his own devising:

> *'Ahem. It is my sworn duty to inform Mr Jotham Allcroft (here present) that this day a complaint has been made against his person for murder, and that he is therefore arrested by warrant of His Worship the Mayor and must come with me, the duly appointed officer, to be brought before His Worship and to answer to the said charge. Stand up!'*

But, with his rear end plugged deep in the container of entrails, Jotham Allcroft could not get up. All he could do in his anger and impotence was kick his feet, wave his arms and weep. Mallender and I regarded him for a few moments, then grabbed his wrists and pulled. He came out with an audible sucking sound and a few minutes later Jotham Allcroft was marched up Fisher Gate to the Moot Hall to answer a charge of murder. Slubbered all over with blood and guts, he was crying like a baby for his mother. It was a sight that people would remember on Fisher Gate for years to come.

Chapter Twenty-eight

Home I went for a change of clothes and, as it was now past ten, straight out again to meet Luke Fidelis at the coffee house we favoured, the Turk's Head. I found him, with pot and cups before him and a pipe in his mouth, perusing the *Preston Weekly Journal*, which had been freshly issued that morning.

'It is confidently predicted that both the Whig candidates have lost, Titus. This is based on an unofficial word from the mayor's office. Sir Harry Hoghton is now a laughing stock. His support has collapsed entirely and Reynolds, for all his greasy efforts in the past year, has never been very popular with our tradesmen.'

'Hoghton will not like being ejected from Parliament, but it's his own fault.'

I settled down opposite Fidelis and he poured the coffee.

'You have heard about the arrest of Jotham Allcroft?' I asked.

'I saw the spectacle on Fisher Gate from my window this morning – and saw you there too. What in God's name happened?'

I related the alarming events in the butchery shed. Far from being concerned for my own well-being, Fidelis thought it amusing.

'Saved by Constable Mallender! There must be a first time for everything.'

'He prefaced the arrest with a speech when the prisoner was

still stuck in the tub – something of his own devising, for it was pomposity itself.'

'I hope he did not ask the man to come clean.'

I refused to encourage, by laughing, Fidelis's regrettable weakness for wordplay – the punning, Penkethman side of him.

Instead I said, 'So, how did you sleep?'

'Not perfectly, but I believe I have puzzled out the vital questions.'

I began filling my pipe.

'Let's hear your conclusions, then, and see if they tally with mine. Start with last night at Drake's shop.'

'Maggie was playing for time. She was ready to make up any story that would get us out of the house and give time, not for herself, but one of her accomplices. I fancy he was actually there in the house all the time, waiting upstairs for the chance to get away.'

'I think it was Drake.'

He nodded.

'And the question is, why did she want him to get away while she herself remained?'

I knew the answer, but I led him on.

'Why, then?'

'To preserve herself, and all her hopes. Absolute blame for the evil deeds of the recent past would naturally fall on the man who runs away, not on the woman who calmly remains. Escaping suspicion, she can enjoy the fruits of the crime.'

'Ah – so you allow the possibility of a murderous conspiracy.'

'That is what it must have been. I saw that at about half past midnight. And to find out the reason for any murder, one must address the essential question. *Cui bono?* Who benefits?'

'We have at least three on our hands, Luke, and maybe four. Was the answer the same in all of them?'

'I am not yet quite sure of that, but perhaps. Let us take them one by one. First, Allcroft. The obvious beneficiary of his death is Jotham the son, who will inherit all his wealth. We knew the junior Allcroft and his senior had disagreed, but could not see why or how Jotham could have killed his father, and never in fact suspected him. But bring Maggie Satterthwaite into the equation and all that changes.'

'Yes. Until this morning's events I did not fully grasp that. She meant to marry Jotham, of course. He was besotted by her, so much that he tried to kill me for putting her back in gaol.'

'But note one thing, Titus. Maggie and Jotham were very careful to keep their connection secret. If we or the mayor and magistrates had known of it, her whole scheme would have been exposed at the start.'

'*Her* scheme? So you see Maggie actively at the heart of this?'

'Oh, she will pretend she was passive. But she ensnared Jotham and then convinced him that his father must die to bring forward the inheritance. And, of course, she managed the poisoning by herself. She was a proper Lady Macbeth.'

'But, as you've said, this plot could never work unless blame was successfully laid off.'

'Yes, on Drake. And the beauty of the whole idea is that he did not mind. What we learned last night was that, above all, he had to get away. He was hounded by creditors, and on the point of being arrested for debt. I think Drake was always intending to escape his creditors in America. He probably had passage booked on a Liverpool ship – they may even now be at sea – but before he could leave he needed funds. The stratagem, therefore, was for Jotham to provide him with cash, probably by buying his shop's stock. There was some risk, because Drake's many creditors should have first call on the residue of his business, but the risk was mitigated by the secret removal of the stock to the mill. If no one could find it, no one could seize it for the creditors.'

'If only I had pursued Furzey on the matter, I would have known Allcroft was the mill's owner and we should have tumbled to this much sooner.'

'The great usefulness of the mill was its distance from town,' Fidelis went on. There was a certain dour relentlessness about his exposition – perhaps the consequence of his lack of sleep in the night. 'It was safe out of the way and after a decent time Jotham could recoup his money by selling the stuff, and the trinkets and so on, bit by bit.'

Fresh coffee and pipes were brought. I was feeling leisurely now, almost light headed, as one does when days of intense activity have come to an end. I picked up the theme.

'So let's agree,' I said, 'that Allcroft's murder was a three-handed conspiracy, with a very wicked leading hand played in it by Maggie.'

'She is cool, is she not? She is evil, but she has courage.'

Despite everything we knew, and despite (or perhaps because of) her long bamboozlement of us, there was still admiration in Fidelis's voice when he spoke of Maggie.

'But what about the deaths of Antony Egan, Thomas Wilson and Maggie's grandfather? We must decide where they fit.'

'I have some ideas, but hazy as yet. I would like to know your opinion.'

He sat back, like a chess player who has taken his turn.

I gathered my thoughts and began.

'Very well. Remember the role Drake has been playing. He was to shoulder the blame, *in absentia*, for the murder. But he needed to be equipped with a quite different motive for having murdered Allcroft, different from the actual motive, that is – and it was decided this should be *political*. The deception was almost successful. We were led, by the nose, into believing it.'

I lit a taper, put the flame to my pipe, and continued.

'So what we imagined – and were supposed to imagine – was a small conspiracy of Whigs trying to reduce the Tory vote by removing tally captains and so knocking their tallies out of the vote. I don't know how, but I think Wilson and Isaac Satterthwaite thought they had uncovered this imaginary plot themselves and confronted Drake with it. Naturally they had to die or they would have let out the secret.'

'That the plot did not exist?'

'Yes. But in certain ways their deaths served Maggie's and Jotham's turn anyway. They promoted the idea of a political plot even further, because of their having been members of the same Whig group that met regularly with Michael Drake, under the pretext – so goes the suggestion – of a game of cards.'

Fidelis puffed deeply on his pipe.

'A smokescreen,' he said, laying a fairly heavy one himself. 'The thicker they could make it, the more chance of obscuring the real evil underneath. But there is little doubt of two things – that Drake killed Satterthwaite in Fisher Gate and that he did so with Jotham's assistance, since the shot must have been from the attic window above the pie shop.'

I nodded.

'Yes, he was expert with a hunting gun, so I believe, and rabbits are more difficult to shoot than people. I don't believe, however, that he would have contemplated trying the shot from Mrs Bryce's house. Too many people might have seen him – the servants, for instance, and there are other residents.'

'Agreed. But who do you say killed Wilson – Drake again?'

'Yes. He must have lured him to the mill. And I also fancy it was Michael Drake that tried to crack open my head. I thank you again for my preservation.'

'It was nothing.'

Fidelis rubbed his hands together.

'So we are left with Destercore and Reynolds. And Peters, of course, the first we suspected.'

He was the younger, but he was testing me, I felt, just as a master puts a pupil through his exercises.

'I believe Destercore and Reynolds are completely innocent,' I said. 'As to Peters—'

'He remains a puzzle, does he not? Who is the fellow, what is his game, and where is he now? Well, he needs catching, or we will never be sure.'

'He must already be far from Preston. He's too clever to be seen again in these parts. I think he hoped to take Maggie with him when he got her out of Mallender's house.'

'Yes, she played him for as much of a fool as she played the rest of us.'

Fidelis's eyes were gleaming, with that chess player's look again. He was imagining the final crushing moves of the game.

'And there is one more thing, Titus. We must decide where the death of your kinsman fits into the scheme.'

But his move would have to wait for, at this moment, I spotted Barty threading his way between the coffee house's mid-morning customers, and looking one by one into the booths. When he found ours he handed me a note:

Mr Cragg, sir,

Maggie Satterthwaite has asked to see you. They have her in the House of Correction. The Mayor has this morning committed her for trial.

R. Furzey

I handed the note to Fidelis who said when he'd read it, 'I always think the best time for interesting things is now.'

I rose and picked up my hat.

'Yes, I think I will go straight there.'

The Old Friary lay in ruins between Marsh Lane and Friar Gate, but a few of its better-preserved buildings had remained in use. One of these was the House of Correction, where civil malefactors who refused to pay their fines received brief incarceration, and where women prisoners awaiting criminal trial were sometimes sent as an alternative – and a welcome one – to the damp cellars under the Moot Hall.

Maggie's cell was dry and airy enough, about 12 foot square. It had a high, barred window and a brick floor, a single chair, a worm-eaten table and a pallet bed. I found the prisoner disinclined to answer questions or to converse to and fro in the usual way. Instead she pointed me into the chair, perched herself on the edge of the bed, and started to talk.

'You and me, Titus Cragg, and the way things are between us, they're different now, do you see? I can say what I like to you. There's no call for "Yes sir, no sir, three-bags-full, sir." I can say, "Kiss-my-arse, sir," if I want to. See, as soon as they arrested me I lost my place in this town. I've come off, like a loose button-hook off a dress. I'm a nobody in Preston, or an *any*body, either of the two. So I may be locked up just now, but you can also call it some kind of freedom.'

She wore a crumpled dress of plain unstarched lockram, but she herself looked surprisingly fresh, her complexion creamy and her eyes flawless, big and blue. With a little tilt of her chin she flashed those eyes at me in a kind of challenge.

'They won't hang me, you know. Transportation's for me. King's evidence, that's what I am. And them jurors and judges, they'll look at me and I shall fill their heads with thoughts of their own angel daughters – all dimpled and pretty, but not too saucy. That I can do, easy – charm them. Of course, they'll hang Jotham Allcroft, my intended husband, because I'll tell them what he did. And they'd hang Michael Drake if they caught him, because I'll also tell them what *he* did. But the fox has run and he's not for being caught. I suppose, if I am to go to America, we may meet up again, but I hope not for I don't like him, with his lecherous looks and lying promises.'

She was fiddling with her hair, not looking straight at me, but vaguely regarding the space between us.

'The vicar came in first thing. He talked to me about how I must repent and henceforth be good and preserve my soul for going to heaven. But I know it's just a story. The immortal soul! I've watched you gentlemen, you lawyers and doctors and clever folk, and you don't believe in it, not deep down, you just pretend to because the idea of it keeps us poor clods in our places. But I could never let a fairy tale get between me and what I heartily desire.'

In the momentary pause that followed, I risked a question.

'But what *do* you desire, Maggie?'

'To be rich, if you want to know. To have meat every day and never wear clogs and find more than just two changes of clothes hanging in my cupboard. So when I set eyes on Jotham Allcroft in the shop – and, you know, I never saw a man so knocked into next week by the sight of me as him – I knew then that I would have him and all his inheritance, one way or another, and soon I found a way, which *he* could never do, but *I* dared.'

She might have been talking to herself by now, almost dreamily and hardly seeming to expect a response from me.

'The night Antony Egan was drowned, drunk, in the river, was when I thought of it. Tom Wilson and Michael Drake went out late for a breath of air outside my grandfather's house – this is after cards were finished and Reynolds gone across on the ferry, and my grandfather gone to bed.'

'Was Destercore still there?'

She looked at me, momentarily recalled to time and place.

'The agent from London? No, he'd long gone. Not one for cards, him.'

'What happened when Wilson and Drake went out?'

'As I was going to *tell* you, they saw Antony the sot on the riverbank. They saw him lose his balance and slide in down the bank.'

'But you said before that they pushed him!'

She gave me a slow, crafty smile.

'I lied about that. But they might as well have, for all the help they gave him. They just stood on the bank in the shadows and had a laugh. He'd lost his hat and they threw it in after him, they said. They thought it was great sport and were still laughing about it as a prank when they came back in the house, they were that callous. And when I'd taken stock of it all I said to them that they could get rid of some more Tories before the election, if they'd a mind to it, and that I knew one they could start with. It went off from there. First a joke and then dead serious. Well, I couldn't believe my luck next, when my – what shall I call him? – my *beloved*'s Tory father turned up staying at the very inn where I worked. It were easy, after that. Easy for me, any road, because I find men don't look at what I do – they look at my bosom, and my bottom, and my ankles and my neck. Their eyes do have a way of taking their minds off the job – like yours are now, don't think I don't see it.'

In the middle of her speech I had raised my hand to interrupt her, like a child in a dame school. Now she tilted her head back, giving permission for me to speak.

'Is all this your confession, Maggie?' I asked. 'Is it for writing down?'

'No, this is for you alone, Mr Coroner. I'll be telling it them again, don't fret. I'll be telling them all, every bit.'

'What will you say about the murder of your grandfather, then, that housed you, fed you and loved you?'

'Love? He never! What he was like behind the closed door, that's what you should know, but it's a long story. Granddad was old, his time had come and any road I had nowt to do with his killing, nor with Wilson's neither. You'd have to talk to Mr Michael Drake about them.'

'Shouldn't I talk to Hamilton Peters too?'

Following all the callous ugliness of what she had been saying, a delightful smile now lit her face. She closed her eyes.

'Oh, aye, Hamilton,' she whispered. 'I tell you, I never had so much joy out of a man as him.'

Then, opening her eyes, she spoke more deliberately, and more harshly.

'He knew how to give pleasure to a girl, he did, and that's why I liked him. But, see, he's a rover, a fly-by-night, though I admit I was tempted to go off with him, even that first time, which is what? More than a year ago.'

'You knew him then?'

'Yes, but I thought better of it, for all the fun we had.'

'Why exactly was he here – do you know?'

'Some political business, he had. It were his visit to Ferry Inn, when he bedded me, that got me dismissed.'

'But you said Wilson—'

'Did I? No. He'd have liked to do it to me, of course. So would Michael Drake. But I don't let just anyone have me, Titus Cragg. I am not a common whore, whatever Grimshaw and his clack will say about me.'

All this time she had been sitting upright on her bed, but now she sprang to her feet and took two steps to the window, looking up through the grille to the sky, where high white clouds scudded across the blue.

With her back turned to me, she said, 'Well, you can nearly leave me now, Titus Cragg. I've had my say, except for one thing. I brought you here because it were you, and your doctor friend, ruined what I thought would be my life as a rich farmer's wife. Well, now I've been dwelling on it, I want you to know that maybe you've done me a favour, when all's said and done. In America, I hear, it's kiss-my-arse for everybody, you see, and I can hardly wait to get there.'

She turned around with a coquettish twirl, parted her lips in a smile so wide that it would challenge any man to say it was not a truthful one.

'So, it would be churlish of me not to thank you, wouldn't it, Mr Coroner? Well, so I do, and now you may kiss my—'

She extended her hand.

'What would you say to my hand?'

I was so surprised that I kissed it.

Chapter Twenty-nine

I WALKED AWAY WONDERING if I had been listening to the ravings of lunacy. According to Fidelis, when I told him later, this was precisely the effect Maggie was trying for.

'For a person facing the gallows, to be mad is a perfectly rational object,' he said.

I am not so sure. Maggie was not the kind of girl who would deliberately swap the noose for a cell in Bedlam. Transportation was what she was set on, and that would depend upon her convincing the court at trial that she was a poor put-upon girl, quite sane, who had fallen into wickedness by the persuasion of men.

With her beauty and quick wit, this ought not to be difficult and it, too, was a rational object. America had suited Moll Flanders well enough, and it would probably agree with Maggie Satterthwaite just as much. But all the same I think there truly was a vein, at least, of madness in Maggie's discourse. She had been perfectly reckless in what she said to me, admitting the utter venality of her 'love' for young Allcroft, owning that the murder of old Allcroft was all her idea, and confessing to unnumbered sexual acts with Hamilton Peters and, by implication, other men. Despite her airy confidence about the future, in her ability to survive, Maggie Satterthwaite's fate was still in considerable doubt.

Elizabeth had gone to visit her cousins at the Ferry Inn and I would have to tell her later of the new information Maggie had given me about the death of her uncle, though whether this could be relied upon as being true I was not sure. I made my dinner at home a quick one, knowing that Furzey and I still had not engaged a room for the two inquests on Monday, and that we must settle on witnesses. Only four would be needed, I thought: a pair from the many on Fisher Gate who saw Satterthwaite fall, Dick Middleton who found Wilson, and Fidelis for his medical opinion. Their summonses would have to be issued today, but there would be no need for detailed investigation into responsibility for the deaths. I knew now that criminal proceedings were in motion and that all that would be required of the inquest was to record how death occurred. The rest would be for the assizes.

When we had discussed all this, Furzey told me that if I went out to the Moot Hall now, I would be just in time to hear the announcement of the election result, which had been deferred from noon to two o'clock. We locked the office and went together, finding a tightly packed crowd about to hear from Mayor Biggs on the hall's steps. Shifting from foot to foot, and waiting to hear their fates, the four candidates were ranged under the portico behind the mayor.

'As recording officer and mayor for this ancient borough of Preston,' he intoned, 'I, William Biggs, hereby declare the votes cast in the late election to have been . . .'

The crowd stirred and then was still. Their murmuring ceased.

'For Mr Nicholas Fazackerley . . .'

He paused, looked up as if to make sure all were duly listening, then returned his eyes to his paper.

'Three hundred and ninety-one votes.'

There was a solid cheer and a few boos. The votes looked enough to take Fazackerley back to Westminster.

'For Mr James Shuttleworth, three hundred and eighty-four votes.'

This was greeted by a thinner, reedier cheer, but one that still prevailed over a few Whig catcalls.

'For Mr Francis Reynolds, two hundred and thirty-one votes.'

There was a loud hurrah from half a dozen in the crowd, though whether in support of Reynolds himself, or to cheer his defeat, was difficult to tell.

'And finally, for Sir Henry Hoghton, fourteen votes.'

This was what the people had been waiting for. They erupted into a cacophony of derisive whoops and yells, whistles and slogans, caperings and slappings on the back. Hoghton, to the delight of nearly everyone present, had been humiliated.

The mayor and two defeated men retreated into the Moot Hall while a musical band no fewer than sixteen strong, which had formed up in the coachyard of the Bull Inn opposite, marched out carrying drums and brass instruments. It formed up opposite the hall steps while men came running out behind them with a pair of carrying chairs gaudily festooned with flowers, tinsel, bunting and paper garlands. These were placed in line astern of the band, ready for their occupants who were, of course, the two victorious candidates. The town wanted to see them chaired.

The new MPs were supposed to put on a show of resistance while being led to their chairs, though in the case of old Fazackerley the reluctance was quite genuine: to lurch precariously on a flower-decked chair being mobbed by a thousand drunken revellers was the last thing he was likely to enjoy. For young Shuttleworth, on the other hand, this was his first election, a new and shining experience, and he showed his enthusiasm by waving his arms and clapping his hands.

The band struck up *Lillibullero* and set off around town on a long, looping progress. The two chairs bobbed along, hoisted high above the jostling ruck on the shoulders of a team of burly porters, with bells around their hats and knees. Nicholas Fazackerley sat holding on grimly to the arms of his chair, with a fixed, painful smile across his mouth. Shuttleworth held himself more loosely, laughing and blowing kisses as he processed through the borough that he had fought for and won. Looking at him I remembered the halting speech I had seen him try to make that morning in the rain, how he had misjudged the crowd and their ideas about the most important issues of the day. He looked as if he had learned much in the last week and, watching him, I felt a perverse surge of optimism for the future, as one always does, however delusively, when the young take up burdens previously carried by the tired and the cynical.

In all this commotion I lost sight of my clerk. I myself did not follow the procession far, but I sheered off and returned to the Bull Inn where I engaged a room for the inquest hearing on Monday. I went on to the addresses of the two chosen witnesses of Satterthwaite's death, and finally to Dick Middleton. With his defect of speech, he did not want to answer the summons, and I had to speak to him in stern terms before he agreed.

Returning to the office, dismally aware of the work I had left undone during the past fortnight – mundane legal work of the dullest but, unfortunately, the most fee-worthy kind – I picked up a pile of testaments, leases, and matrimonial agreements and brought them to my desk. As I dumped them down in one heap, a sheet of paper, folded and sealed, was swept from the top of the desk to the floor by the down-draught, and I bent to retrieve it. It was a letter, which I had not previously noticed, addressed to me.

I broke the seal, wondering how long it had been waiting for me. It was a single sheet, written on both sides. I glanced at the signature before beginning to read. It was unsigned and yet, as I read, its author soon became apparent:

Dark Waters

Cragg,

*I do not owe you any explanations, but before we parted
the Satterthwaite woman told me you took an interest
in her case. I write merely to urge you to abandon that
interest – and to abandon her to whatever judicial fate awaits
her, which I hope will be the gallows. I now know what
I was too besotted to apprehend before: that she is a witch,
or worse, and wholly undeserving of pity or indulgence.*

*I met her first when I came incognito to Preston last
year, and thought she shone with vivacity and beauty like
a pocket sun surrounded by provincial dullness. I was
on political business, meeting the upholders of a certain
gentleman with a stake in these islands, now living on the
Continent. But I did not forget Maggie (nor she me) and
we resumed our dalliance this year when I returned, under
another false flag, to gather more intelligence. My master
is interested to know the names of his most formidable
enemies in Lancashire, and we thought this election an
apposite moment to collect the information. It was easy
to worm my way into the confidence of Whigs such as
Hoghton, Satterthwaite, Drake and Wilson. I had become
especially friendly with Drake, and it was he that I was
meeting at the windmill – we were to go shooting – when
you saw me as you passed by on the road. (Did you know
that I saw you just as you saw me?) But I never suspected
Maggie's role in the murder of Allcroft, or her connection
with Drake, for by then I was growing infatuated. When
she was arrested I mistook it as a sign, not of her guilt, but
of the corporation's prejudice against her, so I played angel
and got her out of prison. We both knew then that I would
be forced at once to flee – as indeed I have – but she would*

*not flee with me. Of all people, she told me that she
wanted to go with Drake. Drake! Is there any fathoming
the passions of a woman? Or the perfidy?*

*I therefore beg you, do not help her, Cragg, or offer her
comfort of any kind. She is depraved even in the eyes of
your depraved correspondent. She deserves whatever she gets.*

There the letter ended, and I laid it on the desk. So, I thought, Maggie had even made a fool of Peters, the self-assured spy. He thought he knew everything yet he left town in the belief that her fancy lay towards Michael Drake. How much more he would have hated her had he found out about Jotham Allcroft!

With this consummate display of deception filling my thoughts it was impossible to address the legal papers, so I went into the library and, as I still do every Friday, sat at the desk to record the facts in my journal. I was beginning to feel a certain satisfaction now. Even though the run of inquests that flowed from this case was still not finished, I felt a sense of completeness, of arrival at the desired end.

In my writing I made a special effort to set down everything I could of what Maggie Satterthwaite had said to me in the House of Correction that morning. Finally I copied in Peters's letter and then, putting the journal away, I sank into my comfortable chair, determined to distract myself by finishing the last part of *The Man of Law's Tale*. I picked up the book and read how the unfortunate Constance was cast adrift in a rudderless boat yet again and, defying all laws of likelihood, ended back in Rome where her frightful adventures had started. Reflecting on the neat circularity of her life story, I dropped off to sleep with the continuing raucousness of the election's end echoing distantly in my ears from outside, and the logs of my library fire hissing gently in front of me.

*

A vast, final election feast was to be laid on that evening in the open air of Market Place. Every elector was invited with his wife, so that more than 700 places were laid, on long trestle tables. Six beeves, a dozen pigs and sheep and 100 chickens were roasted for the occasion, and 300 gallons of ale were provided to wash it all down.

Elizabeth and I, however, were not there. We supped quietly alone in our dining room, listening to the joyous din being made by the feasters not 100 yards away. I picked disconsolately at my herring and potatoes, knowing she was looking at me askance as she ate. Finally I broke the silence.

'I know, I know. It's entirely my fault. I forgot to vote, and if your name isn't on the poll list, you don't get a ticket to the feast.'

My wife's severe expression did not soften a fraction.

'I was so looking forward to it, Titus. Our friends are all out there, enjoying themselves.'

'I know and I am sorry. But I was entirely caught up in this case, you see. And, anyway, my heart has not been in the election since I uncovered some of the things that have been going on.'

'To have tickets, all you needed to do was go through the polling hall. You did not have to cast a vote.'

I sighed but had no answer. Being too busy is rarely an excuse and, as she pointed out, I could have registered a *suffragium non fero*.

We did not stay up late and the party was still in full flow as we went upstairs.

'Oh! Titus, I forgot to tell you.'

I was brushing her hair, which I liked to do at night. As well as making her even more beautiful to me, it pleased her senses and made her dreamy and, sometimes, amorous.

'Lorris delivered a book this morning while you were out,' she said. 'Did you find it?'

'My rebound Aesop! I must see it.'

'It's in the hall.'

'I'll fetch it and we shall read something from it.'

So, having administered the last stroke of the brush, I went down to fetch the small volume. I found it hidden out of sight under a copy of the *Gentleman's Magazine* on the half-moon table. I am always delighted by the neat parcels that bookmen make, with smooth new brown paper, tied with string and sealed with wax. I broke the wax, cut the string and took the book upstairs.

Elizabeth sometimes liked to work her embroidery in bed while I read aloud to her. She did so now as I settled in at her side with the book in my hand. The festive sounds from outside were still audible, but slowly diminishing, as the guests began to go their ways.

Before opening it I examined the new binding itself, on which Lorris, as usual, had done an expert job. The cover was of fine kidskin, like satin to the touch and best tobacco to the nose. The gold leaf for the motifs on the front and back covers, and the titling on the spine, was skilfully laid in, and inside the boards he had used a lovely marble paper. Finally he had sewn the pages anew with red and yellow silk threads, which he gathered in neat seams at the top and bottom of the spine. It was a binding, I thought, to last the length of our children's lives, should we ever be blessed to have any.

'So what will you read?' Elizabeth asked. 'I hope not one of those self-satisfied fables in four or six lines that end with nothing but a commonplace.'

'No, I have one that bears on the case of Maggie Satterthwaite. In fact, it helped me to—'

'Maggie! How could I have been so terribly mistaken about that girl?'

I had earlier given her a detailed account of all that had passed between us, and read to her from the relevant section of my journal.

'It can be difficult to spot madness when it has method.'

'I don't think she is mad, only bad. Like a fruit rotten within. The skin looks fresh and beautiful enough but underneath the flesh stinks.'

'That is Peters's opinion also. You both took her side before.'

She laughed.

'I did not think I would ever be bracketed with the devious Mr Peters. But I suppose you are right. Neither of us knew then that she had killed. So go on, what is this fable that bears on the case?'

'It is *The Scarecrows and the Foxes*.'

And so I read the story of the two scarecrows who observe a pair of foxes creeping from the woods to steal chickens, and how the fox abandons the vixen, as he thinks, to save himself, but she turns the tables and outfoxes the fox.

'What is the moral at the end?'

I read it out: '*There is never honour amongst thieves.*'

'That is a dull moral,' Elizabeth said. 'I can give it a better.'

'Which is?'

'It is better to bluff than to run.'

'And that is exactly my point about Maggie. It is just what she has done.'

'The cunning vixen. Was she brought up on Aesop, I wonder?'

I turned and kissed her on the shoulder.

'If Drake and Maggie were Mr and Mrs Fox, what of the scarecrows, I wonder? What do we learn from them?'

'They are poor blameless souls looking on. They are like us, Titus.'

'I don't feel so blameless tonight,' I said. 'I am very penitent that we did not go to the feast.'

She rolled towards me and, to show I was forgiven, tenderly gave me back my kiss.

'Oh, you and I don't need to feast to be happy, Titus my love. Perhaps we do better without roast chicken – eh, Mr Scarecrow?'

Epilogue

THE SCARECROWS AND THE FOXES
A Fable attributable to Aesop

M R AND MRS SCARECROW, standing together in a field, were accustomed to seeing a dog-fox and a vixen slip each night from the covert and run across the field to the farm, where they would kill a chicken for their supper.

After a time the farmer lost patience. Taking up his bow, and calling his dog, he resolved not to rest until he had killed whoever it was that lived in the covert and was stealing his chickens.

The vixen, spying his approach, cried out, 'Husband, we must fly! The farmer is coming to kill us because we stole his chickens.'

The fox was afraid, but cunningly he thought of how he might escape being killed by the farmer.

'Yes, fly we must,' he said quickly. 'We will go on my count of three. One – two – three.'

The fox jumped out into the open and took to his heels, congratulating himself that he would get away while the farmer chased after his wife, who was the slower runner. But his mate played a cleverer hand. She did not run into the open, but crouched low in the covert and watched her husband flee into the distance while the farmer gave chase.

After some time the scarecrows saw the farmer return, well satisfied. The body of the fox was slung over his shoulder.

'Good vixen,' he called, when he saw his victim's wife taking the evening sun at leisure in front of the covert. 'Come home with me and celebrate, for I have killed the thief that stole my chickens.'

'Willingly,' she cried. 'How shall we feast?'

'On roast chicken,' he replied.

Watching the farmer and the vixen go in together, Mr Scarecrow began to lament.

'Alas, that we cannot eat roast chicken, like the farmer and the vixen,' he cried.

'No,' said his wife. 'The price of chicken is too high. We are better off as we are.'

Background Note

1. POLITICS

BY 1741 THE terms Whig and Tory, which had once stood mainly for attitudes of mind, had begun to define parliamentary parties. Whigs, who governed the country for most of the eighteenth century, were modern, metropolitan and supportive of the Protestant settlement of 1688, and of the later Hanoverian succession to the throne. The Tories were country-minded and conservative, often with a nostalgic affection for the ousted Stuarts.

The country was ruled by a coalition of the King (the second of four successive German Georges), his ministers and Parliament. In the 1730s the most powerful figure was Robert Walpole, the first British 'Prime Minister'. Walpole had an unrivalled ability to manage George II, while maintaining a majority of Whig MPs to vote with him. He carefully kept out of foreign wars and, though there is some truth in his enemies' charge that this only provided more money for filling his own and his cronies' pockets, the policy was genuinely beneficial to trade (including, it must be admitted, the slave trade).

By the 1741 election Walpole was losing his grip. The bribing of MPs with sinecures infuriated the public, as did taxation (too high and on the wrong things), the size of the army (too large), the cost of defending German territories (not our business), and attacks on British shipping by the Spaniards. Meanwhile the Pretender, James Edward Stuart, still claimed the throne from faraway Rome. The Jacobites had been in long-term decline, yet some felt that this government's unpopularity had revived them, especially in country areas.

In about 1740 a new group of dissident Whigs grouped around the heir to the throne, Frederick, Prince of Wales. Lord Bolingbroke wrote them a manifesto, entitled *The Patriot King*, for a new kind of monarch, like King Alfred the Great, who would unite the country under the supposedly fundamental principles of English government: common law, ancient rights and economic, military and naval security. All these ideas were encoded in the masque *Alfred*, and in its rousing hit tune, 'Rule Britannia!', which was first seen privately by the thirty-three-year-old Frederick and his friends at Cliveden House in the summer of 1740. The Earl of Derby's son, Lord Strange, who in my story mounts the play in Preston on the eve of polling, was one of the prince's friends, and had probably been present at that original performance.

The general election of May 1741 went badly for Walpole. Although there were only 94 contests (two at Preston) for 558 seats, his support in the new House of Commons shrank drastically. By February 1742, after deaths and further defections, his majority had disappeared, and he resigned.

2. MONEY

Readers may wonder about the system of money in Cragg and Fidelis's time. The smallest single unit of account was the farthing and the largest was the guinea. Values rose as follows: 4f. (farthings) = 1d. (penny); 12d. = 1s. (shilling); 20s. = £1 (pound). A crown was 5s. and a guinea 21s. Other common coins were the halfpenny, sixpence and half-crown.

The value of money is hard to express in modern terms. A boy could get $1^1/_2$d. for an hour's wood-chopping. A labourer earned between 10d. and 1s.3d. for a day's work, while live-in servants earned £3.10s. to £5 a year, on top of their board and lodging. A shopkeeper might live on annual profits of about £30–50, also the sort of money earned by a craftsman in a high-value trade. A middle-class family would be quite comfortably off on £350, while anyone with £500 or more was regarded as rich. Government sinecures could draw £2,000 or more, out of which underlings were paid to do the work, if any was involved. A very small handful of super-rich landowners had incomes in excess of £25,000.

Here are a few prices I have picked up from various sources:

½d. – a pint of milk or half a loaf of bread

1d. – a day's fee for a child at a dame school or charity school

3d. – postage on a one-page letter going 80 miles, paid by recipient

5d. – 1lb (500g) of butter or cheese

6d. – dinner of cold meat, bread and a pint of porter beer

6d. to 1s. – a pamphlet or paper-covered book for popular reading

1s. – a music lesson

1s.6d. – to dry-clean a coat

2/6 – 1lb of candles

4/6 – petticoat for a working woman

4/9 upwards – 1lb coffee depending on quality

5/7 – worsted stockings

6/6 – bridle for riding horse

7/6 – 1lb cheap tea or a new novel by Samuel Richardson

10/6 to £1.15s. – men's wigs

16s. – silk stockings

£4 to £15 – a riding horse depending on age and condition
5gn. – a silver watch or half-length portrait by provincial artist
£22 – a year's rent for a single man's small apartment in London
£77.6s. – a new four-wheel coach
£350 – freehold on a house in Soho, London
£20,000 – lottery prize in 1769

Now read on for an extract from
The Scrivener,
the latest Cragg and Fidelis story

Chapter One

STANDING IN THE doorway, with medical bag in hand, Luke Fidelis peered into the shadowed room until its main features had resolved themselves: the outline of the low pallet bed; the man's gaunt, ghostly face looking steadily upwards; the pale hand resting motionless outside the covering blanket. The doctor went to the window and pulled aside its rough curtain to admit more light but, in doing so, let in a damp gust of air from off the Moor. Picking up a stool beneath the window, he placed it beside the bed and sat, depositing his bag on the hard mud floor. The prostrate man's breath was shallow but absolutely regular, as if he reposed with not a single care. Fidelis spoke in a low voice, his mouth close to his patient's ear.

'Adam. Adam Thorn. I am Dr Fidelis come from Preston at your wife's request to attend you. Do not fret about the fee – there won't be one.'

Fidelis touched Adam's brow and found no fever. He felt his wrist. The pulse was even, and so was the heart, which he checked by pressing a silver listening-trumpet to the chest, and placing his ear on the earpiece at the narrow end. Next he felt with soft fingers around the contours of the skull. Finally he drew a candle end and tinderbox from his bag, lit the wick and leaned across to peer with the help of its light upon Thorn's face. His skin was dry, his lips cracked, his eyes staring in his head. Fidelis shielded the light from those eyes for a moment with his hand, then revealed it again, and noted how the pupils contracted in response. By this he determined that the automatic processes of the body were continuing as normal. But was the man conscious? Was he aware?

Standing, he returned to the window and dropped the curtain again, then crossed back to the door and ducked his head as he passed into the main room. Here a child of three sat playing on the ground and a baby grizzled in its cot, while another sucked at the breast of its mother who sat on a rough bench beside the cheerless fireplace. This was the month of June, in the year 1742: far from cold enough to make a fire essential for warmth, though this had not been much of a summer in the north country, and the doctor knew that Dot Lorris, his landlady, would have a log burning back at his own room in Preston, and glad he'd be of its comfort when he returned home on this damp day.

'You have no fire, Amity,' he observed. 'Do you not cook?'

Amity Thorn unplugged the child from the nipple, and let it loll back against her shoulder, dreamy with milk. With her free hand she pulled up her dress to cover the breast.

'I'll cook tomorrow. There's not the fuel for a fire every day. I have to learn thrift, with him the way he is . . .'

She cocked her head towards the inner room.

Fidelis sat down at the worm-eaten table on one of the room's two chairs. To learn thrift, you first had to have something to be thrifty with, he thought, looking around the bare room.

'Well,' he said, 'I've had a look at him, and now I want to know more about how it happened.'

'I wasn't there. I didn't see.'

'But you found him, didn't you?'

'No, it was John Barton that found him and brought him home.'

'Barton the horse-coper up at Peel Hall Stables?'

'That's him.'

Barton's yard had been part of a dismantled estate that centred on Peel Hall, now more or less of a ruin on the edge of the Town Moor, to the north-east of Preston.

'Where did John Barton find him, then?'

'Out on the Moor, lying on the ground. It were near the Bale Stone. John Barton saw him and heard him moaning.'

'When was this?'

'A week ago now.'

'A week? Has he been lying like that for a week?'

'Yes, except the once, he's neither moved nor talked, just sort of twitched sometimes. He gave over the moaning after we'd got him to bed.'

'What about food and drink?'

She nodded to the table where a spoon and porringer lay.

'He's been taking soup and milk off the spoon. I have to pull open his mouth, mind, but he's been taking it.'

'Did you not think to send for me or another doctor before this?'

'I had old Mother Greenshaw in to look at him – the wise woman. She told me what to do – if he'd take it, give him the soup and milk and porridge and maybe a beaten egg and some brandy, and just wait, and he might come round. Was that all right, what she said?'

'It's not bad advice. My own would not have been very different. Did you follow it?'

'As well as I could, only he's not come round, has he? He just lies there staring, staring. It frightens me.'

'You said he was like that "except the once". What do you mean by that?'

'After he'd been in bed a bit, he seemed to revive, like. He started groaning again, then I could make out some words. Babbling he was, and I saw he was moving one of his arms.'

'What was he saying? Did he give any indication of what happened to him out there?'

'No, he was only thinking about how he felt. I came to feed him and he kept on lifting his hand and trying to bat away the spoon, saying "rich, rich" meaning the food was too thick for him, or too flavoured, I guessed. The same way, he couldn't stand too much light, or noise.'

'As if all his senses were heightened? It's a possibility.'

'Well he were grateful to me. He kept saying I was precious to him. It were touching.'

'So how long was it before he lapsed into the state I have just seen?'

'He went on with his babbling for an hour or more. Then when I went back in to him he was lying still again, just breathing quietly. I talked to him but it seemed he never heard. When the baby screamed, he never flinched and he made no more fuss about the food I gave him. He's been like that since. If he doesn't come round, what am I to do? There's no one here but me and the little ones.'

'Have you no family anywhere – someone who can come and help?'

'There's nobody, only Peg.'

'Peg?'

'His eleven-year-old niece that he's had charge of since her ma's died.'

'Does Peg live here?'

'Not now. She's gone into service as a housemaid. He thought the world of her, him. But we couldn't afford another mouth to feed even before this. Now I don't know what I'll do.'

'Can you make any money on your own account?'

'There's the little I get from selling my eggs at market. We have a few birds. But most of our money came from bits of work he did, for farmers and gardeners and such. He got some good pay at harvesting, which we put aside to help us through winter. But I had to pay the wise woman, and then there was the brandy to get. So I've had to spend.'

'If you're very short you can go to the parish. You'll be allowed something until your husband recovers. I'll put in a good word with the church warden. In the meantime, I'm afraid there is nothing more to be done except to care for him with warmth, food and drink, as best you can.'

'What is the matter with him, doctor?'

'He has suffered a seizure of the brain. There is also an injury to his skull, a lump from a bang on the head. It's difficult to know which came first. The head injury could have caused the seizure, but just as likely he got the lump by falling down after the seizure. They very often do happen over their own accord, seizures. They make the sufferer insensible so that he falls to the ground.'

'But Adam will get better? If not, I don't know what I'll do.'

'I regret it's impossible to be sure, Mrs Thorn. He might come round at any time, or stay the same indefinitely. Or thirdly, I am sorry to say, he might suddenly be taken from us, without any warning whatsoever.'

She rose and deposited the child in the cot beside the baby, and went to a side table. There she took a scoop of cold gruel from a pot and poured it into the wooden porringer. After placing this on the table, she picked up the eldest child from the floor and balanced it upon her knee to feed it. The somewhat battered and dented spoon carried the gruel inefficiently, but by working fast she managed to force a high proportion of the thin liquid into the mouth, though the child pulled faces and wriggled with dislike of its dinner.

'It will be terrible to live with such uncertainty – if we can live at all.'

Suddenly the child on her knee twisted around and one of its hands grabbed at the spoon. In surprise Amity let go and it fell, clattering off the edge of the table and bouncing to the floor. Immediately Fidelis stooped to retrieve it.

Before he returned the implement to her he glanced at it. Though damaged, pitted and discoloured, it had once been a fine piece of spoonery – the shank heavy and with the remains of chasing along its length, and a nobbled end, as of some figure now unrecognizable. He turned it over: there were four black pits on the shank, square in shape and black where dirt had compacted in them. Amity held out her hand.

'Give it back, doctor, if you please. I must feed him quick or he won't take it at all.'

'Of course. Here.'

He gave her back the spoon and, for the time being, thought no more about it, while they talked of Amity Thorn's hard life, and of what she could do to alleviate it.

'Remember to go to the church warden as soon as you can,' he said firmly, thinking at last it was time to leave. Then his eye caught sight again of the spoon, which lay in the now empty porringer on the table.

'And there is one more thing I should mention,' he said, pointing at the bowl. 'That spoon of yours looks silver. I fancy, if you clean it up, that it will raise a sum of ready cash in town.'

She picked up the spoon and turned it in her hand.

'This dirty old thing? Adam brought it back a month ago, off the Moor. You don't mean it's worth something?'

'It might be. Where did he get it?'

She shook her head.

'As I say, I reckoned he must have picked it up off the Moor, or somewhere about. It were all muddy and stained: just an old spoon, as I thought, though he did say different.'

'What did he say?'

She gave a short, melancholy laugh.

'That it was treasure. "Treasure trove, is that," he said. He's done it before – come home with some brass farthing he'd found on the Moor and said it was treasure trove. He was bitten with this idea that some old soldier had buried a big lot of silver up there a hundred year ago. But he'd got himself killed and the secret died with him, so the silver was never found. Adam even told me he'd gone to Preston to talk to the Recorder to prove it were true.'

'The Recorder? Mr Thorneley?'

'I don't know his name. Adam kept on about looking for it but I just said if poor folk ever do find such things they get them taken off them, as sure as the Gospel, so what's the use? He shut up about it after that, but I'll give you a warrant that he never gave over looking for it. That was his way.'

Fidelis looked carefully at the underside of the spoon's shaft, and showed it to her.

'Well, I don't know about any treasure, but I am saying that, if these pits on the underside of the handle are hallmarks, then it really is made of silver – assayed silver. Maybe that's what Adam was trying to tell you when he was saying "rich" and "precious". He was talking about the spoon you were feeding him his gruel with.'

Her face fell. She had imagined she was the precious one. The doctor gave her back the spoon.

'So you can exchange it for some silver coin. Do it, Amity. Buy some wholesome food for the little ones, and for Adam too. Marrowbone broth is always recommendable.'

Fidelis got to his feet and returned for a last look into the darkness of Adam Thorn's room. As before, nothing there moved, only two tiny winking sparks of light from Adam's eyes, which every few moments were extinguished and immediately reappeared.

Then he returned to where Amity was, bade her good day and

ducked out into the drizzle. He put his hat on his head, turned up the collar of his coat and strode off towards town.

You, the reader, might very well suppose, in order to recount all this to you, that I, Titus Cragg, must have been loitering about under the dripping eaves of the Thorn house, peering in through chinks in the window sacking, listening at the door, committing the conversations I heard to memory. In reality, I was not: all that afternoon I was in Preston town, more than a mile distant from the Thorn house, seeing to my practice as an attorney-at-law and my work, which I hold to be equally important, as the town Coroner.

But how, you must ask, can words describing an event in the world seem so convincing – so real – when their author never himself observed the event? It is a question that often bedevils a law court. It doesn't matter how many times witnesses are warned to tell only what they directly saw and heard, they will run on with the gossip of chair-carriers, and chambermaids' tittle-tattle, taking the jury with their story-telling into the realm of speculation, and soon into a state of firm belief. Many poor innocents have gone to the gallows in those realms and states of fantasy, but their necks were not the less truly broken for it. Stories and lies are so knitted together with facts and experience that they can never easily be disentangled – not in a law court, and not in life.

In a book, then? That, you may suppose, is my aim. The events I have just described were long ago and nobody's neck depends on whether or not you believe my writing. Nevertheless, let me reassure you: every word of what I have written about Dr Fidelis's visit to the Thorns is true, for I had it on the following evening detail by detail from the lips of the doctor himself, and assiduously committed it to my journal before going to bed.

And the reason I set it down here will be clear in due course.